A Strange Death

By the author

Letters to an American Jewish Friend:
A Zionist's Polemic

Across the Sabbath River:
In Search of a Lost Tribe of Israel

Grand Things to Write a Poem On:
A Verse Autobiography of Shmuel Hanagid

Yehuda Halevi

Hillel Halkin

A Strange Death

The Toby Press

A Strange Death
First Paperback Edition 2010

The Toby Press LLC
POB 8531, New Milford, CT 06676-8531, USA
& POB 2455, London W1A 5WY, England

www.tobypress.com

ISBN 978 1 59264 280 9, *paperback*

A CIP catalogue record for this title is
available from the British Library

Printed and bound in the United States

To Marcia

ADMINISTRATION
BUILDING

CEMETERY

APPELBAUM

 GELBERG   SYNAGOGUE

TO ←————————   FOUNDERS'   STREET
BINYAMINA

EPSTEIN

AARONSOHN

V
T

DAVIDESC

THRESHING FLOOR

ZICHRON YA'AKOV

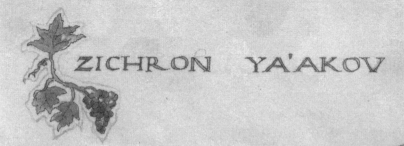

TO WADI MILIKH

HAIFA

LANGE HOUSE

TOWN
SQUARE
AND
PARK

STREET

⊣───⟶Z

FOUNDERS' STREET

BENEFACTOR

ASHKENAZI

RIBNIKER

GRAF HOTEL

STABLE

NEIDERMAN

WINE

YSER

STREET

1920
5720   תר"פ

ZAMARIN

Chapter one

Sometimes, tired of being asked how we came to Zichron, I gave as the reasons a brown dog, a full moon, and two bottles of local white wine. If it wasn't the whole truth, you couldn't say it was none of it.

We arrived in Israel, Marcia and I, in 1970, intending to settle in Jerusalem. Or rather, outside of Jerusalem, on an acre of stony land, with a view of old, terraced hills. We had both lived in Jerusalem before, and if nothing else it was a city that inspired longing.

But that spring in Jerusalem it seemed that whoever had longed for the place had returned to it all at once and was looking for somewhere to live. The doors of the real estate offices reopened behind you before they had time to shut; the boom gripping the city since the 1967 war was at its height. One day we answered an ad for a country villa that led to a converted chicken coop with a view of the road to Tel Aviv. Columns of buyers filed through it as though it were the last shelter on earth. The asking price was a transcendent sum, and it was clear that it would be seen, raised, and called before the day was done. We called for time-out.

And so we set out to visit friends in Haifa, driving down to the coastal plain and heading north. On our left was the smog of Tel Aviv and unseen beyond it the sea, to which the smudge of the mountains of

Samaria ran parallel on our right. Citrus trees rose and fell in dark swells against the red clay of earth and tiled roofs. Rows of wicked cypresses hedged them around, lit by the flames of runaway bougainvilleas.

Beyond the city of Hadera sand dunes set in, blown by the sea winds from the old Roman port of Caesaria. The hills to the east loomed closer now, mountain and sea on a collision course. Soon, as though struggling to its feet, a first spur of the Carmel rose ahead of us in a steep talus.

The road crossed some railroad tracks, wriggled around the base of a limestone cliff, and ran along stands of windmill-leaved banana trees, their fruit encased in plastic bags of the same Mediterranean blue that flashed briefly out toward the horizon.

We pulled into a filling station at the foot of a hill that was said by a sign to be thirty-five kilometers from Haifa and three from Zichron Ya'akov. This was a town neither of us had been in. I didn't know many things about it. One was that it was one of the first Jewish farming colonies established in modern Palestine toward the end of the nineteenth century; another that Ya'akov was the Hebrew name of Baron James de Rothschild, in whose honor the town was named. Somewhere I had heard or read of a Jewish spy ring that had operated in it during World War I. And wine was made there, as declared by the labels on the bottles of Carmel-Mizrachi, the country's largest vintner.

A salt breeze blew through the window of the car. After the austere air of Jerusalem, it felt like a damp caress. I paid for the gas and suggested driving up the hill to Zichron. Perhaps we might find a cold drink there.

The sea came into view at the first hairpin turn of the climb. So did a mirrorwork of fishponds that had been hidden by the tree line. Thin embankments sliced them into panels that glittered in the setting sun. Then we were around the last bend, with a view up the coast to the old Crusader fortress at Atlit. We passed a picnic grounds, entered the streets of the town, and parked in a public square with a small park.

Perhaps nothing is ever remembered as we first encountered it, since memory is a palimpsest on which time erases and we rewrite the same story many times. So, if I recall crossing the street to the synagogue at the square's far end – that plain stone building with its Hebrew-numeraled clock face, built by the French architects of James de Rothschild's son Edmond to stand in the center of town with the sober authority of a parish church – and seeing old Tishbi ride by on his donkey, the inseparable four legs on which he sat, a blue-capped satyr, while it chauffeured him anonymously about town (for when I asked him years later what he called it, he simply grinned with the three yellow teeth that were stuck like the prongs of a pitchfork in his mouth and said, "Donkey"), or Carmeli the druggist, who liked to close early, walking smartly up the block in his tan blazer, in one hand a panama hat and in the other the leash of his white poodle whose manicured toenails clicked against the pavement like high heels, this does not mean that I saw either of them that day. There were to be enough other days when I did – long summer afternoons cooling indolently into evening as the town prepared to lock up and go home – to include them in this story, along with the basketed shoppers waiting for the bus to take them back to the government projects on the outskirts of town, the teenagers lined up by the public telephone at the post office to make their assignations for the night, the jungle-hatted farmers riding their bucking tractors back from the vineyards and fields, and the children crowding the felafel stand next to Shlomo Toker's appliance store before going home to tell their mothers they weren't hungry and could they please go out for one last game of hide-and-seek; or else, with another rub of the slate, Asheri, the little cock's-crow of a greengrocer, dragging crates of vegetables into his store in which he wisely thumped the chests of melons in seven languages, or, burly as a wine barrel, Mordche, the last Mohican of the wagon drivers, swapping tall tales and the black-market rates of leading currencies with his cronies while his mules dreamed in the courtyard of the legendary Graf Hotel, wherein even the most fastidious of European travelers, as promised by Baedeker's *Guide To Palestine and The Middle East*, could find "tolerable accommodations for the night" if reminded to look for them by the sound of the sun splashing into the sea in the year nineteen-hundred-and-seven.

Had he paused at the entrance to the hotel, the traveler could have seen in all directions to the ends of "the new Jewish colony of Jacob's Memory," at the almost precise midpoint of which he would have stood. Sixty-three years later this was no longer the case, although the intersection that we had reached of Hameyasdim and Hanadiv Streets, Founders

Street and the Street of the Benefactor, as the philanthropic Edmond was called by the colonists, still formed the town's commercial hub. It was a hub that had seen better days, though, for the center of Zichron was more *éclatant* then, as befitted a little outpost of Frenchdom in the Levant: not only the newly opened hotel (whose elegant façade with its twin flagpoles for the Ottoman crescent and the Star-of-David, and its fancily-lettered Maspero Cigar sign, was now shared by a shabby barbershop and a defunct dry cleaner's, while the rear of the premises, where Miriam Graf had served meals in the white-linened dining room and her husband Alter had shown silent movies to the accompaniment of Munjak the fiddler, was occupied by the cottage chocolate industry of Mr. Emmanuel Turskanov of Riga, son of a former bonbon czar of the Baltic), but also the arabesqued fences around the front yards of the houses that were torn down to make way for the sidewalks installed after World War I; the gas lamplights in their glass hexagons, which – if he lingered a while longer in the doorway – the traveler might see lit, one by one, like the candles on a birthday cake; and the ornamental pool in the middle of the intersection, drained after a drunken Arab horseman sailed into it one night and was found nose-down among the water lilies in the morning. There were times when I saw these vanished splendors too, or imagined that I did, so lost in some yarn of Moshe Shatzman's or Yanko Epstein's that had Edmond de Rothschild himself driven by with a clatter of coach wheels on one of his grand *tours d'inspection* to the brassy strains of "Carry To Zion Pennant and Banner" played by the town band from the proscenium in the park, I would not have pinched myself. But that was later. Now, I saw none of this – saw only a perpendicular pair of shopping streets whose low, red-roofed buildings looked badly in need of a facelift. A swirl of diesel fuel, tobacco smoke, and frying mashed chickpeas settled into the littered curbs by the side of old newspapers, fallen candy wrappers, discarded good-byes, and the fatigued cries of homeward-wheeled infants: the detritus of an Israeli town at 6:45 P.M. of a fading June day.

Marcia and I crossed Founders Street and continued along the Street of the Benefactor, which ran beneath leafy pipal trees down the other side of the hill: past Aminadav's grocery; past the kiosk of the potato-nosed Parsee; past the gift shop of Avraham Baer and the liquor store of his brother Yitzhak, known as Gift Bear and Wine Bear; past Miriam's wool store, emptying of its gossip of housewives; past Yafia Cohen's open doorway, in which, ruddy as a sailor and nearly as bald as a monk, sat Yafia Cohen on the observation deck of her folding chair, a white lace kerchief around her neck to shield the sunburn on her widowed breasts that peered wistfully out from the crevice of her calico dress; past Carmeli's drugstore, where Carmeli was locking up (funny: hadn't I just seen him by the synagogue?) while his poodle scratched at the stairs leading down to the street; across Jabotinsky Street under the blank stares of the crazy tinker and his wife taking the evening air beside their jars of cabbage and pickles set out to sour in the sun on the stoop of their one-room hovel that smelled like a pestilence; past Motl Sokolov, putting his donkeys to bed for the night; past Benedik's hardware store, by which Meir Benedik, an army fatigue cap riding high on his honeyed haystack of hair, paused to rest with a fifty-kilo sack of cement outside the barred window through which Yosef Davidesco was shot to death by the Stern Gang in 1946; past the ruined house hit by an Iraqi bomb in the '48 war; past Yigal Neiderman drinking Turkish coffee at a table in his yard with his Bedouin riding buddies. Further down the hill, where the Street of the Benefactor swung sharply to the right and disappeared on its way out of town, rose the tall brick chimney of the winery.

We crossed to the opposite sidewalk and turned left into Wine Street, past Ora and Micha Rosenzweig's house, in front of which Ora stopped trimming her lontana bushes to glance up from the very spot she had stood in when the shots rang out and Davidesco's killers turned and ran to their getaway car, passing so close that she could have touched them; past Shmuel and Sonia Bloch's house, where Sonia, who hadn't spoken to Ora since their fateful quarrel over a lost library book, was picking snap beans in her garden; past Tsvi Zuckerman, who was not on speaking terms with the Rosenzweigs either; past Akiva Weissfish tinkering with his lawn mower; past the Lundins' house; past the limit of the town itself, for before us was only a copse of pine trees, and beyond it, partially glimpsed through their branches, a premonition of unbounded space.

At the bottom of the pine copse, a dirt road branched off to the left. We followed it along a contour of the hillside, beneath which, half-screened by olive trees that gave way to a hedge of vine-laced acacias, the ground fell away in vineyards and orchards. Although the drop to the valley below us was only a few hundred feet, its sharp tilt made one feel an almost vertiginous height, so that, coming to a clearing in the hedge, we stopped to marvel at the view. We were looking east into the oncoming night, which even on the longest of summer days descended quickly in this place, or rather, seemed to thicken out of the air like a purplish-gray batter into which the last light had been poured.

Already the fields in the valley, down which ran a ribbon of road, were dull in the twilight; beyond them, ridge after ridge, the Carmel rose to a massif. On our right, a promontory of the town, a last human headland, dipped down to meet the valley; small houses and stone walls huddled beneath the winery, whose chimney rose like the spire of a cathedral. Beyond the furthest wall, a horse did figure-eights in a field, trying to clear a rope from a hind leg; with an awkward leap it was free and ran whinnying toward the field's end until brought short by its tether. The blossoms of the acacias stung the air with a dusty tartness. Goat bells tinkled. We listened, reluctant to tear ourselves away until the last trickle of light had been stirred into the stiffening night.

"Matsati!"

A dog with a hobbyhorse head and short, stubby legs was barking at us from a driveway. The voice called in crisp English:

"Matsati! What the devil are you making that racket for?"

A handsome, white-bearded man, his hand gripping a pipe bowl, appeared at the top of the driveway.

We apologized for the disturbance.

The pipe gestured generously out toward the view, as if pleased to share it. "Quite all right. 'Tsati, when will you learn this is a public thoroughfare? I say, you must be Amurricans."

He gave the vowel a slurred sound, tweaking the colonials.

"And you're British."

"Good lord, no. South African, my boy, a bloody Boer. Matsati, you brute, would you kindly stop slobbering over... but you haven't told me your name, dear. Mah-syah? Lovely. Rather Roman. Mine's Izzy. Israel Traub for short. You'll have to excuse my dog's manners; he's a native of the Middle East. Well, do come and join us for a sundowner. My wife and I were just sitting down to one."

We accepted the invitation. A drink was what we had driven up the hill for, and if we made it a quick one we could still get to Haifa for dinner. The hobbyhorse dog played wickets with our legs while we followed our host to a raspberry-colored cottage on a lawn. "Oh!" Marcia exclaimed. She had stopped by a miniature pond surrounded by a dwarf forest of nasturtiums and was staring at two stone figures on its shores: one a coiled cat, regarding the water with lidless eyes, and the other a bathing woman hugging her breasts. A strong, squat sense of kinship extended between them.

"Do you like them?" Izzy Traub asked. "Rhoda made them. Cat's a cheeky fellow. Matsati, haven't you been fed yet? Rho! Rho-o-ow! Don't tell me she's still in the shower."

Matsati stood nosing an empty bowl. A bell jingled as the cottage door opened and Rhoda Traub emerged bearing a tray with two glasses. A short, slender woman in a silvery caftan, she arched quizzical eyes at her husband.

"We've got guests," Izzy said. "'Tsati treed them. Hand them those drinks and I'll fix us two more. D'you know he didn't come home last night until the wee hours? Quite the dog around town."

While the rake wolfed his supper, the four of us sipped our drinks on the terrace. "Local poison," Izzy Traub said. "Whisky and a spot of sweet *ver*-mouth from the winery over there." He pointed in the direction of the brick chimney, which was hidden by a huge carob tree. "I believe you chaps call it a manhattan. Wonderful place, New York."

"Cheers," Rhoda said. It was easy to like the Traubs. They had come to Israel, they told us, as volunteers to fight in Israel's 1948 war of independence. South Africa, they had decided, was finished, a country of white masters and black slaves. Yet there remained something brightly pukka in their manner that kept one half-listening above the crackle of melting ice for the click of a croquet ball or the rustle of a servant girl's dress. After the war they had tried farming and had lived for several years in Jerusalem.

"What brought you to Zichron?" Marcia asked.

"We didn't plan it that way," laughed Rhoda, as if recalling a clever joke played on her. "It was because of Edmond de Rothschild. Back in the fifties, the family in France decided to have him exhumed and reburied here with all the honors. I suppose they wanted him out of the way. The architect who designed the mausoleum was a friend and asked me to do some sculpture for the grounds. We came for a fortnight and never left. Zichron was a marvelous place in those days, wasn't it, Izzy?"

"Marvelous. Little old grannies in white kerchiefs. Do you remember, Rho, how the cows came home from pasture? Each knew its own house. They'd peel off when they got there as if dancing a reel."

Rhoda Traub swatted a mosquito. "That's all gone now. No one's kept a cow in years. The farmers grow their grapes and buy their milk in plastic bags. The old barns are collapsing. Beautiful stone things and no one gives a hoot." She had a habit when talking about something of cocking her head and squinting fretfully, as if wondering how to model it in clay.

"All these natives care about is the linings of their pockets," Izzy Traub grumbled into his pipe.

Rhoda murmured assent. "Still, the place isn't totally ruined. It has atmosphere, say what you like. And such quiet." As she paused to let us hear it, a donkey brayed with the panicky sound of someone being mugged. "That's one of Motl Sokolov's," she said. "People are thick around here, but they aren't bad sorts. You see them as part of the landscape. You might as well get cheesed off at an olive tree."

"They're peasants," Izzy said. "Stubborn, greedy, pigheaded Jewish peasants. And the stories they tell! Beats *The Arabian Nights*. About as much truth in them, too. Why, *hel*-lo, you've finished your drink. Here, I'll fill you up again."

He captured my glass and went off to replenish it. Marcia reminded me of dinner in Haifa.

"Nonsense," Rhoda Traub said. "You'll eat with us. I'll throw something together in a jiffy."

The day was drifting off course and it didn't seem to matter. Overhead a golden button, Vega or Arcturus, slipped through the satin vest of the sky. Rhoda set the table with a checkered cloth on which she laid silver and crockery; Marcia went to the cottage to telephone Haifa; Izzy produced a bottle of chilled winery hock; and we sat down to eat. The conversation flowed easily, tacking back and forth like the bats in the mothy night. Yet I was having trouble following its progress; it was easier to concentrate on the crickets tuning their bows; and whole sections of it faded in and out like a program on a car radio when you're driving through a series of tunnels.

"...The grape harvest starts in August," Rhoda Traub was saying. "And on the street leading down to the winery is a bakery. On mornings when there's an east wind, you wake up smelling fresh bread and wine. It's like a whiff of Paradise...."

"...Another glass?" Izzy Traub asked. "No? Why did I open a new bottle? Come on, lad, don't let down the home side. Here, I'll fill you right up...."

Over freshly baked scones, Rhoda told us she had driven a lorry in the South African army during World War II. Izzy served in Egypt; he saw the Pyramids and missed El Alamein. They met after being demobbed, in a little fishing village where both had gone to sketch and Izzy to flee a career in barristry.

"I love the sea," Rhoda said. "And the mountains. Where else in this country do you have them together like this?"

Someone was snoring.

At first I thought it was me, groggy from the wine. Yet when I sat up with a start, the sound continued, although apart from Marcia, who was clutching my arm, no one seemed to have noticed. Rhoda Traub had risen to clear the table, Izzy was relighting his pipe, and Matsati lay ears down on the lawn, jaws working like a nutcracker at the splintered remains of a bone.

Khhhhhhh-hhhhhhhaaaaa.

Marcia's fingers dug into me.

"What's that?"

Izzy looked up, puzzled, from his pipe.

"That sound."

He chuckled.

"Oh, don't mind him, dear. That's old Tito."

"Who?"

"*Tyto Alba.* Our barn owl. It's his adenoids."

"Coffee?" Rhoda Traub asked, returning from the kitchen.

"Look!" Marcia said.

A round, orange, monstrously inflated moon had risen so swiftly

13

behind the winery that none of us had seen it come up. Out of breath, it hung there, puffing its gouty cheeks. A bat flitted across it. The wheezing of the barn owl, coming now from here and now from there, made it seem that the earth had fallen asleep and was breathing like a drunk in a ditch.

There was magic in the air. Still, Marcia surprised me when she asked the Traubs if they knew of a house for sale. She had never expressed an interest in small-town life.

"Can't say that I do," Izzy Traub replied. "There is a piece of land, though."

"Where?"

"Right next door." He aimed his pipe at the huge carob tree. "Care to see it?"

He led us beneath the tree and onto a sloping field. A flood of light from the spongy moon had washed the stars from the sky. In their place, the vista now twinkled with the constellations of near and distant villages.

"On a clear day you can see Mount Tabor in the Galilee," Izzy said. The lights of Haifa shone like a far galaxy.

"Whose land is it?"

"Ephraim Ashkenazi's. A local farmer. He stopped me in the street the other day to tell me I could have first crack at it. So it's destiny you two turned up here tonight – unless it's just coincidence."

Izzy's tone made it clear that he had little use for coincidence.

"If you give me his number," I said, "I'll call him right now."

"By God, let's drink a brandy to that," said Izzy Traub.

*   *   *

Ephraim Ashkenazi was a short, smiling farmer with muscular arms and a white jungle hat to shield him from the sun, which in mid-morning whipped brutally down. Each of us flanked by a second – I by Izzy Traub, Ashkenazi by a thin-lipped, liver-spotted man introduced as Gedalia Kruppik, who sat without removing from his mouth the cigarettes that burned down in them like fuses – we chatted in the shade of the Traubs' carob tree about the weather and the grape crop while I watched a lizard doing push-ups on a rock. Ashkenazi was selling a dunam, a quarter of an acre. This comprised the bottom half of a property that ran down-hill from the house on Founders Street in which he had been born and his deaf old brother still lived. But although it was selling for a fraction of what it would have cost near Jerusalem, there wasn't enough of it for the vegetable garden, the fruit trees, the chickens, the goats that Marcia and I dreamed of having.

"It's too small," I said, looking at the dunam, which began below three rows of citrus trees that Ashkenazi was keeping for himself.

"Small?" Beads of sweat glistened on his forehead. "A dunam is a legal building plot. Ask Gedalia."

"We want more land."

His glance wandered out toward the skullcap of Mount Tabor on the horizon. "Look, I'm a farmer," he said. "You don't have to tell me about land. It hurts to sell even this much. But a dunam is plenty. You'll have your hands full just weeding it."

"I like weeds."

"So do snakes."

Gedalia Kruppik flicked away the last half-inch of his cigarette and eyed me with interest. "Ezra Goldstein has two dunam next to this," he said.

"I didn't know Ezra was selling," Izzy remarked.

"He will," Kruppik said. He had the eyes of a small-town sheriff and a head like a large, speckled egg.

I turned to Ashkenazi. "It's a deal if you throw in the citrus trees."

"You can plant your own," he said.

"I want these."

"The bottom row."

"The bottom two."

"Congratulations," Kruppik said, stepping between us. "I get my two percent when you get title."

I was too bewildered to ask what two percent that was. Ephraim Ashkenazi had a dazed look. We exchanged addresses like men whose cars have met in an accident and Gedalia Kruppik led him off the field along a footpath running toward Wine Street.

*   *   *

Ezra Goldstein was a tree lover too.

When the two dunams he sold us were surveyed, the border

between us ran through the trunks of two plum trees. We offered to pay extra to move it.

Goldstein refused. The plum trees had always been his. He would pay us to move the border the other way.

We said no. If he felt that strongly about it, the border could stay where it was. I didn't doubt the trees were old. Their branches were shaggy and split by the weight of the yellow fruit that soon would ripen on them. But they didn't look cared for; how attached to them could he be? Just to reach them meant scrambling down a steep drop at the rear of his yard, no mean task for a man in his sixties who walked with a cane and carried his belly like a feed sack. Unlike most of the old-timers in town, he had never been much of a farmer. He had left Zichron as a young man to seek his fortune in Paris, where he had worked for twenty years as an upholsterer in the *quartier juif*, bringing back a wife – a would-be opera singer, it was said – who went mad and was kept, screeching arias of frustration, under lock and key. "*Vous parlez français alors?*" he had asked with a watery wink while we negotiated the sale of his land, as though sharing a secret against Kruppik. "*C'est une langue de la plus grande importance pour un jeune homme d'esprit.*" It was rumored that he had acquired in the French capital the abhorrent vice of eating snails, which he gathered every autumn when the first rains released them from their summer sleep and consumed by himself like a miser counting his coins.

One day in the snail season, we drove up from Jerusalem to meet our architect on the land. It was time to determinate the exact location of our house. Should it be toward the bottom of the property, permitting a shorter driveway, or further up, where the ground leveled off? The more it did, however, the more the view of the valley disappeared, leaving only the foreshortened hills; by the time you got to the plum trees... the plum trees! All that was left of them were two stumps. They had been mangled with an ax, their hacked branches flung on the ground like clothing after an orgy. Goldstein! I ran to his house. He was out. That evening I got him on the phone.

"Goldstein!"

"Heh?"

"How could you have done it?"

"You! You made me." His voice was aggrieved, the injured party's. "They were my trees. I watered them as a boy. I offered to pay you for them."

"For God's sake," I said. It was as if the true mother in the story of Solomon had torn her baby limb from limb and accused the false mother of murder. "There was enough fruit for us both."

"We'd have fought over it. I wanted us to be good neighbors."

If he did, it was discouraging to think that one of us was a madman. The next time I saw him in town, his belly pendulous above the belt supporting it like a truss, I crossed to the other side of the street. By the time I could bring myself to speak to him again, we were already living in our house.

Chapter two

That first winter, it rained and rained. Apart from going into town to do our shopping, we clung to our house like shipwrecked sailors. It was right after the Yom Kippur War and we had a baby; no telephone and no prospect of one, no lines being available; and no one to talk to except the Traubs. "We should have stayed in Jerusalem," Marcia said as we lay in bed one night, listening to the rain make off like rats with our new garden soil.

"Mmmmm," I agreed. I was reading.

I had a book contract. It was my first and it had happened by accident. While on a visit to New York, I had gone to see a literary agent. Our conversation languished until I began to talk about the town in Israel to which my wife and I had recently moved. The agent perked up. "There's a book there," she said. "How much longer will you be in the city?" A week, I told her. "Bring me a proposal tomorrow," she said.

I brought her a proposal, saw four publishers in a week, received two modest offers, and accepted the larger one. It wasn't for much, but it would be enough to get by on for a while. The only problem was the proposal. It had been written in an hour. It had fooled two publishers, but it didn't fool me. I had no notion of the book I was supposed to write.

Marcia turned her face to the wall. "Don't fall asleep with the light on," she said.

* * *

Edmond de Rothschild, the grandson of Amschel Meyer Rothschild, progenitor of the fabled banking dynasty, did not actually found Zichron Ya'akov. When he first appeared on the scene, the village was a year old and bore the name of Zamarin, inherited from a hilltop hamlet whose absentee landlord removed its Arab peasants upon selling it. Its 350 colonists had arrived from Rumania in the summer of 1882, sponsored by the Lovers of Zion Society, a Zionist organization that preceded Herzl by over a decade. Four other agricultural colonies, the first Jewish farming communities on biblical soil in a millennium, were established in Palestine that same year – in which, following an outbreak of pogroms in Russia in 1881, thousands of other European Jews began their epic migration to America.

Difficulties met the colonists from the start. None had farmed before and their crops did poorly. The men worked in shifts, half of them spending the week in the mud-and-wattle huts they had bought, half staying with their families in an Arab khan in Haifa. Soon all were sick with dysentery from contaminated well water and malaria from the mosquitoes that infested the swamps between the Carmel and the sea. Next, they ran out of money. Some packed their bags and returned to Europe, while others drifted off to Jaffa or Jerusalem. In June 1883, on the holiday of Shavu'ot, the Festival of the Giving of the Law, the remaining colonists were forced to pawn their Torah scrolls to buy food. In late August they cabled the Alliance Israelite, a world Jewish organization headquartered in Paris: *Si l'on n'assistera pas au plus vite possible, nous serons tous perdus* – "If not helped as soon as possible, we are lost."

Their appeal was answered with a speed that was divine and in a tone hardly less so. In Rumania, an emergency session of the Lovers of Zion, told that the organization's coffers were empty, was dispersing in gloom when a special-delivery letter arrived from Paris. Sent by a French Jewish official named Veneziani who had recently toured Palestine, it said:

"It is my pleasure to inform you that I have been able to interest a most distinguished and well-positioned gentleman in the plight of the colony of Zamarin and its inhabitants. At the present moment, I am not at liberty to disclose the name of this estimable personage, whose dear wish it is to support your colony and to enlist it in the great enterprise we have before us, namely, the resettlement of the land of Israel. His one condition is that he alone shall be the colony's sole lord and that all things in its domain be under his rule, no other person having the right or privilege to interfere in its affairs or howsoever to challenge his will or pleasure...."

For two days, the Society debated this unusual offer. Then it cabled back:

"The plenary session fully accepts your proposal. We request to be informed of the name of our benefactor and of the exact nature of his plan."

A reply arrived promptly. The man who proposed to pay the colonists' debts, assume responsibility for their future expenses, and be crowned their absolute monarch was Baron Edmond de Rothschild.

On October 14 the colonists sent the baron a letter of acceptance that concluded:

"And now we wish to assure you that we are in your hands; the lands of Zamarin are yours; we too are entirely yours; we will accept without question or challenge whatever official you send to oversee us; we promise to undertake all that he commands us in your name and to obey in its entirety every order that he gives us.

"With perfect faith, Monsieur le Baron, we await the generous, enlightened, and vigorous measures by which you propose to make of our starving and indigent families a village of Jewish farmers who will, aided by your generosity, wisdom, and benevolent guidance, earn their bread by the sweat of their brows in this holy land, the land of our fathers."

This letter bore fifty signatures, among them an Ashkenazi and a Goldstein. When shortly afterwards, however, an Alsatian Jew named Elias Scheid arrived in Haifa and asked the colonists to officially deed their lands to the baron, several balked; they had left Rumania as free men, they protested, and were not about to enter the house of bondage now. Although at first Monsieur Scheid sought to expel the holdouts from the colony, he agreed to pass the decision on to Paris. Meanwhile, he settled the colonists' debts, redeemed their pawned Torah scrolls, and placed each on a stipend of twelve francs per month while moving the women and children to more comfortable quarters in Haifa and ordering all the men back to Zamarin for a daily work regimen. This began every morning with a bell for reveille; continued until a second bell tolled the noon lunch break; resumed with a third bell; and ended in the evening with a fourth announcing that the day was done. Edmond de Rothschild's new vassals grumbled but obeyed.

* * *

And so, a generation after the freeing of the Russian serf and the emancipation of the American slave, Jewish settlers in Palestine indentured themselves to the youngest son of a parvenu family of French nobility. The colonists of Zamarin were not alone in this regression to feudalism. Three other new Palestinian colonies, Rishon le-Tsiyyon and Nes Tsiyyona in the south and Rosh Pina in the north, pledged fealty to Edmond de Rothschild as well. By the mid-1880s, his fiefdom included hundreds of families and tens of thousands of dunams, and it was to multiply many times more in the years to come.

The promised guidance was not long in reaching Zamarin. On the next ship from Europe came an *architecte*, an *agronome*, and an *administrateur*, while a doctor, druggist, midwife, rabbi, schoolteacher, and ritual slaughterer were procured locally. The architect moved the colony half a kilometer to a more level site, where Founders Street was cleared the width of several carriages and prefabricated wooden cabins were brought from abroad. At right angles to it was laid the Street of the Benefactor, which accommodated a stone synagogue, a schoolhouse, and an administration building. New lands were acquired in the surrounding valleys and distributed to the farmers. European plows and oxen were bought; fruit trees were planted on the hillsides; grapevines were ordered from France. The colonists' wages were paid in scrip that could be spent in one of the village's three stores, each run by the widow of a pioneer freshly buried in a new cemetery beyond the south end of Founders Street.

By the time Edmond de Rothschild arrived on his first visit to Palestine in the spring of 1887, he was able to find in the renamed colony of Zichron Ya'akov (to which he came from a tour of his settlements in the south and a stopover in Jerusalem, where he unsuccessfully negotiated for the purchase of the Wailing Wall) a bustling community of seventy houses and nearly 400 residents apart from his own personnel. A photograph from those days shows Founders Street, unpaved, from the north: its wooden cabins stand behind picket fences and an oxcart rolls down it past half-a-dozen bearded men in mixed Turkish and European dress.

The baron and his wife spent four days in Zichron, inquiring into the lives of its inhabitants with the thoroughness of trained social workers. The day before their departure was a Sabbath. After services in the synagogue, Edmond de Rothschild rose to address the colonists. He lauded their devotion; extolled the virtues of hard work; adjured them to obey their superiors; entreated them to respect their Arab neighbors; exhorted them to keep faith with Jewish tradition and raise their children in the Hebrew tongue; and assured them of the gratitude of posterity and his own undying support. The next day, serenaded by the rifle fire of mounted Bedouin who had come to see "the Sultan of the Jews," he and the baroness left for Jaffa to board the ship that carried them back to France.

*   *   *

Edmond de Rothschild was to return four more times to review his Palestinian empire. Each time he sailed from France on his private yacht, visiting Zichron after anchoring in the nearby Arab fishing village of Tantura. His stays were shorter than the first one, sometimes lasting only a few hours, and although he generally gave notice of his arrival, he once appeared without warning like a schoolmaster surprising his pupils and was detected only as his cavalcade began its final ascent up the hill.

As a rule, he was greeted by an assembly of the colonists at the entrance to the village, where he was welcomed with speeches by the eldest and bouqueted with flowers by the youngest before going to the administration building to inspect the books. Then he rode off to see his latest innovations: The winery built with the finest French know-how, the new grape stock brought from America to combat the phyloxera rot, the soap and perfume factory utilizing the pungent flower of the native wild acacia tree. Next came a stop at the schoolhouse to quiz the children in arithmetic and their prayers, followed by a sampling of the colonists' houses. Poking his head into pantries and running a finger over lintels, he would praise a dwelling for its cleanliness, chide a mother for failing to drape a crib in mosquito netting, and ask a scruffy farmer when he had last been to the public bathhouse. Once, coming across a volume of Shakespeare on a shelf, he ordered the housewife who had displayed it for his benefit to read the Bible instead; another time, discovering an Arab working in a colonist's carpentry shop on the Sabbath, he decreed a boycott of it. A tour of the *dépot*, the general store, aroused his ire when he found the latest fashions from Paris on a clothing rack. Before his next visit, the colonists put away their good clothes and greeted him in the work shifts and house smocks that thrifty Jewish peasants were expected to wear.

Flanked by his officials, Edmond de Rothschild then walked to the synagogue while the villagers importuned him with their petitions as though he were Caesar approaching the Forum – a scene that never failed to exasperate him, who had already done so much for them. Inside the building, he addressed them in a French that was translated into Yiddish. Tall and slim, his black beard whiter with each visit, he cut an elegantly Mosaic figure as he dictated his commandments for life in the Promised Land. Like Moses, he was now brimming with confidence in the new world he was creating, now in despair at its backsliding, for which his invariable remedy was yet another enterprise to rally his querulous flock. Stone houses to replace the wooden cabins. A new colony on the hillside opposite Zichron to the northeast, named Meir-Shfeya after his grandfather Meir, and another in the hills beyond it, called Bat-Shlomo for his Uncle Solomon. A glass factory on the sands of Tantura to make bottles for the winery. Plantations of mulberry trees for a silk industry. Thoroughbred milk cows imported from Brittany. And still he brooded. Once, having delivered his traditional sermon, he concluded its exhortations with the biblical admonition, "Lest the land vomit you out when you defile it, as it vomited out your forefathers before you," declaiming the words in their biblical Hebrew in a voice choked with emotion before departing for his waiting yacht.

And like Moses, no sooner did he turn his back on the children of Israel than trouble broke out. From the beginning, relations between his officials and the colonists were strained. The colonists resented their subordinate position while unabashedly helping themselves to its fruits; the officials considered them a stiff-necked lot, fawningly ingratiating in their patron's rare presence, lazy, contentious, and grasping when he was gone. Lording it over them, they punished them for offenses ranging from failure to tip their hats to their superiors to lodging overnight guests without permission. The country they were stationed in was primitive and poor, populated by illiterate Arab fellaheen and ruled by Turkish warlords so venal that the art of bribery was considered a social grace. It was difficult to endure the heat and boredom; difficult not to go Turk oneself. Like Roman proconsuls, they saw sedition everywhere and helped to spread it.

Soon after Edmond de Rothschild's first visit, open rebellion broke out. Although at first the baron backed his administrator, who drove several of the rebels from the village and had one thrown in a Turkish jail, the tyrant was soon transferred to another post. His successor declared an amnesty, relaxed the *ancien regime's* draconian rules, and even encouraged the formation of a village council that was granted a modicum of home rule. Among its accomplishments were the founding of a Loan Society; a public library stocked with over 500 books and subscribing to seven dailies and periodicals; a Pilgrims Fraternity that journeyed to Jerusalem on Jewish feast days; a Wayfarers Association to house passing travelers; a Volunteer Fireman's Brigade; and a brass band whose musicians were dapperly collegiate in their high collars, dark smoking jackets, and gleaming ensemble of tubas, trumpets, cornets, slide trombones, and French horns.

The band was on hand to welcome the baron on his second visit to Zichron in 1893. Yet even as he listened to the stately airs of "Onward, Jordan" and "Land Of Our Forefathers' Pride," the debts of his colonies were growing. In Zionist circles in Europe, hard questions were being asked. The heroic pioneers of 1882, it was rumored in Warsaw and Odessa, had become the sybaritic citizens of a little welfare state, the only exertion demanded of them being the collection of the monthly stipends that sustained them after deducting the cost of the Arab labor hired to work their fields. In 1891, sent by a concerned Lovers of Zion Society on a fact-finding mission to the Rothschild colonies, the Hebrew writer Ahad Ha'am published a report that stated:

> It is commonly observed that all the Rothschild millions that have
> gone into Palestine have failed to yield a single clear success from which
> might be learned what [economic ventures] to pursue and what to avoid.…
> Yet without a doubt, one empirical truth has been established by the baron's
> colonies, namely, that among the greatest hindrances to successful coloniza-
> tion is the promise of unlimited financial support. Indolence, demoralization,
> dishonesty, deceit, wastefulness, loss of self-respect, and other harmful traits
> have been the results of this system.… There should be an immediate end to
> the financial subsidy of all colonists.

Edmond de Rothschild was not easily swayed by criticism. Yet after his
third visit to the Holy Land in 1899, he took Ahad Ha'am's advice. A year
later, he liquidated his Palestinian holdings, turning their management
over to the Israelite Colonization Association or ICA, an organization
authorized by him to put the colonies on a self-paying basis. His officials
packed and left. Ten wagons were needed to transfer their furniture from
Zichron Ya'akov to Tantura, from where it was shipped for sale to Beirut.

The new management was determined to clean house. Reaching
the conclusion that Zichron lacked the land to support its population,
it decreed that half the village's farming families would have to leave.
The colonists responded by going on strike. ICA cut off all support. The
colonists pooled their meager resources and survived for two years by
a system of mutual aid that came to be known with prideful assertion
as "the time of the commune."

For the last time, Edmond de Rothschild came to the rescue.
Purchasing two large tracts of land to the south of Zichron, twice the
extent of the original colony, he divided them among the farmers, each
family receiving its share of hillside for fruit trees and vineyards and bot-
tomland for grain. It enabled them to eke out a living while buying back
their land in yearly installments paid to ICA, whose role was slashed to
providing technical assistance. In the other Rothschild colonies, similar
arrangements were made. The feudal days were over.

*   *   *

The new century also brought other changes to the Jews of Palestine,
who then numbered a mere 50,000, most of them anti-Zionist tradition-

alists concentrated in Jerusalem. Indeed, the world Zionist movement was at an ebb. Plagued by internal dissension, it had lost much of the enthusiasm of the first Zionist Congress convened by Theodor Herzl in 1897. Yet starting in 1904, the year of Herzl's death, a new wave of Zionist immigration, or *aliyah* as it was called in Hebrew, began to arrive from Russia and the pace of Jewish settlement quickened again.

This wave came to be known as the Second Aliyah, to distinguish it from its predecessor. The two were opposites in many ways. The First Aliyah was composed mainly of families, the Second of unmarried youngsters; the former was conservative in behavior and outlook, the latter freethinking and free-living; the Rothschild colonists aspired to the life of a landed gentry in the Holy Land, the "Muscovites," as they were called by the Arabs, to a proletarian existence inspired by Russian revolutionary ideals. In time their leaders, men like David Ben-Gurion and Yitzhak Ben-Tsvi, were to become establishment figures, and eventually, prime ministers and presidents of the State of Israel. Upon their arrival in Palestine in the early 1900s, however, they were fiery radicals seeking to exploit the newness of the Zionist venture for the construction of a utopian world.

It was inevitable that the two groups should clash. The Muscovites scoffed at the Rothschild colonists, calling them armchair farmers and shtetl squires; the colonists resented the newcomers' brashness and lack of respect for the experience of their seniors. Heightening the tension was the Second Aliyah's campaign to make the First employ only Jewish labor. In principle, the colonists were not opposed to this. In practice, inexperienced Jewish field hands being more expensive and less productive than Arab ones, principle was honored in the breach, leading to strikes, boycotts, and blows.

This was why the farmers of Zichron were happy to welcome another group of immigrants who settled in the village in 1912. These were Jews from the faraway kingdom of Yemen, several hundred families of whom, convinced by rumors of the resettling of the Holy Land that the coming of the Messiah was nigh, made the trek across the barren sands of Hadhramaut to the Arabian Sea port of Aden, from which they sailed to Port Said and thence to Jaffa. In Palestine, where they acquired a reputation for industry and religious piety, the dark-skinned Yemenites found work that they were not finicky about performing for less than

Messianic wages. The colonists were glad to employ them, while the Muscovites reproved them for their lack of class consciousness and set about organizing them in the revolutionary cause. Soon many were living along a footpath to the northwest of Founders Street that was given the name of the Street of 1912.

Zichron grew. By the eve of World War I it boasted three streets; nearly 100 buildings (including a hospital, a bank, and a first sea-view villa, built by a wealthy Jewish couple from England); running water; a stagecoach service to Haifa and Jaffa; one automobile owner; two licensed bottlers of seltzer water; and 1000 inhabitants divided into six categories – colonists, ICA officials, independent professionals and artisans, Second Aliyah laborers, Yemenites, and Arab help quartered in the farmyards. It was the second largest Jewish village in Palestine and it took pride in being called by its sister colonies, with a mixture of mockery and envy, the "little Paris" of the East.

A little place in a big world. A postcard that reached it in those years, found by me in the deserted Graf Hotel (but I'm getting ahead of my story), was postmarked 1914 and addressed to:

> Zicron Jacob
> Near Haiffa
> Palestine (Syria)
> Ottoman Empire.

And then came the world war, bringing the collapse of the Ottomans and an episode called the Nili affair, and no one envied Zichron any more.

*   *   *

"Nili" was a Hebrew acronym formed from the biblical verse *netsach Yisra'el lo yeshaker*, "the destiny of Israel doth not lie," which was the code name of a pro-British spy ring that operated against the Turks, who had entered the war on the side of the Germans soon after its outbreak. Organized and run by Jews from Zichron and the vicinity, the ring functioned from late 1916 until the following autumn. Its main activity was gathering intelligence on Turkish defenses against the British army, then inching its way eastward from Egypt across Sinai. Some of this information may have played a role in General Allenby's rout of the Turks at Gaza in November 1917, with which the British conquest of Palestine began.

Even after the fall of Gaza, however, this conquest proceeded at a crawl. Although Jerusalem and Jaffa were taken soon afterward and Jericho was entered early in 1918, the Turks then dug in and retained control of northern Palestine until the war's final days. By then the country was in a shambles, its economy in ruins, its populace hungry, its peasantry decimated by forced conscription and repeated requisitions of animals and crops. When the 500-year-old Ottoman Empire finally toppled in Palestine, Lebanon, Syria, and Iraq, its inhabitants' endurance had been stretched to the breaking point by Turkish rapacity and the hardships of war.

It was the original slowness of the advance in Sinai that had led to the Nili ring's formation. Despite conditions in Palestine, the British seemed in no hurry to get there. After the failure of their abortive landing at Gallipoli and two Turkish assaults on the Suez Canal in 1914–15, they were content to wear the enemy down with diversionary tactics like Lawrence's guerrilla strikes in the Hejaz. The main theater of war was Europe. Until reinforcements could arrive from there, the British command in Cairo was reluctant to risk an all-out campaign.

Yet each day that passed brought new trials to the population of Palestine and fresh anxieties to its Jews, not wrongly suspected by the Turks of siding against them. Although the Turkish government had looked askance at Jewish settlement in Palestine before the war, too, Zionist interests had been defended by the consular intervention of the Western powers. Now, with the onset of hostilities, these consulates were closed. Jewish leaders were arrested; the use of Hebrew was partially banned; Jewish religious courts were shut down; all expression of Jewish national sentiment was forbidden; and expulsions of Jewish residents were carried out, culminating in the eviction of 10,000 Jews from Jaffa and Tel Aviv when the British offensive in Sinai began. The threat of mass deportation hung in the air. Sentiment for an Islamic holy war against the infidel inflamed anti-Jewish emotions, while news of the Armenian genocide bore out the lengths to which the pashas in Constantinople were prepared to go in defense of their crumbling empire. A quick British victory alone, so it seemed, could stave off disaster.

Such was the conclusion reached by two friends, Aaron Aar-

29

onsohn of Zichron Ya'akov and Avshalom Feinberg of Hadera, during a series of meetings in 1914–15. Aaronsohn was the elder of the two, a dynamic bachelor in his late thirties who had come to Zichron as a boy, the eldest of his family's six children; studied natural science in France on a Rothschild scholarship; and acquired an international reputation as a botanist and the discoverer of *triticum dicoccoides*, the elusive wild ancestor of cultivated wheat. Feinberg was thirteen years younger. The manager of an experimental farm of Aaronsohn's near Atlit, on the coast between Zichron and Haifa, and the fiancé of his sister Rivka, he too was a son of First Aliyah parents and had studied in France. The more introspective and romantic of the two, he was at the same time a crack horseman and marksman and a natural leader of men.

Both Aaronsohn and Feinberg knew every cranny of Palestine; both were passionate Zionists; both believed that, besides hastening the war's end, spying for the British could lay the groundwork for post-war English-Jewish collaboration. It was a bold scheme for two men who had never engaged in espionage before and had no organization at their disposal, or even the assurance that their intended beneficiaries were interested in their services.

It took a year for them to establish a network of agents and to forge contacts with the British in Egypt, who were suspicious of a Turkish trap. Meanwhile, they were joined by two more co-conspirators. One was Aaron's other sister, Sarah; older than Rivka, a strong-willed and physically striking woman of twenty-four, she had left – homesick for her family and native land – a Turkish-Jewish husband in Constantinople and journeyed back to Palestine through Anatolia, witnessing on her way the slaughter of the Armenians. The other was a rover named Yosef Lishansky, whose picaresque career in Palestine had most recently involved heading a Jewish armed guard service in the south. By the end of 1916 the network was in place and Aaron Aaronsohn, having left Palestine by feigning a trip to neutral America, was installed in Cairo as an adjutant with the British general staff.

* * *

The operation is poised to begin. Ill-starred, it runs the swift and deadly course of a melodramatically plotted thriller.

The British establish a regular rendezvous with the spies by means of a small freighter that drops anchor off the coast of Atlit. Yet after a few successful liaisons the ship fails to reappear, and in January 1917 Avshalom Feinberg and Yosef Lishansky, both rumored to be in love with Sarah Aaronsohn, set out to reach British lines by crossing the dunes of northern Sinai. Near El-Arish, Lishansky is found by a British patrol with a bullet wound in his arm. In Cairo, he tells Aaron Aaronsohn that Feinberg was killed by Bedouin marauders, from whom he himself managed to escape with a slight injury.

Aaronsohn believes Lishansky's story. Fearful, however, that news of Feinberg's death will prove demoralizing to the Nili's operatives, he sends Lishansky back to Palestine, where the coastal drops are renewed, with strict orders to keep it a secret. Lishansky moves to Zichron with his wife and two children and runs the ring with Sarah, whose lover he becomes, while telling the spies that Feinberg has been sent to a pilot's course in England so that future contacts with Egypt can be conducted by air.

The work proceeds. The freighter anchors off the coast on moonless nights, men row or swim ashore from it, and waterproof bags are exchanged: lengthy intelligence reports for British gold that covers the ring's expenses and is dispersed to the Jews of Palestine – partly to keep them from starving and partly to keep them from talking, since too many are aware that something is afoot. The British are pleased with the information and press for more. But while Sarah is looked up to by the members of the ring, Lishansky is resented as an upstart. In April, the two sail for a conference in Egypt that becomes a long stay when a series of mishaps strands them there. When they finally return to Zichron in June, they discover that Sarah's brother Tsvi, who has been in charge in their absence and is envious of Lishansky, has spread tales that he murdered Avshalom Feinberg in the desert.

Sarah and Lishansky do their best to hush Tsvi up. Throughout the summer of 1917 they seek to persuade the British, now stalled at the gates of Gaza, to abandon their tactics of frontal assault and outflank the Turks to the east, in the thinly defended sector of Beersheba. Yet the British continue to batter away unsuccessfully at the Turkish trenches while precious days slip by. Half of Jewish Palestine, it seems, knows of the ring's existence and it is only a matter of time before the Turks find out, too. Leaders of the Jewish community, terrified of a fate like the Armenians', threaten the Nili ring with dire consequences unless it disbands. Especially hostile are the organizations of the Second Aliyah, which view the Nili's ties to the British as a political challenge. In August, Sarah and Lishansky are forced to leave Zichron and move their base of activity to Atlit. In September, the noose tightens further. Avshalom Feinberg has a cousin, Na'aman Belkind, who is a Nili agent in the south. Fearing that Feinberg is dead, he sets out for Egypt to uncover the truth. He is caught by the Turks and interrogated until he tells all he knows, which is a great deal.

Sarah and Lishansky realize that time has run out and request an evacuation of the ring members by sea. But it is already too late. On the night of October 1, during the harvest festival of Sukkot, the Turks cordon off Zichron Ya'akov, where some of the spies are spending the holiday with their families. The dragnet is drawn. Arrested and tortured, Sarah obtains permission to return home for a change of clothes, takes a hidden pistol, and kills herself. The other ring members are transferred to a prison in Nazareth and from there to Damascus.

Only Yosef Lishansky manages to slip away. The Turks put a price on his head, scour the countryside for him, and threaten to raze Zichron to the ground if he isn't found. The colonists send search parties to look for him and ask other Jews to do the same.

The hunted man heads north and falls into the hands of Hashomer, a clandestine Second Aliyah organization. After debating whether to hide him or hand him over to the Turks, it chooses to kill him itself. Shot and wounded, he gets away and reaches the Lebanese border; then, finding no one to shelter him, he turns and heads south again, hoping to reach British lines. For a week he travels by night and hides by day, stealing food and horses until, sick and exhausted, he is apprehended by the Turks on October 20. A week later General Allenby turns the Turks' left flank near Beersheba and by Christmas he is in Jerusalem.

Zichron is spared. Lishansky stands trial in Damascus with the other ring members. He and Na'aman Belkind are sentenced to death and hanged on December 15. The remaining spies are sentenced to prison terms and released by the British at the war's end.

Of the Nili ring's leaders, only Aaron Aaronsohn survives the war. At odds with other Palestinian Jewish leaders, especially those of the Second Aliyah, he is nevertheless a member of the Zionist delegation to the Versailles peace conference, where his close relations with the British make him a key figure. A prominent political role in Mandate Palestine is forecast for him. Yet in March 1919 he is killed when a British military airplane that he is on goes down in the English Channel. Although there are rumors of foul play, no proof of it is advanced.

* * *

The Nili affair went on stirring passions in Palestine after the war. It became a permanent subject of controversy, the archetype of such subsequent national dramas as the Arlozorof murder case of 1933 and the sinking of the gun-running *Altalena* in 1948, pitting the Zionist Left against the Zionist Right with bitter divisiveness; for while the Left pilloried the spies as irresponsible adventurers, the Right glorified them as martyrs who helped steer Great Britain to the pro-Zionist stance of the Balfour Declaration. And yet the further afield the argument ranged, the less it touched on the inhabitants of Zichron, who were more interested in the stories that circulated among them of barrels of British gold buried in the town at the time of the spies' arrest.

The years of the British Mandate passed Zichron by in other ways as well. With the political ascendancy of the Second Aliyah, Jewish agriculture was concentrated in kibbutzim and moshavim, collective settlements to which Zionist pioneers flocked from Europe, thus marginalizing the private Jewish farmer. Concomitantly, a flood of immigrants pouring into the country settled mainly in its large cities, turning them into thriving centers. Zichron was left behind. It continued to grow slowly, acquiring electricity, paved sidewalks, and a fourth street named after Herzl, while losing a portion of its population when the Arab farm hands and their families were driven out of the farmers' yards in the 1930s. Once a conspicuous point on the sparsely dotted map of Jewish Palestine, it shrank in importance as the map filled in.

Was it already in those years that the town commenced its fall into hidden disrepair? Viewed from the street its old center, though shabby, was still lived in, rented by merchants who did a brisk trade, and even maintained after a fashion. Yet the minute you peered behind this façade into the old farmyards at its rear, you discovered a world of devastation, a secret Pompeii of moldering ruins, gaping windows, rotting rafters, fallen roofs, and heaps of rubble that could only suggest some calamity of nature, an earthquake or cyclone, that had spared nothing but the venomous weeds.

Yes – and the doves who gurgled in their shadowy roosts and rose as one bird with a titter of wings when I entered their Augean realms. Once they had shared these derelict yards with the hens laying eggs in the staved-in coops and the geese in the bone-white straw. They had seen the mules hitched to the rusted plows, the sheep prance to pasture through the gateless stiles, the ducks splash in troughs that had died of thirst long ago. They had cooed to the donkeys tied to the tethering rings that hung from the walls like knockers without doors; joined fluted voice to the neigh and the bray of the empty pews of the stables and barns; lullabied from their desolate cotes the Arab children in their tumble-down shacks. Now they piped and thrummed forlornly, perched on the skeletons of shutters whose paint was stolen by the sun, on the moldy leather of old harnesses suspended from rotten pegs, on the spindly limbs of unfruitful trees, on naked roof beams whose smashed red tiles were strewn like potsherds on the ground. CHARD CARV, they said. RSEIL. UX FRE.

It was not ancient Hittite or Etruscan. When pieced together, the tiles bore the names of their makers, Fréres Roux and Guichard-Charvin & Co. of Marseilles, their trademarks a cleft heart and a honeybee. They had been imported by Edmond de Rothschild's French architects, along with the lumber for the roof beams and planked wooden ceilings; the square or hexagonal red floor tiles, manufactured by F. Rouvier Gils, its symbol an olive wreath, of Salerne in the department of Var; and the cast-iron clasps of the louvered shutters made by German Templar carpenters in Haifa. These were in the shape of tiny human busts and came in both sexes: the women with round, Second-Empire bonnets above wavy tresses, corsages on their diminutive breasts, the men Roman centurions who – where grasping hands had not pried them from their sentry boxes in the walls – still stood sternly at their posts like the forgotten toy soldier in the children's verse.

A hilltop village transplanted from Languedoc or Provence, nestled among vineyards and olive trees, the Mediterranean a blue brush stroke below: no one could say Edmond de Rothschild hadn't tried. But something insidious had laid waste his plans, sweeping into his town like a sirocco in which the pariah dogs prowled at night. It had smashed the slender stable where he kept his curried horses, covered his honest stone synagogue with chintzy slabs of speckled marble, replaced the old schoolhouse with a new telephone exchange shaped like a giant white die, chopped down the tall pine trees planted by his gardeners in the park in the town square, ripped out the fountain in their midst with its mouth of a yawning lion, abandoned to the elements the Greco-Roman water tower with its ceramic plaque in his honor, and barred with vines the broken steps leading up to its roof, which – despite the three-story, prison-gray apartment building built at the intersection of Founders and Benefactor Streets – was still the highest vantage point in town. When one fought one's way to the top of it past the stings of fugitive roses, one could easily imagine, looking down on the havoc below, that the only artillery shells ever fired at Zichron – a few rounds from a British frigate that landed in a field outside town, sending the Turkish rear guard scurrying toward Damascus – had been a catastrophic bombardment.

At its rear, where it faced away from the street, the tower sloped earthward along a stone ramp supported by arches like an aqueduct's. Up this massive structure, constructed to be used only once, a team of oxen had pulled the big tanks that held the town's water supply, pumped from a spring below the winery.

"My, they were something," our neighbor Ora Rosenzweig said to me one morning as I sat in her kitchen sipping tea. A late spring shower had fallen, teasing open the honeysuckle buds outside her window. "They were made of copper, those tanks, and studded all around. At sunset they caught fire."

"What happened to them?"

"What happened to everything? They were sold for scrap, just like the fountain in the park – just like the old filigree benches. The trees in the park were so thick that a dozen couples could sit beneath them and each think it was alone. The town cut them down for firewood."

It was said without rancor. Ora's house on Wine Street was in perfect repair; her husband Micha's farmyard was as spotless as her kitchen; the rest was beyond their control. The town was not doing badly, expanding to the western ridges overlooking the sea as a first trickle of outsiders moved in and property values rose. As far as the farmers were concerned, its old center was the family attic. They had the right to keep what junk they wanted there without strangers poking around.

But poking had become an obsession. Now that the rainless summer had arrived, I spent long hours exploring, slinking behind buildings and scaling fences like a thief, shinnying through open windows and up stony walls, descending into dank cellars where the dung beetles crawled, bruising knees and cutting fingers on splintered sills and broken glass. I became an expert on old methods of construction; I came to know the different generations of floor tiles and the permutations of the floral patterns painted like cheap wallpaper on the peeling plaster of old walls; I could tell at a glance when a house had last been lived in, whether it was renovated before being abandoned, whether it was built under the British or the Turks. "Are you looking for British gold?" Marcia asked about these forays, which led each time to the same wrecked yards full of flotsam, the same worthless heaps of debris, the same deserted laborers lean-tos with their sordid pin-ups and disemboweled mattresses, the same outhouses stinking of ancient excrement. The objects I brought home – discolored bottles, mildewed books, bits of old farm implements, a stack of grimy index cards on which was written every saying from the Talmud beginning with the Hebrew letter *heh* – were of no value to anyone. Once I came across a dentist's chair that I tried cranking up and down while the leaves of a chinaberry tree rustled overhead like pages in a waiting room. Another time I pushed open the door of an old barn and found myself looking at stacks of yellowed newspapers. Dropping down among them, I read of the Japanese invasion of Manchuria and the Spanish Civil War.

Once, too, I ran into Betsalel Ashkenazi, Ephraim Ashkenazi's deaf old bachelor brother. I had taken a shortcut to town through his yard and stopped to examine a broken barrel pinned beneath a sheet of corrugated tin.

"No strength."

I looked up to see a scarecrow of a man, baggy pants belted tightly at the waist to keep them from dropping to his ankles. The lid of one buttony eye was half shut. He pointed at the tin sheet, beside which lay a torn boot. He made a circle with his arm to encompass the yard, in which the weeds grew shoulder high. "Snakes," he said. He swung an imaginary scythe to cut the weeds. He made an angry fist and let it fall. "No strength."

I touched the barrel with my shoe.

His good eye stared at me. Seizing me by the elbow, he dragged me toward the back of the yard, past an open shed full of discarded boxes and crates in which strings of shriveled garlic swung from the roof beams next to a corroded lantern and a snapped winnowing sieve. Still faintly visible on a wall of bleached boards were the names "Esther" and "Dinah."

"My cows." He tapped his chest and made squeezing motions with his fists, one over the other. "Eight." He lifted eight fingers and pointed to the barrel. He had been deaf for so long that he thought his condition was universal. He flapped his hand like a man shooing hens. "Gone."

The boards groaned in the afternoon breeze as though in pain.

He stood there, the stuffing fallen out of him and half an eye pecked away by the birds. He shooed with a flap of his hand the invisible ghosts of dead hens.

Gone.

Chapter three

S o you like haunted houses," Ze'ev Neiderman said one June day as we trod a carpet of blue blossoms fallen from a row of jacaranda trees. "Let's see how you like this one."

Neiderman was a retired school principal. Beneath his straw hat, a high forehead dropped to a stern aquiline nose and pale eyes the color of lake water that had dampened the mischief of decades of pupils in the local Nili School. I had recently made his acquaintance and had been promised a tour of the old Lange house.

"When I was a boy, I thought this place was a castle," he said. "This was the main entrance."

Before us rose an archway set in a high stone wall. Two iron tracks on which had slid the missing halves of a portcullis met in a parabola beneath it. A row of portholes ran along the wall's top.

"The servants," Neiderman said, "appear to have taken the day off. Shall we enter?"

We stepped into a courtyard, careful to avoid getting snagged on the thorn bushes. Although the house's two wings were deserted, their fluted columns and fretted parapets had withstood the elements more bravely than the town's other ruins. Michael Emil Lange and Nita

Rosalind Bentwich Lange, Neiderman told me, had come to Zichron shortly before World War I. Nita was the second eldest of the eleven talented and eccentric children of a prominent Anglo-Jewish family, a popular belle and honors student at Cambridge – at which, a religiously observant young lady, she had walked the three miles from Girton College to synagogue and back every Sabbath. Michael, an Orthodox Jew too, was a wealthy heir and aspiring social reformer who had unsuccessfully stood for Parliament on the Liberal ticket. Soon after their marriage, they resolved to start a new life in Palestine. In Zichron Ya'akov, where they struck up a friendship with the local physician, Dr. Hillel Yoffe, a Russian Jew with socialist sympathies, they bought eighty dunam and built the residence they called Carmel Court.

Neiderman fanned himself with his hat while pointing out the riding stable along the east wall through which we had entered; the one-story south wing with its rooms for guests and servants and its portico bearing the Hebrew date 5674; and the Langes' own three stories on the north side, with a veranda facing the courtyard and a corneled balcony looking out toward the sea. I stood shading my eyes from the sunlight, trying to picture the scene on a summer day long ago: the metal gates swung open on their gleaming tracks; the Yemenite livery boys washing down the foaming horses brought back from a morning ride; the Arab gardener watering the English flowerbeds of pansies, petunias, sweet Williams, and forget-me-nots that had splashed with bright Cambridge colors this yard where the gray thistles grew.

"Let's pay a call on Michael and Nita," Neiderman proposed.

We climbed the steps to the veranda. The door to the house was nailed shut and we helped each other through a paneless window. "I used to sneak into this courtyard to see how the English lords lived," Neiderman said. "This window was made of stained glass. It had scrolls of roses on it. I always wondered what they looked like from inside with the sun shining through."

We were in the Langes' drawing room. Imitation marble columns, their plaster-of-Paris gouged by vandals, set off a space at one end of which stood a fireplace with a carved wooden frame. The walls had gaping holes where their fixtures were torn out. Piles of refuse covered the fleur-de-lis design of the floor tiles. Neiderman kicked an empty food can, which rolled away to reveal a used condom. "Disgusting," he said. "This place has become the town brothel."

We wandered into the kitchen through a pantry, in whose wall was a ritual washstand inscribed with the initials M.E.L. and N.B.L and the Hebrew verse, "And ye shall draw water with joy from the springs of salvation." We descended to a den on a wooden staircase missing part of its banister and re-ascended to a top-floor bedroom whose windows had had a grand view of the sea before the unpruned trees blocked it. A doorway opened onto a terrace. I followed Neiderman outside.

"The Langes didn't live here long," he said, making room for me against a balustrade. "Soon after they moved in, the war broke out. As enemy nationals, they had to return to England. The Turkish army commandeered the place. There were German pilots billeted here, blond young men who flew sorties from airfields in the Valley of Jezreel. We children hung around the gate when the trucks brought their rations, because they sometimes threw us sweets. Once a boy was crushed against the gatepost. We scraped off his body and carried it away. The Turkish officers didn't lift a finger."

"You must have prayed for the English to come."

"I wouldn't say that," he said. "We were only children. To tell the truth, the grown-ups didn't talk about it, either. They were simple people. They lived for each day."

Even with a spy ring beneath their noses?

"I suppose some people knew about the Nili. My father knew more than most, because he was *mukhtar* of the village. That was a headsman appointed by the Turks. When he felt Zichron was in danger, he asked Sarah to stop. Later, she must have wished she had listened. You've read Aryeh Samsonov's book?"

I had. Most of what I knew about the town's past came from it. Samsonov was a local farmer who, in the 1940s, wrote a history of Zichron, the only one in existence.

"You'll find a different version there. Samsonov was my cousin and I don't like to speak ill of him, especially when he's only been dead a few months. *De mortuis nihil nisi bonum* and all that. But he wrote his book with British gold. For years he went every week to get his half-pound sterling from Alexander, Sarah and Aaron's youngest brother.

That book is sheer Aaronsohnia. Men like my father, pillars of the community, are hardly mentioned in it. I'll never know the half of what he did. My mother, who's outlived him by forty years, was such a gossip that he never told her anything. And now she's about to join him. The blessed soul has been sinking from day to day...."

The swift transition from filial piety to irreverence and back again had left him breathless.

"Then there really was British gold left in Zichron?"

"Let us say that if most people came out of the war poorer than they went into it, some did the opposite."

He was eager to get back to the Langes, who returned to Zichron with the victors.

"Carmel Court was a busy place in those years. The British were new in Palestine and local Englishmen were a find for them. There wasn't a visiting official from London, or a touring member of Parliament, who didn't put up here for the night. Nita was a ravishing hostess.

"One day she went tree-planting with a group of schoolchildren. The next morning she was dead. Of a ruptured appendix, it was said. But there were rumors that she had taken her life."

"How?"

"Poison, I suppose. That's generally how it was done in those days."

Ze'ev plucked and sniffed a blossom from a wisteria vine that had spread over the terrace from below. "Some said it was because she was childless. Or because her husband was less than a man." He gave me a profound look. "Who knows? The Langes didn't mix with us townsfolk. We weren't educated enough. After Nita died, Michael went to Europe to be treated for depression. I believe he had the privilege of being the first Palestinian to be put on the couch. One day he returned. He told the driver who brought him from the port to stop down below, took a gun from his luggage, and put a bullet through his brain."

Neiderman pointed to the remains of a carriageway leading to Carmel Court's back entrance. Sky-blue leadwort and orange lontana flowered faithfully in the circle that the carriages had swung around.

He gazed down disapprovingly. "I sometimes think that in our centuries of wandering, we Jews forgot what it was to have a home. Why bother keeping up anything that you'll just have to leave in the end?

When I was a student at the American College in Beirut, I took a course in civil engineering. One day there was a lecture about something called 'maintenance.' It was a new concept for me. When things fell apart in Zichron, they stayed that way."

On our way out, we passed back through the Langes' drawing room. Neiderman paused to admire the oak frame of the fireplace.

"What grace! It must have come from Damascus. No carpenter in Palestine could have done such work." He ran a hand over its inlaid design. "It's a wonder no one's made off with it. If I were younger, I'd do it myself."

* * *

The following day, in the dead heat of the afternoon when even the horseflies were asleep, I returned with a hammer, a screwdriver, and some rope, pried the frame loose, and dragged it to the car. I tied it to the luggage rack, covered it with a blanket, and drove back through the empty streets of the town.

As I turned into Wine Street, Ora Rosenzweig flagged me down from her garden. "What do you have there?" she asked.

I got out and lifted a corner of the blanket..

She clapped her hands with delight. "Good for you! I told Micha to take it years ago."

"I was put up to it by Ze'ev Neiderman," I apologized, telling her of our visit to the Lange house.

"Ze'ev has a morbid sense of humor," Ora said, "but he was a good teacher and a good principal. You won't hear much about the old days from him, though, even though he's older than I am. He was away most of the time studying. You should talk to Yanko Epstein."

"Who is that?"

"You *are* new in town!"

No one, Ora said, knew as much as Epstein about the history of Zichron. No one could tell a story as well, either. He lived with his son and daughter-in-law on Founders Street. "I have an idea. You know the new museum next to the bus station? He's its director. He's promised to give us a preview before it opens. Why don't you come with us?"

I would be glad to. Meanwhile, I had done the Lange house. What did Ora suggest for me next?

She wrinkled her brow. "You might try Tsvi Aaronsohn's old place, opposite the glazier's on Herzl Street. It hasn't been lived in since his daughter Yardena died. I wonder if there's anything still in it."

* * *

The front door was locked and plastic shutters barred the windows of the deserted home of Tsvi Aaronsohn, the brother left in charge of the Nili ring while his sister Sarah and Yosef Lishansky were in Egypt. I jimmied up a shutter, pushed open the window, and belly-rolled across the windowsill. Then I stood breathing dust while my eyes grew accustomed to the dimness.

There were four rooms, all strewn with refuse as if their tenants had just moved out and not yet returned to clean up. The first two were full of old kitchen utensils, empty bottles, cartons of rags, bent curtain rods, burned-out light bulbs, twisted hangers, unraveled straw mats. A large gecko did a headstand on a wall, its skin as translucent as the imitation parchment of the torn lampshade lying on the floor by a rusty Primus stove.

A sea of printed matter – books, newspapers, circulars, school notebooks, old magazines, mimeographed pages escaped from their staples – covered the floor of the third room. Tsvi Aaronsohn's family had read widely in several languages. There were French copies of *Readers' Digest* and a volume on *Traits d'économique domestique*. There was a German physiology textbook, Arthur Koestler's *Spartakus*, and Part II of *Faust* in old Gothic print. Also De Lacy O'Leary's *Colloquial Arabic With Notes On The Vernacular Speech of Egypt, Syria, and Mesopotamia, and An Appendix On The Local Characteristics of Algerian Dialect; The London English Matriculation Course* and *The Revised London English Matriculation Course*; and *Principles of Navigation, Cook's Traveling Handbook for Palestine and Syria, The Selected Dialogues of Plato, Teach Yourself Sailing, Life On The Mississippi, The Stories of Robert Louis Stevenson,* and H.G. Wells' *Capital, Labor, and Human Happiness.*

Half-hidden beneath the Wells was a pasteboard photograph of a woman. I picked it up and turned to look at the Hebrew books. Old school texts. A government pamphlet on medical care. Translations of European novels of the 1920s and '30s. Volumes printed in Eastern

Europe on paper so poor that the pages fell apart when turned. A small, tattered book called *Sarah, Flame of The Nili.* I added it to the photograph and went to the fourth room.

More odds and ends lay about. An empty container of cleaning fluid. An open can of black shoe polish that had caked into rock hard as basalt. Half a chessboard. In a corner lay a stack of neatly folded, black-bordered mourning notices announcing with great sorrow the death of Yardena Aaronsohn, *May her soul be bound in the bond of life.* Nearby was a battered suitcase. I opened it, gagged at a clotted pudding of dead cat, retreated through all four rooms, and vaulted back into the fresh air. The photograph of the woman and *Sarah, Flame of The Nili* were still in my hand.

Back home, I examined them. I looked at the woman first.

Badly faded, she was young and appeared to have been musical, for she was posed beside a one-legged table on which lay a violin and mandolin. The white of her dress blended into the white of her arms and her throat, giving her a spectral appearance. Only her hair, pulled back in a bun, and the dark points of her eyes remained prominent.

I turned her over. In a scratchy hand on the photograph's back was written in French, *Zichron Jacob le 3 Fevrier, 1910.* Beneath that it said in Yiddish:

"Dear beloved sister, brother-in-law, and dear baby Yardena,
I am sending you my picture and hope it finds you in good health.
Your loving sister,
Tova."

I lay down Tova, the aunt of baby Yardena, and picked up *Sarah, Flame of The Nili.*

The thin, paperbound volume was barely a hundred pages long. Its author had used the pen-name "A Simple Soldier" and dedicated the book to Rivka Aaronsohn, the youngest of the six Aaronsohn brothers and sisters, "who with chaste devotion and intrepid love has served, and still serves, as a priestess in Memory's temple." On the flyleaf, underneath the date "Passover, 1940," appeared the handwritten inscription, "To Yardena with best wishes and kisses." It was signed "Alex" and "Rivka."

Beside the handsome flourish of the first signature, the crabbed letters of the second were painfully plain.

"The year: 1914..." began the little book. "Yes, then too there was a war. Young people today may need to be reminded that Germany, Austria – in those days a great power – Bulgaria and Turkey were allied against England and France. And the Land of Israel was in the hands of the Turk...."

Aimed at a juvenile audience, *Sarah, Flame of The Nili* proceeded to tell the story of the Nili spy ring and the woman who headed it. Sarah Aaronsohn's childhood in Zichron Ya'akov.... Her marriage to a Jewish merchant from Turkey.... Her return to Palestine during the war to find an espionage network being organized by her brother Aaron and her sister Rivka's fiancé.... Her relations with him and with Lishansky, which A Simple Soldier indignantly defended. ("There were some at the time who sought to sully the purity of Sarah's name. They gossiped about her and Avshalom Feinberg, about her and Yosef Lishansky. Even in the Holy of Holies there will be those ready to tread with unclean feet.") Feinberg's death in the desert and Lishansky's return from Egypt....

It was familiar ground and I skimmed over it. The spies' work.... Their worsening situation.... Na'aman Belkind's arrest.... The ring's roundup.... Sarah's ordeal....

Suddenly, I slowed down.

"The people of Zichron," A Simple Soldier wrote, "felt they would go mad if they had to hear the screams of the tortured prisoners any longer. But there were also four women who ran through the streets of the town, laughing and jeering at each scream. And though we may leave their eternal damnation to others, let it be known that each was requited in her way. The first died a strange death shortly after the death of Sarah. The second went mad and died in horrible pain. The third became an invalid and has been bedridden for years. The fourth lived out her life in disrepute. And of all the villagers, let us fondly remember Yosef Epstein, who stopped one of the women from hitting Nisan Rutman when he was in chains. But not the local physician, Dr. Yoffe, who failed to come to the aid of the prisoners or to intervene for Sarah in her agony."

I read the passage a second time. Why did it grip me more than anything else I knew about the Nili affair? Perhaps because the story of the ring, for all its drama, had been scrutable until now. Heroism and passion, though not everyday occurrences, were perfectly human. But this ... *there were also four women who ran through the streets of the town, laughing and jeering at each scream* ... this was monstrous. It belonged to another world, an infernal one of Gorgons and Furies.

A Simple Soldier moved on. Grandiloquently, he pursued his tale to the end, where it merged with the great nature myths of the Ancient East, the fructifying gore of Tammuz and Astarte. Sarah's suicide.... The hunt for Lishansky.... The trials and hangings in Damascus.... The first rains of autumn falling on Sarah's fresh grave. "And since then each flower, tree, and blade of grass in our land has had in it something of the great torment and lofty hope of our saintly Sarah. The secret of her life is one with the secret message of the universe, which dies to come to life again each year – one with the secret message of eternity."

It was not the prose of an old doughboy, this book given as a gift to their niece Yardena by Rivka Aaronsohn and her brother Alexander. Who had written it?

* * *

"That's easy," said Nissim Carditi, the town librarian. "Your simple soldier was a captain in the British army."

He rose from his desk and went with the heavy limp of childhood polio to an inner room. "These are all by the same author," he said, taking three slim volumes from a shelf. The first was *Sarah, Flame of The Nili.* The second was a short biography of Aaron Aaronsohn. The third was entitled *In The Garden of Thought (From An Observer's Notebook)* and attributed to the authorship of ***X. On its dust jacket was the handsome photograph of a young man in military uniform. Taken in profile, he had a faultless nose and wavy hair cleanly parted. The brow was in perfect repose, the eye firmly marbled: the head of a sculptured Greek kouros.

I opened the book. On its front page was the notice:

"In 1942–43 there appeared three editions of this little volume of reflections. Now Aaronsohn House has republished a new edition for today's reader in which the name of the author is revealed: Alexander Aaronsohn."

I had been meaning to visit Aaronsohn House. Open to the public, it stood behind a picket fence near the old water tower on Founders Street.

I asked Nissim to check out *In The Garden of Thought* for me.

* * *

In the street outside the library, Ephraim Ashkenazi, a jungle hat strapped to his chin, was preparing to mount his bicycle, a fat-tired vehicle that looked like a child's first two-wheeler. With him was Amnon Broner, Carmeli the druggist's brother, a man with a sad face that had furrows like dueling scars. "Watch out you don't scrape your knees against the pavement," he said to Ephraim.

Ephraim slapped Amnon's back. "You'd never guess from his wrinkles," he told me, "that Amnon was once our star athlete. If he hasn't pawned them, he has a pound of gold medals at home."

Soon they were reminiscing about a historic tug-of-war against a Haifa team.

"There were eight of us," Amnon said. "Me and seven of our biggest farm boys. But when those lugs from Haifa showed up, my heart sank. They were stevedores from the port, every one of them. Each could lift a crate of oranges with one hand. Before we knew it, they were hauling us in like a bucket up a well."

The Zichron team was skidding toward defeat when the rope miraculously snapped. "Those Haifa boys were backing up so fast that they went flying head over heels. There were bodies scattered around like after a train wreck. They picked themselves up and ate so much melon while waiting for a new rope that their muscles grew soggy. In the second round, we won."

"It was a lucky thing Amnon brought along a razor," Ephraim said, poking my ribs.

I headed for Aminadav's grocery. Outside it Bad Ginger, the red-headed policeman, was writing a parking ticket, an act regarded in town as no better than a quisling's. Nearby, the state lottery vendor had fallen asleep with his chin on his table.

The grocery was in its usual chaos. Customers stood waiting while Aminadav tinkered with a torn tape in his cash register and his Arab helper crawled about on the floor, mopping up milk from a torn plastic bag. Small and cramped, the store had once been twice as big. However, Aminadav and his partner had quarreled; neither had agreed to sell out to the other; and they had built an inner wall, on either side of which, as though by a process of cell division, a new grocery came into being half the size of the old one. The customers split in two, too, each faction sticking to its side of the wall as though the other were barred by a picket line.

Next, I went to buy pastries at Mayunka Pomerantz's cafe, whose window was draped with a blanket to keep the cream cakes from melting in the sun. At the tables, the talk among the farmers taking their morning break was of grapes: of tonnage and sugar content, of prices at the winery, of crews of Arab pickers, of cabernet and semillon and sauvignon and carignan. The harvest was about to begin.

I headed home with my bags past the sleeping lottery vendor; past the kiosk of the potato-nosed Parsee; past Gift Bear and Wine Bear; past Miriam's wool store; past Yafia Cohen in her folding chair; past Carmeli's drugstore. Black-bordered flags of grief on the pipal trees announced with sorrow the death of. I wondered who posted them. Never seen, he came and went, a fleet herald, at an hour that was neither day nor night.

Outside Benedik's hardware store, Meir Benedik was measuring lengths of chicken wire. Meir had a large stock of jokes. "Did you hear about the Zichron farmer who went to Paris on his honeymoon?" he asked.

"What about him?"

"The passenger next to him asked where his wife was and he said, 'She's already been to Paris.'"

I crossed the Street of the Benefactor to Wine Street, passing the Rosenzweigs' house, passing the Blochs, passing the Weissfishes, cutting through the empty lot behind the Lundins. Little globules of snails clung to the undersides of the caper plants, seeking cover from the jackhammer sun; at night they were gone, leaving silvery trails in the moonlight, only to return the next day like a false dew. Although it was only midsummer, the big almond tree behind our house had already ripened its nuts in their blackened hulls and was dropping its leaves like a prize pupil handing in an exam ahead of its classmates.

I put away the groceries, then went to my desk and took the

woman named Tova from her drawer. Her spectral skin had as though faded even more, leaving her eyes, dark and knowing, in empty space.

Ask, said those eyes, and you'll know too.

You were one of the four women, I guessed wildly.

The dark eyes mocked me. Of course not. Her sister was the wife of an Aaronsohn, a Nili member himself.

Chapter four

Ora Rosenzweig was at the back door. "Come," she said. "We're on our way to the museum."

Micha was waiting on the corner in their jeep. We drove past the bus station and parked opposite the cemetery by a lawn planted on the grounds of the old village threshing floor.

A stone walk crossed the lawn to a glistening round white structure, by which puddles of freshly dried stucco lay splattered on the ground. From it, like a section of scroll, a curved wall unrolled to one side. A ceramic mural on the wall depicted the first colonists of Zichron in terra cotta relief, doll-like figures in heraldic fields of wheat ears and grape clusters interspersed with columns of names. Arranged alphabetically, these were the same names that appeared on the letter of fealty sent to Edmond de Rothschild in 1883. I scanned the first column:

Aaronsohn, Ephraim Fishl and Malka
Aaronsohn, Kalman and Hannah
Abadik, Leib and Rivka
Abadik, Shlomo and Tova

There were still Abadiks living on Founders Street, one the town veterinarian; Malka and Fishl Aaronsohn were the parents of the Nili leaders Sarah and Aaron; and Kalman, if not Fishl's brother, must have been a nephew, uncle, or cousin. Many of the first settlers had come in extended families. Even in the early years, let alone after decades of marriage among them, the old clans of the town were densely tangled.

"I found them!" Ora called. She pointed to the names:

Hoyser, Meir and Mira-Golde
Hoyser, Ita

"Your poor mother," Micha said. "She was left all alone when your father died and now she's all alone again."

"Micha! Mira-Golde – " Ora didn't finish the sentence. "Good morning, Yanko! How long have you been standing there?"

"Morning of light!"

Judging by his grin and quick blush, the man who answered with the Hebrew version of the traditional Arabic greeting might have been standing behind us for some time. He was slightly below medium height and wore a blue beret and thick glasses. "It was a ticklish business, Ora," he said. "You wouldn't have wanted your mother in one line with your father's first wife; they would have looked like a threesome. And if I had written his name twice, there would have seemed to be two of him. Who's the young man?"

Yanko Epstein and I were introduced. Then, pointing out a large bell by the entrance to the white structure, the original gong rung by Edmond de Rothschild's overseers to summon the colonists to their labors, he opened a security gate with a key, fitted a second key into a heavy glass door, opened that too, and pressed a light switch.

The word "museum," I realized as the fluorescent lights flickered on, had misled me. I had expected antique utensils, period costumes, old tools and artifacts, the tangible relics of the past. Yet what was displayed in the cave-like, windowless room we stepped into, with its oddly carpeted ceiling from which tufts of fabric hung like woolly stalactites, was only the past's black-and-white image. Dozens of photographs covered the walls, frame against frame. It was like being inside an overstuffed family album.

Yanko Epstein stood proudly in the doorway. "I'll hang more," he said. "There are pictures I haven't found yet."

It wasn't clear where they would go. The walls were as crowded as the Louvre's.

"Well, have a look." His voice was rough, as though hoarse from a cold.

The Rosenzweigs were already standing before a blown-up photograph of the town fire brigade, taken in the 1890s. With their battleaxes and visored helmets, the firemen called to mind ancient warriors storming a city under siege. Some struck heroic poses on their ladders. Others struggled with a coiled length of hose like Laocoon and his sons wrestling with the serpent in the sculpture by Polydorus of Rhodes. A bugler stood by, his half-raised instrument ready to sound the charge.

Yanko Epstein went over to the next picture, an old shot of the town band. With a wooden pointer he had picked up, he tapped a figure. "Here's your father's brother, Yeshaya Hoyser," he told Ora.

Ora regarded the figure. "So that's what he looked like," she said.

She had never seen a picture of her uncle, who had left for America before she was born. She only knew he had lived in New York and moved to San Francisco. "He was never mentioned in our home. He and my father quarreled when he left. Once I asked a friend who was going to California to look him up. She found him in the phone book and he said, 'If your friend is the daughter of my brother, I don't want to hear about her' and hung up."

She and Micha went from photograph to photograph, identifying dead relatives and acquaintances, emitting little gasps of surprise or dismay at living ones changed or forgotten, querying this face or that form. Epstein walked beside them, his pointer behind his back. From time to time, he tapped with it professorially.

I wandered ahead. The pictures were arranged chronologically, starting with a blurry one of the first pioneers boarding a ship in Rumania. There was a portrait of a grandfatherly Edmond de Rothschild; old views of the village; shots of the colonists with their oxen and plows. There were posed sittings of the baron's officials and the village elders, distinguished-looking men with whiskers and watch chains. In a large frame captioned "Heroes of The Nili" were Sarah and Aaron Aaronsohn, a nattily dressed Yosef Lishansky, and a moody-eyed Avshalom Feinberg. Below them were faces I didn't recognize and then one that I did. Its features were clearer: the cheeks full, the chin round, the lips slightly parted as if about to speak. But the dark points of the eyes were unchanged.

Tova. Last name: Gelberg. My ghostly musician. Next to her was Nisan Rutman.

I passed a group of workers, deep in mud, draining the malarial swamps between Zichron and the sea, and stopped before a column of horsemen.

Yanko Epstein came over. "1926," he said. "A memorial procession to Sarah's grave." He tapped a lead rider. "That's me."

Out of focus, he was hard to make out.

"I'm clearer in this one." I turned to some heavily made-up youngsters mugging for the camera. "1921. Our drama society put on *L'Avare*." He tapped an angular figure. Wearing a black bowtie, it peered rakishly over the shoulder of a young lady with a lipstick-smeared mouth. The face was thinner and sharper than that of the man standing next to me. A jaunty lock of dark hair fell over the forehead and a thin mustache grazed the upper lip. The assertive jaw jutted toward the viewer.

"Moliére's *Miser*?"

"We put it on in the cellar of the winery. I was out plowing the fields and had no time for rehearsals, so I wrote my lines on slips of paper and attached them to the plow handle with laundry pins. That's Ezra Goldstein." I wouldn't have recognized in the slim actor the corpulent snail eater who hacked apart the plum trees. "And the sweet thing with all the lipstick is Yafia Cohen."

Old Mrs. Cohen, whom I had passed the other day on a chair by her front door, one hand tugging at the dress that had fled naughtily past her knees to let the breeze peek at her underpants?

Yanko Epstein accompanied me past a picture of the town council and another of a female choir in sunbonnets. He touched my elbow by a group of young men kneeling in front of a man on horseback.

"That's me."

The mounted man wore a colonial jacket, breeches, and riding boots, and sported a hip holster attached to a shoulder strap. Magisterial, he verged on middle age. The face was fleshier than the young actor's, the dark hair combed back from a widow's peak whose lower slopes had eroded. The kneeling youths were dressed in uniforms of short pants and white shirts.

"Were you coach of the local football team?" I asked.

If he felt my urge to tweak him, he gave no sign of it. "Those boys were under my command during the Arab Revolt," he said.

The next photograph, in which four Arabs in robes knelt gripping long rifles while a second row stood behind them, could have been the rival squad's. It too had a leader, a portly man with a mustache and a resplendent *keffiyeh* on his head.

"Who are the Arabs?" I asked.

"What makes you think they're all Arabs?"

"Aren't they?"

"One isn't."

I searched in vain for the ringer.

He tapped the portly figure. "That's me."

"You?"

He grinned, the victor in our duel, and called to Micha and Ora: "Come see me with Sheikh Mukbil's gang from Sindiani!"

The Rosenzweigs laughed at the photograph. Yet before Epstein could say more, Micha, who appeared to know what it would be, yawned and remarked that there was work in the vineyards and Ora would like to see her parents.

"Her wish is my command," Epstein said gallantly, leading us to the last quadrant of the circular room. There, in a large frame, the founding couples of the village were marshaled, two by two, in columns as though in a senior yearbook. Young and old; thin and stout; clean-shaven and bearded; shy and bold-faced; bareheaded and wearing a carnival of caps, fezes, derbies, top hats, kerchiefs, bonnets, and shawls; leaning intimately toward each other or facing stonily outward like carved Pharaohs and their consorts, the Class of '82 was a varied but uniformly grave-looking lot.

And indeed, I thought, looking at their solemn faces, was there not a time before its decline into a common household totem when the camera had been a feared temple deity, the pilgrimage to it a sacred rite? In Zichron this had begun with rising early and taking a holiday to make the day's trip to Haifa. It had meant dressing in your best and taking care not to crease or wrinkle it on the long wagon ride; descending the stairs from the busy street to the grotto of a picture studio, where backdrops of foamy seas, snowy crags, verdant hills, and pearly lakes – of the Alps, the Hebrides, the Pyramids, and the Taj Mahal – stood stacked like giant postcards; choosing, along with one of them, whatever cape or caparison, walking stick or other accouterment, caught your eye in the crates of costumes and props; composing before a mirror your face for eternity, since the journey was unlikely to be made twice; then, freezing it into a mask beneath the arc lights while the keeper of the shrine dropped the silver oracle into its box and vanished, a priest donning vestments, beneath his black cloak; and lastly, returning to the humdrum bustle of the Arab *souk* to await the god's pronouncement, which told the truth more faithfully than the wandering gypsies who sometimes descended on Zichron to read palms on the threshing floor.

Yanko Epstein tapped the glass frame. "I've got them all here, every one of them. It wasn't easy." He spoke with the air of a shrewd philatelist. "Here are your parents, Ora. I did my best."

At first I thought he was referring to the quality of the reproduction. Ita Hoyser's short hair fell on either side of a round, girlish face. Although her husband was turned toward her, his light eyes stared, above a droopy moustache and close, curly beard, meditatively into space. He looked young for a widower on his second marriage…until, my glance straying, I caught sight of him in the same pose, this time gazing distractedly past a thin, aristocratic woman in long earrings and an embroidered blouse. Sadness veiled her eyes, as though to hide her approaching death from them.

Ora read my thoughts. "I didn't have a photograph of my father. But neither," she added with satisfaction, "could Esther-Leah find one of him with her mother. Both of these were spliced from the same shot of him."

She sighed. "I was five when he died. That's how I remember him, with that dreamy look. If he wasn't reading, he was thinking. I don't suppose you knew him well," she said to Epstein.

"No one did," Epstein said. "He was a man of few words. I'll tell you a story about him. He and Itzik Leibowitz had bordering vineyards.

Once I rode by while Leibowitz was pruning his vines. I stopped to talk and let my horse wander onto your father's land. I was the village field guard. Who could object to her snacking on a few grape leaves?

"Leibowitz and I were chatting when your father appeared in his vineyard. He looked at my horse and went like this." Yanko Epstein rolled a wrist back and forth in the local sign language for a question mark. "'Mr. Hoyser,' I said, 'the horse is mine.' He heard that and did this." Epstein pointed to himself, then to Micha, held up two fingers side by side, and swiveled his wrist again. "I called back, 'Mr. Hoyser, I know we're not partners, but my horse is working for you too.' Well, he nods at that and shows me his thumb and forefinger with a little space between them. 'Don't worry,' I said, 'I won't let her eat too much – and that was the end of our conversation. How do you get to know a man like that?"

He surveyed the faces in the picture frame.

"There's not a one of them I don't remember. Not one that didn't dandle me on his knee."

He walked us out to the lawn, the pointer still in his hand. The Rosenzweigs went to their jeep and I lingered with him by the ceramic wall. "Tell me," I asked, "what relation to you was Yosef Epstein?"

He took a step backward, as if to get me into focus. "What makes you ask?"

I told him about reading *Sarah, Flame of the Nili.*

"He was my father."

"And those four women?"

"What about them?"

"Who were they?"

His jaw jutted like the young actor's. "Some things are best forgotten," he said.

"Is it a secret?"

"A secret?" His hoarse voice was scornful. "The whole town knew about it. It happened right there." He pointed toward Founders Street. "You want to know who they were?"

He raised his pointer to the ceramic wall.

Tap.

Lerner, Yisra'el and Tsippora.

Tap.
Goldstein, Alter and Adele.
Tap.
Blumenfeld, Binyamin and Gita.
Tap.
Appelbaum, Avigdor and Perl.

"There," he said. "There's your secret. If you want to know more, you can ask them. They're all across the street."

*   *   *

I entered the cemetery through a gate and roamed about in it.

It had grown much like the town itself. At its center was an old section, its small, crowded, and poorly kept graves, many telling of untimely death in doleful epitaph and homespun verse, dating from Turkish times. Around them, starting with the British era, were wider avenues and bigger headstones, while further back a new neighborhood overlooked the sea. Although there were still some vacancies in the old part, most of these had, as though in fear of squatters, wooden signs saying "Taken" or "Reserved."

Two plots, each surrounded by a low iron fence, stood out at the juncture of British and Turkish sections. The first contained a pair of graves: a plain one with a modest stone saying "Sarah" and Sarah Aaronsohn's mother Malka's. Pebbles were heaped on Sarah's grave in the old Jewish custom of paying homage to the dead. A bouquet of fresh roses had been placed on top of them.

The second fenced plot was larger. In it were buried Nita and Michael Lange; the Langes' friends, the country doctor Hillel Yoffe and his wife; and a sister of Nita's who had lived at Carmel Court after the Langes' deaths. Geraniums grew there, and rosemary for remembrance, and slim, straight cypresses, tightly ranged like pallbearers. Suicide was a crime in rabbinic law, which ruled that those desperate enough to commit it be buried "beyond the fence." How typically Jewish to obey the law by outwitting it, making a badge of distinction out of a badge of shame!

Not a breath of air stirred the cypresses. Beneath them, where mother lay with daughter and old friends were together again, death seemed a not intolerable thing.

I found the first of the four women to the left of the Langes. She was

Tsippora
(Daughter of Aryeh Tsvi)
Lerner
A Builder of this Village
Who Died
On the 7th of Shevat, 5703
May Her Soul Be Bound in the Bond of Life.

She lay beneath a king-sized slab of marble together with her husband Yisra'el, the son of Rabbi Yehoshua Lerner, who had died three years before her in the Christian year 1940.

Alter and Adele Goldstein were buried singly, separated by a narrow strip of earth. They were on the other side of the Langes, he

The Industrious Farmer
Cultivator
And Public Servant
Born in Rumania 5630
Died the 21st of Adar, 5695;
she

The Industrious Farmwoman
Daughter of Meir Tsvi
Born in Rumania 5635
Died the 23d of Tishrei, 5700.

Hot and getting hungry, I wandered on, past the graves of founders and farmers, of graybeards and youths, retracing my steps up and down the jumbled rows as if looking for an address in the interminable streets of a town whose names kept repeating. I passed Alexander Aaronsohn and his father Fishl. I passed Meir Hoyser, the son of Yitzhak Hoyser of Focsani and the father of Ora Rosenzweig. I passed Tsvi Aaronsohn, in whose house I had been, lying next to his wife Sarah Hinde, the daughter of Shimon Gelberg and the sister of the spectral Tova. I passed Ze'ev Neiderman's father, Yisra'el Yehuda Neiderman

A Builder and Dedicated Public Servant
of this Village,

after whom Ze'ev's son Yisra'el Yehuda Neiderman was named. I passed Aryeh Leib Neiderman, the first Yisra'el Yehuda Neiderman's father, and Aryeh Leib Neiderman, Ze'ev Neiderman's brother – for the old Jewish practice had persisted in Zichron of handing down to grandchildren the names of dead grandparents, which skipped a generation like certain genetic traits.

I walked on past the grave of Aryeh Samsonov, Ze'ev Neiderman's cousin, whose book I had read; past Ya'akov Ashkenazi, the uncle of Ephraim and Betsalel; past Tsvi-Hirsh Graf, the first proprietor of the Graf Hotel, bitterly reproached because

Of thy beauteous inn thou wast the proud keeper,
But of all that thou sowed, Death was the reaper;

past the grave of

Mathilde Klein
Née à Paris le 29 Fevrier 1864
Décédée à Sichron Jacob
Le 19 Avril 1892,

whose epitaph was the verse from the Book of Ruth: "Whither thou goest I will go, and where thou lodgest I will lodge; thy people shall be my people, and thy God my God." *Pauvre* Mathilde Klein, who had converted to Judaism and married the colony's second physician, Dr. Alexander Klein, following him to a wasteland to die of malaria, puerperal fever, homesickness, or whatever else his meager stock of medicines couldn't cure, after which he returned to Paris to seek a new wife and career, leaving her lodged in this stony soil without a pebble of it on her grave.

It took a while to stumble upon the

Dear Man
Beloved and Loyal Father
Industrious and Indefatigable Public Servant
Binyamin
The Son of Aryeh Leib Blumenfeld
A Pioneer and Builder of the Town of Zichron Ya'akov
May His Memory Be Blessed
Who Died on the 13th of Sivan 5709
At The Age of 85.

Beside him lay the

Dear Woman and Esteemed Mother
Gita Blumenfeld
A Founder and Pioneer of Zichron Ya'akov
May Her Memory Be Blessed
Who Died on the 14th of Adar 5714
At The Age of 72.

Compared to such inscriptions, which could have been toasts at the Rotary Club that met in the town hall on alternate Monday nights, the crudely rhymed griefs of earlier years were keenly eloquent. After-dinnery, too, was the epitaph of the

Dear Man
Pioneer Farmer
And Public Servant
Avigdor, Son of Yitzhak Aharon
Appelbaum
Born the 15th of Elul 5638
Died the 23d of Sivan 5714.

But where was Avigdor Appelbaum's wife Perl? He was buried at one end of a family row that included his brother Shmuel; Shmuel's wife Miriam; and another brother, Meir. Perl was nowhere in sight. On Meir's far side lay Miriam Neiderman, Ze'ev Neiderman's mother,

A Founder and Builder of this Town,

who had died shortly after our excursion to the Lange house.

"Well, well! I had no idea the two of you were acquainted."

I looked up to see Ze'ev Neiderman, come to pay his respects in a plaid jacket, orange shirt, and green tie. "Actually," I said, "I was looking for Perl Appelbaum."

He knew the story of the four women. My interest in it puzzled him, though. "Epstein is right," he said. "Who cares what some foolish housewives did in the days of the Turks?" He had no idea where Perl might be; she had died when he was a boy. Carefully he placed a pebble on his mother's newly unveiled headstone and leaned forward to inspect it, clucking his tongue. "Look how these cracks are puttied up! I call that shoddy work, don't you?"

I asked why his mother was buried with the Appelbaums.

"It was one of her many miscalculations. She didn't want to waste money on a plot beside my father because she had no intention of dying. By the time she realized she was mortal someone else was installed there, so she decided to move in with the Appelbaums She just forgot to inform Meir Appelbaum's widow. A few days after my mother died the widow came to visit her husband's grave and had the shock of her life. She wanted my mother moved, but I said no. One burial is enough for a single lifetime."

"Meir's widow should have put up a 'Reserved' sign," I said.

"You're quite right. The grave robbers in this town don't bother with the bodies; they steal the graves themselves. Would you like to see mine?"

He was already leading me to it. "This plot needs to be swept," he said critically, glancing at a scaly mat of brown cypress needles. "Well, what do you think?"

What could anyone think? "It looks the right size," I said.

"Does it? Let's see."

The former principal of the Nili School lay down on his future grave, crossed his hands and feet, and shut his eyes as though embalmed, an orange and green mummy. After a while, he opened his eyes and sat up. "It fits like a glove!" he exclaimed. "Would you like to try it?"

He rose, took off his plaid jacket, and brushed the dead scales from its back. "I didn't think so," he laughed gaily, taking me by the arm. "Come, walk me back into town. You can leave Perl Appelbaum for another day. She's not going anywhere."

We passed through the cemetery gate and crossed to the other side of Founders Street, where he stopped to tip his straw hat to a tall, freckled man coming out of the bus station. The man tipped a black fedora back.

"*Mi'eyfo?*" asked Neiderman.

"*Mi'Heyfo.*" Only the old-timers in Zichron pronounced "Haifa" to rhyme with "Where from."

"I was visiting an old friend in the hospital," the freckled man explained. "We went to high school together in nineteen-oh-eight."

"And how are you yourself?" Neiderman asked.

"I can't complain. Bless God for each day."

The black fedora was raised and lowered again.

"That's Ben-Hayyim," Neiderman said when we parted. "He makes me feel young. Imagine that: high school in oh-eight! I was a year old then."

"How many men his age are left in town?"

"Of those who matter?" He stopped to count. "There's Ben-Hayyim. There's Epstein. There's Moshe Shatzman. There's … no, he's a baby like me. The rest are all pushing up daisies."

*　　*　　*

"Took a turn around the cemetery, did you?" asked Izzy Traub. "I don't suppose you came across Ruth Efrati's grave there."

We were having drinks on the Traubs' terrace, looking out at the twinkling night. From the darkness came the snores of *Tyto Alba*. A light breeze fanned the musk of the ripening pods on the great carob tree.

"No," I said. Marcia and I had only met Ruth once. She and her husband had had a weekend place on the other side of the Traubs.

Izzy said:

"Ruth was a local girl, a relation of the Aaronsohns. Her brother, Yoram Efrati, runs Aaronsohn House. Carries on as if the spy ring were still operating, I'm told. She married a chap from Tel Aviv and moved away. Then she inherited the land next to us and they built on it.

"There was a huge cypress tree there, the biggest I've ever seen. A stupendous old thing! People would come just to look at it. But the peasants in this town have queer notions about cypresses. Trees of death and such rot. Ruth told her husband to cut it down.

"The poor devil didn't know what to do. He wasn't superstitious and didn't want to cut down a town landmark. The more he put it off, though, the more Ruth pestered him. She told him it was either the tree or her. She wasn't setting foot in that house as long as it stood there.

"They stayed away for a while. Then, one night, I heard sounds in their garden. *Hel*-lo, I thought, they're back. But when I went over in the morning, no one was there. The odd thing was that the earth around the tree had been turned as if a trench had been dug and filled in. At first I reckoned it was a wild boar. They sometimes come up from the valley to root – big brutes. But it was a bit too tidy for that.

"A week or two went by and that cypress turned the color of a sprayed weed. Ruth's husband drove up from Tel Aviv and called me over to have a look. He wanted to show me the tree was diseased. I didn't say anything; I didn't know who the poisoner was. He went off and came back with some workers and they cut the bloody thing down. Christ! It was like butchering an elephant.

"Well, they started coming up again for weekends. Spent summers here, too. Then one year they went to Europe. While they were there, their daughter was in a car accident. Ruth booked the last seat on a flight to Israel and left her husband behind. The girl wasn't badly hurt. But when Ruth got off the plane.... Now what was the name of that Japanese Red Army chap who shot up the airport?"

"Kozo Okomoto?"

"Bob's your uncle! It was a ghastly business. It took a whole day to identify her body. Now she's beneath a cypress in the cemetery. Shame!"

A town of tree murderers.

Chapter five

The perfect trim of Aaronsohn House stood out in contrast to the dereliction around it. There were in fact three houses, all painted pink, in a single compound on Founders Street. On the low, padlocked gate of a picket fence hung a sign informing the public that the entrance was around the corner – where, down an alleyway named Nili Lane, a wall sloped to a higher gate on which a second sign announced that admission was on Mondays, Wednesdays, and Thursdays between the hours of nine and one. There I joined a party of tourists composed of a lone Israeli, some French hikers with walking boots, and a middle-aged couple from South Orange.

We were admitted to a gravel courtyard by an attendant. A young lady with eye shadow that looked applied by a paint brush introduced herself as our guide. Once we had bought our tickets in the archives building and seen the exhibit there, she said, she would show us the house in which Aaron Aaronsohn had spent much of his life and his sister Sarah had ended hers.

The exhibit consisted of two glass cases in which were displayed specimens of the wild wheat whose discovery had made Aaron Aaronsohn's scientific reputation; photographs of his family and of the Nili ring; and old documents and newspaper clippings. Several publications on a table were for sale. I was leafing through a volume co-authored by Yoram Efrati and entitled *Nili: A Tale of Political Daring* when we were summoned to the courtyard for our tour of Aaron Aaronsohn's house.

He had built it, our guide told us as we followed her through a latticed portico and a front door, so as to have a private place to live and work in while remaining with his family. Yet like its exterior, with its stone tower crenellated like a chess rook, its rooms struck one as excessive for a bachelor scholar's retreat. Although not large, their inlaid Damascene chairs and tables, the Persian rugs on the floors, the patterned Turkish drapes on the walls and on the divan of the sitting room, and the heavy blue velvet curtains on the windows had belonged to a man with expensive tastes. So had the double-posted bed and mirrored commode in the bedroom, which bore the wild wheat design that was Aaronsohn's personal crest. Next to it stood a bookcase with a remnant of the botanical volumes carried off by the Turks to Damascus, where their pages, our guide said, were used to wrap butter in the *souk*.

A second bookcase was in the sitting room. While the hikers gathered round it to read the titles of its leather-bound French novels, the man from South Orange fingered the ornamental silver swords that hung crossed on a wall above a photograph of Avshalom Feinberg. Then all turned to look as a concealed wooden wall panel flipped open at our guide's touch. Her narrative was as practiced as the dramatic pause that preceded it.

"When the Turks saw they could get no information from Sarah by torture, they decided to transfer her and the other spies to Damascus via a prison in Nazareth. She wrote a farewell note and managed to deliver it to safe hands; then she asked to wash and change her bloodied clothes and was led down the street to this house. The Turks had searched it and expected no surprises. They posted guards at the doors, removed the manacles from Sarah's hands, and let her enter by herself. She took a pistol hidden behind this panel and went to the bathroom with it. This way, please."

We trooped to the bathroom, in which stood a sink, an old metal washtub, a primitive floor scale, and a partition screening a toilet. Bending to lift a hidden trapdoor from which wooden stairs descended to a tunnel, our guide showed us the secret route by which Yosef Lishansky had escaped on the night the Turkish army surrounded the village.

"Sarah could only pray that Lishansky would survive her. She stepped behind this screen, put the pistol to her mouth, and pressed the trigger. The bullet passed through the top of her spine, paralyzing her from the neck down. The Turks sent for the town doctor, Hillel Yoffe. Sarah's first words to him were, 'For the love of God, I beg you to kill me!' But although she kept pleading in the days that followed for him to end her life, he refused to do so. Her greatest fear was of becoming delirious and revealing secrets.

"She passed away on the fourth day. Since no fabric could be bought for her shrouds, she was brought to the cemetery wrapped in mosquito netting. The Turkish curfew was lifted for her funeral and the townspeople came to pay their last respects. She died as she had lived: a heroine of her people. Are there any questions?"

A Frenchman wanted to know why Sarah had not fled with Lishansky.

The reason, our guide replied, was that she had felt responsible for the other ring members and did not wish to abandon them.

Was it true, asked the Israeli, that Yosef Lishansky had murdered Avshalom Feinberg in the desert to have Sarah for himself?

The eye shadow underlined a frown. Neither Sarah nor Aaron had believed that calumny for a moment. Its falsity was proven after the 1967 war, when Feinberg's remains were dug up by Israeli soldiers in Sinai with the help of an old Bedouin who corroborated Lishansky's story.

The woman from South Orange inquired about the bathroom scale.

That, our guide said with a smile, was an unusual item for its day. "Aaron Aaronsohn was a prominent figure in more ways than one. He fought a daily battle with his waistline. Once, before the war, when Jamal Pasha, the Turkish governor, threatened to hang him for his insolence, Aaron told him: 'Do it and the gallows will snap with a sound that will be heard around the world.'"

Back in the courtyard, someone asked about the third pink house.

"It was the family's. All the Aaronsohns grew up in it and Sarah's younger sister Rivka still lives there. Thank you for having come."

The visitors drifted off through the gate. I introduced myself and asked to speak to Yoram Efrati.

Efrati's office was in the archives building. A short man, he did not rise from his armchair to greet me, making me bend across his desk to shake a stubby hand. "I understand you're the Traubs' new neighbor," he said.

"Yes," I said. "They told me you were related to the Aaronsohns."

"On my mother's side. She was Sarah and Aaron's first cousin. How can I help you?"

"I'd like to use your archives."

"You're welcome to them. But they're too extensive to browse in. We have prearranged files for your convenience. Fill out this form and you'll be brought what you need."

He handed me a mimeographed sheet. At the bottom I agreed to acknowledge the assistance of Aaronsohn House in my research and to submit any publication for prior review.

I replaced the sheet of paper on his desk. "I've used archives before," I said. "Your first clause is standard. Your second is unheard of."

An eye twitched. "We're not a public institution. If you knew the defamation to which the Aaronsohns and the Nili have been exposed over the years, you would understand our need to protect ourselves. What aspect of the Nili story interests you?"

By now I knew the passage from *Sarah, Flame of The Nili* by heart. He made a dismissive gesture.

"You may think it trivial," I said. "But it made me curious."

"Did it? It shouldn't have. Those women were hysterical. The Turks were threatening to burn down the town and everyone blamed the Nili. They shut their eyes to the greatness of the moment and thought only of saving their own necks."

"Which were in real danger. Everyone knew what had happened to the Armenians."

He shrugged. "All I can tell you is that those four women and their husbands belonged to Dr. Yoffe's circle. Yoffe hated the Aaronsohns."

"Why?"

"Part of it was political. Yoffe believed in socialism; Aaron despised it. Part was personal. The two were friends until Aaron failed to recommend Yoffe for a medical position. Those women were under his influence.'

"That's all you know about them?"

"Two of them are mentioned in Sarah's farewell letter. You'll find the text of it in my book. The only one of the four I remember being talked about in Zichron was Tsippora Lerner. If a child of hers got into trouble at school, people would say: 'What can you expect? The father is a Lerner, but the mother's a bad bird.'" He smiled at the double pun: a *lerner* was Yiddish for a diligent student, while *tsippora* in Hebrew meant "bird." "You won't find that kind of gossip in our files, of course."

And the fourth lived out her life in disrepute.

"I suppose," he said, "that you could see it as a tragic clash between the village and the Nili. But true tragedy takes place between equals. Today the Nili is honored by the entire country. Just yesterday a kibbutz school was here, dozens of children from the political camp that reviled the Nili for years. Who remembers your four women?"

"I'd like to find that out."

"I wish you luck. When it comes to those years, there were two kinds of people in Zichron: those who knew more than they told and those who told more than they knew. The only kind left now is the second."

I left him drumming stubby fingers on his desk and bought a copy of his book on my way out.

* * *

Nili: A Tale of Political Daring was a scholarly if partisan history of the spy ring, published in 1961. I began at the end of it, with an appendix that contained thumbnail sketches of the ring's members. One read:

"Gelberg-Rutman, Tova. Born in 1893 in Zichron Ya'akov. Her father was a cooper in the winery. A friend of Sarah, Alexander, and Rivka Aaronsohn, she was active in the Nili from the beginning and traveled widely in Palestine collecting intelligence. During the Turkish arrests in Zichron, she was apprehended with her fiancé, Nisan Rutman from Hadera, and sent to Nazareth and then to prison in Damascus."

She was full of surprises, Tova was. Besides belonging to the Nili ring, she had married the spy assaulted by the four women, Yoram Efrati's "hysterics."

I turned to Sarah's farewell letter. Scribbled hurriedly and not always coherently on the morning of her suicide, it began with instructions for paying off the spy ring's debts and continued:

"According to a report I heard the [Turkish] governor give the [local] commandant, I saw him give him these three names: Appelbaum, Feitelson, Madursky from Hadera. I think they told them of our work, they quite simply informed on us.

"We're in a very bad way. I worst of all, because all the blame is on me. I've been beaten terribly and kept chained. Remember to tell those who come after us what we went through. I don't believe we will live after they've informed and probably told the whole truth. Soon there will be news of who has won [the war] and you'll see my brother[s?] and tell them of our tortures and say that Sarah asked for every drop of her blood to be avenged properly. Revenge on our Jews and especially on the government [under?] which we live. No pity as they had none on us. Believe me, I have no more strength to suffer and would rather kill myself than suffer any more at their filthy hands. They say they're sending me to Damascus, they're sure to hang me there. I'll be all right if I can get hold of some small gun or poison. I don't want them to torment my body any more. It's even worse for me because I see my father suffering for no reason. Well, the day will come and they'll be reckoned with, if not [by?] us then remember we were brave and died without talking…. Tell the Zichron council that when judgment comes they'll pay. We worked to pave the way and happiness for our people…. Let them gloat, Perl and that rotten Adele. It's all right, I'm not a hateful woman and I say gloat. I have no time for bastards. I did my best for my people and the good of my people, and if my people is lowdown…. So be it!

"Maybe Yitzhak can go on foot to look for Yosef [Lishansky] in the hills after the army leaves the village in a day or two, so that we at least know what's happened to him. They're searching for him everywhere.

"He mustn't give [himself] up. Better to kill himself.

"They've come. I can't write any more."

The letter ended there.

I checked the thumbnail biographies. "Yitzhak" was the Nili spy Yitzhak Halprin (1890–1960), also a native of Zichron.

I didn't know why Sarah spoke of only two of the four women,

Adele Goldstein and Perl Appelbaum. Perhaps the others hadn't been mentioned by her interrogators, who were unaware that she had lived in Turkey and understood their language. What she had heard, though, put Perl Appelbaum in a class by herself. She was not only a cheerleader at the arrest of Nisan Rutman. She was of three informers who turned the ring in.

*   *   *

As I was passing that Saturday afternoon through the town square, which was closed to traffic on the Sabbath, I spied Micha Rosenzweig and Yanko Epstein sitting by the plastic chess table in the park. With them, waiting for the afternoon prayer to begin, was the sexton of the synagogue, who doubled as the town slaughterer. I sometimes saw him, a sly-looking man with a trimmed, silver-fox beard, walking down the street with a hen dangling from each hand, its tail feathers spread in alarm like an upended petticoat.

Micha was talking about his team of grape pickers from the West Bank. Now that the harvest had begun, they were brought to work every morning by an Arab straw boss or *ra'is*. This past week the *ra'is* had been sick and Micha had had to pick them up himself near the old "green line," the border between Israel and Jordan erased by the 1967 war. He couldn't believe the traffic streaming across it at five-thirty in the morning. "It just kept coming. Cars, vans, pick-up trucks – each with five, ten, twenty Arab workers. To tell you the truth, I don't know what I'm growing grapes for. My *ra'is* makes more money than I do. I pay him ninety pounds a day for each picker, half of which he keeps for himself. He packs twenty of them into his truck, makes two runs a morning, and goes back to bed for the rest of the day."

Yanko Epstein clucked his tongue sympathetically.

"And mind you, he doesn't pay a cent in taxes. I give him cash and get no receipt. I don't even know his last name. Go find an Arab named Mahmoud."

The sexton glanced at his pocket watch. From the playground at the other end of the square came the shouts of children on the slides and monkey bars.

"But what choice do I have?" Micha asked. "My last Jewish picker worked till noon on his first day and said he was tired and going home. I can't even get Arabs from around here. Not long ago I asked a fellow from Faradis to work for me. He laughed at me and said, 'I live in a finer house than you do.'"

Faradis was the Arab village just up the road toward Haifa.

The sexton whipped off his sunglasses like a challenge, revealing light, cloudless eyes. "It's your own fault!" he accused. "The Arabs are taking over. You should have driven them out instead of begging them to do your work. Why, in '48 you stood shotgun over Faradis to keep them from running away! Do you know why they won't work in your fields? It's because they're sure that one day they'll own them."

"You know," Epstein said so mildly that perhaps I only imagined seeing him flinch, "you may not have been here at the time, but they once did own most of the fields around here. Breiki. Um-ez-Zeinat. Sindiani. Suberin. Hubeizi. Igzim. Kafr Lam. Tantura. Ein-Ghazzal." He tolled them like a drum roll for the dead. "You won't even find them on the map today. Only Faradis. And don't tell me that story about it."

"*Only* Faradis, eh?" The sexton stabbed the air. "You're right. I wasn't here. I was in Russia in 1948. I saw what was done to the Crimean Tartars for collaborating with the Germans. They were packed off to Siberia, every one of them. You should have done the same."

"That's not what your Torah says, is it?" Epstein asked. "Doesn't it tell you not to oppress your neighbor?"

"The stranger," I helped him out. "Ye shall not oppress the stranger, for ye were a stranger in the land of Egypt."

The sexton turned to look at me. I had never seen him without his glasses. A fox-fur beard, a foppish face; a cruel slant to the cloudless eyes. "A scholar!" he exclaimed, as though sniffing a hidden danger. "We have a scholar in our midst. Don't tell me about the Torah! The Arab is not the stranger. The Arab is Amalek. The Torah says, 'The Lord will have war with Amalek from generation to generation.' The Torah says, 'Thou shalt blot out the remembrance of Amalek from under heaven.' We should have learned from the Russians!"

"But why the Russians?" Epstein asked. "Why not the Swiss? They're made up of French, Germans, Italians. They fought each other for hundreds of years. Look at them now. Wouldn't you rather have Switzerland?"

"Switzerland!" The very idea was outrageous. "This is the Land of Israel, not Switzerland!" The sexton glanced at his watch again and rose to go. "Switzerland," he muttered, shaking his head incredulously. He had an odd gait when he walked, bobbing up and down like a buoy on invisible waves.

We watched him head for the synagogue. "You know," Epstein said, "I believe he'd slaughter them all if he could, the way he slaughters a chicken."

"You don't really think we can get along like the Swiss," Micha said.

"Why not? I have a brother in Zurich. I've been there five times."

"Jews and Arabs aren't French and Germans."

"No! They're closer! The Arabs know that. It's we who have forgotten. You have to know how to talk to them. Once I had an argument with a village sheikh about Abraham. You know, they say he was the first Moslem and that his favorite son was Ishmael, not Isaac. I told that sheikh, 'Listen: if someone came to your village and wanted to know what had happened in it long ago, would you send him to the young men or the old?' He said, 'The old, of course.' 'Well,' I told him, 'tell your ears to listen to what your mouth just said. Our Torah is older than your Koran.' He laughed and didn't say another word."

"It's their laughter I don't like," Micha said. "We have a cleaning woman from Faradis. During the war last year she said there were fights there over who would get whose house in Zichron when we were dead." He got gloomily to his feet, a big, tired-looking man with another week of harvest ahead of him. "And don't think she hasn't staked her claim on ours."

"Well, have a good week," Epstein said.

He and I were left alone. I waited for him to rise too, but he remained, thoughtful, at the chess table. "Faradis," he said. "I'll tell you why they stayed in Faradis."

I had heard the sexton's version before. Fearing their hired hands from the nearby Arab village would join the growing flight of refugees, it was said, the farmers of Zichron had guarded them to make sure they stayed put. I had never bothered to inquire whether there was any truth in the tale or whether it was a confusion of history with one of those jokes that the farmers were the butt of.

"It was right before the British left," Epstein said. "There was fighting everywhere."

He was talking about the spring of 1948, shortly before the state of Israel was declared.

"We had taken the offensive. The Arabs were on the run. But their villages around here were holding on. They were dug in and full of armed irregulars.

"We had the forces to clean them out. It wouldn't be easy, though. And so I was asked by the army to go to each village with an offer. If it laid down its weapons and put itself under our protection, we'd guarantee its safety. Otherwise it would have to face the consequences.

"I was the man for it. I had lived with those Arabs. I knew them from the effendi to the thief. 'Abu-Yussef,' 'Father of Yosef,' they called me, after my son, the way they called each other. A field guard isn't a farmer, up in the morning and in bed at night. For years I was awake when the town slept. I saw things – knew things – that no one did."

The gruff voice eddied as though around an invisible shoal and flowed on.

"I started with Faradis. It was the nearest village and the weakest. I rode there on my horse, gathered the village elders, and told them of the army's offer. If they agreed, I said, I'd come back that night with an officer. '*Ahlan wa-sahlan*, Abu-Yussef,' they said, 'but don't come at night. Come by day – and bring all the soldiers you can.'

"I understood them. They wanted a deal. They just didn't want to be suspected of cutting it secretly. I came back the next day with some armored cars and a loudspeaker and told the village to lay down its arms. The elders were there, trying their best to look surprised. We pretended to parley. They told the villagers they had no choice but to accept our terms, and we collected some weapons and left.

"Next I sent word to Tantura, down by the coast. The message came back that it was too dangerous to meet there, so we rendezvoused at night in a dry creek bed. The *mukhtar*, Sheikh Da'ud el-Hindi, was there; so was Mustafa Barimi; so was someone from the Dafiki clan. 'Look,' I said. 'You've heard about Faradis. We've taken Haifa. We've taken Acre. We've taken Jaffa. Your people are running like mice. Give us your arms and you can keep your homes and fields.'

"'Abu-Yussef,' they said, 'we would if we could. But Tantura isn't Faradis. We've lost control to the young hotheads and they're spoiling for a fight. They'd rather be dead lions than live dogs.'

"They begged me to keep our meeting a secret. The next time I saw them was after the battle of Tantura. They were squatting on their rear ends with their hands on their heads. '*Ya* Sheikh Da'ud,' I said to Da'ud el-Hindi. 'It wasn't the dogs you should have listened to, it was their master.'

"I went by night to Ein-Ghazzal, dressed as an Arab. I rode a donkey, because too many people knew my horse. I tied it to a tree near the house of the Sa'abi brothers, Ismail and Otman, and knocked on their door. They were scared to death to see me. I could tell I wasn't a welcome guest. They said a meeting with the village elders was out of the question. The Arabs of Faradis were traitors. It would never happen to Ein-Ghazzal.

"I rode to Igzim and spoke to Mahmoud el-Madi; he told me what I had heard in Ein-Ghazzal. I rode to Suberin and met with its three big clans, the Hajj Mahmouds, the Abulbadis, and the Hamadis. They said the village would rather flee than surrender and be disgraced. 'Do us one kindness,' they said. 'Keep the Jews from destroying our homes until we return.' 'Know,' I answered, 'that if you flee now you will never return.' They never did.

"I rode to the camp of the Arab-el-Hamdun. 'We'll do what Um-ez-Zeinat does,' they said. I rode to Um-ez-Zeinat. They said they would follow the lead of Sindiani. I rode to Sindiani and met the elders. They agreed to turn in their arms. Their one condition was that I be there. I promised to come back in a few days with the army.

"A few days later we came to Sindiani. The village was empty. Even the moths were gone. They had all headed east, taking Um-ez-Zeinat and the Arab-el-Hamdun. I ran into some of them in a Jordanian refugee camp after the '67 war. They were living in hovels. 'Why didn't you keep your promise?' I asked. 'Abu-Yussef,' they answered, 'the world of Islam would never have forgiven us.'"

He fingered a square of the chess table. "Well," he said, "now you know why they stayed in Faradis."

"Yes."

"No, you don't."

His gaze was sharp behind his glasses.

"They stayed because they had no balls."

And still he made no move to leave the table, although he had plenty of time to do so while I pondered his words. It was getting dark. The playground was emptying out. I glanced up through the branches of the trees for the three stars that marked the end of the Sabbath. Had they really been as thick as Ora Rosenzweig recalled?

"They were thick," he confirmed.

He leaned toward me confidingly. "I had better places than this to take my girlfriends. But if you want to hear a story about lovers in this park, I'll tell you one that even Ora doesn't know. It happened during the great war."

Although there had been many wars, only one was deserving of that title.

"The Turks had fenced off this park for their officers. One day a friend of mine, Dov Leitner, told me he had seen a local woman trysting with one of them here at night. That wasn't something you could tell me in those days and expect me to leave it at that. I told Dov I'd look into it."

He pointed toward the back of the park. "There was a hole in the fence back there. I crawled through it after dark and hid in a bush. I sat for an hour, chasing away the sting-gnats, until I heard a sound. It was the woman. She had crept through the same hole and was checking to see that her dress hadn't ripped on the fence. Then she sat on a bench near me. Now I couldn't move. Those gnats were driving me crazy."

I could believe it. Tiny things with noiseless wings, they stung like iodine in a wound.

"After a while I heard voices. Three officers let themselves in at the gate with a key. I recognized the middle one. He was the army doctor, Adel Bey. The other two were hanging onto him. I could see they were drunk. They staggered so badly they couldn't keep to the path. 'Oho!' I thought. 'This is even better than Dov said.'"

"I glanced back at the bench to see what the woman was doing. She was gone.

"I looked around and didn't see her anywhere. That was odd. There wasn't time for her to have crawled back through the fence. She had vanished into thin air.

"The three officers began to stroll around the park. I had to try not to laugh, because none of them could walk a straight line. Adel Bey's two friends kept calling the woman's name, laughing and shouting. He tried to hush them.

"That's when I spotted her.

"The three of them, you see, had decided to have some fun with her. The more the merrier, eh? But that wasn't for her. She hadn't bargained for more than the doctor. Now she was hiding in a bush like me.

"There was nothing to do but wait for them to get tired. And when they did, I had some business with her. What a woman did with her life was her own affair, but this was a matter of Jewish honor."

A first car, getting a jump on the new week, passed through the square, skirting the no-entry signs at either end of it.

"The officers kept shouting and swearing. They started toward me down a path. Their arms were linked and each time one stumbled he pulled the others after him. Just as they passed me, Adel Bey lost his balance and fell. I didn't wait to see where he landed. I jumped from my bush and made for the fence like a rabbit.

"I was halfway through the hole, with my behind in the park, when there were shots. If those officers hadn't been too drunk to see straight, I'd have had to patch my only pair of work pants. I ran up the street without looking back and bumped into Dov Leitner. He had heard the shots and come running. 'Dov,' I said, 'why did you tell me that woman was carrying on with an officer? It's more like a regiment.'"

The Sabbath was over. Men drifted out of the synagogue, wishing each other a good week. The sexton went to the no-entry sign on the corner and wheeled it away on its round base.

Yanko Epstein stood up from the chess table. "Don't think that doctor didn't pay for it," he said as though loathe for me to think he had been bested.

"How?"

"That's a story for another time."

"Let's make a date."

"I'll be at the museum Tuesday morning."

I walked him toward Founders Street. "Did you ever have it out with that woman?" I asked.

"Of course," he said. "She wasn't a bad sort. It was wartime and her husband was in Egypt. She lived next to the park and it was easy for her to sneak into it."

"Who was she?"

"A woman from town."

"I meant her name."

I had a growing stack of index cards at home, each with a name on top.

His jaw jutted. "I thought I told you some things were best forgotten."

The sexton had finished wheeling the sign and started up the street for the second one at the square's far end. He wagged a finger at us as he passed. "Watch out! Watch out for him!" he warned.

It wasn't clear whom he was addressing.

Our ways parted at the corner. "Have a good week," Epstein said.

He turned to go to his house on Founders Street and I headed home down the Street of the Benefactor. From the houses along it came the voice of a television announcer, back on the air after the Sabbath. As there was only one channel in Israel, you could follow the program from house to house. It would be a quiet Saturday night in Zichron. It always was.

* * *

Arriving that Tuesday at the museum, I found the gate and door locked. No one opened when I knocked.

I waited by the ceramic wall, watching the tractors chug up the hill from Binyamina with their wagons of grapes for the winery and chug back down again. After a while I crossed the street and walked through the open gate of the cemetery.

A handful of people, too few for a funeral, was gathered by a grave.

An unveiling, perhaps, or a memorial. I kept to the old section, wandering idly until an inscription caught my eye. Stooping to read its chiseled lines, I saw they were a Hebrew poem. It went:

> *My wife, didst thou speed to this place*
> *In woe, and best me in life's race,*
> *Rather than labor vainly on,*
> *Always asking: Lord, how long?*
>
> *God and man could not avail thee*
> *On the day that hope did fail thee.*
> *Learning and knowledge thou didst pursue.*
> *Didst thou not know that these fail too*
> *And fill the heart with grief and rue?*
>
> *Before thy time, thy time hath passed,*
> *And thou hast left behind at last*
> *Thy sorrows that outlived thy joys,*
>
> *Bereft of four of thy dear boys.*
> *Even thy comforters could find*
> *No comfort for thy heart that pined.*
> *Zion weeps for thee and thine.*
> *Thy darling daughter mourns for thee.*
>
> *My heart will ever long for thee.*
> *O gracious, pure, and blameless soul!*

Beneath this was carved:

> *"Mira-Golde, wife of Meir Hoyser."*

It was the grave of Ora Rosenzweig's father's first wife, the sad woman with the long earrings. Ora hadn't mentioned her burying four of her sons. The cemetery was full of children's graves, little stone reliquaries shaped like jewel cases, but this was rare loss even for those days.

The bitter grief of a bookish man. Only after studying its oddly arranged stanzas did I realize that Meir Hoyser had written an acrostic, one of the oldest Hebrew verse forms. Read from top to bottom, the first letters of the first fifteen lines, plus the first word of the sixteenth, spelled "Mira-Golde bat Ben-Zion," Mira-Golde the daughter of Ben-Zion. The "darling daughter" of line seventeen was Ora's half-sister Esther-Leah Berkowitz, the frail old widow I sometimes saw rocking on her porch next door to the old water tower.

I passed the fenced enclosure in which Sarah Aaronsohn lay with her mother Malka. The wreathe of roses was gone from her grave, its place taken by white lilies.

And then, as you sometimes find a lost object only by forgetting about it, I was in front of the grave I had been looking for. It was not far from Sarah's, hidden from it by a spreading cypress tree. On a plain, weather-cracked marble plaque atop a low gray stone was written:

> *Here Lies the Woman Perl Appelbaum*
> *Daughter of Reb Hayyim*
> *Born 5632*
> *Died the 27th of Av, 5682.*

I made a quick calculation. Late summer, 1922. A woman of fifty.

The first died a strange death shortly after the death of Sarah.

The Woman. Not the Esteemed Mother, or the Industrious Farm Wife, or the Builder of This Village. Buried alone, away from her husband and his family.

I returned to the museum. There was still no sign of Epstein.

I ran into him in town, talking to Yosef Blum, the farmer who lived beyond the Traubs at the other end of our dirt road. Blum was leaning against his tractor, which was hitched to a wagon of grapes. They were examining something in Epstein's hand.

"Come, see what I've got here," he called to me.

It didn't seem a cause for celebration: a small, old photograph, frayed at the edges, of half-a-dozen whiskered men around a table.

"I found it this morning in an old file cabinet of The Savings and

Loans Bank," he said. "No one knew what it was. But I did! It's the inaugural meeting of the first board of directors in 1906. I'll have it enlarged and framed."

He seemed as pleased as if it were a lost Rembrandt.

"Did you forget our date this morning?"

His eyes widened behind their thick lenses. "Of course not. But this is a find."

I proposed trying again.

"It's a busy week. Today I'm going to Tel Aviv. Tomorrow I have a class of schoolchildren at the museum. Friday there's a meeting of the Burial Society. I'll bet you didn't know I was its president. Come to the park on Saturday afternoon. I'll be where I was the last time."

"How are the wife and daughter?" Yosef Blum asked.

"Just fine," I said. "And yours?"

He was the tallest farmer in town, and next to him Epstein, with whom he was still talking when I stepped out of Aminadav's grocery a few minutes later, looked even shorter than he was.

Over lunch I told Marcia about my morning.

"It could have been anything," she said of Perl Appelbaum's death. "She could have been scalded by a kettle or bitten by a bee. What difference does it make?"

"Plenty. According to Sarah's farewell letter, Perl betrayed the spy ring to the Turks. In that letter, she asks to be avenged. And years later her brother Alexander writes in a book that Perl, who is buried in the cemetery like an outcast, was punished with a strange death. What does that suggest?"

"That there are more interesting things to talk about. Why don't you ask those old-timers you hang out with?"

"You don't have to sound jealous."

"I'm not. I just don't like it when you go for a walk and don't come back."

"I'm usually back in half an hour."

"Last Saturday it was two and a half."

"I ran into Epstein and Micha Rosenzweig in town. If we had a phone, I would have called from there."

"If we had a phone, I wouldn't feel that you'd brought me to a desert island with a child. With two children."

She was pregnant.

"*I* brought *you?*"

That was often how our arguments began.

Chapter six

I don't know. A heart attack? Cancer? She was a nice woman. It's not as if she was murdered."

It was Yafia Cohen's first day back in her folding chair next to Miriam's wool store and she had marked it by putting on her rhinestone earrings and daubing bright lipstick on her mouth. She was wearing a bathrobe over her pajamas and a print kerchief that hid the white tufts of her balding head.

"Good to see you back," I said.

"Hello, sweetheart," she said to my daughter Talya, who was perched on my shoulders. "Yes, they all say the town wasn't the same without me. And next week I have to go back to the hospital for more tests. At my age, if the doctors don't find what they're looking for, they find worse. It was better in the old days. My mother belonged to a society called Righteous Lodging. She sat up nights with the sick, fetched the doctor if he was needed, things like that. I helped run errands and brought hot meals that she cooked. No one died by themselves the way they do now. You got better care from your neighbors than you get from the nurses today. Don't bump your head against the sky, sweetheart."

It was then that I asked how Perl Appelbaum had died.

She remembered nothing strange about it. "The Appelbaums lived at the far end of the village. My mother never sent me that far. Some young man might have run off with me." She sent a coy finger to her chin as if in search of a lost dimple.

Talya squirmed on my shoulders.

"I wasn't as pretty as you, sweetheart. But all the farmers' daughters were jealous of me. They called me 'the princess' because of the way I dressed. My father was a schoolteacher. He would never have let me marry a farmer."

"Home," Talya said.

"I was once thrown out of a farmer's house. I was friends with his daughter and used to eat lunch there. Once I said, 'How come you eat only bread and herring? In my home we eat all kinds of things.' Her father rose from the table and shouted, 'Get out!'"

I wished her health and started down the street. By Carmeli's drugstore, I heard her call. I turned and she motioned me back.

"Home, Abba!" Talya urged.

"I think I remember something about Mrs. Appelbaum," Yafia Cohen said. "She wasn't right in the head before she died. Maybe that was the strange death."

Something wet ran down my neck.

* * *

"A brain tumor. And her son died of the same thing. Odd, isn't it?"

Ben-Hayyim poured himself a brandy and reached out to pour me one, too. Despite the tremor in his freckled hand, not a drop spilled on the tablecloth.

"Odd," he repeated of the Appelbaums.

If Ben-Hayyim had a first name, not even his wife ever used it. Perl Appelbaum, he said, had come to Zichron from Russia by herself. She was a "cultivated lady," the only farmer's wife to own a piano.

Two oil portraits hung on the wall. They were of Ben-Hayyim's elder brothers.

"They grew up in France," he said. "My father died of yellow fever when I was a baby. He was dead six hours after it hit him. The farmers took about as long to divide up his land. My mother left me with my grandmother and went to Paris to get it back. In the end she won her case, but by then my brothers were in school and stayed in France. One was killed at Verdun. After the war, I went to look for his grave. Do you know how many men died at Verdun? Half a million. Try finding a grave in half a million."

His parents were from Russia like Perl Appelbaum. "That made a difference. The Russians were a cut above the Rumanians. They were the circle around Dr. Yoffe. That's why I was brought up to believe I was a little genius who was sent to school in Jerusalem to become a rabbi. I never became one, but I have held my own in life's wars."

His head had the same slight palsy as his hand. It made him nod when he spoke, as if for emphasis.

"I remember the summer I came back from Jerusalem. We were winnowing on the threshing floor and someone said I was blocking his wind. You need a good breeze to winnow. The other farmers took his side. I shouted at them, 'Who do you think you are? You, you're the son of a harness maker! You – of a shoemaker! You – of a carpenter!' They were simple people, the Rumanians. My father came from Russia and read books."

I had run into Ben-Hayyim outside the synagogue, of which he was president, and he had invited me home with him. Often now, going into town on some errand, I ended up chatting in the street or in Pomerantz's café. Most of the old-timers were happy to reminisce. They didn't have much else to do. Everyone but me had already heard their stories

Sometimes I introduced myself. Seeing her rocking on her porch one morning, I went up to Esther-Leah Berkowitz, Ora Rosenzweig's half-sister, the "darling daughter" of her mother's tombstone.

"Yes," she said. "Those four boys died of malaria when they were little."

"Your mother must have died of heartbreak."

"Oh, no." She seemed surprised that I thought hearts broke so easily. "She fell off a ladder and died of complications from a miscarriage."

The poem on her mother's grave was the wordiest she remembered her father being. In writing, too. "I'll show you something," she said. She went into the house and came back with a worn copybook.

"He wrote down the important events of his life here. They don't fill a page. Look at this: *1893: My daughter born.* And here's the next time I'm mentioned: *1916: Esther-Leah married.*"

"In the middle of the war," I remarked.

"Yes. A week after my wedding the Nili tried enlisting my husband. I said to him, 'What, *I* married a spy? Never!'"

She had distrusted the Nili ring from the day she realized the spies were in it for the money. A dressmaker had shown her a freshly minted English coin. "She told me it was from the Aaronsohns and I thought, 'So that's what it's all for – to buy Sarah dresses!'"

The Aaronsohns were stuck-up. But the end was terrible. "Don't ask me about it. I can hear Sarah's screams to this day." She helped care for Sarah after she shot herself. "I changed her sheets and primped her pillows. She only spoke once. She had fainted and someone revived her by rubbing her with eau-de-cologne. It got in her eyes and she said, 'Can't you do anything right?'"

She remembered Perl Appelbaum's death, too. "Perl had married off her eldest daughter that year and then … ." Her hand rose slowly, passing over her chest and throat as if ferreting out a hidden illness before coming to rest on her forehead. "Something happened up here. There was nothing strange about it. Alexander must have wanted to sound scary. He liked to impress people. He walked around in those years like an English lord, in a gold-buttoned jacket and a white captain's cap."

Ben-Hayyim didn't think much of A Simple Soldier, either. "Alexander had half of Zichron on his payroll after the war," he said. "He had a following of toadies. If you weren't one of them, you had to watch out. I was once threatened by two goons of his for being against his speaking at a memorial service for the Nili."

He poured us both another brandy.

"It was in the synagogue. When he rose to speak, his brother Sam got up and shouted that it was a mockery for the martyrs of the Nili to be eulogized by a lecher. Alexander made a sign and Sam was given the bum's rush. He was a bum, all right, but it was true. Alexander was a degenerate."

He nodded vigorously.

"He had a thing for the little girlies. He liked his fruit fresh, if you get what I mean. He had them brought to him, fourteen years old, fifteen. The Aaronsohns owned an olive grove beyond the cemetery. He had a pavilion there to which he took them, a regular boudoir. Once I put my two mules out to graze in the next field and found him in the grass with one of his little friends."

He laid a freckled hand on my arm, as if to restrain my swelling outrage. "It started with Tova Gelberg. She's dead, so it's no sin to say it. She was Alexander's first *maitresse*. When she was too old for him, he passed her on to Nisan Rutman. But life, my friend, has a sense of humor. Man proposes and God disposes. In the end Rutman ditched her and ran off with some young baggage, who then left him for a younger man. Now he's alone in an old-age home in Haifa. Do you know what the Bible says about that? 'He that diggeth a pit shall fall into it; and whoso breaketh a hedge, a serpent shall bite him.' No, my friend, I don't know what Alexander had in mind when he wrote that about Perl Appelbaum. Maybe he dreamed it. The Talmud says, 'A man sees in his dreams what he dreams in his heart....'"

Tova Gelberg had become a mysterious traveling companion. Wherever it was that I was headed, I kept running into her.

There was nothing mysterious about Perl Appelbaum's death, though. Although Ben-Hayyim was wrong about the brain cancer, he had the right organ. The cause of death was listed in an old town registry that Nissim Carditi kept in a back room of the library. Large and bound in black, its pages were ruled into vertical columns. The first entry, dating to December 1919, was for a three-month-old infant who had died of "infantile atrophy." Next came a two-and-a-half-year-old victim of malaria.

I looked for Perl in the summer of 1922. She wasn't there. The only name I knew from that year was Nita Lange's. No. 41 on the list, she had died on February 14, at age 38, of "Intestinal colics and paralysis of the heart."

It was a curious diagnosis. After appendicitis and suicide, it was a third version of Nita's death.

But where was Perl? After playing hide-and-seek with me in the cemetery, she was at it again.

I found her in 1921, on August 31, the 5th of Elul, between No. 34,

Lena Ashkenazi ("Suicide by setting herself on fire"), and No. 36, Ita Hershkowitz ("Septicemia"). Parents' Name: Unknown. Born: Russia. Occupation: Housewife: Cause of Death: Encephalitis.

Compared to what had killed others in Zichron in those years – "old age," "weakness," "prolonged intestinal illness," "Valaneor disease," *"maladie du coeur," "élancement"* – this had a solid medical ring.

Nor, despite the discrepancy in dates, had Perl died twice. The puzzle was easily solved. As elsewhere among Jews, tombstones in Zichron were sometimes unveiled after a year, sometimes after a month, and sometimes after a week. Perl had died in 1921; the unveiling took place a year later. The stone carver, however, mistakenly thinking her dead but a week, had inscribed the wrong year on her grave, subtracting a mere seven days from the ceremony to arrive at the day of her death.

A Simple Soldier had blown the whole thing up.

A pity, because he would have made a logical murderer. He even had a license to kill. He had issued it to himself in his *The Garden of Thought*, in which he declared that "God created man to be the master of his own life. The soul of man is a spark of God. When it flares into a fire, man is freed of all human constraints."

It was a curious little volume, a collection of epigrams and reflections originally published in the 1920s in a weekly newspaper column. Divided into sections with names like "Love," "Holiness," "The Way To Beauty and Happiness," "Suffering and Its Fruits," and so on, it seemed less the work of a single soul than of a team of eccentric authors – a romantic, a libertine, a moralist, a mystic, a stoic, a cynic, and an aspiring *Uebermensch*, all companionably sharing the same bachelor digs in which they stayed up late at night discussing Nietzsche and Khalil Gibran. About "The Way to Happiness" this odd fellowship had reflected:

"To hope for the best – to be ready for the worst – this is the secret of the believer's serenity."

Also:

"If our sensual perceptions were not effete, we would always know how to behave. The secret of life is to let sensual perception command and the mind find the way to obey."

Of Love it had observed:

"There are men, few and far between, from whom lust is not a staircase descending to a wine cellar where they besot themselves but a ladder ascending to God."

And:

"A young girl dreams of a wondrous love.... But the child does not know how to plant her imaginings in the soil of Life, how to weed them with the hoe of Faith and water them with the waters of Desire. Therefore her dream is but a night flower that wilts in the morning light of Reality.

"But if she were to remain faithful to it – if she were to wait for the morning of its fulfillment – it would bring her Knight of Love to her, adorned in bright glory. He would appear before her rapt eyes while she was milking the cows or sewing in her alcove, standing at the cook-stove or typing at the office. His burning love would clothe her in queenly robes while her faithful longing would crown him her prince forever."

The Knight of Love had not only had "a thing for the little girlies," he had had a philosophy for them:

"From the earliest age, the child must be prepared to welcome with a tremor of joy the sexual impulse when it awakens, to receive it as a great and wondrous gift of divine grace. Children must be educated for the priesthood of sex."

He had fancied himself a naturalist, too. In a section called "Mysteries," he wrote:

"I once knew a lady with an unusually keen eye who thrilled to everything in the universe. One day, after long hesitation, she confided to her brother, her life's guide, that all houses with cypress trees around them were doomed to tragedy. Ever since then, brother and sister have continued to observe this truth. In all places and countries, they have seen that the cypress bears a curse. Its place is in the cemetery."

That explained Ruth Efrati's cyprophobia. It came from her cousin the cosmo-vibratory Rivka, the last of the Aaronsohns, a recluse never seen in the streets of the town.

Besides also reflecting on loneliness, motherhood, hygiene, athletics, and nutrition (Alexander favored vegetarianism but was opposed to the fad of tomato juice), *The Garden of Thought* contained a sketch of a dancing party.

I had just been hearing about such parties from Yafia Cohen. "People say to me," she told me from her folding chair, "'Yafia,' they say, 'you have so many memories, you should write them down.' But who would read them? All anyone wants to do nowadays is watch television. It's ruined everything. In the old days, the village was one family. We mourned and celebrated together. And the young people! The fun we had! The dances!"

"What did you dance?"

"What didn't we! The waltz. The *lancers*. The one-step. The two-step. Dances you had to know how to dance, not the jumping up and down they do now. Everyone wanted me for a partner because my boyfriend's roommate was a wonderful dancer who paid his rent by giving me lessons. That was the year I acted in a play. I don't remember its name."

"*The Miser.*"

She stared at me as if I were a ghost.

Alexander had written:

"Cigarette smoke. The smell of beer, sausage, sour pickles, sweat, and dust. The groaning of an old gramophone. And couples, many couples, dancing in the narrow aisles between the tables.

"The moment a woman sets foot in such a place, she ceases to belong to herself and becomes the chattel of the dancers. And what for? To execute the most ridiculous set of movements that man created in God's image ever stooped to.

"From out of a box, like canned, tasteless food, comes music. And the couples, as if they were nursery children again, begin to move. Most pay no attention to the rhythm. What rhythm can there be when men and women pass from arm to arm with no soul-link between them?

"A husband sits sadly looking at his wife, who drifts by him with a stranger. And as though hiding in a corner, his face pale with anguish, stands a young man. He is watching the girl he loves cling to a lout who is getting her drunk on hollow words. Now the two slip outside....

"When she returns with hay in her hair and dirt on the back of her dress, she is met by mocking eyes. The young man's heart shrivels. A flower has been plucked and trampled. Tomorrow the trampler will smirk at his triumph.

"The unclean handprints of her partners smudge her gown. Never mind: it can be washed and ironed. But her befouled body and soul – these will haunt her all her life ...."

Why, there's Tova, I thought. Tova Gelberg.

Chapter seven

Yanko Epstein was not in the park that Saturday. An hour later he still hadn't turned up. There was no one but the crazy tinker and his wife, slowly progressing along the benches. Both in their Sabbath best – he in the socks and shoelaces he did not normally wear, she in a clean dress instead of her usual dishrag-colored house smock – they kept opening and closing the distance between them.

It began with the tinker, who held a pocket knife in one hand and a large apple in the other. Sliding down the bench away from his wife, he cut a slice of the apple and popped it in his mouth. After a while, she sidled up to him. For a while they sat side by side, regarding the apple as if to see what it would do; then, without offering her any, he moved away and cut himself another slice. This time, as though to catch him napping, she waited longer before edging back. Once more they sat with their knees almost touching until he bolted again.

They were already on their third bench, advancing and retreating like a pair of courting squirrels. When, passing their room opposite Carmeli's drugstore, I heard them arguing, his voice was a tongueless howl, hers a twitter like an injured sparrow's. She liked to sun herself beside her jars of pickles on the steps while he mended the watering cans and kerosene heaters brought to him for repair in the stable he shared with Motl Sokolov's donkeys. No one knew whether they had gone mad in the Nazi death camps or had always been that way.

Most of the small band of men gathered in front of the synagogue for the afternoon prayer were wartime survivors from Europe. Although the founders of Zichron were Orthodox Jews, the agricultural life had not lent itself easily to the clocks and calendars of ritual observance, and somewhere along the line, gently and without shock, religion had passed away like an old grandparent. Apart from Ben-Hayyim, the sole farmer I now saw was Yisra'el Tishbi – who, trading his donkey for a walking stick, made do on the Sabbath with three legs instead of four. Yet he was in no way diminished, for the dark suit and black derby that replaced his blue work clothes made him look like a prosperous broker.

Such transformations were common in town. There was Meir Benedik's father, the owner of the hardware store, which he ran in a mixture of Hungarian and bedlam. There was Menachem Friedman of the stationery store, who had begun as a penniless refugee with a number on his arm, peddling used books on the sidewalk. There was Gift Bear, his German accent thick as strudel, whose brother Wine Bear prayed only on Yom Kippur. There was Mordecai Bushnik the blacksmith, who had fought in the Red Army, and Karol the mechanic, who had a garage near the winery, and still others. Once a week, while their neighbors mowed the lawn or washed the car, they stepped out as princes among their people in jackets, neckties, hats, and polished shoes, their prayer shawls in velvet bags beneath their arms like the portfolios of bankers.

There was still no sign of Epstein.

I glanced up at the sky. Furrows of crimson cloud ran across it, shirred and banked at the edges like earth thrown up by the plow, portenders of autumn.

The clouds had turned a smoky purple and the tinker and his wife had left the park when I rose to go. From within the synagogue came the dull chant of prayer, the sexton's nasal cries bobbing up and down at the head of it. Though he spoke an Israeli Hebrew, he reverted when he prayed to the native accents of Eastern Europe, his "t" changing to "s," his "ah" to "aw," his "o" to "oy."

Oy was right.

* * *

"Do you think he's avoiding me?" I asked Ora Rosenzweig about Epstein a few days later. We were in her living room, a bowl of chocolates before us on the table. Next to it was a ceramic sculpture of three backgammon players.

"Whatever for?" she said. "He's always glad to find someone new to talk to. No one in town has the patience for him except me. I can listen to him for hours and still feel sorry when he goes, like a child at the end of a bedtime story. But you can't expect him to be punctual. He keeps time like an Arab. He spent his whole life with them."

"Well, I'm tired of chasing after him," I said.

"You should talk to Moshe Shatzman. He knows a lot and he's straight as an arrow. Just don't get him started on Epstein."

There was no love lost between them. "Yanko," Ora said, "was never well-liked in town. He had charm when he was young, but he was wild – a brawler, always getting into trouble. Today he's a different man. It's as if all the bluster had sunk to the bottom and the mellowness risen to the top. You should see him with visitors to his museum. The elder statesman of Zichron! I just wish he weren't so pro-Nili."

She shared the anti-Nili views of her half-sister. "They came from my parents. My father was a socialist like Dr. Yoffe. He was the one farmer in town who wouldn't employ cheap Arab labor and hired only Jews – Yemenites, Russians, anyone willing to work. He even gave them Hebrew lessons. I remember him sitting with them on the floor at night, all around the same book."

Ora's mother was a "Muscovite." She had met Meir Hoyser in Zichron during the war, as a refugee from Tel Aviv. They both hated the hysteria around the Nili, "all that bowing and scraping."

The other farmers thought her father queer. "They would have thought that of anyone who read more than the daily paper, let alone Hegel and Schopenhauer. Those were philosophers, weren't they? I remember their names on the bindings of the books that my mother gave away when he died." Her voice choked easily when she spoke of him. "Most of them went to Dr. Yoffe. Alter Goldstein took a few, too."

"The husband of Adele?"

"My goodness, how did you know? She was crazy as a loon, that woman. Once Alter woke in the middle of the night to find a sheet over his head. He pulled it off and saw a candle on either side of him. Adele was sitting by the bed in a black dress, keening as though for a corpse."

The second went mad and died in horrible pain.

Ora didn't know about the pain. "She died like anyone. You can't believe every word Alexander wrote. Have a chocolate. They'll be collectors' items soon. Emanuel Turskanov is going out of business."

I was sorry to hear that. There was nothing special about the bonbons sold by Turskanov – who, with his lofty brow and stallion's mane of white hair that tickled the black scarf he always wore, strode about town with the princely and distracted air of the last scion of a deposed royal house. Yet waiting to be brought them while inhaling the soupy aroma of melting chocolate in the doorway of the old Graf Hotel, of which he was the last occupant, differed from being handed a box with a pink ribbon over the counter of a confectionary shop.

On my way out, I bent to look at the backgammon players. One had just cast the dice; another arched a long, jointed body over the board; a third, a young kibitzer, looked on. The dice thrower must have said something funny, for the tall man was smiling. But the kibitzer, intent on the dice, was too absorbed in the game to have heard it.

"What sculptor made this?" I asked.

"It wasn't a sculptor," Ora said. "I made it for a ceramics course I took with Rhoda Traub."

"It was a sculptor."

She gave me a suspicious look as if my admiration were a ruse, then said in self-exoneration:

"But that's just what he looked like, Mizrachi! He had a body like a question mark. He owned the general store when I was a girl. There was nothing you couldn't buy there: spices, mouse traps, fly paper, cough sugar, iron griddles, heat rash powder, lamp wicks, dress fabric, combs, silk ribbons, cans of halva, coffee beans packed in little baskets woven from palm shoots, bags of tobacco, sheets of cigarette paper. He spent all day playing backgammon with his friends on the sidewalk, taking snuff and drinking coffee from little cups."

"You should do more things like this," I said.

"That's what everyone tells me."

Outside her house, the perfectly still air gave a nervous flutter, an atmospheric palpitation. Ora sniffed it like a deer.

"There'll be a *hamsin*," she said.

* * *

The *hamsin* was howling the next morning when I walked to Moshe Shatzman's house on a new street facing the sea. There were those who got violent headaches from these winds, hot-tempered, panting lunatics that blew from the desert in autumn and spring. Others were exhilarated, or quite literally electrified, jumping from the shock when they touched metal doorknobs or appliances. It had to do, the scientists said, with a surplus of positive ions.

I walked up a flagstone path and rang the bell. A cross-eyed woman blocked the door with the instinctive stance taken by housewives against salesmen and canvassers. She regarded me doubtfully while the wind blew my words back at me.

"Father's in his room," she said. "I'll ask him."

She did not invite me in and shut the door in my face. The man who opened it again, still fumbling with the top button of his shirt, did not resemble her. He was on the tall side, with an upturned nose and a head of snowy hair neatly brushed across the hairline, an erect, good-looking man despite his age.

"Well," he said after hearing me out. He had an unwavering glance. "Did Ora really say that? Straight as an arrow, eh? " His mouth crinkled at the corners. "Well, well. Ora!" I had taken that for agreement when he said: "So you want to hear stories about the old days? I'm not the man for you. I don't have the time and I'm not well." He laid a hand on his heart. "Find someone else."

"Such as who?"

"Try Yanko Epstein."

"I've done that. I want to hear things from different angles."

"Oh, Epstein knows all the angles," Moshe Shatzman said. "Don't you worry about that. He's the storyteller. I'm just a farmer. He's your man."

The door lunged at me, chasing the fleeing wind.

* * *

I chose a cold, wet morning. A wintry wind blew the last leaves from the pipal trees, whose dark bodies bore the lashes of the rain. Rivulets of water ran down Benefactor Street, forming little whitecaps in the gutter. It was early and the street was empty except for Sa'adya, the miniscule Yemenite street cleaner. Dressed in a child's yellow rain slicker, he was hitching his little donkey to its barber-pole-striped cart in front of Motl Sokolov's stable, which had once housed the mounts of Edmond de Rothschild's officials and the horses that pulled the Haifa stagecoach. So tiny were the three of them, man, donkey, and cart, that, standing in the vaulted entrance, they might have emerged from an underworld inhabited by gnomes. I followed the pointing forefinger, still faintly visible on the stable's wall, that had guided the traveler to the now empty Graf Hotel.

A bar on a window moved easily. A faint attar of chocolate lingered in the room into which I had dropped. It was empty except for a stack of old cartons. A corridor ran past it to a jerrybuilt wall. Beyond that, where the hotel's lobby had been, were the barbershop and defunct dry-cleaner's facing Founders Street.

The rain beat an irregular tattoo on the roof, rising to a gunfire crescendo and tapering off in a lame retreat. I followed the beam of my flashlight into the corridor and from there to the other rooms. Emmanuel Turskanov had made a tidy exit. Gone were the tables, oven, burners, vats, ladles, conchers, and molds that had been the tools of his trade; nothing remained but some old jute sacks, a single slipper, and several feet of copper tubing that were trampled in the moving. Dark splotches of chocolate on the floor had hardened into a sterile lava, across which a mournful ant wandered.

I had returned to the corridor and stepped into an alcove when my beam fell on something dark. Lying in a puddle of water, it was a small desk, three of its legs sticking up like an overturned beetle's. The fourth, broken, splayed outward.

A drop splashed into the puddle. I pointed the flashlight above me. Overhead, rotted by a leaky roof, a caved-in ceiling had brought the desk crashing down from an attic storage space. Its single drawer, knob pressed against the ground, was jammed shut. This opened when I pulled the desk from the puddle, spilling its contents on the floor. I swept them up and took a quick look at them.

They consisted of various items. Many were picture postcards, some of old Hollywood movie stars. The brightest had a colored illustration of a mooning couple on a bench. The woman with a rose in her hair and a pink dress spangled with gold sequins, the man with a pink bow-tie and a straw boater, the two looked dressed for an Edwardian ball. A smiling cupid gazed down on them through an open shutter in the sky, which was emblazoned with the verse:

I've loved you long with all my heart
'Neath sun and stars, in shade and shine.
Earth cannot greater bliss impart
If you will be my Valentine.

There was also a large number of letters, written by different hands. Most had letterheads that said:

J. P-CORNEY
MANUFACTURER OF ALL KINDS OF
HEMSTITCH GOODS, LAUNDRY BAGS, BRAIDING,
CORDING, COVER, & BIBS
FOR THE TRADE
59–61 FULTON STREET
BROOKLYN, N.Y.

Or else:

OFFICE OF

J. P-CORNEY

MANUFACTURER OF

STAMPT LINENS, ART EMBROIDERY

AND TINTED NOVELTIES

59 & 61 FULTON STREET

In addition, there were two photographs. One was a studio portrait of
a little girl, a toy goat between her knees, posed against a backdrop of
cliffs and crashing surf. The other was of a large crowd of Jews, men,
women, and children, standing on two stories of a stone building, their
heads covered with the same motley of hats, caps, kerchiefs, shawls, and
fezes worn by the couples in Yanko Epstein's ensemble of the founders
of Zichron. Those on the top story were squeezed between the railing
of a balcony and several doors at their backs. Bundles and packages lay
at their feet. The Jews on the ground floor stood in front of three large
archways. Small domes on the roof showed the building to be Arab. I
had no idea where or what it was.

* * *

Examined at leisure, the letters mailed to the Graf family in Zichron
Ya'akov from the Fulton Street business of J. P-Corney turned out to have
been written by three people: Jeanette Corney; Jeanette's sister Bracha
or (a childhood nickname) Buka Hoyser; and Bracha's husband Yeshaya
Hoyser, the uncle of Ora Rosenzweig's who, before she was born, quarreled with her father upon leaving for America.

He wrote in Yiddish, in a cursive hand difficult to decipher. Bracha's letters, on the other hand, were easily read despite their lack of
punctuation, as were Jeanette's. Both women wrote in French to their
brother and sister, Alter and Rebecca Graf, and in Yiddish to their parents, Miriam and Tsvi-Hirsh Graf – the latter the "proud keeper" and
first proprietor of the Graf Hotel whose bitter tombstone accused Death
of reaping what he sowed.

At the time of this correspondence, the hotel did not exist. After
reading it, however, I understood Tsvi-Hirsh's epitaph better.

The earliest of the letters was dated May 8, 1902. It was posted from Marseilles, where Yeshaya and Bracha Hoyser, in her eighth month of pregnancy, were in transit from Palestine to New York. They had only six hours before boarding a train to Le Havre and Bracha apologized for not buying her parents a gift.

The Hoysers disembarked in New York on the morning of May 17th and wrote to their family in Zichron the next day. They had traveled third class and had a good passage, and they were now staying with Jeanette and her husband, a fellow Zichronite who had Americanized his family name of Karniel. On the floor above their Brooklyn apartment the Corneys operated two "factories," one employing eight seamstresses and sewing machines and the other turning out hand embroidery.

Bracha gave birth the following month. "I'm happy to inform you," Yeshaya Hoyser wrote his in-laws, "that yesterday, the 28th of June, at 5 P.M., Buka and I became the parents of a very ugly little girl." The girl was named Chana and had a difficult first month, for on July 31 Bracha wrote Rebecca that her baby had been *gravement malade,* though *grace à Dieu* she now was better. The doctor and medicines had cost a large sum, leaving no money to buy Rebecca the bolt of silk she had asked for. In closing, Bracha sent Alter her love.

By the time this letter arrived in Zichron, however, Alter was no longer there. Together with his mother, he was visiting another brother, Tsolik or Charles, who was living in London. From there, they planned to continue to New York, where the Hoysers had moved to a ten-dollar-a-month flat near the Corneys and Yeshaya had found work in a sweat shop. He was making eight dollars a week and hoping for a raise, and Bracha, responding to an account of her family's economic woes, wrote back:

"My dear beloved parents first I write you that praise God we are well I pray God we hear the same from you if things are so bad with you over there over here you could make a living from a farm you would only have to raise chickens and geese and sell the eggs and we could all be together as for Rebecca I think she could earn five or six dollars a week in Jeanette's shop."

Things were hard for everyone in Zichron. It was "the time of the commune," when the rebellious farmers had barely enough to eat – and to make matters worse, the phyloxera rot had devastated Tsvi-Hirsh's vineyards. Still, he was not eager to be a chicken farmer in New Jersey.

Soon after receiving Bracha's letter, he asked Jeanette for a loan to tide him over, occasioning an apologetic reply in which she explained that all her "capital" was sunk in her business. She had already spent more than she could afford on the Hoysers, not to mention her promise to pay for her brother's and mother's steamship tickets to New York. Tsvi-Hirsh then wrote Alter, who was still in London, asking him to please go at once to Paris and purchase new grape stock for the vineyards.

Alter, though, did no such thing. He and his mother stayed in London for nearly a year while the Hoysers continued to urge him, Rebecca, and their parents to join them in New York. They also sent news of their baby, reports of purchases and pay raises, descriptions of illnesses and recoveries, expressions of homesickness, regards from relatives newly arrived from Rumania, and recurrent appeals for more mail. In October 1903, on the eve of the winter planting season, Tsvi-Hirsh and Rebecca mailed a joint plea to London. "*Cher* Alter," wrote Rebecca in a better punctuated French than her sisters':

"Yesterday we received a letter from Buka in which she wrote that she has already sent you money for a ticket to America. I don't understand why you haven't done anything about the vines. What are you waiting for? If you don't act, and we still have no vines for next season, it will be all over with us…. Dear Alter, don't go to America! The life there isn't for you. You can lead a far nicer and more peaceful life here, and Papa will leave you everything, the house too. My dear brother, don't throw away your one chance and that of your dear parents – you, who can live happily here and make them happy by your presence…."

To which Tsvi-Hirsh added in Yiddish, in angry letters whose strokes slanted downward like fist thumps:

"Alter! We can live well from our three hectares of vineyards but if you don't save them now there won't be nothing to save! You won't find a better life nowhere, so think again about America because it's not for you. God help us to help ourselves…."

In the margins Rebecca had added the postscript:

"*Cher* Alter, I beg you a thousand times not to go to America. But if you must anyway…."

The rest of the sentence was smudged by time or tears.

"Did Alter ever get the vines?" asked Ora Rosenzweig from the sink, where she was washing dishes. I had dumped my finds on her kitchen table, on which they were spread like a peddler's wares. Micha, in his undershirt, was examining the photograph of Baby Chana, the little girl with the toy goat.

"There's no sign that he did," I said. "Maybe that's why Tsvi-Hirsh gave up farming and opened a hotel. Alter went to New York. Look at this."

Ora came over to regard a postcard addressed to him, care of a friend in the Bronx. The sender proposed meeting Sunday morning at the Corneys – "*à la famille Cornet.*"

She examined the postmark. "October 20, 1905. He must have returned to Zichron to take over the hotel when his father died."

That was in 1906. And with Charles in London and Alter, his two sisters, and their mother in New York, Death and Rebecca would have been the sole beneficiaries of Tsvi-Hirsh's estate.

"It wasn't just the Grafs," Micha said. "The young people were leaving in droves then. There wasn't enough land for them to farm. One of my Aunt Rivka's family set out for Australia, got as far as the Philippines, married a half-caste, and was never heard from again."

"What else could have been expected from a tribe of gypsies like the Jews?" I asked. "The wonder isn't that, twenty years after he came home to the land of Israel, all but one of Tsvi-Hirsh Graf's children had left it. It's that after twenty years of crop failure, hunger, malaria, Rothschild bureaucrats, Turkish despots, and the Angel of Death, he and Rebecca still fought to stay on."

"I wouldn't make too much of Rebecca," Ora said. "She left for America herself after Tsvi-Hirsh died. She wasn't like my father. He honestly thought it was a sin for a Jew to leave this country. That's why he and my uncle fought. I don't suppose you came across any mention of him."

"As a matter of fact, I did."

I was sorry the minute I said it.

"It's not very flattering," I warned

She came to the table and took a seat, wiping her hands on her apron.

At the end of a letter of her husband's, Bracha Hoyser had scribbled a note to *Ma trés chére soeur Rebecca.* Halfway through it she wrote:

"How is my brother-in-law's little girl and why do you never write me news of her and her father you know that even if he is a fool he still is a brother so do write my dear."

"The little girl was Esther-Leah," I said of the old lady in the rocking chair on Founders Street.

"A fool? Are you sure that's what she wrote?"

"But still a brother. *Tu sais meme qu'il est fou c'est un frére.*"

"I'll tell you something." There was bitterness in Ora's voice. "Bracha Hoyser was right. My father was a fool to think anyone but himself could live by his ideals."

"I don't believe it!" Micha Rosenzweig exclaimed.

"You never knew the man, Micha."

"What man?" He held up a postcard. "It's Jackie Coogan. She must be ten years old here. And look at Douglas Fairbanks."

Ora went to Micha's side of the table. "Oh, my Lord!" she said. "I saw him in that. It was…" She shut her eyes. "*The Thief of Baghdad.*"

"*The Thief of Baghdad*?" Micha ran a finger over Douglas Fairbanks' mustache as if to see if it was pasted on. "He dressed like an Arab in that. This is from *Robin Hood.*"

"Oh, I'll say! A fine Robin Hood he would have made with that bandanna and an earring! He wore a pointed cap with a feather in *Robin Hood.*"

Ora turned to me. "These cards must have belonged to Carmela Graf, Alter's daughter. We girls collected them. We saw all those movies at the hotel. Alter added a big room at the back and bought a projector. I never had money for a ticket, so he'd wait until no one was looking and let me in for free."

She glanced at a postcard of *Ben-Hur.*

"That movie theater! The whole town squeezed into it on Saturday nights. There was a show at seven and at nine. Leybl Munjak accompanied it on his fiddle. He sat behind a wooden crate that hid him from the audience. He played fast tunes to the funny scenes and slow ones to the sad ones."

"Well, I'll be damned!" Micha said. He held up the photograph of the Arab building.

"What is it?"

He scratched his head with a beefy hand. "This looks like the Khan Zakhlan. It had two stories just like these."

The Khan Zakhlan, I knew from Aryeh Samsonov's book, was the caravansary in Haifa in which the first families of Zichron had stayed after arriving from Rumania. If Micha was right, I had found the earliest photograph of them in Palestine.

Ora and I looked over his shoulder. Pressed against the railing of the second-floor balcony, the Jews with their packs and bundles looked like steerage passengers on a ship. The photographer had been standing on their level with the ground-floor Jews beneath him. "Do you recognize anyone?" I asked.

Neither did. "But this photograph was taken a hundred years ago," Micha said.

"I'll go to Haifa and compare it with the building."

"You can't. It was destroyed in the '48 war."

"Show it to Yanko Epstein," Ora suggested. "He'll know."

"The Khan Zakhlan," Micha said. "How about that!"

Chapter eight

Iswallowed my pride and stopped Yanko Epstein in the street to tell him I had found something in the old Graf Hotel that might interest him.

"Why don't you bring it to the museum tomorrow morning," he said. "I have a class of eighth graders at ten. I'll be finished with them by eleven."

At eleven the children had just gotten off their bus and were milling by the ceramic wall. Two teachers, a man and a woman, shepherded them inside. Epstein stood supervising them, hands behind his back. "They were supposed to go from here to Aaronsohn House," he explained, "but they went there first instead. That's just as well. Now I can set them straight."

I said I would wait outside.

"Why outside? Come in and sit down. You have something from the Graf Hotel for me? I have something from the Graf Hotel for you."

He grinned like a gambler over a hand of cards.

The children trooped into the museum. Taking out his ring of heavy keys, he opened a glass case, removed a scuffed, leather-bound volume, and placed it on a table. "Have a look," he said to me above the din of thirty voices trapped in the cave-like room.

"Quiet, you all! We still have to do the synagogue, the winery, the Lange house, and the Rothschild grave, so let's listen to what Mr. Epstein has to say."

There was in the male teacher's harried voice a hint that, after the Rothschild grave, he still would have several hours of night school to teach.

I opened the leather volume while Epstein picked up his wooden pointer and went to the head of the class. As irked with him as I was, I felt sorry for him. Entertaining the odd visitor to his museum was an agreeable sinecure for an old raconteur. Having to lecture unruly schoolchildren seemed unjust.

Yet he appeared to take it in stride, waiting importantly for the bubble gum to stop popping and the last whispered conversations to end. My eye fell on the first page of the leather volume.

Washington's Birthday, 1907. Hurrah!
Marcus E. Madden, Boston, U.S.A.
Daniel J. Casey, Boston, U.S.A.
James E. Krugg, Washington, U.S.A.
Harry Knell, Dragoman.
Rah! Rah! Rah! Tiger!!!

3rd March, 1907.
We arrived here today and found the Hotel Graf
very clean and comfortable, and everything entirely
satisfactory.

Gregory H.R. Mellor
London

March 5, 1907
Sir William & Lady Creary have stopped here and
found it pleasant, cooking excellent, & met attention &
courtesy from the staff. We think the hotel ought to have
every success.

I was looking at the hotel's guest book, which began with a college cheer soon after Alter Graf's return from New York. Staked to a graduation-present trip (as advertised by Cook's Tours in my 1907 Baedeker) to "The Holy Land & the Near East, With Special Attention to Pilgrim Sites & The Footsteps of Our Savior," the three Princetonians must have whiled away their evening at the hotel singing old frat songs. It was perhaps fortunate that the Crearies had missed them.

Yanko Epstein cleared his throat. The room was as quiet as it was likely to get. "Well, now, children," he began. "Good morning and welcome to the Founders Memorial of Zichron Ya'akov. Let's begin your visit by going back a hundred years. The land of Israel was not then what it is now. It was a wilderness named Palestine in which few Jews lived. The Bedouin roamed by day, the jackal and hyena howled at night, and the Turk ruled with a tyrannous hand. Yet from that wasteland went forth a clarion call that was heard in the exile of Rumania by 350 men, women, and children, who set out for these shores from a port on the Black Sea."

His delivery was elevated – his notion, so it seemed, of what his office required.

"Here is the *Thetis*, the ship the colonists sailed on. After arriving in Haifa, they lodged in an Arab khan. I don't have a photograph of it to show you, but it was there in the months that followed that they became a single family, possessed by one dream and one goal: to strike roots in the land of their fathers and till its soil. Let no one say, boys and girls, that their path was strewn with roses. Every hardship you can imagine...."

I turned the page.

Had a really good time at the Hotel Graf. The dinner was real good and several of our party had to ease off several buttons.

Mr. and Mrs. A.J. Hawke
Ingersoll, N.Z.

Miss Lotham has been agreeably surprised at finding such a

comfortable hotel in this out-of-the-way place. The landlord
is most obliging and eager to please.

August 12, 1908
Just arrived at somewhere from nowhere. To missionaries
and others it is the Holy Land – but to me it is the Stony Land.
But after arriving at the Hotel Graf, I forgot all my troubles.
Mr. Graf's kindness to me will be one of my pleasant memories
on the conclusion of a Trip Around The Cities Of The World
By Cycle.
Langston Carter,
World's Second Cyclist

"…It wasn't long," Epstein was saying of the colonists, now living on
the land they had bought, "before they were on the verge of starvation.
One day a Jew named Veneziani, who was on a mission for the Baron
de Hirsch, passed through the new colony and saw a group of men and
women clearing stones in a field. Do any of you know who the Baron
de Hirsch was, children?"

No hands went up.

"He was a wealthy French Jew who also thought that Jews should
return to the land – but not to the land of Israel. He believed in Argen-
tina, the country of the future, where he was founding Jewish colonies.
And so Monsieur Veneziani reined in his horse and said from the saddle,
'Why are you growing stones in this desert? Come to the Pampas, the
true land of milk and honey.'

"And then, children, a man stepped forth and said: 'Monsieur, if we
have to eat stones we will eat them, but we will not budge from this place.'
Veneziani was so struck by this answer that he went back to Paris and
told another rich Jew, Baron Edmond de Rothschild, about it." Epstein
tapped a photograph. "That man's name was Meir Leib Hirshko, and
his grandchildren and great-grandchildren live in this town to this day."

"Excuse me," the woman teacher interrupted. "Wasn't it Sarah
Aaronsohn's mother Malka who said that about the stones?"

Epstein measured her with a look. "The name of that man was
Meir Leib Hirshko."

"But we were told at Aaronsohn House...." She had the petulant air of a defrauded shopper.

"Young lady," Epstein said, "I hope that when you're as old as I am, you'll have learned not to believe all you're told. The Baron de Rothschild, boys and girls, was most impressed with Monsieur Veneziani's report. And so he decided...."

I turned another page.

After suffering almost every modern inconvenience, including a night of horrors on a Russian steamship, our group of Scottish pilgrims is happy to testify to the cordial, refreshing reception at the Hotel Graf.

Contente de la propriété et de la bonne table de l'hotel Graf.

Honig echt, Butter frisch,
Reines Bett, guten Tisch,
Finden wir in Graf Hotel.

The number of languages in the guest book was large. Beside English, French, and German, there was Turkish, Greek, Russian, Chinese, Japanese, Polish, Hindi, Arabic, and something I took to be Welsh. Ottoman Palestine had enjoyed a brisk tourist trade, even if the roads were unsafe and the traveler, as advised by De Lacy O'Leary's *Colloquial Arabic*, had to keep in mind such complex rules of etiquette as "In eating and drinking with the natives, only the right hand should be used"; "Thanks must always be given to God, not to the person who has conferred the benefit"; and "It is a grave discourtesy to refer to the women of the family of one's host. If an inadvertent inquiry betrays a consciousness of their existence, it is proper to add, 'I take refuge with the Lord of the Daybreak.'"

The hotel did not have many Hebrew-speaking guests. Traveling Jews generally put up with friends or relatives – or, if they were pioneers of the Second Aliyah, slept by the roadside. Two young "Muscovites" who treated themselves to a room observed cuttingly the next morning:

What a beautiful place Zichron would be if not for
its inhabitants.

To which a local patriot replied:

Once a man came to a town and asked a boy who lived there,
"Why are there so many dogs in your streets?" Whereupon the
boy answered, "There are indeed many curs here, sir, but
none of them are ours; they are visitors like yourself." I hope
this is read by the "comrades" and "comradesses" who
have been befouling the air of our lovely colonies for a long
time.

One of the last entries before the First World War was made by

Henry Morgenthau
American Ambassador to Turkey,

no doubt on a visit to his friend Aaron Aaronsohn. Morgenthau – later
to serve as Secretary of the Treasury under Franklin Roosevelt – sat on
a committee of American Jewish financial supporters of Aaronsohn's
agricultural projects. More than any other foreign diplomat, it was he
who, prior to America's entering the war on the side of England and
France, labored to protect the Jews of Palestine from Turkish excesses.
Which Epstein was now up to.
"…In 1914, children, we still thought of ourselves as loyal Turkish
subjects. A group called the Gideonites, founded by a young man from
Zichron named Alexander Aaronsohn, even volunteered for the Turkish army. We gave it a grand send-off to the recruitment office in Haifa
in a wagon flying two flags – the green Turkish one and our own Jewish
blue-and-white. Let me tell you, that blue-and-white flag didn't fly long.
The Turks threw those volunteers into work gangs and forced them to
pave roads like common prisoners – and when they asked for grease
for their wheelbarrows, they were told to use the spoonful of olive oil
they were given each day to dip their bread in. That was the beginning
of our political education.

"In 1915 came the locusts and wiped out our crops. Now there was not even bread to eat. For a slice of it you could buy one of the Armenian women who had fled to Palestine from the Turkish massacres in Anatolia. Have any of you read *The Forty Days of Musa Dagh*?"

No one had. But they were listening.

"In '16 came the pest and killed all the farm animals the Turks hadn't made off with. We burned their carcasses and covered them with lime. By now, we had been through the ten plagues of Egypt. And it was then that an agronomist from Zichron Ya'akov, Alexander Aaronsohn's older brother Aaron...."

So began the story of the Nili ring.

He told it as if it were still fresh in his memory, tapping out four faces in their square picture frame. "Yitzhak Halprin, Re'uven Schwartz. Menashe Bronstein. Tova Gelberg. These were the four young men and women from Zichron who joined the ranks of the spies. But spies, children, is a dirty word. 'Patriots' is a better one. They weren't out for themselves. None of them stuck their heads in the hangman's noose for the fun of it."

The Nili [handwritten margin note]

Though hearing the story for the second time that morning, the children stood hushed.

"On the second night of the Feast of Booths," Epstein told them, "the whole village was at a wedding celebration. Every man, woman, and child was there. Suddenly, word came that we were surrounded."

Then came the search for the spies. The arrests. Lishansky's flight. "The Turks gathered us all in the synagogue. You'll be going there, so try to imagine it. We took the Torah scrolls from the Holy Ark and the head of each family passed before them and swore to find Lishansky. I can remember Yisra'el Neiderman, the head of the village, crying as he made us swear. Crying tears of blood, children! But no one turned Lishansky in. No one informed on anyone."

"But didn't Sarah write in her farewell letter...?"

"I know what Sarah wrote," Epstein told the male teacher. "And I say it's not so." He had a slow, deep way of flushing, the blood spreading through his cheeks as if they were made of absorbent cotton. "The only one who blabbed was Na'aman Belkind, Avshalom Feinberg's cousin from the south. And don't think we weren't frightened. We knew what the Turks had done to the Armenians. Neiderman was a strong man; he stood there weeping."

For a while, as he related the ordeal of Zichron, his speech had lost its stiffness. Then, continuing with the fate of the captured spies, it reverted to it. The eighth graders grew fidgety again. The teachers glanced at their watches. Epstein cleared away the last of the spy ring's corpses, briefly described the town's post war recovery, and concluded with Baron de Rothschild's last visit to Zichron.

"The baron, dear boys and girls, was glad to see that his labors had borne pleasant fruit. And so, I hope, have mine. Enjoy the rest of your tour."

There was a rush for the door. In the winter sunlight the children scattered on the lawn. Epstein said goodbye to the teachers and returned to where I stood waiting.

"Well?"

I wasn't sure if he was asking about his talk or what I had brought him. "You spoke well," I said. "It's just a shame that there's so little curiosity at that age. I wonder if it's worth the effort."

His eyes rebuked me. "But who will tell them if I don't?"

"Then do." I handed him a manila envelope. "This is what I found. Micha Rosenzweig says it's the Khan Zakhlan."

He gave me a skeptical look, pulled the photograph from its envelope, and went to the doorway to hold it to the light. For a long time he stood there, as if my presence had been forgotten. From the lawn came the receding cries of the children, rounded up and driven to the synagogue.

He turned to me, flushed with excitement. "It's the Khan Zakhlan, all right! The camels and horses passed through these archways into an inner yard. The colonists stayed in the top-floor rooms. They're here, every one of them!"

He studied the photograph, moving it back and forth.

"My eyes aren't what they used to be. I'll recognize them all when I have this enlarged. I'll hang it next to the *Thetis*."

I told him where I had found it.

"In that pantry off the hallway," he mused. "You know, the hotel had a piano in the sitting room. Sometimes, if there weren't any guests,

Alter Graf let us young folk come over. Someone would play the piano and we'd dance. After a while we'd fly out of the room and down the hallway."

He had to go. He was late for a meeting of the Burial Society. His gaze rested on me, speculative.

* * *

Marcia had begun taking driving lessons. How had we thought she could live in a small town without a license? Meanwhile, though, she had no mobility. Talya had few playmates. There was no way to contact anyone without walking to the pay phone in town – and once there, you had to wait in line and be overheard by those waiting behind you. "It's raining," I protested when asked to call friends in Jerusalem and invite them for the weekend.

When the rain stopped, I put Talya on my shoulders and set out. A rainbow spanned the valley beneath our house. We had them often, luscious arcs that floated to the ground in sunbeamy fizzes beyond the winery. "I'm going to steal one to put in your hair one day," I told Talya.

"Bad Ginger will 'rest you," she said.

Our friends weren't home.

We started back. Instead of turning at our corner, I kept going downhill toward the winery.

"Where, Abba?"

"To find the end of the rainbow."

"But it's gone."

So it was, melted in a sky of brilliant blue.

We passed Benedik's hardware store and the bombed-out house next to it and the great bottle yard of the winery, its dusty empties so innumerable in their crates that no amount of human thirst could refill them. Athwart the bottom of the street stood the winery itself, massively blocking the way as if to catch the stray grape that tried tumbling past it. A distant rumble of machinery throbbed from within, deep and mysterious like the engine of a ship.

We started down the potholed road that led out of town to Wadi Milikh, the ancient Salt Pass that had routed the commerce of the sea to Damascus and the interior of Asia. Halfway there was the spring from which Edmond de Rothschild's engineers had pumped water to the copper tanks on Founders Street. Bir el-Hanazir, "Pigs' Well," the Arabs had called it, because of the wild boar that came there to drink. "It had a stone watering trough you could gather a whole herd around," Micha Rosenzweig had told me. Now the town had taken what was left of it, run it into something that looked like a bathroom pipe, and let it drip out the other end as though from a leaky faucet into an algae-choked pool by which stood a Russian artillery piece captured in the Six Day War. Pig's Well was a memorial picnic grounds.

We cut through the picnic grounds and entered a vineyard in a hollow, treading on a rug of violet campion spread on the muddy earth. Still glistening with raindrops, the bare vines rested knotty arms on each other's shoulders. Arab workmen were pruning them, piling whips of wood while singing giddy snatches of song.

We headed toward the Bedouin shack that stood at the hollow's far end. Winter flowers daubed the fields. Purple stork's bill; sky-blue irises; white-petaled jonquils striped yellow like peppermint sticks; swan-necked cyclamens, beaked buds tucked into downy leaves as sumptuous as brocade; unopened anemones, crumpled like discarded red tissues. Loose mounds of earth marked the fresh tunnels of the mole rats. A woodpecker typed a message on a tree.

Bright notes struck the air. A flock of goats trooped from behind some trees. A tall male with a chestnut beard pranced ahead of it, a tin bell jaunty on its chest. A matriarch stepped from the shack in flowing greens and mauves. She stooped to lift a stone and flung it at the lead goat's feet. "Hhahhh!" she called.

Her cry brought it up sharply, the flock bunched bleating behind it. A dark, curly-headed goatherd strode at the rear. He wore an old, double-breasted jacket and held one arm stiffly by his side, its fingers hooked into his belt. Next to him walked a she-goat, her swollen udders reaching nearly to the ground. A red blob swung between her legs.

The goatherd unhooked his arm. From his jacket he withdrew a baby goat. Carefully, its uncut umbilical cord dangling like the string of an opened gift, he set it on the ground. It wobbled but kept its footing. He reached into his jacket and brought forth two more little goats. The woman grunted. Talya squealed with delight.

"*Ta'ali,*" the woman said.

I put Talya down beside the newborn kids, already at their mother's teats, nosing past the bloody afterbirth. The goatherd opened the spigot of a metal drum and ran water into a tin trough, washing his blood-stained hands before letting the flock drink. With quivering bleats it jostled to the water.

"*Ta'ali.*" The woman took Talya's hand and ran it over the soft, skinny rumps of the kids. They wiggled peevishly, intent on the warm milk.

"*T'fadlu.*" She pointed to the door of the shack.

"Abba, there's childrens there," Talya said. Their mother behind them, three dark, curly heads were at the door, peering out.

But although Talya wanted to play, the winter day was too short. "Some other time," I told her. And yet, the world so bright and new, what other time could one wish for?

We climbed the slippery hillside to the Binyamina road and headed back into town along the south end of Founders Street, past Yanko Epstein's museum and the bus station; past the new water tower and the office of the Civil Guard; past the old houses of the farmers; past the flower store, the nut store, Ata Clothes and Bank Discount; past Shlomo Toker's appliance store; past the felafel stand with its golden balls of chickpeas crackling in oil. It was a few minutes after four and the town was coming to life from its siesta.

Down the street in his blue work clothes rode old Tishbi, reading a newspaper on his donkey. Parking the donkey by the curb, he tied it to a lamppost, stuck the paper in a saddlebag, took his walking stick from the girth, and hobbled into the bank. On the sidewalk in front of Pomerantz's café the lottery vendor was setting up his table. Inside the café a chrome espresso machine shone on the counter.

Mayunka Pomerantz, backed by shelves of cakes and pastries, was working the machine while chatting with two customers. One was Ben-Hayyim. Pomerantz was telling them about his grandfather – who, it appeared, had worked as a male nurse in Dr. Yoffe's infirmary.

"If it hadn't been for your grandfather, Mayunka," said the man sitting with Ben-Hayyim, "no one would have come out of that infirmary alive. Next to malaria, Hillel Yoffe was the leading cause of death in this town. Your grandfather knew more about medicine than he did."

He was a sardonic-looking man, with thin hair combed back over a balding head.

"Yoffe knew a lot about medicine," Ben-Hayyim said. "He was just too busy talking politics to practice it."

Steam hissed from the espresso machine. Mayunka brought coffee for me and a soft drink for Talya. About Dr. Yoffe, he couldn't say. But his grandfather had saved many lives. One belonged to a Torah scribe, who expressed his gratitude with two gifts: three grains of wheat, on each of which was written a verse of the Priestly Blessing from the Bible, and an egg inscribed with all eight chapters of the Song of Songs.

"Three grains of salt would be more like it," Ben-Hayyim said.

"It must have been an ostrich egg," said the man with the thin hair.

"An elephant egg," Ben-Hayyim said.

"It was an ordinary egg," Pomerantz assured them. "I saw those grains of wheat myself. My grandfather kept them in a silver snuff box."

"What happened to them?"

"The box was stolen."

"Mayunka ate the egg for breakfast," said the thin-haired man.

Patiently, Pomerantz explained that the contents of the egg had been extracted through a pinhole before the Torah scribe wrote on the shell. One day, its fame having spread to Jerusalem, a curator arrived from the National Museum and persuaded his grandfather to donate it. It was probably sitting in a drawer to this day.

"You should ask for it back," Ben-Hayyim said.

"Let Yanko Epstein exhibit it," said the thin-haired man.

"Epstein wouldn't exhibit an egg," Ben-Hayyim said. "He'd exhibit a photograph of himself holding it."

Outside, the sun was low in the sky and the winter breeze was turning nippy. Afternoon shoppers crowded the street. Tishbi left the bank, mounted his donkey, and clucked it into motion. A wealthy man, he owned large tracts of farmland. Cars tooted a salute as he U-turned in front of them. Someone called out:

"*Ya* Tishbi! You should be declared a historical monument!"

Tishbi raised his prod in acknowledgment.

We passed Aminadav's grocery and stopped at the kiosk of the potato-nosed Parsee to buy a paper. "Kissinger In Israel: New Israel-Egypt War Soon If No Sinai Agreement Reached," the headline said.

Throwing a long, two-headed shadow, we turned the corner and headed down the Street of the Benefactor, saying hello to Ephraim Ashkenazi on his bicycle and greeting Yafia Cohen in her folding chair.

"How are you today?" I asked.

"God be praised." Her standard answer, it implied that God would one day have some explaining to do.

We turned into Wine Street. In the swinging love seat on his porch, Tsvi Zuckerman was sitting with Ze'ev Neiderman.

Zuckerman lived next door to the Rosenzweigs, who didn't talk to him. Their feud had begun long ago, in British times, when he built a fence encroaching on the Rosenzweigs' property. After failing to convince him that it was on their side of the border, they broke off all relations.

"Why didn't you go to court?" I asked Ora.

"With his brother a court clerk in Haifa? We wouldn't have stood a chance."

I never asked Zuckerman for his version. He was a retired bus driver, a small, unctuous man with a scent of mouthwash. But I did, one day, ask him about Gita Blumenfeld when told that her daughter had married his brother. "That's so," he said. "She had trouble with her legs when she was old. She couldn't walk."

The third became an invalid who has been bedridden for years.

"She was married to a bully. Once he wanted to welsh on a written agreement with someone, so he knocked on the man's door, asked to see his copy, and poured ink all over it. That was Binyamin Blumenfeld."

"And Gita?"

"Do you have a few minutes? Good. I'll tell you a story.

"My brother who married their daughter was a gifted fellow. Not a genius, but an able young man. After the war he taught himself English and stenography and got a job as a court clerk in Haifa. That may not sound like much. But in those days, when the farmers ate bread and onions, being a court clerk was next to being God.

"At the time that my brother was courting the Blumenfeld girl, he was living in a rented room in Haifa; every Friday he came home for the Sabbath in Moshe Arizon's coach that let its passengers off by the synagogue. Gita Blumenfeld was dying to have him for her son-in-law. He had to pass her house on his way home, and she used to wait by her front door and scream when she saw him, 'Here comes my prince!' The most shameless flatterer would have had more shame. There was my mother, waiting for her favorite son while Gita dragged him into her house. By the time he came home, it was dark and the Sabbath candles were lit.

"That was just the beginning. After a while he began eating his Friday night meals with the Blumenfelds and then he began sleeping there. My mother didn't get to see him until synagogue let out the next morning.

"She was terribly hurt. If you plant a garden and one plant does better than the others, you water it and care for it more; if something then happens to it, the blow is much worse. She went to Gita Blumenfeld and said, 'Look, love is a big thing. Why can't we share my son between us? He can eat his Sabbath meal with you, but let him sleep with his family.'

"'Mrs. Zuckerman,' Gita Blumenfeld answered, 'I'll tell you a story.' And this is the story she told:

"'Once upon a time, there was a woman with an only son she loved dearly. What didn't she do for him? She cooked his meals, she laundered his clothes, she cleaned his room, she polished his shoes, she brought him a mug of hot milk when he went to bed at night and stood by his bed while he drank it. He couldn't imagine loving anyone more. "Mother," he told her, "even when I'm married I'll come every morning to say hello."

"'One day the boy married and went to live with his new wife. His mother rejoiced. It's a happy occasion when you marry off a son. And yet the night after the wedding, she couldn't sleep. Had her son's wife brought him his mug of milk? Would she make his breakfast the way he liked it? Would she remember to iron his shirt? At the crack of dawn she was up and about, waiting for him to come. Seven o'clock passed. Eight o'clock. Nine. She began to worry. What could have happened to him? At noon he walked in, yawning and stretching.'" Tsvi Zuckerman puffed out his little chest and stretched his short arms. "'"Son," she said, "where have you been?" He said, "Mama, don't you know that one night with a wife is better than ten mornings with a mother?"

"My mother never forgave Gita Blumenfeld for that. Not even after the wedding. Not for as long as she lived."

Chapter nine

 It had rained all night in short, violent bursts and I braked as I neared Yanko Epstein, who was leaving his home on Founders Street, to keep from spattering his shoes. With a shine on them, a tweed sports jacket, a striped tie, a gray pullover, a blue wool scarf, and his blue beret, he looked like a man bound for somewhere.

I rolled down the car window. "Where to?"

"To the bus station." He had no umbrella or even a raincoat. "To Tel Aviv. To pick up the enlargement of our photograph and bring it to the framer's."

Westward, rising over the village, a gray bar foretold a new squall.

"Stay right here," I told him. "I'll be back in ten minutes. I'll drive you."

"Eh?"

He rolled his wrist back and forth.

"It isn't a day for waiting for buses. And it is our photograph."

He hesitated. "There was something else I had planned on doing in Tel Aviv."

"There's no problem. I'll take you anywhere you want."

Ten minutes later we were on our way.

We headed down to the Haifa-Tel Aviv road, the fishponds below us half in sunlight, half in shade, the sea stroked in rough charcoal by a dark, scudding sky. Out where the breakers fell frothing on the shore, the rain was already beating down. For months I had pursued the man sitting stiffly beside me, fingering the beret in his lap. Now that I had taken him captive, I had no idea how to begin.

It was he who broke the silence as we crossed the railroad tracks at the base of the Carmel. "Well, now," he said as though we had halted in front of a photograph in his museum. "The Arabs called that cliff up there Hushm el-Carmel, the nose of the Carmel. In the summer of 1916, Bashir el-Hamdun camped on top of it with his Bedouin. It was the year after the locusts."

He made it sound like "last winter" or "the autumn before last."

"The farmers had planted sorghum that year in the fields beneath the cliff. The village posted guards in them. There were three of us: Yitzhak Halprin, Yitzhak Bronstein, and myself. We had horses, old breech-loading Mauser rifles, a lookout tower near a spring, and 8500 dunam to keep an eye on."

I flicked on the wipers as the first drops of rain hit the windshield.

"That summer, the pasture on the Hushm was thin. Every night the Arab-el-Hamdun sent their cows down to graze in our fields and every night we drove them off. We never caught any of them because they scrambled back up when they heard us. It's not so easy to catch a running cow in the dark.

"One night we caught one. She was about to calve and she was slow. We tied a rope to her and tried pulling her back to our camp, but she just lay down and wouldn't budge.

"Well, there are two ways of getting a cow to her feet when she's not in the mood. One is to twist her tail until the bone breaks and she jumps up from the pain. It didn't work with this cow. She had a tail like a garden hose.

"That left the second way." The mischief of the memory stirred the gravelly bottom of his voice. "We lit a fire under her. That got her up. It got her up so fast that she ran into the bushes and set them on fire, too. She was burned to a crisp. We scraped what we could from her bones and ate it well-done. It was wartime and we hadn't tasted meat in months.

"The next morning, Sheikh Bashir came looking for his cow. Not that anyone had sent her to graze in our fields, mind you. Oh, no. She had just wandered off by herself. 'Maybe you saw her?' he asked. 'Maybe we didn't,' we said. So off he goes to look for her and pretty soon he finds her carcass. Back he comes hopping mad and black with soot. 'I wouldn't have minded so much if you had stolen her,' he said, 'because that would have shown you knew something about cows. But how could you burn my best milker when she was about to calf?'

"It didn't do any good to explain it was an accident. 'I'm going to Caesaria right now,' he said, 'to lodge a complaint with Ahmed Bek.'

"That was no joking matter. Ahmed Bek was the Turkish governor. If he found us guilty of killing Bashir el-Hamdun's cow, the village would pay a stiff fine.

"There was nothing to do but get to Caesaria before him. And I was the person to do it, because Ahmed Bek knew my father, who was *mukhtar* of the village before Neiderman. I saddled my horse, grabbed a big pot of honey, which was scarce in those years, and rode off.

"I knew I'd get there first, because Bashir el-Hamdun had to return to his tent to change his clothes. '*Ya* Ahmed Bek,' I said when I saw the governor, 'I have a matter with you concerning the Arab-el-Hamdun. But first I have regards from the bees of Zamarin, who ask to be remembered to you.' I gave him the honey and told him how the Bedouin's cows had been eating our sorghum, and how we kept chasing them away, and how one kicked over a lantern and set herself and our fields on fire, and how Bashir el-Hamdun found her and mounted his horse and galloped off ahead of me to Caesaria. 'You can see that Allah has given me wings,' I said, 'because I overtook him on the way. You can expect him at any moment.' Just then I saw Bashir through the window. 'It would be only fair to the sheikh,' I said, 'if you questioned him without me,' and I went to the next room and put my ear to the door.

"Bashir el-Hamdun didn't know I had been there before him. He told Ahmed Bek his story and Ahmed Bek said:

"'*Ya* Sheikh Bashir, do you know what beef costs nowadays in the butcher stalls? Had you told me that the son of the *mukhtar* killed your cow for her meat, I might have believed you. But who can believe he deliberately burned her?' Then he summoned me and pronounced judgment. The Arab-el-Hamdun, he said, were to blame for the death of the cow and had to pay for the damage to our fields and leave the Hushm. Sheikh Bashir was fit to be tied. There was nothing to be done about it, though. Ahmed Bek's word was law in the whole province of Caesaria.

"That was my first job as a field guard. And it was the last we saw that year of the Arab-el-Hamdun and their cows."

Of Bosnian extraction, Ahmed Bek hailed from one of the old Moslem families of the Balkans that had been brought by the Turks to Palestine. It was he who presided over the interrogation and torture of Sarah Aaronsohn.

"He and my father were on good terms," Epstein said. "He was once even our guest at a Passover Seder. He brought his wife, which Moslems never did. She wore her veil to the door and took it off when she stepped inside.

"That was before he became governor. He and my father had quarreled over some land and made up, and my father wanted to be friendly. But he had to get in the last dig all the same, Ahmed Bek. After my father blessed the wine, Ahmed Bek didn't drink any; that much of a Moslem he was. But when my father blessed the matsos and passed a basket of them around the table, Ahmed Bek didn't eat his either. He sat holding it to the light as though candling an egg. We all stopped chewing and stared at him. After a while he turned to his wife and said, 'It's all right, my dear, you can eat.' 'Ahmed Bek,' my father said, 'this matso is in memory of the bread of affliction that our forefathers ate when they left Egypt. What were you looking for?' 'You'll excuse me, my friend,' Ahmed Bek answered. 'I once heard a Greek monk say that you Jews slaughtered a Gentile child every year and baked your matso with its blood. I wanted to see if it was true.'

"My father turned white. No one spoke. Ahmed Bek burst out laughing and said, 'But you and I know what terrible liars those Christians are, don't we?'

"That was Ahmed Bek. He had a crazy streak. He knew me when I came riding to Casaria that day ahead of Bashir el-Hamdun. This tree was a baby then."

We were passing the huge eucalyptus tree at the turn-off to Caesaria. Finger-like, its exposed upper roots seemed to lift it off the ground by a prodigious exertion of force. The rain was driving eastward, over the mountains. Epstein said:

"Jewish field guards were new in the village. It had hired Arabs until then. That was Rothschild's idea. He thought it took a thief to know one. He didn't know how right he was.

"I'll give you an example. One night Halprin and I left Yitzhak Bronstein in camp and rode off to the vineyards in Um-el-Tut to pick some grapes. There were Arab watchmen there. 'Give us your saddlebags,' they said, 'and we'll pick your grapes for you.' Before we could count to a hundred, they were back with two bags full of muscat grapes. We could see that something wasn't right. They were in a hurry to get rid of us and they couldn't have picked those grapes so fast.

"We rode back a ways and pulled off the path and waited. Sure enough, some donkeys come along, loaded with grapes and driven by three Arabs. We ordered them to halt. Two of them took off and escaped, but we nabbed the third and brought him to Zichron. He was from a large clan in Suberin. We turned him loose and said his family would hear from us.

"It didn't wait to. The next morning the head of it, Amin el-Hajj Mahmoud, came to see us. 'I want you to know,' he said, 'that that wasn't the thief you caught last night. It was the middleman. The thieves were your own watchmen.'

"We learned from that. We learned from everything. You had to be careful. You saw things you wouldn't have believed.

"There were wild boar in that sorghum. They came from the swamps near the sea. Once a party of Christian hunters from Haifa passed by with two guides. The guides were brothers. They asked permission to hunt in our fields and we gave it. The boar did more damage than they would do.

"It was early summer and the grain was high. The hunters went off into it and after a while we heard shots. Then they stopped and there were shouts.

"I rode off to see what had happened. One of the brothers was lying face down. A wounded boar was goring him. He had his head covered to protect it and the boar was slicing his back: left, right, left, right, the way you'd work a man against a wall. The hunters just stood there.

They didn't dare shoot for fear of hitting him. His brother grabbed an ax, ran to the boar, and swung.

"The boar swerved to one side. A hunter fired. The boar fell to the ground. So did the brother with the ax.

"We ran to them. The boar was dead. The two brothers were lying there. The one with the ax was moaning. He wasn't hurt. The other brother had no head."

"What – ?"

"Chopped clean off like a rooster's. We found it in the sorghum. The hunters strapped the boar to one side of a camel and the corpse to the other and brought them both back to Haifa.

"You couldn't be too careful. One night Halprin and I were riding from Um-el-Yamas to Ras-el-Eyn. We were passing a stand of mulberry trees when we heard something rustle in the brush. We were sure it was a boar. We fired and galloped off before it could charge.

"When dawn broke, we rode back to see if we had killed it. We had. But it wasn't a boar. It was a donkey with two crates of fruit. It had wandered off from a caravan of merchants.

"It could have been a human being. Yitzhak Bronstein almost killed a man, a deaf mute he mistook for an animal at the spring. I stopped him at the last moment.

"You had to be careful. You had to be careful! That was the long and short of it. You didn't learn that in a day."

As if fretting whether he had been careful enough, he sat turning his beret in his hands while we waited in a line of cars at Hadera Circle.

I could have gone on listening. He had dropped his museum-guide tone and knew how to shape and pace a story and knot it with a twist at the end. Still, it wasn't the way he told his stories that most entranced me. It was the world they were about.

Jews and Arabs were already rivals in this world for the prize of Palestine. Yet seen from the perspective of a Jewish state that had just fought another frightful war with its neighbors, this rivalry seemed magically benign. Its two sides, neither aware of how quickly the weaker would pull a country from beneath the stronger's feet, lived without walls between them. Their tensions were balanced by familiarity and respect. You missed much of the point if you thought only of the Moslem landowner half-credulous of anti-Semitic libels or the Bedouin sheikh outwitted by a young Jew. The point was also that the Moslem felt sufficiently at ease among Jews to make a joke of it and that the Jew had triumphed on the sheikh's own terms, by the sheikh's way of doing things. It was the Jew's way of doing things, too.

This was a First Aliyah phenomenon. Unlike the "Muscovites," the colonists of the Rothschild villages had wanted to change only their own lives, not the world. The world, however backward, could stay as it was. They accepted the need to fit into it and they did – until World War I swept it away.

As a phenomenon, it didn't last long. The parents of Epstein's generation were immigrants to the Middle East and his children grew up under a British Mandate in which all was changing anyway and the rivalry was turning into a murderous blood feud. Yet for a generation there lived in Palestine a unique breed of Jew: native-born; confident; even cocky toward the Arabs around him; yet master of their language, their culture, their traditions, and their skills – of the plow, the saddle, and the gun.

It wouldn't do to romanticize. By now I knew the farmers of Zichron well enough to know that Epstein was an exception. He was the only moderate among them, all right-wingers who took pride in their understanding of the devious Arab mind and dealt with their field hands from a stance of Jewish superiority. And yet these dealings, observed in the streets of the town, were warm and conducted in fluent Arabic – an anomaly in Israel, where Jews and Arabs did business in Hebrew. There wasn't a farmer above the age of fifty who hadn't grown up with Arabs in his backyard; hadn't worked side-by-side with them; didn't have lifelong ties with their families. If such a mixture of intimacy and class distinctions made you think of blacks and whites in the old American south, you had to remember that those linked by it had been more equal before the crushing Arab defeats of 1948 and 1967.

The Israel that inflicted these defeats was ruled politically by a Left that, from the moment it seized the reins of leadership in Jewish Palestine in the 1920s, had preached the brotherhood of Jews and Arabs and practiced their separation. In theory, Second Aliyah socialists like Ben-Gurion were for Arab-Jewish cooperation; in reality, they fought

for an all-Jewish economy and all-Jewish institutions from which Arabs
were excluded. The supporters of the parties they founded were still like
that. We had friends in Jerusalem who thought only fanatics voted for
the Likud but who, like northern liberals vis-à-vis Negroes, had never
been in an Arab home and had no notion of what Arab life was like. Any
child in the world Yanko Epstein grew up in knew more about Arabs
than they did.

Perhaps relations in Palestine might have developed differently
had this world not vanished so quickly after World War I. But there was
no way of knowing – and in any case, the right-wing Zionist opposition
in those years was a European product little influenced by First Aliyah
mores. Indeed, political organizations in Palestine having been banned
by the Turks, the Rothschild colonies produced no politics to speak of.
Their one attempt at them, which ended badly, was the Nili affair.

"That same summer," Epstein replied when I asked him when he
had learned of the spy ring's existence.

He gave the beret a last turn.

One evening, he said, Yitzhak Halprin failed to show up for work.
He and Bronstein made the rounds by themselves. They said nothing
when they saw Halprin the next day. He was older than they were and
had served in the Turkish army. It wasn't for them to tell him what to do.

A few days later, though, it happened again. This time they were
peeved. They were griping about it on the watchtower when two horsemen rode up from the south. The two stopped to water their horses at
the spring and one approached while the other hung back.

The rider who approached was Yitzhak Halprin. "Oh," he said
when asked where he had been, "Sarah Aaronsohn forgot a shawl in
Hadera and asked me to fetch it." Then, turning to the second rider, he
called, "Yosef Lishansky, come and meet some friends." A small, dandy-
ish man with red hair and a red mustache climbed down from his horse
and joined them. They drank coffee together and the two horsemen
continued to Zichron.

The next day, he and Bronstein pressed Halprin for the truth. He
might live next door to the Aaronsohns and think the world of Sarah,
they said, but he hadn't ridden all the way to Hadera for a shawl. "You're

right," he told them. "I'm involved in something big." He was going to work for an organization that would help free the country from the Turks.

That was Epstein's first knowledge of the Nili ring. It was his first encounter with Lishansky, too. There were to be three others.

The second took place a year later, at the Aaronsohn farm in Atlit. Lishansky and Sarah were seeking new recruits for the spy ring and had invited some young farmers from Zichron to a meeting, including two of Epstein's five brothers, Dov and Tsvi. There was a rumor that Alexander Aaronsohn would be there. "I went along as the driver," Epstein said. "We had a wagon and the only mule left in the village. She was a draft dodger."

His laugh was short and severe, a dry cough.

"You can give my father credit for that mule. He didn't work in the fields, but he had an eye for animals. Once he was sitting outside our house when a stray mule wandered by. 'Yanko,' he said, 'go see who that mule belongs to.' I followed it to Moshe Arizon's yard and came back. 'Go offer twenty-five pounds for it,' my father said. 'Twenty-five?' I said. That was an awful lot for a mule. 'Twenty-five,' he said. I went and bought it from Arizon for twenty-five pounds and it was worth every one of them.

"When the Turks took to confiscating our farm animals, that mule was given a deferment because she had a boil the size of a fist on her forehead. I wasn't smart enough to give her a boil, but I was smart enough not to lance it. Every few days I squeezed out just enough pus to keep it from bursting. Each time the Turks came back, our mule was turned down again."

Alexander wasn't at the meeting that day. He wasn't even in the country. He had left America, to which he had sailed early in the war with his sister Rivka, and was with his brother Aaron in Egypt. Word had been spread of his return because the young Zichronites looked up to him and would have followed him anywhere. They once did follow him as far as Rishon le-Tsiyyon, a Rothschild colony in the south. A feud had broken out between the two villages. They set out with him at dawn, rode hard all day, reached Rishon in the evening, and galloped through its streets, cracking their whips and challenging the southerners to a fight until they apologized.

Neither Dov nor Tsvi joined the spy ring. "My father talked them out of it. He sat us down when we came home from Atlit and said, 'I want to tell you about Pleven.'

"None of us had heard about Pleven. My father said it was a town in Bulgaria, near the Rumanian border. When he was a child, there was an uprising there. The Turkish general who put it down was Osman Pasha. 'By the time Osman Pasha finished with Pleven,' my father told us, 'it was a heap of ashes.'

"He didn't have to say any more. He wasn't against the Nili, he was just afraid of the consequences. He was on good terms with Sarah personally. He was on good terms with everyone. He only stopped being *mukhtar* because he gave up his Ottoman citizenship when the war broke out. He thought it would keep us out of the Turkish army."

"Did it?"

"My brothers weren't drafted. But that was because they had *wasikas*."

A *wasika* was a military exemption. The easiest way to get one was to hold a job classified as vital for the war effort. The longer the war dragged on, however, the more jobs the Turks dropped from the list. In the end, the only one left was chopping down trees for wood to stoke their troop trains. The Jewish contractor in charge of the work put Dov and Tsvi on his payroll and pocketed their pay. "By the time I turned eighteen and was eligible for the draft," Epstein said, "there were more Jewish boys on that payroll than trees in the forest. There was no room for me.

"The next best thing was flunking the medical. If a mule could do it, so could I. On the day of my call-up, my father gave me ten Turkish pounds. I put them in a money belt, went to the induction center in Haifa, and came home with a *wasika*. The only time I was asked to take off my clothes was to open the money belt.

"That put me in the clear. I just had to be careful not to set foot outside the village without my *wasika*. There were Turkish military police everywhere. They inducted you on the spot if they found you without your papers. I kept mine in the pocket of my work pants."

Those were the same pants he had almost had to patch because of the woman in the park.

"A few weeks went by and we young folk decided to throw a party.

We needed to let off some steam. We picked a Saturday night and hired Arn Klarineter. Arn played at every celebration in the village. We paid him in advance in sorghum and lentils. That was easier to get hold of than money.

"That same night, it turned out, Moshe Arizon's daughter was getting married across the valley in Shfeya. The Arizons were counting on Arn to play his clarinet at the wedding. They just hadn't bothered to ask him, because everyone thought someone else had already done it. When Moshe's son Meir came to take Arn to the wedding, Arn said he had a previous engagement. Meir tried reasoning with him: how could a party compare to a wedding? But Arn was an honest soul. He had given us his word and he would keep it.

"Well, a wedding without music is about as cheerful as a stove without a fire. Meir Arizon went home, came back with a pistol, and carried Arn and his clarinet off to the wedding at gunpoint.

"Meanwhile, the boys and girls began arriving at our party. Pretty soon someone asks, 'Where's the music?' We wait a while longer – no Arn. 'He must have forgotten,' I said to Itzik Leibowitz. 'Let's go get him.' We went to Arn's house.

"We knock on the door – Arn's wife opens it. 'Where's Arn?' 'What, don't you know?' she says. 'He's gone to play at the wedding in Shfeya.'

"That riled me. 'Listen,' I said. 'We're going to Shfeya to get him.'

"'How will we do that?' Itzik asked.

"'Leave it to me,' I said.

"We took our *wasikas*, rode the mule across the valley to Shfeya, and tied it at the entrance to the village. The wedding was in the schoolhouse. It was a summer night and the windows were open. I spotted Arn by one of them, sitting on a bench. The guests were eating dessert. 'Here's what we'll do,' I told Leibowitz. 'You'll stand outside the window. When the clarinet comes through, run with it to the mule. I'll meet you there with Arn and we'll ride back to the party.'

"When dessert was finished and everyone got up to dance, I joined the wedding. I was dressed for our party, so they all took me for a guest.

"Moshe Arizon was the dance master. He arranged the couples for a *lancers*. I stole up on Arn from behind. The clarinet was next to him. I kicked the bench on its far side to make him turn toward the noise, grabbed the clarinet, stuck it under my jacket, backed up to the window, and passed it to Leibowitz.

"By now the couples were all lined up. Meir Arizon gave the signal and Arn Klarineter reached for his clarinet. Then he slid his hand along the bench. Then he looked beneath it. Then he opened his mouth wide.

"What's wrong?' Meir asks. 'My clarinet's gone,' says Arn. Pretty soon everyone at the wedding is on their hands and knees looking for it. I went outside and slipped back in as if I had just arrived from Zichron. 'Arn,' I said, 'what happened? Your clarinet is waiting for you at our party.'

"'My clarinet?' he says.

"'Yes,' I said. 'If it could play without you, I wouldn't have come.'

"'But it was just here,' he says.

"'If it was just here,' I say, 'what's it doing in Zichron?'

"He was too befuddled to think straight. 'Come on,' I said. 'You'll believe it when you see it.' I led him to the mule and the three of us squeezed onto it and rode to Zichron. The wedding guests never saw us leave. They were still beneath the benches and the tables.

"We got to the party and Itzik Leibowitz went inside while I made Arn stand still to straighten his tie. When Arn entered, the clarinet was on a chair in the middle of the room. He was afraid to pick it up. His hands were shaking so hard he couldn't play. In the end, though, he got over it and we danced all night. The next day I disappeared."

I leaned toward him to hear better. A big semi-trailer was passing us, hissing on the wet road. The traffic was growing thicker as we neared Tel Aviv. Dirty spray kicked up by the cars in front of us fouled the windshield.

"I only slept a few hours that night. In the morning I rose early, put on my work clothes, and took the mule. I had a ten-box field to plow in Wadi Mina that I wanted to finish in a day."

A "box" was a strip of land two hundred meters by seven. "You plowed it with a mule in a single round, half the width going and half coming back. If you were in a hurry and wanted a double swathe, you used an outrider. I rigged one to the plow and took along the son of a field hand to sit on it.

"We were on our third or fourth box when I saw a column of men at the top of it. Some were on horseback. Soldiers, I thought. But as we got closer I saw that only the horsemen were in uniform. The others were draft dodgers, rounded up that morning in the Arab villages.

"They waited for us to reach them and an officer asked to see my *wasika*.

"I put my hand in my pocket – it wasn't there. It was still in my party pants.

"Well, go explain to a Turkish officer that you left your *wasika* at home. I was marched off so fast that I barely had time to tell the boy to leave the plow and ride back to my father.

"'Where are they taking us?' I asked. 'To Haifa,' someone says. That was a good day's walk. I didn't look forward to it on two hours' sleep and the only Jew among twenty Arabs. Luckily, I knew one of them. He was Amhamed Sa'id from Suberin and he was a prankster. I fell in beside him and we started to talk.

"Sure enough, he joked all the way. It helped to keep up my spirits. 'Don't worry,' he said, 'we'll be home soon. The war's almost over.' 'What makes you so sure?' I asked. 'Why, look at the men we're with,' he said. They were a sorry-looking bunch. 'Any one of them can lose the war single-handed.'

"In Haifa we were given uniforms and put on a train to Samah. From there we were sent to a base near Kuneitra, on the Golan Heights. The word was that we were going to boot camp and then to the front. Meanwhile we sat around in tents. One day we were given a few hours' leave to go into town.

"Amhamed Sa'id and I went into Kuneitra. 'You know,' he says, 'this is our chance to make our getaway.' I was thinking the same thing. If we didn't do it now, we'd end up ducking shells in a trench. 'Let's walk back to Samah,' I said. 'We can hitch a ride there on a farmer's wagon.'

"'Just stroll down to Samah in our uniforms?' Amhamed Sa'id says. 'We won't get very far. I have a better plan. We'll find a store in Kuneitra and swipe two brushes and a can of paint.'

"'And paint ourselves invisible,' I said. I thought it was one of his jokes.

"'Not at all,' he says. 'There are telegraph poles all along the road. Each has two numbers, one in Arabic and one in German. That's to help the repairmen find them if they're bombed. If we see soldiers, we'll pretend to be repainting them. You'll paint in German and I'll paint in Arabic.'

"'What will we pretend to be if we're bombed?' I asked.

"'Deserters,' he says.

"He had a head on his shoulders. We found a store in Kuneitra and I took the owner to the back while Amhamed Sa'id made off with two brushes and a can of white paint. Then we set out for Samah. Each time we saw troops we stopped and painted numbers on the poles. It worked like a charm."

We were in the streets of Tel Aviv.

"It took a few days to get to Samah. Now and then we passed a village and Amhamed Sa'id went and cadged some food. Once he said to me, '*Ya* Ya'akub, do you know why we're the only soldiers in the Turkish army who could get away with this?' 'No,' I said. 'It's because,' he says, 'we're the only ones who know all the numbers up to ten.'

"From Samah we cut across the Galilee. We crossed the Valley of Jezreel at night, slept the next day, and headed up Wadi Milikh and over the hills to Suberin. From there I walked the rest of the way myself. It was the middle of the night when I knocked on my parents' door. I was still in uniform. I saw a curtain move on the window and heard my mother say to my father, 'You better go have a look. There's a poor devil of a deserter out there.'"

Yanko Epstein drew back his arm, brushing mine as it rested on the floor shift.

"Left," he said.

I was almost at the corner and had to jump lanes while hitting the brakes, taking the turn with a squeal of tires. I didn't know Tel Aviv. I didn't care for it. It was a hasty, graceless place, grown too fast and old before its time.

"Right." He made the same motion with his other arm, as if pulling on the reins of a horse.

"You never learned to drive, did you?" I asked.

"No. I should have listened to Edwin Samuel."

Edwin Samuel was the son of the first British High Commissioner in Palestine. Epstein had worked as his bodyguard. "I went with him everywhere. Once we had a flat tire. I got out to help change it and he said, 'My good man, first learn to drive.' He even offered to pay for my lessons, but I told him a horse was good enough for me. Bear right. That was ... when was Arlozorov murdered?"

"1933."

Chaim Arlozorov was a Zionist socialist leader shot to death on a Tel Aviv beach. Two members of the right-wing Revisionist Party were accused of his murder and acquitted.

"Edwin Samuel had been romancing Arlozorov's wife. After the murder he received a death threat, a drawing of a dagger dipped in blood. Major Strange of British Intelligence asked a friend of mine, Yosef Davidesco, to recommend a bodyguard. Davidesco said, 'I've got the man for you: Ya'akov Epstein from Zichron Ya'akov.'"

We were driving through the south of the city, in dingy streets.

"I took the job because Samuel lived in Haifa. That was nearer to Safed, where my wife was in a sanatorium with TB. Turn into that side street. I left my little boy and girl with their grandparents and rented an apartment in Haifa. Once or twice a week Edwin Samuel would say, 'Epstein, take the day off and come back tomorrow,' and I'd go visit my wife. Those were the days he saw Mrs. Arlozorov. Park here."

He was out of the car before I had pulled up the handbrake.

I locked the car doors and followed him to a photography shop. The sun was out, glinting off the puddles on the sidewalk. The window of the shop featured the stock-in-trade smiling brides and plump barmitzvah boys. Judging by the dust on them, the brides were already nursing babies and the bar-mitzvah boys were serving in the army.

Yanko Epstein was standing by the counter, a pasteboard enlargement of the Khan Zakhlan in his hands.

He was too absorbed in it to look up. The faces of the Jews on the upper floor stood out clearly now, like old coins that had been cleaned. The ground-floor jews remained indistinct in the shadows exhaled by the archways.

The counter of the shop was cluttered with photographs and albums. On the wall behind it, an Alpine landscape advertised a German camera.

"Well?" asked the owner. A friendly man, he wore rubber bands on his shirtsleeves.

Epstein looked up from the enlargement.

"No one," he said. He sounded baffled. "Maybe with a magnifying glass...."

The shop owner handed him one.

He held the enlargement in one hand and passed the glass over the balcony of the Khan Zakhlan. Then he ran it back the other way, playing it over each face like a spotlight. It dropped to the ground floor and probed among the shadows, then rose to the balcony again. It lingered on a figure; released it; came back.

"I suppose this could be Mordecai Bronstein."

It was said without conviction. He laid the enlargement on the counter.

The owner of the shop picked it up and scanned it. "Tell me," he said. "Are any of these people still alive?"

"Not a soul. The children you see were grown up when I was a child."

"Then that explains it."

Epstein stood frowning while the owner slipped the enlargement and the original into an envelope. He took a hundred pounds from his wallet and laid them on the counter.

The man regarded the money sadly. "Mr. Epstein," he said, "I normally charge three hundred pounds for a job like this."

"Eh?" Yanko Epstein's brows shot up as if to say: *Three hundred pounds for a picture in which the only face that looks familiar isn't even Mordecai Bronstein?*

"I'll make it two hundred. I wouldn't do this for anyone else."

Epstein took the magnifying glass, placed it on the hundred pound note, and went to the pay phone at the back of the store.

The owner pocketed the money with a sigh. "I don't know why I let him do this to me," he said.

He busied himself with some negatives while I studied the landscape on the wall. After a while, I found myself listening to Epstein's conversation. He was talking to a woman. "Yes, Bella...:" he said. "Yes, Bella, that's so.... That's so, but we've always been logical.... Yes, of course..."

His gruff voice was tender. "I still am a romantic, you know that.

I haven't changed…. Of course. But I have a driver who has to get back to Zichron. I can't keep him waiting…."

He didn't have to. I could drive back without him and he could take the bus he had planned to take in the first place. But it wasn't for me to tell him what to do or to object when he said, "We'll just have to make it some other time." He blushed easily, I had already noticed that. "What? …Of course. Your wish is my command, Bella."

He hung up and rejoined us. "You know," he said, gazing at the Swiss landscape, "that could be near Zurich, where my brother Yeshayahu lives. He owns a pharmacy." He took the envelope and shook the owner's hand. "Come up to Zichron some day. We have a nice little cemetery. I'll give you a special price on a plot."

"Mr. Epstein," the owner said, "one more special price and you can bury me right now."

On the sidewalk, beneath a sky that had clouded over again, Epstein stopped me as I started toward the car. "Let's get something to eat," he said. "There's a good place a few blocks from here."

We walked through a shabby district of workshops and warehouses. The streets were too narrow for the traffic pouring into them. Scooters and bicycles fought cars and trucks for right of way. Pools of rainwater had formed on the sidewalk where the pavement had crumbled. The elements had stripped the paint and plaster from the buildings, reducing them to the color of soiled Band-aids. "You must miss the days when there were sand dunes here," I said.

"Never!" he answered. "Every time I see what's been built in this country, I thank the Lord. Not long ago I traveled to Beersheba; the road ran through green fields all the way. I remember that road. It passed through wilderness."

His vehemence took me aback. Yet by what right did I expect him to be as nostalgic as I was for a past that was his and not mine?

The place to eat served fast food and had a large clientele of flies. Our waitress was a dark-haired woman with a good body and a bad complexion. Epstein ordered for the two of us and whispered something in her ear.

"You're lucky my boyfriend didn't hear that," she said.

"You can tell him," he answered, "that if I were forty years younger, he wouldn't stand a chance."

She went off and he said with a grin, "Women are like toys. You can play with them, but gently." He picked up a salt cellar and put it down again. "If I had done what my brother did, I would have married her."

He was talking about the woman he had spoken to on the phone. "She didn't want to live in Zichron and I wouldn't move to Tel Aviv. I took the advice I gave my brother Meir-Itzik. His wife had asthma and the doctors recommended a drier climate, so he decided to move to Jerusalem. I said, 'Meir-Itzik, you're a farmer. You can always find another wife. Where will you find another farm?' He sold it and moved anyway."

The waitress returned with a tray on which were two glasses, two Coca-Colas, and two dishes, each with a pair of lumpy pastries.

He pointed to my pastries as if they were a riddle he'd made up. "That one's sweet and that one's salty," he said.

I bit into the sweet one.

"Wrong! Sweet after salty! Salty before sweet! I'd have thought a fellow who cared for the old days would have known that."

He made me eat my stale, salty pastry first while telling me an Arab folktale about two brothers who set out on a journey with a camel loaded with sugar and salt. They were on their way to Damascus to argue their case before the great qadi and were taking a long time getting there. Both, inexplicably, were named Ali, their problem being that their father had willed his fortune to one of them without saying which Ali he had in mind.

There was a clap of thunder. I began counting the seconds until the lightning, then remembered it was the other way around.

One of the Alis, it seemed, was a bastard. His legitimate brother was the rightful heir. The clever qadi managed to find this out.

I yawned. I needed some fresh air.

Yanko Epstein finished his cola. "What do you think of her?" he asked of the waitress. "She reminds me of a stripper in a Paris nightclub Yeshayahu took me to."

He rose from the table, pushed back his chair, and reached for his wallet. "It's on me," he said grandly.

He left a big tip.

Chapter ten

Thunder cracked again, louder and nearer. It began to pour as we reached the car. The parking ticket under the windshield wipers was soaked. Epstein watched without comment as I wrung it dry and stuck it in the glove compartment.

"Shall we go to the framer?" I asked.

"Eh?"

"To frame our photograph." I was eager to see it on the wall of his museum.

"It's too late," he said without glancing at his watch. "He'll be closed."

"It's only twenty after twelve." No one closed for the midday break before one.

He put the envelope on his knees and placed his blue beret on top of it.

It was slow getting out of Tel Aviv. A flooded intersection had backed up traffic. Not until the city was behind us did I ask:

"When was the third time you met Lishansky?"

He didn't need to think about it. "When Na'aman Belkind was caught."

It was Belkind who doomed the Nili by trying to reach British lines in Sinai in order to find out what had happened to his cousin Avshalom Feinberg, suspected by him of having been murdered by Yosef Lishansky in the desert.

"Belkind was caught by a Turkish patrol and brought to Beersheba. He told the Turks he had gone to visit Bedouin friends. They pretended to believe him and drugged the food they gave him. He spilled the beans. He gave them a full list of the Nili spies."

"I never understood," I said, "why only he was hung with Lishansky in Damascus."

"He was caught trying to contact the British."

"The whole ring was in contact with the British."

He had no answer to that. Belkind was arrested in early autumn, between Rosh Hashana and Yom Kippur. That Friday night, while his family was eating its Sabbath dinner, a message came from Sarah via Yitzhak Halprin. "Yanko," Halprin said, "Sarah needs a favor. Some people have to get to Beersheba in a hurry."

Beersheba was 150 kilometers away. "Go hitch your mule," Halprin said. "Moshe Arizon will give you a carriage. The passengers will be waiting by his house."

Although the rain had stopped, the wet road sizzled like a griddle. Epstein said:

"I went home and told my father. 'So it's that, then,' he said. He knew about Belkind. 'Did you promise her?' he asked.

"I said, 'Yes.'

"'Then keep your promise,' he said.

"Two people were waiting at Moshe Arizon's, a man and a woman. The woman was veiled. The man had a horse. He tied it to the back of the carriage and climbed in with the woman. They didn't talk much. When they did, it was in whispers.

"The main road to Tulkarm was heavily patrolled. I took the back way through Um-el-Haras and whipped the mule on to Kakun. There was a little khan there where I stopped to let it rest. I gave it its feedbag and asked my passengers if they wanted coffee. They didn't, so I went to get some for myself.

"I had just stepped out again when a carriage pulled up from the other direction and stopped next to ours. The driver was Nisan Rutman. His passengers and mine began to argue. It was about our continuing to Beersheba. Someone in the other carriage said, 'Don't do it! You're heading straight into the fire! Straight into the fire!' The voice was Yosef Lishansky's.

"They argued for a while. Then my passenger untied his horse and rode back to Zichron. Lishansky climbed out of Rutman's carriage and into mine. 'Turn around and head back, Yanko,' he said.

"We started back. Lishansky didn't speak. Neither did the woman. Just once she said, 'Here, take this pill. You'll feel better.' I thought it was for his nerves. They were shot by then. But he was sick with a fever."

The woman was Belkind's sister Sonia, a doctor from Haifa. "The man with the horse was named Fein. He was a Nili spy from the south. When news came of Belkind's arrest, Lishansky went to Beersheba with Rutman to try to free him. He thought he could do it with bribes. But it was too big for that. He knew what would happen if Belkind talked, so he began to plan a jailbreak and sent Fein to consult Sarah. Sarah was for upping the bribe. She was sending Sonia Belkind to Beersheba with more money."

"But why was Lishansky coming back?"

"He had realized his plan wouldn't work. It would have taken a whole army to free Belkind. He was coming to tell Sarah.

"It was getting light out when we reached Zichron. Lishansky asked me to take him to Atlit. 'I have to see Sarah right away,' he said. 'If you don't drive me, I'll walk.'

"I had already pushed that mule more than I should have, but I couldn't let a sick man walk twenty kilometers, so I swung around the village and cut back toward the coast through Wadi Milikh. Near Fara-dis I stopped to rest the mule. The sun was coming up. Lishansky was too tense to wait. 'I'll get out and walk,' he said, 'and you can pick me up along the way.' Sonia Belkind and I must have fallen asleep, because the next thing I knew the sun was high. We didn't catch up with him until we were nearly at Atlit. He had walked the whole distance in three hours, that little man – and with a fever!

"Sarah was there. Lishansky went inside to talk to her and then she came out and asked me to take Sonia Belkind to Haifa. 'Miss Sarah,'

I said, 'this is as far as I go. My mule is half-dead and the other half has to work tomorrow.' It was the only time in my life I ever said no to her; she could make you feel small for doing that. 'Well,' she said, 'at least come in and have a cold drink.' I didn't do that either. I knew she shared a room with Lishansky."

"You didn't like their being lovers."

"I never said they were."

"No. They just shared a room."

"They didn't tell me what they did there." He laughed his hoarse cough of a laugh. "I grant you, a woman who stoops to spying doesn't stop there. What is it to surrender your body when you've already surrendered all else? He had a family. She wouldn't have done it if she had thought there was a way back. But she didn't love him. He was tough, Lishansky – a little bantam of a man, but a man. I never believed he killed Feinberg in the desert. But he wasn't in Sarah's league."

Sixty years later, he still sounded jealous. He must not have been the only young man in Zichron to have been in half in love with Sarah Aaronsohn himself.

"Still," I said, "his life meant more to her than her own."

"That had nothing to do with her feelings. She wanted him to reach British lines. She made him swear to get to Egypt and tell her brother Aaron what had happened. That's why he broke his promise to me to turn himself in."

"Lishansky promised *you* to turn himself in?"

"Yes. The last time we met.

"Sarah had asked for an evacuation by sea. The British refused to risk it while the moon was full, so she came to Zichron to spend the holiday with her family."

There was always a full moon on the first night of Sukkot, the seven-day Feast of Booths.

"On the second night of the holiday, there was a wedding party at the Schechters. Some of us were standing in the street outside when we were told that the Turks had surrounded the village.

"We didn't know what to make of it. It could have been an ordinary search. The party broke up and I went home to get my *wasika*. My father was sitting on the bench in our front yard, smoking a cigarette.

Just then Sarah walked by. She was coming from the Gelbergs' and had crossed to our side of the street. She saw my father and asked:

"'Do you think it's routine?'

"'Miss Sarah,' my father said, 'you should know better than that. It's not for deserters this time. It's for you.'

"'Really?' she said. 'Do you think so?' And she walked on back to her house.

"Lishansky was there with Yitzhak Halprin. Sarah told Halprin to find Lishansky a safe place outside the village where he could wait to see how things turned out. They left through the tunnel in Aaron's bathroom and went to the hill behind the winery.

"The Turks strung Sarah up by the wrists and beat the soles of her feet to make her tell them where Lishansky was. The only sound in the village was her screams. They seemed to come from next door, because we lived close by. Epstein. Bronstein. Karniel. Halprin. Aaronsohn."

He ticked off the houses

"The next day, they gathered us in the synagogue. You heard me tell the children about that. Ahmed Bek gave us twenty-four hours to find Lishansky. He said that if we didn't he'd round up the heads of the village and send them to Nazareth with the spies. That's when those women of yours carried on."

It was his first mention of them since the morning outside the museum.

"What made them do it?"

"They were scared."

"That's no reason to laugh at anyone's screams."

"No one laughed at any screams. They hit and cursed Nisan Rutman. They wanted to show the Turks they were against the spies. My father saw them from the window. He went outside and made the three of them stop."

"You mean the four."

"There were three of them. Adele Goldstein, Tsippora Lerner, and Gita Blumenfeld."

"You're forgetting Perl Appelbaum."

"Perl never left her front porch."

"Then why did Alexander – ?"

145

"Where was Alexander?" he interrupted angrily. "Where was Alexander during the war, when we scraped and starved and lived in fear? In America with his little sister, sucking up to rich Jews at dinner parties! We didn't see him again until he came riding into town with the British on a white horse. Do you know why Rivka Aaronsohn has never been to my museum?"

"No."

"Because she knows I know the truth. 'Miss Rivka,' I once said to her, 'I was here then. You weren't.'"

He waited for his anger to pass.

"Only Halprin knew where Lishansky was. He and Re'uven Schwartz were still on the loose. The next morning the Turks took Alter Albert, Schwartz's father-in-law, and marched him through the street. They whipped him while he cried, 'Re'uven, where are you?'

"Schwartz turned himself in. Halprin decided to do the same. First he came to tell me where Lishansky was. 'Try to get him to surrender,' he said. 'But he's promised Sarah not to, so you may have to use force.'

"I took my brother Yeshayahu and two friends and we went to the hill. Lishansky was behind a tree. He saw us and called out. All we saw was the barrel of his rifle.

"I walked up to it. 'Yosef,' I said, 'you don't stand a chance. The Turks have caught everyone. They'll slaughter us like the Armenians if you don't turn yourself in.'

"He kept pointing the rifle. I said, 'They're torturing Sarah. I'm surprised you don't hear her screams up here.' Watch out for that car."

An old pick-up cut in front of us at Hadera Circle.

"'Yosef,' I said, 'I'm asking you to do it.' 'Is that all?' he says. He had a funny smile. 'All right,' he said. 'I'll come down tonight.'

"We believed him. We could have used force. There were four of us. But I thought he had that much honor.

"After Yeshayahu and I returned home, a Turkish soldier came to the door. He told us our father was on the list for Nazareth and under house arrest.

"Father took it calmly, but Yeshayahu and I went to see Ahmed Bek. '*Ya* Ahmed Bek,' I said. 'Yosef Epstein's sons have combed the hills for Lishansky and this is his reward?'

"'Combed the hills and found not a hair!' he said with his crazy laugh. But he called an adjutant and asked for the list. My father was the only member of the village council on it. Ahmed Bek crossed out his name and wrote another.

"The next day those on the list were sent to Nazareth with the spies. For a while, no one heard from them. Then they smuggled out some mail.

"One of the letters was from Fishl Aaronsohn, Sarah's father. He wrote his in-law David Sternberg that the Nili had buried two barrels near the big custard-apple tree in his yard.

"Sternberg asked me to dig them up. But the Aaronsohn place was well guarded. You couldn't just dig there in the middle of the night without knowing exactly where those barrels were.

"I went to Hayyim Rothstein the smith and had him make me a metal prod with two handles. Then I scaled the Aaronsohns' fence after midnight. The ground was still soft from the rain that fell on the day of Sarah's funeral. I probed around the tree and found nothing. I wanted to go back a second time but Sternberg said, 'That's enough. If Fishl thinks the barrels are in his yard, you can be sure they're somewhere else.'

"He knew old Fishl. After Lishansky was caught, Fishl was released from prison and came home. 'Where are those barrels?' Sternberg asked. 'Near the custard-apple tree,' Fishl says. A week goes by and Fishl's Arab field hand comes back too. 'Those barrels?' he says. 'I buried them myself. They're in the olive grove, near Alexander's pavilion.'

"We dug them up, slung them in sacks, carried them to Sternberg's house, and opened them. They were full of...."

"Gold!" I lunged at the sentence he left hanging.

"Guns. Bolt-action .303 caliber Lee-Enfield rifles, disassembled and stored in grease. A Colt revolver, too, and an antique, pearl-handled pistol. Sternberg took the pistol and I took the Colt and a rifle and gave the others to my brothers."

He didn't believe any gold had been left. "The Aaronsohns' money came from their connections with American Jews. After the war, my father asked Alexander to pay back part of what the Nili cost the village. We spent a fortune on bribes alone when the arrests began. He might as well have talked to the wall. Even the spies got nothing. Only Nisan Rutman."

"Why Rutman?"

"You'll have to ask him."

"I'm told he lives in an old-age home in Haifa."

"He did."

"Ben-Hayyim says he still does."

"Ben-Hayyim says a lot of things."

"Where does he live, then?"

"Nowhere."

"But – "

"He's dead! He died last week. His obituary was in the papers."

His tone was the same as when I bit into the wrong pastry.

"Well," I said, miffed, "that sometimes happens at his age. Did he leave any family?"

"Just a brother."

We crossed the railroad tracks at the base of the Carmel. "Rutman had spent the night with Tova Gelberg. A group of us came out of the synagogue after Neiderman's speech. We worked our way up the street, searching every house for Lishansky.

"When we reached the Gelbergs', we went through all the rooms. There was nothing suspicious. The next house was the Appelbaums'. Perl was on her porch. She caught my eye and went like this, back toward the Gelbergs.'"

I took my eyes off the road to look at him. He gave his head a sideways flick.

"We went back and searched again. This time I noticed something. A pillow on the floor of Tova's room had been pushed against the bed. I moved it and there was Rutman.

"He didn't put up a fight. 'I'm coming out,' he said. 'I've come from Hadera to turn myself in.'

"He didn't say how he was planning to do that from beneath Tova's bed. We took him to the street and a Turkish soldier tied his hands and led him to the Lange house. That's when those women came along. Tsippora Lerner slapped his face; Adele Goldstein hit him with her shoe and Gita Blumenfeld egged them on. Perl wasn't with them."

"Alexander wrote that she died a strange death."

He said nothing.

"What did she die of?"

There was a scraping sound in his throat as if something were stuck there. I turned to look at him again. His jaw was tight. A flush had spread through his cheeks. "If you don't mind," he said, "take the back way up Wadi Milikh." We were nearing the turn-off at the gas station below Zichron. "My son owns a vineyard there that I want to look at."

I drove to the Faradis junction and turned right. After a kilometer, he told me to stop.

The vineyard ran to the road. The vines gleamed in the sunshine, dark and muscular, their long shoots dangling above the puddles of rainwater like fishing rods.

Epstein rolled up the cuff of his pants and stepped into the vineyard. The earth squished beneath a shoe. Quickly he withdrew it, sucking up mud.

He surveyed the scene grimly. "He hasn't done much," he said.

"Your son?"

"Yosi?" He gave a parental humph. "No. The Arab worker we hired." He stamped his shoe to shake off the mud. "Today it rained. But what about the rest of the week?"

As we passed the winery, he asked:

"How much is five times fifty?"

"Two hundred and fifty."

"Two hundred and fifty pounds and he hasn't begun to prune the shoots. I don't know what we're paying him for."

I dropped him off at his house on Founders Street. As I turned the corner into our dirt road I saw, out over the sea, a fresh bar of gray rising quickly like mercury.

Chapter eleven

I

f there was anything unusual about Perl Appelbaum's death, the town council failed to notice it.

According to its minutes, whose thick volumes were kept on one library shelf with the old death registry, the council met three times the week Perl died. Present on each occasion were Councilmen Steinberg, Schwartz, Temshis, Arizon, Pomerantz, and Epstein. Their first meeting was on a Saturday night, the 27th of August, 1921. It began with a discussion, joined by the town druggist, Mr. Broner, of the precarious financial state of his pharmacy. Next came the complaint of Rabbi Orlansky.

Zichron's rabbi was troubled that, having heard that day of a shipment of wine due to leave for Haifa port the next morning, several grape growers had desecrated the Sabbath by driving their wagons to the winery and parking them there to assure themselves the job of hauling it. This was especially grave, the rabbi said, because if the rabbinical sages in Jerusalem got wind of the matter, they would publish notices declaring the produce of the winery "libational," the equivalent of wine used in pagan sacrifices and forbidden to Jews to drink. It was imperative, therefore, to punish the Sabbath violators by giving the job to someone else.

This was responded to by Councilman Epstein. Although the

rabbi's complaint had merit, he observed, it was crucial for the cargo to reach the port on time, since the ship waiting for it was scheduled to sail on Monday. The council resolved, therefore, firstly, to forbid the offending farmers to transport the wine; and secondly, to request the presence of a British constable at the winery on Sunday morning to ensure that law and order prevailed there.

The final item on the agenda was the case of Mr. Gruper, who had come, said the minutes, "to complain about his neighbor, Mr. Pervis… who has not only besmirched his good name with wild accusations but has sought to press charges against him with the British police for the attempted rape of Mr. Pervis's wife, the smashing of Mr. Pervis's dishes, and yet other offenses. Mr. Gruper furthermore stated that under no circumstance would he continue to live next door to Mr. Pervis. He asked the council to summon Mr. Pervis for a judgment and to compel him to withdraw his complaint to the police."

The council declined to get involved and advised Mr. Gruper to seek redress from a British justice of the peace. In addition, Councilman Epstein suggested that greater care be taken in the future in letting outsiders like Mr. Pervis settle in the village. Anyone wishing to buy a home in Zichron should be required to obtain either the unanimous agreement of the council or the general approval of the populace. The proposal was not put to a vote.

On Monday, the 29th of August, the council met to debate three more issues. The first was a plan to lower the price of meat by contracting its delivery to a single wholesaler. This was opposed by Mr. Samuel Aaronsohn, appearing as an interested citizen. "If we grant a monopoly to any one supplier," he argued, "he will end up feeding us carrion, and at prices higher than we pay now, no matter what his contract stipulates." The plan was shelved.

Next came the plea of Hayyim-Ber Schwartz to release his grain that had been impounded on the threshing floor for non-payment of taxes, which he promised to remit upon receiving the first installment from the winery for his grapes from the current harvest. The petition was granted.

Finally, the council considered the request of Mr. Samuel Aaronsohn's brother, Mr. Tsvi Aaronsohn, to connect his new house (in which, years later, I was to find a large number of books, a photograph of a woman, and a dead cat in a suitcase) to the town water supply. Since the house stood at a distance from the nearest water main, a decision on the matter was postponed.

The council met once more that week on September 1, the day after Perl Appelbaum's death. It discussed the pharmacy again; debated linking Zichron to a new coastal road being built by the British; considered selling the coming olive crop on the branch to an Arab picker; voted to grant the grape growers exclusive rights to hauling wine from the winery, thus avoiding a repeat of last Saturday's incident; and heard a report on Hinde Sokolowitz, who wanted 200 piastres to repair her broken oil lamp. Councilman Steinberg recommended granting the money while warning against buying Hinde a new lamp, since he knew her well and could vouch that "no matter what we buy her, she will say it is no good." The sum was approved.

I turned back to the beginning of the volume. It started with the autumn of 1918, soon after the British entered Zichron. The council members at that time were the same men who had served throughout the war: Avigdor Appelbaum, Moshe Arizon, Binyamin Blumenfeld, Yosef Epstein, Alter Goldstein, Zeyde Goldstein, Alter Leitner, and Yisra'el Lerner.

I recognized all those names. One belonged to Yanko Epstein's father and one to the father of his friend, Dov Leitner. Zeyde Goldstein's son Ezra had chopped down our plum trees. Moshe Arizon, the operator of the stagecoach to Haifa, had married off the daughter from whose wedding Arn Klarineter's clarinet was stolen. The other four councilmen were the husbands of my four women.

They were no longer such a mystery, these women. All were married to prominent citizens of Zichron who were friendly with each other and with the "Russian circle" of the town doctor, Hillel Yoffe. They disliked the Aaronsohns like him. They were frightened and angered by the spy ring's existence, for which their husbands stood to be blamed if it was uncovered.

It was – and Yosef Lishansky slipped away. The Turks threatened to take the council members hostage. The four women were desperate to convince Ahmed Bek of their husbands' loyalty. Publicly abusing Nisan Rutman, a Nili operative from Hadera whose local girlfriend, a spy herself, had a tainted reputation was a good way to do it. Perhaps the other three knew in advance that Perl Appelbaum was about to reveal

Rutman's hiding place; perhaps they ran into him by chance in the street. In either case, their tactic worked: when the list of detainees for Nazareth was drawn up, their husbands were not on it. The only councilman to appear there was Yosef Epstein, who had come to Rutman's aid.

The Gorgons and Furies were ordinary women. Not terribly likable perhaps – none was remembered fondly in town, though of Perl Appelbaum no one had much to say – but all too human nonetheless.

*　*　*

The war had hardly ended when a public campaign was launched against the council. The minutes from a December 1918 session reported:

"Mr. Lerner wishes to announce in the council's name that its difficult situation does not allow it to continue its work. This is especially so because there are farmers in the village who have spared no opportunity to slander and besmirch the council members and spread false rumors about them. The council therefore tenders its resignation and asks for a new council to be elected ...."

This was in fact a political ploy. "After a long debate," the recording secretary continued with a straight face, "the council... resolved not to accept the council's resignation. A special judiciary committee was appointed to try those guilty of slandering and besmirching its members." Yet no one was tried and soon afterwards the council resigned for good and was swept from office in new elections. Of the incumbents, only Yosef Epstein and Moshe Arizon were returned. Two of the new men elected, Councilmen Steinberg and Schwartz, were openly identified with the Nili. It had all the markings of a political coup engineered by Alexander Aaronsohn, who had ridden into Zichron in his captain's uniform with a British reconnaissance unit on the heels of the Turkish retreat.

Apart from the council's minutes, historical documents from the town's past were scarce. "You can blame Aryeh Samsonov for that," Nissim Carditi the librarian said. "He went from house to house collecting everything he could and asked to keep it even after his book was published, since he was working on a second edition. But there never was a second edition and now no one knows where all that material is. I've spoken to Samsonov's widow and can't get a straight answer. First she told me there were cartons in the basement full of her husband's research. Then she said she didn't know what was in them. Now she's not sure there are cartons at all."

Perhaps it was her way of getting back at Zichron. "She was Samsonov's third wife. He brought her here from the city. She hated this town. She might have thrown it all out. Unless he gave it to someone before he died."

"Like who?"

"You might try Aaronsohn House."

"You try." We both knew you might as well ask to see the archives of the Kremlin.

*   *   *

"Poison!" Izzy Traub said. "It had to be. What's yours?"

I took the traditional manhattan. Marcia, off alcohol for her pregnancy, chose juice.

"What exactly is encepha-whoosis?" Rhoda Traub asked.

"An inflammation of the tissue of the brain. The symptoms include headache, vomiting, muscular tremors, personality changes, drowsiness, stupor, coma, and occasionally death."

"I believe it was known as brain fever when the world was young," Izzy said. "Which of those things besides occasional death did your Appelfeld lady suffer from?"

"Appelbaum. Ben-Hayyim thought she had a brain tumor. Yafia Cohen remembered her behaving strangely. Esther-Leah Berkowitz said something was wrong upstairs. Alexander Aaronsohn wrote that she died a *mitah meshunah.*"

"A *mise meshuneh!*" Izzy gave the Hebrew words their Yiddish pronunciation. "What my mother in South Africa wished on the neighbors when their dogs ate our chickens."

"Exactly. Alexander could have made it up, of course. But his sister Sarah asked for vengeance and Yanko Epstein looked as if he had swallowed a frog."

"He was just clearing his throat," Marcia said.

"But how could Epstein be the only person in town to know she was poisoned?" Rhoda Traub frowned as though looking at a painting in which a detail was wrong.

"Elementary," Izzy said. "Because he dunnit."

"Not so fast," I said. "Alexander knew too."

"Then maybe he did it," Rhoda suggested.

"But why," Marcia objected, "would the doctor have called it encephalitis if it wasn't?"

"This doctor could have called smallpox a heat rash. Listen to what Amnon Broner told me."

Running into Amnon in town, I had told him of reading about his father's pharmacy in the council's minutes. Amnon remembered its financial difficulties in those years. Business was poor because the Histadrut, the national labor federation founded after the war, had opened a clinic dispensing free drugs. "In Turkish times," he said, "my father was half a doctor. People who couldn't afford Hillel Yoffe went to him. There were days when the line outside his pharmacy looked like the pilgrimage to Lourdes."

"What kind of physician was Yoffe?"

"A good one. His bedside manners were crude, but he was a first-rate diagnostician."

"Are you sure?" I told him about the case of Nita Lange.

"*Intestinal colic and paralysis of the heart*?" He looked at me unbelievingly. "What year did you say that was in?"

"1922."

"There's your answer. The doctor then was Dr. Cohen. Hillel Yoffe left after the war. Cohen wasn't fit to carry his bag. Intestinal conniptions! That sounds like something he might have written."

"I don't suppose there would have been an autopsy?"

"An autopsy?" When Amnon smiled, he didn't look any happier. His face just creased into deeper folds. "Not unless it was a murder. When someone died in those days we asked the Lord's blessing and stuck them in the ground."

"So it wasn't encephalitis," Marcia said. "So it was a murder. So what?"

*   *   *

On my way home from town one day, I decided to look in on deaf old Betsalel Ashkenazi. I hadn't seen him since his house and the land below it had been sold by his brother Ephraim to a couple from Haifa. The couple had agreed to let Betsalel go on living there until he died or moved to an old-age home.

I knocked, quite unnecessarily, on the door and opened it. It was cold inside. The shutters were closed and there wasn't a ray of sunlight. Knees drawn up to his elbows, Betsalel was sleeping fetally in his overcoat on an iron cot. His shoes, caked with mud, were on his feet. I checked to make sure he was breathing and tiptoed back out.

I cut through his old farmyard, past the ruined milking stalls. On the slope beneath it I skidded and fell on the wet ground. Something sharp cut my hand. Broken glass. I picked myself up and kicked at it angrily, sucking blood from the cut. It didn't budge. I found a piece of wood and cleared the earth around it. A chipped bottleneck emerged, clogged with dirt. I pulled and out with a dull clink came a strange bottle. I dug toward the clink and a second bottle appeared, shaped like the first one.

Made of thick glass, the two bottles looked even stranger when cleaned. Flaring out beneath bullish necks, they were circled by four teardrop-shaped indentations and crimped in sharply further down. Inside them, the crimps formed narrow ledges on which rested a glass ball like a child's marble. Free to roll back and forth, it could neither drop through the space between the ledges nor fit through the neck of the bottle, in which it was trapped like a model ship on a mantelpiece.

Both bottles had writing, the raised characters of which could be felt like Braille even before I scrubbed the dirt away. One said in large letters:

JACOB ASCHKENASI
ZICHRON JACOB
CAIFA

The obverse side said:

THE NIAGARA BOTTLE
BARNET & FOSTER
LONDON, N.

The name of this London firm was on the back of the second bottle, too. Its front said only:

H.M. ROTHSTEIN

I had never seen anything like them. But Ze'ev Neiderman knew at once what they were. "Good lord!" he exclaimed when I brought them to his house, to which he had invited me for lunch. "I haven't seen one of these in ages."

He went to the sink and filled a bottle from the tap. "Watch!" he said. Tilting it gently, he poured from it into a glass. "Now watch this." He tilted the bottle sharply. Instead of sluicing out faster, the flow of water slowed down. "And this." He turned the bottle upside-down and held it over my head. Not a drop fell on me.

"Magic!"

He returned the bottle to an upright position. "Here," he said. "Try it yourself."

I did, with similar results.

"Soda water bottles," Ze'ev explained. "Ship ahoy!" He raised the empty bottle to his eye like a telescope and passed it to me to do the same. "That little marble is hollow. It floats. When a bottle was filled with carbonated water, it was sealed by the pressure of the gas forcing the marble into its neck. It was opened like this." He pretended to push down on the marble while turning away with a grimace to avoid an imagined squirt. "These" – he touched the indentations – "held the marble in place while you poured. See this vertical line? The bottles were made in two halves that were fused with the marble inside. Clever, eh? No bottletops, no openers. They knew a thing or two back then."

He regarded the Braille-like letters.

"Hayyim Rothstein the smith! He lived across the street from us, in the pile of stones next to Benedik's hardware store. It became one when it was hit in 1948 by an Iraqi plane aiming for the winery. The pilot must have seen the chimney and thought we were making atom bombs there.

"We used to hear Rothstein's hammer all day long. It came on the second stroke. The first was his Arab helper's. That gave the rough shape. Then Rothstein gave the fine shape. TONG-tong! TONG-tong!" Ze'ev

Neiderman sang out the tones like church bells. "I used to watch him pump up the coals with his bellows. When I first learned that poem by Longfellow about the smith – you know the one, *Under the spreading chestnut tree, ta-ta-ta-tum, ta-ta-ta-tee* – I thought of him. I was a student in Beirut then. How I loved Longfellow! Listen."

He struck a pose and recited in his Beirut accent, rolling the r's on his tongue like a dentist's drill:

> *Often I think of the beautiful town*
> *That is seated by the sea;*
> *Often in thought go up and down*
> *The pleasant streets of that dear old town,*
> *And my youth comes back to me.*

He bowed to an invisible classroom. His eyes fell on the bottles by the sink. "Ah, yes, where were we? The Niagara Bottle Makers of North London, purveyors to soda water bottlers throughout the Middle East. I will spare you the prologue to *Evangeline*."

We sat down with his wife Ada to a lunch of *ful medammes* – broad beans grown in Ze'ev's garden and garnished, Egyptian-style, with salt, pepper, olive oil, lemon juice, parsley, onion, and slices of hard-boiled egg. His mind was still on the bottles. "And who do you think," he asked, "taught Hayyim Rothstein to make the carbon dioxide for his soda water? A young man by the name of Yisra'el Yehuda Neiderman who had recently returned from working in a brewery in Des Moines, Iowa."

"Your father?"

"My future one. I was a Y chromosome at the time. He had gone to America to work for an uncle and lost his right arm in an explosion. The first thing he did after getting out of the hospital was to teach himself to write again. I have a left-handed letter of his from Omaha, Nebraska. He showed Rothstein how to make CO_2 from the old Roman marble in the ruins in Caesaria. Just imagine: all those Corinthian columns ending up as bubbles in a bottle!"

He waved his fork gaily at the thought.

"Rothstein made the gas for Yankl Ashkenazi, too. They were

partners before then, because Ashkenazi was a wheelwright and Rothstein made the wheels' iron rims. Yankl also ran a grocery store with his brother Binyomin, Ephraim Ashkenazi's father. What a pair of dim-wits! One year there was a comet in the sky and all kinds of prophecies of doom. So Yankl said to Binyomin, or maybe Binyomin said to Yankl, 'Listen here, if the world is coming to an end we're not giving any more credit' – and they didn't until the comet was gone. To tell you the truth, they were typical of Zichron. I sometimes think the reason my father traveled so much was to find someone to talk to. He went to America twice, India twice, Europe, Turkey, Rumania. He was supposed to be looking for new markets for the winery, but who wanted to drink its wine?" Ze'ev made a sour face. "He liked books – Shakespeare, Balzac, serious writers. Whom did he have here? Goldstein and Lerner. They and Meir Hoyser were the only men who read. And Hoyser," Ze'ev said of Ora Rosenzweig's father, "read too much. He once drove his wagon into a tree because he had his nose in a volume of Nietzsche."

I asked about Avigdor Appelbaum.

Ze'ev remembered nothing out of the ordinary about him. Avig-dor remarried a widow from Zichron after his wife died. "After the war he was with my father on Alexander's black list. The British governor summoned all the council members to Haifa and threatened to send them to an internment camp for Turkish collaborators. A British officer slapped my father's face for making everyone swear to find Lishansky."

"The council got off lightly," I said. "*Tell the Zichron council that when judgment comes they'll pay*: that's what Sarah wrote before she shot herself. She also asked for vengeance on informers."

Ze'ev did not believe there were informers in Zichron. "Sarah wasn't clear-minded when she wrote that. She had been tortured for days."

"She was clear-minded enough to hear the names of three people. The first, Feitelson, was an ICA land surveyor who left Zichron after the war. The second, Madursky, came from Hadera." A little research had turned that up. "The third was Appelbaum."

"But why look for informers besides Na'aman Belkind?"

"Only the Turks knew what Belkind told them. Why did they hang him in Damascus?"

"Why shouldn't they have?"

"Because he was no more important than the spies they spared. He wasn't a leader like Sarah or Lishansky. Why hang the one person who talked?"

"He has a point, Ze'ev," Ada said.

"None at all. You can't look for logic in these things."

"I think you can."

"What could it have been?"

"If the Turks were protecting informers, they would have wanted Belkind to appear their sole source. They wouldn't have wanted him around to tell his story."

"But why would anyone from Zichron inform on the Nili? It would only have endangered the village more."

"For the usual reasons, I suppose – fear, spite, or greed. The Turks would have paid well for information."

"Ha!" Ze'ev patted away a sliver of bean with a napkin. "That's a new one. All the Turks did with money was take it. If they thought you knew something about the Nili, they would have reached for their whips, not their wallets."

"I've read Yoram Efrati's account. The Belkind business doesn't add up. According to one version, he was carrying a list of Nili operatives that fell into Turkish hands – an odd thing to take with you while trying to reach enemy lines. According to another, the list was sewn into the lining of a jacket that his wife just happened to send him when he was in prison in Beersheba. Yanko Epstein says he was drugged. That would have made a good story to tell him if he was supposed to think he had said things he hadn't."

"If I were you," Ze'ev said, "I'd treat Epstein with caution. He's not a historian. You should consider him an artist. He has the soul of one. With any education he might have been a writer. He was" – he rose to help Ada clear the dishes – "a fantastical sight in those days. You never saw him with his feet on the ground. They were always in the stirrups. He rode an Arab horse that danced beneath him, decked out with ribbons and tassels and embroidered saddlebags." Pleased with his formulation, he repeated it. "The very soul of an artist, Ada, no?"

* * *

Dropping in on the Rosenzweigs, I found Ora sitting with Moshe Shatzman in her living room. Shatzman greeted me warmly.

"Look who's here! Look who's here!" he said. "I want to thank you. If not for you, Ora and I would still be feuding over that form she wouldn't sign."

"Moshe, what are you talking about?" Ora protested. "Micha and I were among the first to sign!"

"You're wrong," Shatzman said. "I came to ask you to donate your share of the old threshing floor for the museum and you refused. I was so mad I walked out without drinking your coffee." He turned to me. "A few days later I'm with Shalom Bronstein in the street and Ora comes along. 'Hello, Shalom,' she says and walks right by me. I didn't forgive her until you told me what she said about me. Straight as an arrow, Ora, eh?"

His eyes twinkled.

"He's totally confused," Ora said to me. "He came to ask for a donation to the Maccabee Athletic Club."

"Have it your way," Shatzman said. He seemed delighted to be reconciled. "I should have drunk your coffee. The only other time I did that was with Yosef Davidesco. We had gone to borrow a horse for a *fantaziyya*."

Davidesco was the man who had recommended Yanko Epstein for the job of Edwin Samuel's bodyguard. A *fantaziyya*, Shatzman said, was a Bedouin spectacle in which mounted horsemen formed skirmish lines and fired fusillades to honor an important personage. The town had staged one for Rothschild and Alexander Aaronsohn wanted to do the same for a rich American Jewish lady visiting Palestine. "He wanted us to ride Arab thoroughbreds. I didn't own one, so Davidesco took me to borrow one from a Bedouin. Ora! You know the song their women sing when they pound the coffee beans?"

"To let the neighbors know there are guests." Ora sang a few spiraling bars. Shatzman joined in, off-tune, and they laughed.

"Well, this fellow's wife is singing her coffee song while Davidesco and I are in his tent, sounding him out about his horse. The more we talk, the more we see he won't lend it. After a while Davidesco says in Hebrew, 'When I get up, follow me,' and as soon as the coffee is served he stands and says, '*Yallah, ad-dabbur ma mino asal*,' and we both walk out of the tent. That Bedouin was so upset that he ran after us and begged us to take the horse."

"I suppose you thought I'd do the same! You'll get no honey from a wasp," Ora translated for me. "It's an Arab proverb."

"He knew a thousand of them," Shatzman said. "Old Abu-Djaj."

"The Arabs called him the Chicken Man," Ora explained, "because he disguised himself as an Arab egg peddler when he was looking for the murderers of Micha's uncle, Binyamin Kruppik. One day he passed through Zichron and sold eggs to his wife. She didn't know who it was until she found a note from him in her shopping basket."

"No, no, no!" said Moshe Shatzman. "Who's confused now? Who's confused? That happened during the war, when he was going back and forth between British and Turkish lines for the Nili. He had a hatchery in his yard, that's why he was called that."

"He did? Well, that's news to me. I knew that yard. I was the first person at his side when he was murdered."

They seemed about to start another feud.

I said, "I thought it was Micha's uncle who was murdered."

"Both were," Shatzman said. "Well, Ora, I'll be off. Thanks for the coffee. I should have drunk it the last time."

As I rose to shake his hand, my gaze fell on a new sculpture. Done in the style of the backgammon players, it was of a pair of foot-high musicians. One was beating a drum strapped to his neck. The other, wire spectacles on a clay nose, blew gustily into a clarinet.

"Arn Klarineter! It's the spitting image of him."

Both Ora and Shatzman struggled to calculate how I could have met the man, then protested that I couldn't have.

"But I did," I said. "It was at the Arizon wedding in Shfeya."

Shatzman put out a hand to steady himself. "That was before you were born! I was there."

"Of course you were. We bumped heads beneath a table, looking for Arn's clarinet."

The hand went to his heart.

It seemed best to drop the charade. "I heard about it from Epstein," I confessed, relating what he had told me.

"I'll be a monkey's uncle!" Shatzman said. "Did he tell you that? Did he?"

"It didn't happen?"

"It happened, all right. If Epstein tells you he stole something, that's the one time to believe him. But he never rode off with Arn. Say!" He grabbed my arm and pivoted me slightly, as if to face me in the right direction. "Arn was playing his clarinet. He had his back to the window. Epstein came up outside, grabbed the clarinet, and ran off. Some of us chased him, but he got away in the dark. Maybe he did have a mule. But Arn stayed at the wedding. There wasn't music anywhere that night. Do you know what it's called when a rooster wears a peacock's feathers?"

"What?"

"Cock-and-bull."

He added a title of contempt. "Lord Cock-and-Bull! And now he runs that museum as if he built it. A lot he cared when Shalom Bronstein and I were going from door to door."

"Is he always like that about Epstein?" I asked Ora when Shatzman was gone.

"Always. They're complete opposites."

She bent to adjust Arn Klarineter's glasses.

"Look how you've caught him in the middle of a kleyzmer tune," I said, touching Arn's fingers on the clarinet.

"It's probably Dixieland. This isn't Turkish times. It's the roaring twenties. That's why Nissele has pegged pants and patent leather shoes." She put an affectionate hand around the drummer's little waist. "Do you see how one shoe is scuffed? That's where Arn used to step on his toes to let him know he was changing the beat."

I returned to the subject of the two murders.

"There was no connection between them," Ora said. "Davidesco was killed in 1946. Micha's uncle died in the Events."

"The Events" were the Hebrew term for the major outbreaks of Arab violence in the Mandate period. These came in three waves, 1920–21, 1929, and 1936–39, the years of the Arab Revolt. Micha's uncle Binyamin Kruppik, the elder brother of Gedalia Kruppik the real estate agent, was killed in the first of them. If I was interested, Ora said, she had a book that told the story.

* * *

"I was working," wrote Yosef Davidesco, "in the criminal investigations division of the Central Intelligence Department in Jerusalem when word reached me of the Arab attack in which my friend Binyamin Kruppik was killed. I couldn't believe it. I ran to the telephone, spoke with Zichron Ya'akov, and was told it was true. Kruppik was dead. By the time the police reached the scene, the murderers were gone.

"Binyamin Kruppik was a broad-shouldered young man with arms of steel known for his strength and physical courage to all the Arabs of the area, who were careful to stay on the good side of him and his friends. But as the sun was setting on a peaceful Sabbath day, marauders broke into the yard of the little colony at M'rah, which numbered only eight Jewish families, and raked its houses with gunfire. Several colonists were wounded, Kruppik was killed, and farm tools, mules, and a horse were made off with.

"The news of my friend's death made it impossible for me to get any work done in Jerusalem. A few days later I left the capital for Zichron.

"Reports reaching us from the Arab villages east of M'rah indicated that the marauders had stolen more horses from Arab travelers in their retreat. They had headed eastward across the Jordan. Most likely they hailed from there.

"I was hot with rage. Determined to avenge my friend's blood, I began preparing for a trip across the Jordan to track down his murderers."

Davidesco's narrative was one of several appearing in the little book that Ora gave me. Published by the town of Giv'at Ada – a Rothschild colony founded southeast of Zichron on land known to the Arabs as M'rah – it was a memorial volume for local residents killed in Arab attacks. The first of these took place in the summer of 1920.

Davidesco's account of it continued:

"In those days, the Arabs west of the Jordan, having been disarmed by the British government, lived in fear of the armed Bedouin to the river's east. These Bedouin, who dwelt in the Jordan Valley and the Ajlun Hills above it, crossed the river in raiding parties, robbed and pillaged, and rode safely back again. They made a handsome living, and it was taking one's life in one's hands to resist them. It was inconceivable for a Jew or Englishman even to think of tracking them to their lair in search of lost property or its plunderers. This could be done only by pretending to be a Bedouin, and the infidel discovered in such disguise would have the flesh torn from his bones.

[handwritten margin note: Bedouin after British occupation]

165

"This was the expedition I now readied myself for, trusting in my knowledge of the Bedouin's customs, language, and manner of speech to see me through. I acquired a Bedouin robe and headdress, shaved my beard so that only a small chin patch was left in the Bedouin fashion, and outfitted my horse with Bedouin trappings. I found a Bedu friend, Taleb, who was willing to accompany me and we picked a day for him to meet me with his gear.

"My chestnut mare Atalia was a tall, handsome horse raised by Bedouin and trained to pace, trot, and canter in their style. Her black mane and tail gave her a flair that convinced all of her noble blood. The Bedouin, as is known, judge a man by his horse no less than by his clothes.

"In a few days' time my friend arrived and we set out. To prevent word of our expedition from spreading, we spent our first night in a village where no one knew us."

The next morning the two men rode eastward, reaching the Jordan Valley at noon. "We were now," Davidesco wrote, "entering the danger zone. Relations between the Bedouin and the British governor of the area were strained and tempers were running high. There had recently been an armed clash between Bedouin and British soldiers in which men were killed on each side. The government had prohibited the Transjordan Bedouin from crossing the river, which was patrolled by British troops, and the Bedouin, too, guarded the fords against the British. The most contentious of their tribes was the Arab-el-Gazawiyya, known up and down the Jordan Valley for its fierceness. Forced by the government to abandon territory to the river's west, it had moved all its tents to the east, from where it periodically skirmished with the army.

"Looking down on the valley at our feet, I saw a wide plain on both sides of the river, dotted with large and small tents. Among them was the encampment of the Arab-el-Gazawiyya – to which Taleb and I, on a hunch, were now headed.

"Soon we were in the valley. There were no longer any paths, just narrow trails running through the tall grass. We rode on along their winding, unfamiliar course, past swamps and wild undergrowth, twisting and turning uncertainly.

"It took two hours to reach the river. On our way we met a police force from Bet-She'an, whose British commander recognized me. Informed of our plans, he advised me to turn back because of the danger. However, I was too full of ambition and lust for revenge. Toward sunset we reached the Jordan. The narrow trail ran down to a ford whose murmuring water calmed our anxious hearts.

"We crossed the river and rode on to the Arab-el-Gazawiyya's camp. Our sudden appearance startled its inhabitants, who could tell from our garb that we came from west of the river. At a time when the tribe was on the brink of open warfare with the government, such a visit was unexpected.

"We asked for the tent of the sheikh. One of the elders offered to lead us to it.

"The tent was full of Bedouin notables dressed in their finest. It was the month of Ramadan and they had been invited to break the day's fast with the sheikh.

"Several young men ran up to take our horses' bridles. We dismounted and entered. Everyone rose in our honor and the sheikh turned to us and said, '*T'fadlu*, welcome.'

"We slipped off our Bedouin sandals, said hello with a *salaam aleykum*, and sat in the space cleared for us between the notables and the sheikh.

"There was a hush. No one spoke. All eyes surveyed us from head to foot. At last the sheikh broke the silence by announcing the evening prayer. Most of the assembly rose for it, including myself. Taleb stationed himself beside me to prevent any mistakes that might give me away. He needn't have worried. I knew the Moslem prayer by heart and wouldn't have joined it if I didn't trust myself. It passed without a hitch and we returned to our places.

"A few minutes went by and a servant brought water in a jug and poured it over our hands, which we then dried on our robes. This was the sign that dinner was about to be served. Soon it arrived, its many condiments set in a wide circle in the midst of which was placed a large platter of mutton cooked with rice.

"The guests were invited to help themselves and the feasting began. Knowing that my table manners would be scrutinized, I was careful to comport myself in the Bedouin fashion. Silver, of course, there was none; one's only fork, spoon, and knife were one's right hand. In the dim tent whose sole light came from a small lantern that barely repelled the dark night, the meal was consumed with wondrous dexterity, hands moving nimbly from dish to dish and platter to mouth, although sometimes, searching for a choice morsel of meat, you ended up clutching the fingers of your neighbor....

"Each man ate until sated. Then he stepped outside, where boys were waiting with more jugs of water. After washing our hands again, we stepped back into the tent.

"Now came the turn of the coffee. Coffee drinking among the Bedouin is a practically endless ritual. It goes on for as long as the talk does. A bit of strong brew is poured into the bottom of a small cup and sipped lustily, after which the cup is returned to the pourer, half-filled again, and handed to the next man.

"Once a first cup was drunk by all, the conversation began. The sheikh, who was seated beside me, wished me a good evening once more and inquired after my tribe. I told him it was the Arab-el-Hamdun, a tribe living near Zichron. Taleb said the same.

"Most of the gathering was composed of the tribe's elders. The younger men stood outside the tent. Through the opening of the flaps I could see their eyes glowing like coals. Clearly we two visitors were a puzzle.

"Half an hour had passed when I heard a clatter of hoof beats. It was the night patrol, riding off to the Jordan to watch for British troops.

"I slept soundly that night, wearied by the long day's ride. Before dawn I was awakened for the pre-fast meal. Needless to say, I rose promptly like a good Moslem. We then returned to our pallets and slept until late as is the custom of Ramadan fasters, who thus shorten the foodless day. The sheikh had ridden that morning to Irbid to attend a meeting of tribal leaders and Taleb and I rose to find ourselves alone in the large tent, from which we sat looking at the passing Bedouin.

"All of a sudden, a familiar-looking gray mare, ridden by a big, pitch-black Negro, crossed my field of vision. I looked again – there was no doubt of it. It was the horse stolen from M'rah on the day of Binyamin Kruppik's murder. My heart pounded like a hammer.

"Although I said nothing, the keen-eyed Taleb noticed the change in my demeanor and asked the meaning of it. Pleased to hear that our hunch had proved right, he too was now forced to exercise every bit of self-restraint. There, sitting on a horse a few dozen meters from us, was the likely murderer of my friend – and there was nothing to do but hold my peace....

"Toward evening, messengers arrived from one of the tribesmen to invite us for dinner. After prayers we accompanied the man to his tent. The meal proceeded much the same as the night before. At its end more Bedouin dropped by, among them the rider of the gray mare, and the conversation touched on various matters. By and by it reached the subject of Bedouin wars, and then of the attack on M'rah.

"On this occasion, the tribesmen in the tent were among the simpler of the Arab-el-Gazawiyya. As each boasted of his valor, I realized that I was surrounded by the very band of men that had murdered Binyamin Kruppik. I was sipping my coffee from one cup with them! Wishing them to think I was gladdened by news of an attack on a Jewish colony, I asked a few innocent questions.

"One of the Bedouin replied:

"'The Jews were taking their Sabbath rest when we burst into the yard. We had been warned to watch out for one of them, a strapping fellow, and we went straight to his house to take care of him first.

"'As we climbed the front stairs, we heard him struggling with his wife. We crashed through the door and saw a Jew as large as a cedar tree, his whole family hanging onto him to keep him from rushing out at us. He broke loose and charged, but one rifle bullet finished him off. He didn't make a sound. His wife and children screamed horribly when he collapsed in their arms. We ran back to the yard, took a horse and some mules, and made our getaway....'

"The man's eyes glittered like a sword blade at the memory. My blood boiled. My only comfort was that I now knew every one of my friend's murderers. I memorized each line of their villainous faces and thought: 'We will meet again, you dogs!'

"I couldn't sleep that night. I kept tossing from side to side. The next evening the sheikh returned from Irbid and the notables gathered to hear his report. In a loud, blustering voice he announced that the meeting had been convened to make peace between the sheikhs of the different tribes, who from now on would devote themselves to attacking the Jews.

"As the gathering broke up, a few wild-looking young men with unkempt hair invited Taleb and myself to join them on a night patrol. We spent the whole night on horseback. From time to time we encountered other patrols, too.

"I had a wretched feeling. When we returned to our tent in the morning, I threw myself down, bone-weary and furious. I even considered taking Taleb's gun, wreaking vengeance on whomever I could, and lighting out for the Jordan. Yet the chances of reaching it alive were slim.

"The next day the sheikh asked me at last what my business was. I told him: 'I am an outlaw with a government price on my head and I have come to seek refuge with you.' This answer pleased him and he said: 'You will be safe with us. The government does not dare show its face here.'

"Taleb and I spent a few more days with the tribesmen, lounging in their tents by day and riding with them by night. I came to know the plunderers of M'rah well, which only made my frustration worse.

"After a week of this, we decided to head back. Saying we were going for provisions and would return, we set out for Bet-She'an.

"As we neared the Jordan we heard shots. Turning to look, we saw Bedouin chasing us at full gallop. Their hail of bullets told us that we were wanted dead or alive. We spurred our horses across the river and breathed a sigh of relief when we reached the far bank. The next day we arrived safely home.

"A few days later an acquaintance of Taleb's arrived and told us what had happened. Half-an-hour after our departure, a Bedu from Bet-She'an came to the Arab-el-Gazawiyya's camp and informed them of my identity, which had been made known to him by a British officer. The sheikh sent his men to retrieve us and was beside himself when they returned empty-handed. 'So! Deceived by a Jew!' he shouted, raging about the camp."

Two years passed before Yosef Davidesco obtained the vengeance he sought. Then, he wrote, "I crossed the Jordan again with a company of policemen from Haifa, to which I had meanwhile been transferred. We rounded up every one of Binyamin Kruppik's murderers, who were sentenced to fifteen years hard labor."

Among the convicted prisoners was Sa'id el-Bukei'i, the black man who rode the gray mare. I was to run across him again.

*   *   *

Down the lower half of Wine Street we strode, singing as we went:

Here we go to the bakery,
The bakery,
The bakery,
Here we go to the bakery,
So early in the morning.

"Talyushki," I said, "this is the last ride. You're getting to be too heavy. From now on you walk."

"Giddy-up!" Talya said.

The men working in the bakery had aged half a lifetime since dawn from the flour that powdered them a wiggish gray. Sweating from the ovens, they tossed balls of dough to the kneading boards, where three of them worked at a time – one thumping out the round loaves, one spinning the long baguettes, one braiding the hallah rolls as deftly as tying a shoelace.

We bought two baguettes for breakfast, each whispering curls of steam, and started back. Talya held them high over her head. We sang:

Here we come from the bakery,
The bakery,
The bakery,
Here we come from the bakery,
So early in the morning.

We stopped to watch a kestrel skateboard in the sky and to listen to the wooing of two turtles, which clicked like billiard balls each time the male rammed the female, *clack-a-butt, clack-a-butt*. The buds of the apricot trees on the hillside beneath our house were stiff and red from holding in their bloom.

"Cacky-butt, cacky-butt," Talya sang.

The spring days were halcyon, borne on north winds. In our garden, drunk from the scent of the orange blossoms, the bees jabbered excitedly. I went for long walks in the hills, ranging to Shfeya and Bat-Shlomo, and resumed my old rummaging around town, in which I found a wooden wine barrel in good condition and a threshing sled. With its empty sockets from which the chaff-stripping stones had fallen out, the sled looked like a primitive gaming board. In the barrel, the work of Shimon Gelberg the cooper, Tova Gelberg's father, Marcia planted geraniums.

The bombed-out home of Hayyim Rothman the smith yielded a rimmed wagon wheel. From the stone shed behind Miriam's wool store I lugged home an old pirate's chest, filled with fabric that crumbled to dust at a touch as though released from a spell. Such coffers, I was told, had once contained the trousseaus of brides.

I took a shovel and dug where I had found the two soda bottles. In no time I unearthed dozens more. I was standing in a graveyard of them. Although most bore the H.M. Rothstein and Jacob Aschkenazi imprints, there were also some blanks; some that only said THE NIAGARA BOTTLE; one with the trademark of a horse and ALY HASAN and ALEXANDRIE EGYPTE; another with a star-of-David and JAFFA PALESTINE; a crescent-mooned one with BEIRUT and MUSTAFA SAAD. I had uncovered a vast network of soda dealers stretching from the arms of the Nile to the Orontes, far-flung concessions selling bubbles to the thirsty East, each accepting the other's empties and refilling and passing them on, innumerable bottles sold in groceries, peddled on street corners, carried on donkeys to remote villages, hawked by boys shouting through the windows of trains that sped them across international borders, all supplied by the same unflagging source, the great Niagara Bottle makers themselves, Messrs. Barnet & Foster of London, the never-slacking furnaces of whose glassworks glowed by day and by night, the clerks of whose corridors labored over order forms and bills of lading for ports of call where turbaned stevedores rowed out to the ships in lighters – all ended, annulled, brought to a grinding halt by an invention an inch in diameter: the corrugated, cork-gasketed, machine-pressed bottle cap. Never had so mighty an empire fallen to so tiny a conqueror.

The carbon dioxide for the seltzer was produced in Zichron with the help of oleum or $H_2S_2O_7$, which broke down the calcium carbonate of the Roman marble from Caesaria. This I learned from Yankl Ashkenazi's son Yitzhak. To the rear of his house, which stood next to his cousin Betsalel's, was a barn in which I was taking inventory one day, drawn to a large glass amphora that I thought would make a handsome lamp, when its owner appeared behind me. He was short like his cousins and displeased. It took an effort to convince him that my interest in his property was purely antiquarian, my ace in the hole being my knowledge of his father's global connections.

"You don't say!" Both his father and I rose in his esteem. "I never knew those bottles came from London. They were delivered by a trader from Beirut. When my father quit making seltzer, we dumped them down the hill. This jar contained the oleum. That was some soda water! It made you cry like horseradish."

A "dimwit," Ze'ev Neiderman had called his father. He was a simple man himself. Mistakenly arrested by the Turks in the roundup of the Nili, he was soon released because he knew nothing. He had gone to Haifa with a load of grain and been told by his father when he returned, "Get into the house and don't go out. Those crazy Turks think there are spies in the village!"

One day I walked to the old Aaronsohn olive grove beyond the cemetery. Some boys were playing by Alexander's pavilion. There was no sign of its having been the site of sumptuous seductions. Its two small rooms, one atop the other, were connected by a rickety staircase. A few old books on botany and agriculture were on a bookshelf on the top floor. I took one of them, *Florula Cisiordanica, Révision critique des plantes récoltées et partiellement déterminées par AARON AARONSOHN au cours de ses voyages (1904–1916) en Cisjordanie, en Syrie, et au Liban, avec une préface de Fernand Chodat et an avant-propos d'Alex Aaronsohn.*

The boys quit their game to flock around me. I asked if they knew the history of the place.

"It's a fort."

"An old fort. The Jews fought the Arabs."

"They spied on them. Sarah and Abraham."

"Hey, mister, come look!"

Two boys had dragged away a flat rock to reveal a vertical shaft.

"What's down there?"

"Gold!"

I knelt and peered down the shaft. It was too dark to see anything. I took a stone and let it drop. There was a soft thud of earth when it hit bottom.

I walked back into town, past the bus station, past the first homes, past the empty lot in which the old Appelbaum house had stood, and ran into Yanko Epstein on Founders Street. He looked glad to see me. "I see you got my message," he said.

"What message?"

"The one I sent you in my thoughts. What are you doing tomorrow?"

I wasn't doing anything special.

"Then pick me up with your car at nine. And tell your wife you'll be gone all day. I had a dream. I need your help to interpret it."

I walked on home. Outside Benedik's hardware store, Meir Benedik was invoicing cans of paint. "Listen," he said. "A fairy godmother knocked on the door of a Zichron farmer."

"How come?" I asked.

"She'd come to grant him any wish he wanted. 'There's just one catch,' she said. 'What's that?' the farmer asks. 'Whatever you wish for,' she says, 'your neighbor will get twice as much of.' The farmer thinks. He scratches his head. 'Well?' the fairy godmother asks. 'All right,' the farmer says. 'Poke out one of my eyes.'"

Chapter twelve

Y anko Epstein didn't answer when I asked him the next morning where we were bound for. He wouldn't comment on his dream, either. His only response was to guide me past the winery to the Wadi Milikh road and set us on a northeasterly course for the Valley of Jezreel. On the car floor in front of him he had laid a manila envelope, a white cake box, and a brown plastic bag.

The road was a good one – a bit too good, its wide shoulders tempting drivers to treat them as extra lanes. I swore as a car forced me onto one of these, rocketing toward me past a slow-moving truck.

"It was more dangerous in the old days," Epstein remarked. "This road was a dirt track then. Armed robbers hid in the hills and charged down."

He didn't dwell on it, though. Beyond Shfeya, he was reminded of something else. "That's Wadi Mina," he said of a cleft in the hills to our right. "I chased the Gypsies there."

It was his manner to throw out a line like that and make you ask: "What Gypsies?"

"The ones who took the boy from Zichron."

It had all begun with his horse, a bay mare. She was a *saklawiyya*, a pure Bedouin thoroughbred. He had bought the reins to her from Fu'ad al-Hamdun. "That meant I rode her and gave him half the foals. She was the smartest horse I ever saw. She could talk."

The *saklawiyya* talked with her ears. If she sensed an animal nearby, she raised and lowered them; if a human being, she kept them raised. He always knew what she was aware of.

One night she confused him. He was riding past a field of barley by the well of Bir Tata, where the border ran between the lands of Zichron and Suberin, when he saw some stalks of grain ripple. Although it could have been only a breeze, he backed the bay against a tree for concealment. Her ears went up and stayed there. He slipped his Enfield from its sling on the saddlebag. His horse's ears went down. "Well," he thought, replacing the rifle in the sling, "it's only an animal." Up went the ears again and up they stayed. Out came the rifle. Down they went once more. He was still trying to puzzle it out when dark shapes bounded toward him, moving like a wave through the barley. Hunting dogs. He held his nervous horse still while they surrounded her. Behind them came a group of men.

Each of the men carried a stick. He let them come closer, slid home the bolt of his rifle, and called: "Who are you in the night?"

That was a watchman's challenge.

The men answered that they were Gypsies from across the Jordan and were hunting porcupines. A porcupine couldn't run very fast. It was killed with a whack on its bare head. "Come along and we'll show you," they said. He followed them. He was curious to see how porcupines were hunted.

They headed for a cave at the field's edge. A Gypsy stuck his hand inside it. Warm meant the porcupine was home; cold that it was out. The cave was warm and the Gypsies set to work on a trap. Sloping the earth toward the cave, they built a stone enclosure around it. They then took a plant liked by porcupines, placed a small rock on top of it, and propped a larger rock against the smaller one. When the porcupine tugged at the plant and moved the first rock, the second would roll down the slope and plug the cave, leaving the porcupine, which couldn't climb, trapped in the enclosure.

The trap set, the Gypsies went off. You couldn't get a porcupine to hurry.

The next day, riding by the threshing floor in Faradis, he saw the Gypsies camped there. They had a fire going and were roasting a skinned porcupine on a spit. "Come join us," they called. But though they assured him that porcupine was as tender as lamb, it was not anything he cared to eat.

"We Jews don't eat the porcupine," he told them.

"What do Jews eat?" the Gypsies asked.

Just then a hen cackled behind a tent. "We Jews eat the chicken," he said.

The Gypsies roasted him a chicken and asked if he knew of a hyena cave, since that was what they wished to hunt next.

He knew of one. He had seen a gray form approach it in the first light of dawn, suck its ribs in until even its shaggy hair was combed flat, and vanish through a hole smaller than its own girth. Hyenas chose caves with small entrances. This one, he told the Gypsies, explaining where to find it, was sunk like a funnel in a rock face.

The next day he was standing by a vineyard near Shfeya with Yisra'el Neiderman, Ze'ev Neiderman's father, when the same Gypsies passed and said hello. This time they had a small boy with them. "Where to?" he inquired. "To hunt your hyena," they said. Neiderman raised an eyebrow. "Since when do you pal around with Gypsies?" he asked. "Mr. Neiderman," he answered, "I'm not only their pal, I'm going off with them right now to see how hyenas are caught."

The road wound through a mountain pass that separated the Carmel range on our left from the uplands of Manasseh on our right. Trees marked a creek on the Carmel side that ran deep in winter and was now going dry. Past the turn-off to the Druze village of Daliat-el-Carmel, the pass narrowed. Epstein said:

"We reached the cave and a Gypsy said to me: 'Now, *hawajja*, let's see what you have learned. Tell us if the hyena is home.'"

He stuck a hand into the cave and quickly withdrew it. The cave was warm. (He had expected it to be; hyenas scavenged by night and slept by day.) As soon as the boy heard this, he undressed. A scruffy little thing, he looked like an animal himself without his clothes. He was given a rope with a noose at one end and a wooden board with a sharp nail and he squeezed into the cave with them, leaving the rope's free end in the hands of a Gypsy.

Yanko Epstein was still wondering how a naked boy crawled into a hyena den when the shout came from inside: "Pull!" The Gypsies began pulling on the rope, slowly and steadily as if reeling in a kite. Two of them stood at either side of the cave. They had short swords, the kind the Gypsy tinkers made. They didn't wait for the whole hyena to appear. Its hindquarters were still in the cave when its head emerged in the noose. "*Trakkhhh!*" Epstein said. "They let that hyena have it."

The hyena was scarcely dead when the boy called out, "Hand back the rope!" The Gypsies passed it back in and soon there was another shout of "Pull!" and out came a female hyena. The two were a married couple.

The Gypsies killed the female, too, and whooped and hollered, paying the boy no attention when he crawled out of the cave and put his clothes on. You would have thought he had done nothing out of the ordinary. But Yanko Epstein was amazed by his courage. "I have to ask you something," he said to him. "Those hyenas had jaws that could have crunched you in two with one bite. How did you get a noose on them?"

"Oh, that's easy," the Gypsy boy said. "I walked right up and slipped it on them and jabbed them with the nail to make them move. The hard part is holding onto their tails to keep them from rushing out too fast and laughing. A laughing hyena can make you go mad."

That evening he found the Gypsies on the threshing floor, roasting one of the hyenas. Its big rear haunches were over a fire. "We don't eat the forelegs," they explained. "The hyena grips its carrion with them and even the dogs won't touch them. But the hind legs are a treat. They're better than the drumsticks of a turkey. Surely Jews eat the hyena!"

He could see they weren't eager to slaughter another hen and he said, "No, my brothers, our Torah does not permit it. But I can't stay for dinner anyway. I only came to ask you a question. How do you send a small boy into a hyena den with only a nail and a noose, and how does he come out again alive?"

"By virtue of his nakedness," the Gypsies said.

He didn't know what they meant by that.

"That, *ya hawajja*," said the Gypsies, "is because your Torah does not tell you what our holy Koran does. It is written there that when Allah made the world, He first made all the animals. When He finished making them, He made Man. And when Man was made, Allah gathered the animals and said to them, 'This is Man. Look at him and mark him well, for he shall rule over you and his fear shall be upon you and you shall do his bidding.' Then all the animals looked at Man and bowed and said, 'Yes, Lord.'

"Now all this happened in a garden called Eden, where Man and his wife went naked without shame. But when they sinned and Allah made them leave the garden, they grew ashamed of their nakedness and put on clothes. Now, when the animals saw Man and his wife, they failed to recognize them. The fear of Man was no longer upon them and they did his bidding no more.

"Had that boy, *ya hawajja*, entered the cave with his clothes on, the hyenas would have torn him to shreds. But when they saw him naked they remembered Man in the garden and his fear fell upon them again. He had to be obeyed. It was their promise to Allah when He made the world long ago."

We were in the Valley of Jezreel, driving north along its western rim. Green and flat, it stretched to the round cap of Mount Tabor and the hills of Nazareth. Vapors rose from its fields in the morning sun as though from an ironing board.

"I used to cross this valley on horseback when I was courting my wife," Epstein said.

She came from Kfar Tabor, on the other side of the mountain, though he had met her in Binyamina, on her way to visit relatives in Zichron, leaning out a train window. The valley had marked the end of his bailiwick. That was why he was eager to find the Gypsies before they reached it.

They had struck camp one morning and moved on. Coming home from his nightly rounds, he had seen them folding their tents and preparing to head through Wadi Milikh. He slept late, rising after noon. When he stepped outside, he saw a crowd in the street. It was gathered around a weeping woman whose young son had been missing since morning. The boy had been searched for everywhere.

No one but he knew that Gypsies had camped in Faradis. Although he had never known them to have stolen a child, he had heard of such things. When Gypsies camped in an Arab village, mothers kept their children close by.

He saddled his horse and spurred it down to Wadi Milikh. Gypsies traveled with pack camels and moved slowly. Even giving them the better part of a day's head start, he could count on catching up by nightfall.

At the foot of the hill called the Heteri, he went to the tent of Sheikh Bashir el-Hamdun. They had patched things up since the day Bashir's best milk cow was burned. "*Ahlan wa-sahlan*," the sheikh said, inviting him into his tent.

But he had no time for visits. He was looking for the Gypsies who had camped on the threshing floor of Faradis. Sheikh Bashir must have seen them pass. How far down Wadi Milikh had they gotten?

"Not far at all," Bashir el-Hamdun said. "They left it and turned into Wadi Mina. They were whipping their camels and traveling fast."

That heightened his suspicions. Wadi Mina was a poorer route than Wadi Milikh. It wound past the well of Bir Tata, deserted now by the shepherds and their flocks who had watered there at midday, and came out by the village of Suberin. Beyond that were grassy uplands and a descent on their far side through the precipitous Wadi Kisab to the Valley of Jezreel. The only reason for going that way, unless you wished to camp somewhere along it, was to throw a pursuer off your trail.

And the Gypsies had not camped anywhere.

In Suberin he asked Sheikh Amin el-Hajj Mahmoud if he had seen them. "They passed about noon," said Sheikh Amin. "They were heading for Um-e-Shuf."

He cut across open meadow to Crocodile Creek, in whose mouth by the sea Nile crocs were still said to lurk, and stopped to water his horse. From there he followed the narrow paths of the uplands, hedged by walls of ancient stones where they passed through farmed fields. Fresh tracks and camel droppings told him the Gypsies were ahead of him. The sun was low in the sky when he neared Um-e-Shuf. Villagers were bringing cattle home from pasture. "Gypsies?" they said. "They passed by two hours ago, on their way to Hubeizi."

He would find them, then, in Hubeizi. It was close by and Gypsies didn't travel at night.

In Hubeizi he went straight to the home of Abdel-Kadr Hajj Hassan, the village *mukhtar*. Abdel-Kadr was sitting down to supper and invited him to join. He didn't object; he hadn't eaten all day and was famished. First, though, he wanted to know where the Gypsies who had come from Um-e-Shuf were.

"*Wallah!*" Abdel-Kadr said. "That's a strange thing you ask about. They didn't camp here. They passed at dusk and headed for Daliat-e-Ruha. Maybe you can tell me where they were going so fast in the night."

He left Abdel-Kadr without eating and rode on. The night was moonless and he steered by the stars. There was no one to ask at Daliat-e-Ruha. Not a light shone in its blackness. The smell of extinguished dung cooking fires, coming from afar, was all that told him the village was there.

He rode on toward Wadi Kisab. On the high ground near the top of it he saw the silhouette of shepherds' tents. Dogs barked. A shepherd stepped out of his tent. He hailed the horseman and asked who he was.

"I'm a Gypsy from across the Jordan," Epstein said. "I'm looking for my brothers who rode ahead of me."

"They started down the wadi an hour ago," the shepherd told him.

He rode down into the wadi. In the darkness, the trail was treacherous. It ran in places along the steep flank of the ravine and dropped in others to a dry streambed that twisted and plunged. Loose rocks spurted beneath his mare's hooves and the low branches of the willows and ashes forced him to hug her neck. Now and then he had to dismount and lead her by the halter.

At the mouth of the wadi was a farm owned by a rich Turk named Yussuf Bek. Dawn was breaking when he reached it. Yussuf Bek was awake and said, "Good morning, my friend. What brings you here at daybreak? Has a sheep or goat been stolen from the flocks of Zamarin?"

"Morning of light, Yussuf Bek," he replied. "There has indeed been a theft from our flocks, but neither of a sheep nor a goat."

"Then of a cow," said Yussuf Bek. "The theft of a cow is a serious matter."

"This theft," he said, "is more serious than a cow's."

"Of a horse?" Yosef Bek asked. "By God, horse thievery is a plague! I would hang every horse thief I found."

"Worse than of a horse."

"But what is worse than the theft of a good horse?" asked Yussuf Bek.

"What was stolen," he said, "is worth more than the horse of the Prophet."

He told Yussuf Bek about the child. "Those Gypsies?" Yussuf Bek said. "They're on my threshing floor right now. They asked permission to rest there just a few minutes before you arrived. That's why I'm up so early."

We had turned northwest, leaving the Valley of Jezreel behind, though the Carmel was still on our left. We were making a three-quarters circuit around it toward Haifa Bay. "Head for the Checkpost," Epstein said, directing me toward a junction still called by its old British name.

"Did they kidnap the boy?"

"No. I did."

The youngster, it turned out, had gone with the Gypsies willingly. He was playing on the threshing floor with some Gypsy boys and having the time of his life. "He didn't want to return to his mother. I had to grab him and seat him on my horse. If those Gypsies had crossed the Jordan with him, he'd have ended up hyena bait himself."

"A case for Davidesco!"

He considered that. "Yes," he said. "Davidesco would have gone after him."

We had entered the industrial zone of the bay, driving into the smells of the big chemical plants, the stench of solvents and poisons that could eat their way through the periodic table – through the periodic tabletop itself.

"Whew!" he said, holding his nose. And, finding it in his hand: "You know, this" (he jiggled it) "and this" (he covered an eye) "and this" (he tugged at an ear) "made a good field guard. But it didn't mean a thing without this." He rapped his head with his knuckles as if sounding a secret compartment. "The man who taught me that was Yosef Davidesco. I'll tell you how he helped me catch a thief."

Like a giant welder's torch, the big oil refinery spewed fire at the sky.

"One year there was a rash of thefts in the vineyards. My horse and I were working by ourselves. The times were quiet and the village thought we were enough.

"It was early summer. The grapes were no bigger than peas. But it wasn't the grapes the thieves were after. It was the leaves. That's when they're most tender and best for stuffing. A thief doesn't pick grape leaves like a farmer. A farmer does it carefully, a little here, a little there; it does less damage to the vines. A thief grabs all he can. He'll tear off branches, whole clusters of unripe grapes.

"These thieves knew what they were doing, though. They were only taking Alicante. There was a reason for that. Most grape leaves are smooth on the outside and rough on the inside; you stuff them with the smooth side facing out. Alicante is the only leaf that's smooth on both sides. That makes it worth more.

"Every night a different vineyard was hit. I could see I was dealing with professionals. And every night I went looking and didn't find them. Maybe I wasn't looking in the right places." The hoarse voice rippled slyly. "I didn't know how many of them there were or if they were armed; I wasn't that eager to find out by myself. But the farmers were upset. What good was a bed with fresh sheets every night if you lay awake worrying about your grapes? 'Yanko,' they said, 'if you can't find those thieves, we'll hire someone who can.' I went to Davidesco.

"He was working for British intelligence in Haifa. 'Listen,' he said. 'Why wear yourself out and risk your life doing it? A thief is a rope with two ends. If you can't find one end, look for the other.'

"'What is that supposed to mean?' I asked.

"'It means,' he said, 'that it's not enough for thieves to steal. They have to sell what they've stolen. You need to find out where they're selling it.'

"'That,' I say, 'may be what they teach you in British intelligence. But there are dozens of Arab villages around here in which those grape leaves could be sold. I can't start looking in each of them.'

"'You don't have to,' he says. 'Those leaves are Alicante. Someone has to afford them. You'll only find such people in Haifa. Come to my place tonight and get some sleep. In the morning we'll go to the market and catch your thieves.'

"Early the next morning we went to the market. We brought

baskets and pretended to be shoppers. The merchants were just setting up their stalls. All of a sudden Davidesco gives me a poke and points with his eyes to a man and two boys driving a donkey in our direction. I knew the fellow. He was a tall Arab from Ein-Ghazzal named Abu-Mahmoud. Everyone called him Abu-D'nein, 'Mr. Ears,' because he had these two big jug handles on either side of his head.

"Sure enough, the donkeys were loaded with saddlebags stuffed with grape leaves. Davidesco brushed against them and plucked a leaf. We walked on a bit and looked at it. It was Alicante. It even had some broken branch attached to it.

"'Those are your customers,' Davidesco said. 'Let's pick them up.'

"We turned and followed them. When Abu-D'nein stopped to sell the grape leaves to a greengrocer, Davidesco drew his pistol and arrested them.

"We marched them off to the police and they confessed. The two boys were under age and got probation. Abu-D'nein went to prison for a year.

"Let me tell you, that was the quietest year I ever had as a field guard. It made me realize what a hard-working thief Abu-D'nein was. Once I said as much to a neighbor of his from Ein-Ghazzal. 'You don't know the half of it,' he told me. 'Abu-D'nein was in your fields every night. He knew better than your farmers what was in them and when it was ripe.'

"Well, a year goes by and Abu-D'nein gets out of jail and pretty soon the fields are being hit again. It didn't take long for the farmers – "

"Which way?" We were approaching the Checkpost.

"Toward Acre."

Perhaps that was what he had dreamed about. I hoped so. Lunch by the water of the old Crusader town with its Arab fishing port, watching the waves spume over the sea wall, would make up for the dreary arc ahead of us, with its factories, outlet stores, and working-class suburbs.

It didn't take long for the farmers to start complaining again. This time he didn't go to Davidesco. He went to Neiderman, who was head of the Farmers Association. If they wanted the thefts to stop, he said, he needed an assistant. He couldn't do it alone.

Neiderman listened and said, "Yanko, if an assistant will do the trick, I'll find the money for it."

"And I can choose who I want?" he asked.

Neiderman promised him that, too. The two of them got along well, despite the age difference between them.

"And who do you think I chose?" asked Yanko Epstein. "Mr. Ears himself! I went to Ein-Ghazzal and I drank his coffee and I said, 'Listen here, Abu-Mahmoud' – no one called him Abu-D'nein to his face – 'how much money do you make from thieving in a year?' He laughed and said, 'Why?' 'Well,' I said, 'your next court sentence will make your last one seem shorter than a winter's day. I have a better idea for you. I need an assistant. It means working nights, but you're used to that. And you'll get paid every week and those big ears of yours won't have to hear the word "thief" any more. How about it?' He laughed again and said, 'Why not?'

"Neiderman wasn't keen on it. 'Yanko,' he said, 'the Arabs cut off a thief's hand. They don't shake it and take him into the business.'

"'Mr. Neiderman,' I answered, 'the Arabs say that if you want a good watchman, take the thief from the hangman's rope. And you're the last person I'd expect to talk about cutting off hands.' He had only one himself. He sighed and said, 'All right. I just hope you teach him your profession instead of learning his.'

"Abu-D'nein had no horse and had to walk alongside me, but he had a big stride and managed to keep up. And he carried a double-barreled shotgun, which gave us a lot of firepower. We made a good team. The farmers thought so anyway, because the thefts stopped from the moment I hired him. Only Neiderman knew why. He'd smile when he saw me and say, 'Well, how is your new apprentice doing?'

"'Mr. Neiderman,' I said, 'the apprentice isn't him, it's me.' Abu-D'nein knew every thief for miles around. I learned to listen to him. The one time I didn't got me into trouble.

"One night the two of us were patrolling by the coast, near the swamps by the sea. We were next to an abandoned olive grove owned by Hayyim-Ber Schwartz when we heard a strange sound coming from it: *hoooo-oooo... hoooo-oooo...* like that. 'What's that?' I asked. 'Oh,' Abu-D'nein says, 'it's just an owl.' But I was enough of a night bird myself to know it wasn't any owl. It was more like a man trying to sound like an owl – and a minute later we heard it again. 'We'd better see what that is,' I said. Abu-D'nein made no move to follow. 'Come on,' I told him.

"He fell in behind me, but not with his usual stride. After a while I stopped to let him catch up. 'What's wrong?' I asked. 'Look here,' he says, 'it's just an owl. If I were you, I'd leave it alone.' 'Abu-Mahmoud,' I told him, 'I know an owl when I hear one. If you don't feel like coming with me, I'll go myself,' and I rode ahead.

"I didn't head straight for the olive grove. I circled it and approached from the swamp side, where no one would have expected me to come from. The trees hadn't been tended in years; the brush between them was dry and as high as my horse. I couldn't see a thing in it. But I did hear something: it was a grunt like a cow's. I slipped off my horse, cocked my rifle, and said, 'Stand and tell me who you are in the night!'

"'*Ya Hawajja* Ya'akub,' a voice answered. 'Put down that gun. The night is not just yours.'

"A man stepped out from the brush. I knew him. He was a cattle thief named Hassan Abu-Hudeish. With him was Muhammed Liksa of Igzim and a third man I didn't recognize. Each time I tried to get a look at him, he covered his face with his *keffiyeh*.

"'*Ya* Hassan Abu-Hudeish,' I asked, 'what are you doing on the land of Zamarin?'

"'We were looking for lost cows,' he says.

"'And the cows you lost,' I asked, 'do they sound like owls when they're found?'

"He saw I had him dead to rights. '*Hawajja* Ya'akub,' he said, 'this land belongs to Zamarin but the cattle do not. We stole them from the el-Madi family in Igzim and we're driving them to auction in Tulkarm. All we ask is permission to cross your fields to Bir Tata.'

"Well, I was a field guard, not a policemen. What business of mine was it whose cows they were? I just didn't want them eating our crops. 'Follow me and I'll escort you,' I said, and I rode ahead of them as far as Bir Tata.

"When we reached the well and the border with Suberin, I took my leave of them. '*Hawajja* Ya'akub,' said Hassan Abu-Hudeish, 'we want to thank you. And please remember that you never saw us tonight.'

"'Abu-Hudeish,' I said, 'you should know one thing about me. Once my mouth is sealed, it's easier to crack a safe.'

"I turned back and they headed for Tulkarm. As I rode past them

I tried again to get a look at the third man, but he covered his face this time, too.

"Dawn was breaking. I didn't bother looking for Abu-D'nein; he would have walked back to Ein-Ghazzal by now. He knew about those cattle all along. The hoot was a signal to let him know the thieves were coming through.

"I was tired. Instead of taking my usual route home, past the cemetery and down Founders Street, I cut over the hill behind the winery and up to our house from the rear. I watered my horse, put her in the stable, and went to bed.

"An hour hadn't passed when I was woken by one of my brothers. I had visitors from Igzim, he said. I dressed and went to the living room and saw a delegation from the el-Madi family. 'Good morning to you all,' I said, trying to look surprised. 'To what do I owe the honor?' They told me the whole story: how one of them was woken by a sound in the night, and how he went to his barn and found his cows gone, and how he told his brother and *his* cows were gone too, and how pretty soon there were five el-Madis missing their cows and all steamed up about it. They looked for the tracks, and they found them, and they followed them to Hayyim-Ber Schwartz's olive grove, where they were joined by the tracks of a horse, and from there to Bir Tata, where they were lost in the jumble of hoof prints by the well – all except the horse's, which led over the hills to my house. 'And now,' they said, 'you had better tell us where our cows are and why you helped steal them before we go to the police.'

"That was a good question. I should have listened to Abu-D'nein. 'Look,' I said, 'you've been out tracking your cows all night and I've just gotten out of bed. I'll make us all coffee and then I'll tell you what I know.' I went to the kitchen and I took my time making it and I thought: If I tell the truth I'll break my promise to Abu-Hudeish, and if I don't I'll go to jail for his theft. When we had drunk our coffee, I said:

"By Allah, here is what happened. Last night I gave three men and their cattle safe passage across the fields of Zamarin. I didn't ask who they were. My only concern was to see that their cattle did not eat from our fields. But I did hear them say they were taking them to auction in Tulkarm. If you're quick, you may catch them there.

"I never believed they would. But Hassan Abu-Hudeish and

Muhammed Liksa had stopped to rest on the way and the el-Madis caught up with them in the marketplace. Most of the cows were still unsold. The third man was gone. He had managed to get away.

"Naturally, the el-Madis came by to thank me. It was embarrassing. It was worse than that, because when Hassan Abu-Hudeish and Muhammed Liksa stood trial, I was called as a witness for the prosecution.

"I took the stand and answered the prosecutor's questions. Abu-Hudeish and Liksa were sure I would rat on them. But when I was asked, 'Mr. Epstein, can you identify these two men as the thieves you were with that night,' I looked right at them and said, 'No, sir.'

"The judge wasn't prepared for that. 'Mr. Epstein,' he said, 'do you mean to tell me that you escorted these cattle thieves across your land, riding with them every inch of the way, without seeing who they were?'

"'Your Honor,' I answered, 'who they were was none of my business. The night was not just mine.'

"They couldn't get any more out of me. Abu-Hudeish and Liksa were convicted anyway, but I had kept my promise. And that wasn't the end of it."

The end came years later, when he was a married man with children and had a team of field guards working under him. It was the year his wife was in the sanatorium in Safed with the illness she would die from. His little boy and girl were staying with her parents in Kfar Tabor and one day he went to visit them.

It was too long a trip to make in one day on horseback. He rode his horse to the railroad station in Binyamina, padlocked her to a tree with a long chain, and left her there. He wasn't concerned about her. He would be back by evening and there was pasture beneath the tree and plenty of shepherds around to keep an eye on her.

In the evening he returned for her. The whinny she gave him left no doubt that she really could talk. It was a whole speech – not at all complimentary. But she hadn't been touched except for the tip of her tail. The hairs there were braided with red wool.

None of the shepherds could tell him who had done it. "We saw the braid, Abu-Yussef," they said, "but we thought you had made it yourself." That was an Arab custom: for weddings and celebrations you dressed your horse up like a fine lady.

It was a mystery. It stayed one, too, until a young field guard under his command, a newcomer from Poland named Badrak, shot and killed a Bedouin from the Arab-el-Turkeman tribe. It was the time of the Great Arab Revolt. Badrak had been too quick on the trigger and the tribe wanted vengeance. No self-respecting Bedouin went to the police over such a thing.

He told Badrak to lay low and went to the Bedouin to arrange a *sulha*, a forgiveness ceremony involving the payment of blood money. Even after he managed to drive down the price, the Zichron council thought it too high. He went to Neiderman, who said, "That's a lot to pay for a dead Arab." "Mr. Neiderman," he answered, "it's very little to avoid a dead Jew." Neiderman found the money.

The *sulha* was held in a big tent. The entire Arab-el-Turkeman tribe was there. Yanko Epstein came with Badrak and his friends. He didn't tell Badrak what was going to happen. He wanted him to sweat a bit.

The Bedouin seated Badrak in a chair. They put a noose around his neck, tied it to the ridgepole of the tent, and left. Badrak started to squirm. "Just sit still," Epstein told him, instructing his friends to form a circle around him.

All at once the Bedouin women outside the tent began to scream and beat on the flaps. They howled like jackals while the dead man's family poured inside, brandishing swords and calling for Badrak's blood. "Don't let them through, boys," Epstein shouted. The Bedouin pressed forward; the cordon of friends fell back. In the scuffle Epstein cried, "The friends of the murderer ask the family of the murdered man for forgiveness and offer fifty British pounds for his blood." "No!" shouted the Bedouin. "Blood is not money! Blood for blood!" They were about to break through the cordon. At the head of them was a huge black man. He was Sa'id el-Bukei'i, the murderer of Binyamin Kruppik, who had just finished serving his jail sentence.

Badrak was white as a sheet. The practice at a *sulha* was for the family to threaten to kill the dead man's killer until it cut the rope around his neck, signifying the acceptance of the blood money. "One hundred pounds for your son's blood!" Epstein cried. That was the price that was agreed on. "No!" shouted Sa'id el-Bukei'i. "Blood for blood!"

Epstein said:

"He was so worked up he forgot it was a show. I grabbed his arm just as he was about to slash Badrak's throat. It was like wrestling with a mad bull. I held on with all my might while someone else cut the rope and freed Badrak. His knees were so weak so he couldn't walk.

"After the *sulha*, we went to another tent to eat. There was a big tray of food there. Across from me sat a Bedouin who kept staring at me. When he was finished eating, he rose to make room for the man behind him and came around to my side of the tray. He knelt behind me and whispered in my ear:

"'Abu-Yussef, you have a fine horse. You should take better care of her.'

"'I take very good care of her,' I said without turning to look at him.

"'No, you don't,' he says. 'If not for me, she'd have been across the Jordan long ago.'

"I didn't know the man. 'What do you and my horse have to do with each other?' I asked.

"'Abu-Yussef,' he says, 'do you remember how once you pastured her by the train station and came back to find her tail braided?'

"'Of course I do,' I said. 'To this day I wonder who did it.'

"'Turn around and you'll see him,' he says.

"I turned around and said, 'I don't see anyone.'

"'Abu-Yussef,' he says, 'you're looking at him.'

"'It was you?'

"'It was me.'

"'But why?'

"'That braid,' said the Bedouin, 'was a thank-you note you couldn't read. I wasn't always the honest man I am now. Once some friends of mine and I stole a herd of sheep that was pastured near the station in Binyamina. As we made off with them we saw a fine-looking mare chained to a tree in a field. My friends wanted to take her too. "You'll have to fight me first," I told them, "because that horse belongs to a friend." Before we left I wrote a message in her tail.'

"I stared at him like an idiot. I had never seen him in my life.

"'Abu-Yussef,' he says, 'don't you know me yet?'

"'No,' I say. 'Who are you?'

"'I am,' he says, 'the man who stole the cattle from the el-Madis in Igzim with Hassan Abu-Hudeish and Muhammed Liksa and followed you as far as Bir Tata. And because you kept your word and did not bear witness against us, I spared your horse. Know that that padlock would not have done a bit of good. Thieves like us could have picked it in no time.'"

Half-hidden by a waterfront hotel, the minarets of Acre came into view. The sun tossed golden skipping stones on the water of the bay.

"You know," Epstein said, "even after Abu-Hudeish and Liksa got out of jail, I never told anyone but Neiderman about them. He was the one man I knew who could keep a secret as well as I could. For years we had one of our own."

He confided:

"Late one night I saw something in the village that I wasn't supposed to see. In the morning I went to tell Neiderman. He was at home with his wife. The first thing he did was send her off to the kitchen; he knew she had a big mouth. Then he said, 'Talk.' I talked and he said, 'Yanko, I didn't hear a thing. And if you want my advice, you didn't see a thing, either.' We never spoke about it again. He took that secret to the grave with him."

He shifted in his seat, his foot scuffing the brown plastic bag.

"And I'll do the same," he said.

"It was about the Turkish doctor's mistress!"

"That?" My stab in the dark made him snort. "This was serious. It happened later, during the Events."

"Which?'"

"The first."

"In what year?"

He cleared his throat and didn't answer, as if already having said too much.

We were at the roundabout outside Acre. The old Crusader town was to the left. Straight ahead, the road ran up the coast to Lebanon. To the right were the mountains of the Galilee.

"Right," Epstein said.

What on earth had he dreamed of?

I tried thinking of his secret with Neiderman.

Triggered by Arab fears of massive Zionist immigration, the first Events occurred in two clusters: the spate of anti-Jewish violence in 1920 in which Binyamin Kruppik was killed and a bloodier series of attacks in 1921.

Which was the year Perl Appelbaum died.

But how could he have witnessed a poisoning?

It had happened, he said, late at night. He was riding home through the sleeping village, past the cemetery, past the threshing floor, past the houses at the south end of Founders Street. First those on the east side of the street: Abramowitz, Bonstein, Abraham Berkowitz. Then those on the west side began: Yosef Cohen, Hayyim-Ber Schwartz, the Appelbaums, the Gelbergs. Where he saw....

What?

It made no sense.

Whatever it was, he understood its gravity. He was young and needed to talk to someone. Davidesco was in Haifa, working for British intelligence. The next best choice was Neiderman.

Whose calculation would have been simple. If the tracks led to Alexander Aaronsohn. it was best to hush the whole thing up.

And perhaps, too, Perl deserved it.

Not, of course, if Epstein was right about her having betrayed only Nisan Rutman, hiding beneath Tova Gelberg's bed. No one in Zichron, he insisted, had informed on the spy ring itself.

Yet how far could I trust a man who stretched the truth about a clarinet?

And Marcia was right, too. Who cared how Perl had died?

Oddly enough, though, Epstein did. That made two of us.

It had begun with the four women. I had wanted to know what made them act as though possessed. And now that I did, the demons had vanished.

In general, the more you learned about Zichron in those years, the more you saw that people remained who they were. If you wanted to know who did what – joined the spy ring, was for it, against it, took no stand – you had to put the big things aside. The course of the war – the hopes of the Jews – the plans of the British – the right to risk lives that

hadn't asked to be risked: these were not the keys that fit the doors on
Founders Street. To open those, you had to know other things. Who was
related to whom. Who was the neighbor of whom. Who was friendly or
had quarreled with whom. Who was more brave, prudent, adventurous,
selfish, caring, or timid than whom.

I supposed it was always like that, with greater and more terrible
things, too. Revolutions, upheavals, civil wars: you approached them
looking for the grand motives, the historic debates. And they were there.
But they were not what –

"Whoaa!"

I pulled off onto the shoulder. The road was empty except for a
bicycle ahead of us, drawing away in a wavering line. I had been driving
unaware of my surroundings. We were in a long valley, heavily planted
with old olive trees. Mountains walled it on either side. To our left, an
Arab village started on the plain and ran up the lower part of a slope.

"We missed our turn," Epstein said. Not far behind us, a side road
ran to the village.

I made a U-turn and came back to it. "Here?"

He gestured with his hand as if flinging clues up the slope for
me to follow.

The houses in the lower part of the village were widely spaced.
Vegetable and fruit gardens grew around stacks of tires, stripped-down
cars, and piles of junk. Further up the houses were more crowded. Some
were made of raw cinderblock, or stood on stilts with no lower floor as
if they had been built from the top down. It was hard to tell which were
finished or what the signs of completion might be.

"What's this place called?"

"Rami."

The narrow streets were full of children. They darted away like
birds, flying from our wheels at the last moment. The drivers coming
toward us passed on whichever side they could, mounting sidewalks to
do so and once the front step of a house. When such maneuvers were
impossible, they waited patiently to see who backed up first.

We followed the maze of streets upward until we came to a house
by which Yanko Epstein told me to park in a tight space between a
wheelbarrow and a ditch. Stepping out of the car with the white box he

had brought, he regarded the front wheels critically. "If I were you, I'd straighten them," he said.

I agreed with Edwin Samuel. Let him learn to drive first.

Three hours later, the forgotten wheels still turned toward the ditch. I plunged the car into it while maneuvering to clear the wheelbarrow.

I was fuming long before that, however – long before the end of the tedious meal I was made to sit through, a feast of heroic proportions whose preparations began from the moment of our arrival in the house by the ditch. The direction of the kitchen was marked by the smells of Arab spices and the comings and goings of children bearing cups of coffee, glasses of tea, pitchers of soft drinks, dishes of olives, plates of goat cheese, and whispered messages for the ears of our host, who was consulted, so it seemed, over every pinch of salt or handful of thyme added to the dishes frying, roasting, boiling, and braising at the far end of the house. A tubby man wearing pajamas, he received us in a chamber large enough to be a council of state's. High-backed chairs ran along its walls, on which hung photographs of Arab dignitaries. Taken by surprise in his lounging clothes, he greeted Yanko Epstein with shrill cries of excitement, his voice high-pitched like the women's in the kitchen.

A pajama button was missing at the midriff, where a bit of white-haired paunch showed through. He and Epstein had not seen each other in a donkey's age. They had a long list of mutual acquaintances to go through, assign to the ranks of the living or the dead, and reminisce about with some story – generally one of Epstein's that the man in pajamas listened to avidly, shaking his head or wiping away tears of laughter while ticking off amber worry beads. It went like this:

"And so-and-so?"

"*Rah, el-miskeen.*"

Gone, the unfortunate one.

"And such-and-such, the brother of who-was-it?"

"*Tayeb, il-hamd-illah.*"

"He lives? Health be upon him! He worked for Yussuf Bek. Tell me, what of Yussuf Bek?"

"May Allah have mercy on him! He was a fine man. Once I rode at night down Wadi Kisab and arrived at his farm as dawn was breaking. 'Good morning my friend, what brings you here at daybreak?' he asked."

My God, he was going to tell the whole story of the Gypsies all over again! And tell it he did, taking his host on the same long ride up Wadi Milikh, through Wadi Mina, past Bir Tata, Sindiani, Um-e-Shuf, Hubeizi, and Daliat-e-Ruha, down Wadi Kisab to the Valley of Jezreel. I followed him by the place names as though they were the flying mane of his horse appearing at intervals around the bends of a trail.

I had been used. His dream, if there had been one, was of an old friend he had wanted to see; I was simply the chauffeur. Help him interpret it? It was me who needed the interpreter. I could hardly understand a word of their Arabic. Here and there I made out a familiar name among others that meant nothing, as in a long tale about a couple named Mustafa and Alya. Wiping his eyes with a pajama sleeve, our host exclaimed:

"Ai, ai, Mustafa! Ai, ai, Alya!"

It was mid-afternoon when we drank our last cup of coffee, served with baklava from the white cake box, and drove off. The car got as far as the ditch. One wheel came to rest on a section of sewer pipe.

Epstein got out to have a look. "You should have straightened those wheels," he said.

It took another hour to extract us. First the children of the village came flying to see what the Jewish driver had done. Then their older brothers tried pushing us out. Finally, a man came with a tractor and chain.

I drove back to the main road. Acre was to the right.

"Left," Epstein said.

We were on a narrow road again, climbing. It passed vineyards and orchards and headed higher, through pine forests and little meadows in which spring flowers grew. The rocky hillsides glistened with the trickle of the winter's rains in their veins. Blossoming Judas trees waved lilac flags.

Where was he taking me? The road was a switchback now, basted to the side of a mountain. Each time it rose above the tops of the pine trees, the Galilee appeared below, the heavy slabs of its heights supine in sunshine, the afternoon shadows licking them like fog. Then the treetops rose back and the road nosed down and we drove through forests again.

After a while, the road leveled off. There were fields and a village with red roofs.

"Slow down," Epstein said. "It's somewhere near here. It's been ... there it is! Turn in at that gate."

On the gatepost hung a sign of the ministry of religion.

The Tomb of Rabbi Simon bar Yohai?

* * *

Outside the saint's shrine a man at a table was peddling religious artifacts: skullcaps, prayer books, amulets, cheap Sabbath candlesticks. Another man, cross-legged on the ground, sold blessings. A small sum bought you, or the person or endeavor of your choice, the bounty granted Abraham, Isaac, and Jacob.

Epstein stood surveying it all. He was holding the manila envelope.

In front of us was a two-story building, the burial place of the legendary author of the mystic Book of Splendor – the same Rabbi Simon who spent twelve years of study secluded in a cave and of whom it was said that, when he opened his mouth to speak words of Torah, the angels in heaven were so hushed that you could hear the flutter of their wings, while their rejoicing was as great when he was done as on the day the Law was given at Sinai. Once a year, on the holiday of Lag b'Omer, pilgrims met here for an all-night revel. In the morning small boys were given their first haircuts, shorn like sheep in the saint's honor.

Shading his eyes against the sun, Epstein glanced up at the shrine's roof. Then he entered the rectangular courtyard of the building. Through an opening at its far end, religious Jews went to and from the tomb. Balconies ran along the building's second floor, behind which were the doors of rooms.

"I need to get my bearings," he said. "You can look around in the meantime."

He glanced up again, as though scanning the cloudless sky for auguries.

I walked through the opening at the end of the courtyard into a room with a vaulted ceiling. A silent beggar extended a hand as I passed and lowered it like a turnstile. Men chatted by shelves of religious books. A young Hasid in a black gabardine stood chanting at a prayer stand, clapping his hands loudly at the end of each verse as if making sure the saint stayed awake.

The tomb was unprepossessing: a wall niche with a whitewashed plinth covered by a velvet cloth embroidered in gold letters. A man holding a small child was being photographed in front of it. A sign said in the language of the Kabbalah:

"As they above unite in unity, so She below unites in the secret of unity, so that She may be over against them as one against one. The Holy One Blessed Be He will not sit in glory until She is one as He is one, one in one to affirm that the Lord is one and His name is one."

"She" being the Shechinah, God's exiled presence brooding over the world.

I returned to the courtyard. Epstein had disappeared.

"Up here!"

He was calling from a balcony. I found steps to it and joined him. A door at his back was open, revealing a room in which a man in a black skullcap fussed with a kettle on a Primus stove. A laundered towel, some shirts, and a pair of socks hung on the railing of the balcony to dry.

"What do you think?" Epstein said. He looked pleased with himself. By the socks he had propped a large photograph against the railing. It was the picture of the Khan Zakhlan.

I glanced at it and around me. On the roof across the courtyard was a series of domes, one for the ceiling of each room. Apart from its crowd of Jews, the photograph was just like the scene opposite us. We were standing where the photographer had stood, looking down and out.

"You think...."

I hated to say it.

"It's obvious."

But it wasn't.

"You're wrong! Look at these big archways." I pointed to them triumphantly, dark and cavernous in the picture. The ground floor did not have them.

"Look again."

He was right. They had been there, once. You could still trace the line of them, filled in to create more doors. The photograph I had found in the Graf Hotel was of the shrine of Rabbi Simon bar Yohai.

The man boiling water stepped out on the balcony and came over. The shrine's caretaker, he looked at the photograph curiously. Yes, there once had been archways on that side of the courtyard: the pilgrims had stabled their animals inside them and slept in the rooms on the second floor. With the advent of motor transport, the stables were turned into more rooms. Nowadays, though, there were such crowds on Lag b'Omer that nearly everyone slept in tents or in the open. "The saint is a big draw," he declared. He sounded like the saint's impresario.

Epstein handed me the photograph. "In 1894," he said, "a group from Zichron attended the Lag b'Omer celebration. It met a larger group from Rosh Pina; most of the families you see here were from there. Here, it's yours."

Rosh Pina was a Rothschild colony in the Galilee. On the photograph's back was written:

"Too a frend who helped me fiined this."

You might have thought I had boosted him through the window of the Graf Hotel. "When was the last time you were here?" I asked.

"With Edwin Samuel."

"And you just now dreamed of it?"

"What is a dream?" he questioned philosophically. "It's a vision, isn't it? You can say I had a vision."

What he had was an uncanny memory and a fund of knowledge.

We returned to the car and drove down the switchback. The demotion of my photograph rankled. To change the subject, I asked about the man in the pajamas. "An old friend. His village was on our way."

"You might at least have introduced us."

He mulled that over and replied:

"You know, the Bedouin would consider that bad manners."

"So would many people."

"Would they? Well, no Bedouin would introduce you if you walked into a tent with him. It would be like saying you weren't important enough to be known already."

That settled that, then. He was merely being polite.

We reached the main road and turned toward Acre. The sun was low in the west. Even after I lowered the sun flap, it kept getting in my eyes. I said:

"Tell me about Mustafa and Alya."

"Alya?" He gave a start and straightened in his seat. Perhaps he had dozed off, for he repeated, as if having heard the second name alone:

"Alya!"

And, wide awake now:

"I'll tell you about Alya. I've known women on whom God didn't stint – Arab, Jewish, French, and Swiss. None had the beauty of Alya. And the only time I saw her she was dead."

He put up a hand to block the sun, which went on streaming through his fingers.

"She was a Bedouin of the Arab-el-Turkeman. Her father was white and her mother was black and she was the color of a loaf of fresh bread. There wasn't a man in her tribe who didn't dream of her. They went to bed with her image before their eyes and woke with it there in the morning.

"When Alya came of age, her father's tent filled with suitors. Rich sheikhs bid up the price of her. They came from afar to see if what they had heard was true.

"The truth surpassed what they had heard. Alya outshone her own legends. Every suitor fell in love with her. And every one was turned down. Young and old, shy and bold – not a one pleased her. They came like horses and went like donkeys, as the Arabs say.

"The days and months passed. Alya's father, Ahmed Ali, grew impatient. Then he grew angry. The daughter who should have brought him riches was bringing him ridicule. It was whispered that she had a secret lover, a man she was unable to wed. Some said he was poor. Others that he was a Jew or a Christian. Her brothers watched her with seven eyes. At night they stayed awake beside her tent, lying in wait for her lover. They never saw even his shadow.

"And then the rumor spread wings that Alya was pregnant. Her belly was growing from day to day. Her secret lover was a phantom, a demon."

We were coming out of the mountains, the plain of Acre lurid in the sun.

"One day word reached the British police in Zichron that Alya had been killed. Her family was digging her grave when they arrived. It told them she had been milking a cow. A horse kicked the cow, the cow kicked Alya, and Alya died on the spot.

"It sounded suspicious. Honor killings were common among the Arabs. The police took Alya's body and sent for Dr. Cohen to perform an autopsy.

"A Jewish policeman, a friend of mine named Kalman Radin, was assigned to drive the doctor. I told him I was coming along. The case interested me. I.…"

He had wanted to see what so many men had dreamed of. And when he did, it was like looking at a sleeping goddess.

But Dr. Cohen was a practical man. He had no time for the contemplation of corpses, not even one whose splendor was blemished only by a swollen belly. He put on a pair of rubber gloves and reached for his surgical knife. He was about to make the first incision when Sergeant Radin remembered that he had left some important papers in the car. The doctor watched him dash off and said:

"Epstein, before I begin, are you sure you don't have to go somewhere too?"

He was sure. He would stay and help.

The doctor handed him a pair of gloves. They knelt by Alya's body and Dr. Cohen slit it open, stuck a hand in, and passed out the inner parts. "I threw them in a bucket," Epstein said. "It was like cleaning a fish."

After a while the doctor pulled out something red and spongy and held it in the air. "You can tell your friend Radin," he said, "that this was the cause of death. A ruptured spleen, greatly enlarged from malaria." He handed it to Epstein and sewed Alya up for her funeral.

Not only had she not been pregnant, she was still a virgin.

The case was closed. Alya was buried and the suitors went home and found themselves other wives.

Epstein said:

"Let's return to the horse that kicked the cow that kicked Alya. It belonged to her brother Mustafa. He was a good rider who loved to compete. There wasn't a horse race you didn't find him at.

"A few years after Alya's death, there was a big race in the Valley of Jezreel. It was an annual affair. I was on my way back from Kfar Tabor and stopped to see it. Mustafa was there and asked to borrow my horse. 'We'll split first prize between us,' he says.

"'Where's your own horse?' I asked.

"'She threw a shoe and came up lame,' he said.

"'And what makes you think you'll win on mine?' I asked him.

"'I know your horse,' he says. 'I've seen you race her.'

"I said, 'Mustafa, you couldn't have. I never race my horse.' I never did. I had seen too many accidents happen that way.

"'But I saw you,' he says. 'It was on my wedding day.'

"He was right. That was the one time I did it.

"Mustafa married an *abada*, a slave girl. He wasn't golden-skinned like Alya. He was coal-black like his mother and took a bride as black as himself. She belonged to Dib el-A'ayat. Dib was the sheikh of the Arab-el-A'ayata, who camped in the dunes near Pardes-Hanna.

"The Bedouin custom was that, when a slave girl was given in marriage, her owner received a set of clothes from the groom's family. It was brought him on the wedding day by the groom's father: a cloak, a belt, a white *keffiyeh*, and a black headband, all of the best cloth. An outfit like that wasn't cheap. Ahmed Ali had spent all he had on the wedding and didn't have the money for it.

"What did he do? He knew I was friendly with Sheikh Dib el-A'ayat and he sent for me and said: *'Ya Hawajja* Ya'akub, I have a request of you. On the day of my son's wedding, go in my place to Sheikh Dib's tent and fetch the bride. He respects you and won't turn you away for coming empty-handed.'

"I agreed. I felt sorry for him. He had never gotten over the death of Alya; he had counted on her to make him rich. On the day of the wedding, I dressed my horse in her finery and rode to the camp of the Arab-el-Turkeman. Two Bedouin were waiting for me with a she-camel, all decked out like a bride herself. Instead of a saddle she had a broad litter. That was for the bride to ride on. Brides sat in the middle with a bridesmaid on either side while their kinsmen rode around them in circles. Halfway to the groom's tent they were met by his kin, and they traveled together the rest of the way.

"We reached the camp of the Arab-el-A'ayata and went to the tent of Sheikh Dib. He gave me a warm welcome. *'Ahlan wa-sahlan! T'fadl, t'fadl!* What brings you here?'

"'*Allah yezid fadlak*, Sheikh Dib,' I said. 'I've come to bring the bride of Mustafa, the son of Ahmed Ali, to her wedding.'

"'My friend,' Sheikh Dib answered, 'say no more. Take the bride with my blessing and tell Ahmed Ali I have all the clothing I need.'

"He couldn't have been more noble. We put the bride on the

camel with her bridesmaids and started back to the camp of the Arab-el-Turkeman with her kinsmen on horses around her.

"One of the bridesmaids was named Fidi and lived in Zichron with her husband. All three women had little flags. When they reached the halfway point and were met by the groom's kin, they raised the flags high. That was a challenge for the horsemen to snatch one. Whoever did shouted 'Open the way!' and raced with it to the tent of the groom. If he got there safely and planted the flag in the ground, the groom's father owed him and his kin a feast. If someone else caught him and took the flag away, the feast was his.

"It wasn't easy to snatch a flag. A camel is a lot taller than a horse. You had to gallop by at full speed, standing in the stirrups. If you weren't careful you ended up without a horse. And the bridesmaids did their best to keep the flag away from you, because they wanted the bride to get off to a good start with her husband's family.

"A few riders went for those flags and missed. There was laughing and joking and singing of funny songs, and meanwhile we're getting closer to the camp of the Arab-el-Turkeman. 'Ya'akov Epstein,' I said to myself, 'this is your chance to show that a Jew can be as noble as a sheikh.' I rode up behind the camel and said in a low voice, 'Fidi, I'm taking your flag. Lower your arm when I come through.'

"She nodded to let me know she'd heard me. I dropped back and waited for a space to clear around her and shouted 'Open the way!' She lowered her arm and I stood in the stirrups and snatched the flag as I galloped by.

"I turned to look back – there was nothing but a cloud of dust. I whipped my horse and looked again – a storm of Bedouin was pouring out of the cloud.

"Not a one of them could catch me. Some were riding fine horses, but my *saklawiyya* outran them all. When we came to the railroad tracks at Binyamina, she leaped a flatcar without breaking stride. Ahmed Ali was sitting by his tent, waiting for the procession to arrive. I jumped from my horse and planted the flag. '*Ya Hawajja* Ya'akub,' he said, 'what have you done? I sent you to save me ten British pounds for an outfit and you've cost me fifty to feast the sons of Zamarin.' 'Abu-Mustafa,' I answered, 'put your mind to rest. The sons of Zamarin no more need your feast than Sheih Dib needed your outfit. I absolve you of it and wish you a happy wedding.'"

All this was to explain why Mustafa had asked to borrow his horse for the race in the Valley of Jezreel. He told him:

"It wouldn't do you any good if I lent her. She's a one-man horse and lets no one else ride her. You wouldn't get to the starting line on her."

He related:

"In the end Mustafa borrowed a horse from someone else. It was a stallion and fast, with a mind of its own – and when he whipped it to get it to concentrate, it reared and threw him. Nothing much would have happened if his foot hadn't caught in the stirrup. It was a narrow English one, not the wide Arab kind he was used to. The horse left the racetrack and ran through a rocky field, dragging Mustafa behind him. By the time anyone could grab the reins, Mustafa's head was split open like a ripe melon.

"Well, someone had to tell his family. And since the Arab-el-Turkeman camped near Zichron, that someone was me.

"I rode straight to their encampment. Mustafa's mother was spinning wool by her tent. When I told her what I told her, she threw down her spindle and screamed:

"'O Mustafa, Mustafa! What falls from heaven lands on earth! You've been punished for what you did to Alya.'

That was how he learned that Mustafa had killed his sister. Later, he found out how.

"One day he was sitting in her tent. Alya was pounding coffee with a pestle. 'What are you staring at?' she asked. 'At your belly,' Mustafa said. 'What makes it so big?' 'A baby demon as black as you,' she answered. She was only taunting him; she was a virgin and could prove it. But Mustafa didn't know that. He grabbed the pestle and struck the demon."

The Wadi Milikh turn-off was to our right. We'd be home in twenty minutes.

"Keep going straight," Epstein said.

Too weary from the long day to protest, I let him hijack me again. We drove south in the darkness, the Valley of Jezreel on our left.

It turned into an equally long night. There were more old friends he wanted to see, in the town of Um-el-Fahm, near the 1967 border with

Jordan. He didn't have to visit their homes; they came to see him. "*Ahlan, Abu-Yussef, keyf el-hal,* Abu-Yussef," they hailed him through the open window of the car, reaching through it to shake his hand and drag us off to a café where the smoke of cigarettes and grilling meet meat formed a greasy haze. Word of his presence spread. New faces kept appearing to say hello. Men rose from their hookahs and backgammon boards to come over from the nearby tables. A beak-nosed man with a barbered beard brought a tray with half a dozen empty cups, set it down on our table, and issued a challenge. "I haven't played this in years," Epstein said

"This" was a game called *siniyya*, which the younger men in the café had never seen. Soon they were crowding around to watch. The cups were turned upside-down on the tray, a player hid an object beneath one of them, and his rival had to guess where it was. "In the old days," Epstein said, slipping a ring off his finger and under a cup while the bearded man covered his eyes, "the loser paid cash or a penalty. Once, in Um-ez-Zeinat, I made a fellow carry me around the village on his shoulders."

The man with the beard guessed the wrong cup and it was Epstein's turn. He studied the tray like a chessboard, passed a hand over it, reached for a cup, pulled back his hand at the last moment, let it hover above another cup, and turned that one over. The ring was beneath it.

There were cheers and laughter while the bearded man ordered everyone a round of *kanayif*, pancakes filled with crushed nuts and honey. The onlookers slapped Epstein's back. One said:

"Abu-Yussuf, if you were here today we'd still be voting General Zionist."

The General Zionists were a middle-of-the-road party that disappeared in the early 1970s in the merger that formed the Likud. He had worked for them, he told me driving back to Zichron late at night, as a canvasser. Men like him were middlemen, intermediaries between the politicians in Jerusalem and Tel Aviv and the Arab sheikhs and clan heads who delivered the vote at election time. They distributed patronage, lobbied with ministries, helped award contracts. The connections established during his years as a field guard had stood him in good stead.

"I could sling the talk of the peasant, the merchant, the laborer, the sheikh, each in the speech of his village," he said. "I could crawl into their skins. Did you think it was luck I won that game of *siniyya*? All the time I was pretending to look at the cups, I was watching that fellow's face. It was he who told me where my ring was."

He had no illusions about Arabs. He had always had "two hands" for them, one to embrace and one to keep at arm's length. When they were expelled from the farmyards of Zichron in the 1930s, he had led the campaign against them. Arab nationalism was spreading. The Arabs in town were raising their heads. They were demanding a mosque to pray in, a school for their children. He saw the writing on the wall.

He was a nationalist himself. Once, during World War II, he was summoned to the British land office in Haifa to help settle a border dispute between Zichron and Sindiani. The district superintendent was a Nashashibi, a cousin of the mayor of Jerusalem. The Nashashibis were the more moderate of the two clans fighting for the leadership of Palestine's Arabs. Their rivals were the Husseinis. Haj Amin el-Husseini, the Grand Mufti of Jerusalem, had fled the country and was living in Germany as Hitler's ally.

It was King George's birthday. They had their maps spread out on a table. As they were studying them, a brass band marched down the street. They went to the window to look. After a while Nashashibi turned away and said:

"Epstein, let's go back to our maps. This isn't our holiday."

They returned to the table and he said:

"Give it up, Epstein! They're playing us against each other, don't you see? Give up the idea of a Jewish state that they've put into your heads. Do that and we'll live in peace!"

"Like in Iraq?" he asked. The pro-Nazi Rashid Ali had just come to power in Baghdad. Dozens of Jews had been killed in a pogrom there.

"What do you want?" Nashashibi asked. "When the bells ring in Palestine, the Arabs hear them all over. You can't fight the whole Arab world. The Crusaders had armor against our garden spades and we threw them into the sea. It will happen to you, too."

"I'll tell you when I thought of that," Epstein said to me. "It was after the battle of Tantura. I was standing on the beach, looking at the waves. The village behind me was empty. Half its inhabitants were on the threshing floor in Faradis and the other half had fled to Lebanon in boats. I looked at the sea and I thought: who's in it now?"

The refugees from Tantura spent the summer in Faradis. Then they were marched to the cease-fire line with Jordan and forced to cross it. "My sister, Faida Bek, went with them," he said.

Although there was no room in my head for even one more of his stories, he had done it again.

"You had an Arab *sister*?"

"An adopted one."

Faida Bek was the wife of Fauzi Bek, the son of Sadik Pasha. Fauzi owned a farm near the encampment of the Arab-el-Turkeman. Every summer Yosef Epstein sent his sons there with his McCormick threshing machine. It was a new model from America with an internal combustion engine and a toothed cutting bar. The Arabs had nothing like it.

"It took us two weeks to cut Fauzi Bek's grain," Epstein said. "Until then it had taken him two months. It was worth his while and we made some money." It was like a vacation for him and his brothers. They lived well in Fauzi Bek's big house, sleeping in its beds, eating its lavish meals, and waited on by its servants.

In 1924, Fauzi Bek died. He was still a young man and he left behind a wife, Faida, and a small boy.

The following summer, Faida Bek asked Yosef Epstein to send his sons with the McCormick. "By then," Epstein said, "I was the only one of my five brothers left at home. Tsvi and Meir-Itsik had married and moved out, Yeshayahu was in Switzerland, and Dov was dead from the Spanish flu."

Although he was now a full-time field guard, he could rely on Abu-D'nein to manage without him for a few days, and so he sent his father's farm hands with the McCormick to Faida Bek's and rode after them. She met him at the door and burst into tears.

"Faida, why are you crying?" he asked.

"I swear, I thought you were Fauzi," she said. "When I saw you through the window on that fine horse, I was sure it was him coming back. No one sat on a horse the way he did."

They worked all day with the thresher. In the evening he saw to it that the workers were fed and lodged and mounted his horse to return to Zichron. As he was about to ride off, Faida Bek ran out and seized the bridle.

"What is it?" he asked.

"Come spend the night with me," she said.

"Faida, how can I?" he asked. "There are Bedouin all around. If they find out, they'll tear me to pieces. You won't fare any better yourself."

She held on to the bridle. "Please," she begged, "just one night. You don't know what this means to me."

Epstein said to me as we turned into Wadi Milikh:

"Who was I to deny a pretty widow? She had three beauty spots that I remember to this day: here, here, and here."

He touched his face three times in the dark car.

He told her:

"All right, Faida. But first do what I tell you. Send a messenger to the Arab-el-Turkeman and have them gather their menfolk in front of this house."

He could see she thought he was crazy. "Just do as I say," he said.

Faida Bek sent a messenger and the Arab-el-Turkeman began arriving. When a crowd had gathered in front of the house, he took her up to the roof. They stood where the Bedouin could see them and he called down:

"Know, all of you, that from this day on Faida Bek is my sister and I am her brother. As a brother's duties are to his sister, so mine are to her; as a sister's are to her brother, so hers are to me. Speak now or forever hold your peace."

No one spoke. He and Faida Bek were sister and brother. That was a Bedouin rite of adoption, a way of taking a single woman under your protection. It meant he could come and go in her house as he pleased.

"What else could I do?" he asked. "Her wish was my command. And don't think that was the only night I spent with her."

His affair with Faida Bek continued even after he began courting his wife. He was forced to break it off when he became engaged. When she protested he told her, "Faida, know that I still am and always will be your brother. If you want a husband, I'll find you one."

It was a brother's duty to marry off his sister once their father was no longer alive.

Finding Faida a husband wasn't simple. Although she was rich and good-looking, he was choosy. One of the suitors he turned down was a Bedouin sheikh named Muhammed el-Hilu. "How many wives do you have, O sheikh?" he asked him. "Three," the sheikh said. "Come with me to my stable," he said. The uncomprehending sheikh went with him. "Do you see this horse?" he said, pointing to his *saklawiyya*. "She lets only one man ride her. Do you think my sister Faida is less of a thoroughbred than my horse?"

In the end, Faida Bek married a wealthy moneylender, Abdurahman el-Anabtawi. Epstein met him in Caesaria, to which he had gone with a consignment of his father's watermelons. It was the season in which the local melons, as red and sweet as raspberry sherbet, were shipped up and down the coast as far as Beirut and Alexandria. The little port teemed with sellers, buyers, shippers, and moneylenders who had staked the melon growers to advances. One of these approached him and proposed marriage. He was a middle-aged bachelor from the village of Anabta and Epstein accepted.

Faida Bek wed the moneylender and went to live with him in Haifa. When the city fell to the Haganah in 1948, they fled to Faradis. Faida's husband came to see Epstein in Zichron. He wanted to know whether they should stay in Israel or return to Anabta, which was now in Jordan. Epstein advised them to stay. A few days later he went to Faradis to see them. They were already across the border.

"After the '67 war," he said, "I went to Kalkilya on business. There were some people outside the office of the military governor and we struck up a conversation. One of them was from Anabta. I asked if he knew Faida Bek's husband. 'Yes,' he said, 'and Faida Bek too. She was my mother.' 'Then I'm your uncle,' I said. He told me both his parents were dead.

"That time on the beach in Tantura, there was a fellow from the Haganah, a man named Avraham Durian. He knew I had lived my life with Arabs. 'Well, Ya'akov,' he said, 'what do you have to say to them now?' 'What do I have to say to them?' I said. 'I have the book of Psalms for them. By the waters of Babylon, that's what I have. There was a Nashashibi in Haifa who once told me the Arabs have patience. Let's see if they have as much as we did.'

"You know, sometimes late at night, I sit and fiddle with the radio. I tune in to the Arab stations – Cairo, Amman, Damascus, Beirut. All they have at that hour is music. Do you know what they're singing about? The house with the orange tree in Jaffa. The house with the lemon tree in Lydda. Afterwards I can't sleep."

The lights of Zichron shone on a distant hill.

"I miss them. War is war and I fought them when I had to, but I never scorched the earth between us. They live in green fields in my heart to this day."

I dropped him off by his house on Founders Street. He bent to pick up the plastic bag. Its drawstring had opened, revealing the sawed-off barrel of a shotgun.

"I hope you don't mind my asking," I said, "but how come you brought that thing along?"

One foot was already on the sidewalk. "Seeing as how we were among friends, you mean?"

"Seeing as how we were."

"Those friends have a saying," he said. "It takes a man's shrouds to change his habits."

Chapter thirteen

She stood with her back to me in the large gravel courtyard, in blue sandals and a light-blue chiffony dress. Although she gave no sign of hearing me enter at the gate, which I had been told would be left open, she waited long enough for me to take in the scene, that of her slight, girlish figure intent on something I couldn't see and perhaps was even inside her, and then turned to face me. The hand she extended was not meant to be shaken and I took it without knowing what to do with it. "Ah, how disappointing!" she said. "Yoram led me to believe you would be older."

"I'm mature for my age," I quipped. It felt like the start of a blind date.

"He told me to spend no more than an hour with you. He's so worried I'll tire myself out. But we're not counting the minutes, are we?"

She smiled with anxious coquetry, unsure I could be coaxed not to tell on her to Yoram Efrati, and led me by the little hand I still held to the house that was out-of-bounds for tourists. Guiding me through it, she showed me its special effects: the hiding place beneath the innocent-looking floor tiles, the secret compartment magically opened by a button at the far end of the room. "Aaron was so clever!" she exclaimed. Apart from planning concealments and escape routes for his family, he seemed to have delighted in the ingenuity of so many complicated hooks and wires installed like plumbing in the walls.

It was Aaron Aaronsohn who had bought, on one of his trips to Damascus, the inlaid furniture in the drawing room, in which a table was now set for afternoon tea. But it was not he who dominated the room. It was not even Avshalom Feinberg, staring moodily down from a wall. It was Alexander, everywhere on display like a versatile fashion model. Alexander in a gold-buttoned blazer. Alexander in a yachting cap. Alexander in a knotted scarf. Alexander in his captain's uniform, the simple soldier who dedicated *Sarah, Flame of the Nili* to his sister Rivka, "a priestess in Memory's temple."

"Won't you sit down?" said the priestess.

Her hair was dyed the light brown color it must have been on the night when Feinberg, soon to be her fiancé, wrote her a letter from Hadera in the spring of 1911. "Shall we chat a bit, Rivka?" it began. "I imagine right now – it's 9:30 – you're sitting beneath a lamp whose peaceful light falls golden on your hair. The two little snakes at your forehead coil tranquilly. You're reading. Your head is down and your eyes feast on the page. I don't know what's in them, because I can't see them."

She was nineteen. He wrote her a poem:

No, my child! You can't have my love.
You're much too small and too frail.
But I'll tell you as one tells a friend, without shame,
The secret of what makes me ail.

When the angel who fashioned me gave me a heart,
He forged it from one solid mass.
That's why it's not able to love or to hate
By measurements or by halves.

And so when, on my knee, I stroke your soft hair,
Or I hold you tight in my arms,
Everything comes out clumsy and rushed,
As if meant to strangle or harm.

Do you remember how hard you cried when I bit
Your white neck and the crimson blood flowed? This,
My dear, vexed me, believe me, it did,
Because it was only a kiss, just a kiss!

And now do you see why you can't have my love?
I'm afraid…. You're so little and frail.
You're a woman and weak, and you can't understand
The secret of what makes me ail.

Avshalom's last published letter to Rivka was written from Alexandria in late 1915, a year before his death in the desert. She was in America with Alex and he was in Egypt, holding discussions with British intelligence. It was her birthday, and writing by the light of a full moon he pictured riding to her in Zichron. "Faster, old boy!" he urged his horse. "Shake a leg! Can't you feel me tugging at your white mane? Here's Crocodile Creek – here's the bridge – and the hill… and now the cemetery with its white stones and dark graves. Slower, now! They can already hear our hoofbeats in the yard. The dear heart waiting for us has heard them long ago…."

But the vision soon faded. Alexandria was a large, smelly city, "moldy with whores and stinking of bars and drunks"; from the street outside came "soul-shatteringly" loud music. "No, my little Ubi," he wrote, using her family's pet name for her. "The horse is gone. The sandy hill and the rocky path that climbs it grow faint. So does the dear child bathed in moonlight. It's all a dream, just foam on the waves…."

Their relationship had not been a happy one. She was a worrier and hadn't allowed it to be. "For years," he wrote, "I loved you and begged you, abjectly, like a pauper asking for alms, to open a window in your heart, to let in the light, to give hope and victory a chance, to banish the worm gnawing at your heart – and what good did it do? …I went down on my knees, my heart bled until I was exhausted, and in the end I've lost and the worm has won….

"At home, with so much always to do, there was never time to think or breathe. Only now can I make the terrible reckoning, tally up the tragic (the never, never recoverable!) loss; four whole years of our lives, four years between your nineteen and twenty-three and my twenty-two and twenty-six! How the heart cringes...

"I've made up my mind, Ubi. We'll try one more time. I'll do anything, try anything, to put an end to this.... Either I win or I smash up, but something has to give. I'm often tortured by the thought of how we've sinned – to ourselves – to our hopes – to our children – to the future – by waiting so long. Sinned terribly! And I want this to change as soon as possible....

"Enough for now. What more can I say to you, dearest child? I'll shut my eyes and cross my arms on my breast and dream that your head is resting there. Slowly I'll rock you, my little one, and cover you with quiet, burning kisses – hush! don't wake me from my dream – on your brow – on your dear eyes – on your lovely mouth. God in his mercy knows how I need to lean my head against your legs. And here's another kiss – and another – and another...."

Down, downward went the kisses. A servant brought tea and cake. "Oh, yes," Rivka Aaronsohn said. "Women were different in those days. They had... *l'honneur de leur chastété*. They knew the meaning of restraint. To love and to burn. To burn and not be consumed. How important that was...."

It was a sore point between them, her virginity. It came up often in Avshalom's letters. "I send you a thousand kisses, my love," he wrote. "And now that you're covered with them all, nine hundred ninety-nine, there is only one left – one alone that I must give you... But its radiance is not meant for my sinful eyes, its heaven is barred to my impure, greedy lips. Its impossibility will burn them forever and weigh on my heaving breast until I die."

It was said in Zichron that Rivka and Avshalom put off marrying because Avshalom and Sarah had fallen in love, and that Sarah's brief marriage to a Jewish businessman from Constantinople, intended to leave the field to her younger sister, failed to have that effect. It was hard to say. Although affectionate, Avshalom's letters to Sarah, published together with the ones to Rivka, breathed no passion. Yet both correspondences came from the archives of Aaronsohn House and might have been tampered with. In his biography of Aaron Aaronsohn, Yoram

Efrati's co-author in *Nili: A Tale of Political Daring*, Eliezer Livneh, who had full access to the archives, called Sarah's marriage "self-sacrificial."

Was it? From Rivka I could only elicit that this would have been in character. Sarah, she said, had always been fascinated by martyrdom. When she was young, she had liked to read about the Spanish Inquisition.

However you looked at it, the Aaronsohns were a sexually odd family. Only the second and third of Fishl and Malka Aaronsohn's six children, Sam and Tsvi, had families and children of their own. Rivka had no known romantic relationships after Avshalom; Aaron, who died in his early forties, had none at all; and Alexander, two years older than Sarah, preferred young nubiles. I had been told of adolescents procured for him and had had a house in Zichron pointed out to me as that of an elderly woman who was one of his teenage playthings. She was the wife of the thin-haired, sardonic man I had met in Pomerantz's café with Ben-Hayyim.

I knew of no explanation for this, the best I heard being a remark of Yanko Epstein's that the Aaronsohns were too much in love with each other to have much feeling left over for others. Their sense of being special, he said, came from their mother. She had treated them like royalty.

"Oh, but we were!" Rivka Aaronsohn made a wry face. "My grandmother said we were descended from King David."

To Sarah, three years her senior, she had felt inferior. "I was always the little sister. She was so much braver and more beautiful." But Alexander she had adored. His bachelorhood was an act of pure selflessness. "He loved women too much to marry," she said of the Knight of Love. "He wanted to kindle the spark of holiness in them, to raise it higher and higher. How could he have lived with just one woman?"

Her brown eyes, puppyish, queried me. The runt of the litter's, they pleaded for an approving nod or touch. Poor little Ubi! Her girlish figure had never ripened. The vestal virgin tending the sacred flame! Was it for Avshalom she had remained like this, unconsummated, unconsumed, or for her brother? All that worminess, *l'honneur de la chastété*, while he had his girlies in the grass! The whole parade of Ubi-Nubis, starting with Tova Gelberg.

"I've brought you something," I said. "You might say I'm returning it."

Curious, she opened the package I handed her and took out the photograph of the white woman and the tattered copy of *Sarah, Flame of the Nili* that bore her and her brother's signatures. Tova and I had come a long ways together; I felt a twinge at parting.

She clucked her tongue while I told her where I'd found it. "Oh, those eyes!" she said, regarding their dark points. "They *saw*."

"Saw what?"

"Tova was a *voyante*." She held séances, read the future in cards. The cards told her she and Alex would never marry. "We all thought they would. Our mothers were close friends. Alex was ready for it. He was so good to her. But Tova saw he wasn't meant for her – wasn't meant for marriage at all. The spirits talked to her. I once saw one of them move a table."

Her psychic powers were lost when she married Nisan Rutman and went to live with him in Hadera.

"Nisan wanted her all for himself. He wouldn't even let her have her music. And it meant so much to her! If she was playing the piano when he came home, he'd make her stop. He was a *jaloux*."

"And a miser to boot," I said. I had heard that from Gabi Asiag, the son-in-law of Yosef Blum, the tall farmer who lived down our road. Gabi grew up in Hadera. Although Rutman, he said, owned thousands of dunams of orange groves, the greengrocers in the market saved him their rotten produce because they knew it was all he would pay for.

"Him and his groves!" The mention of them made her petulant. "He was more married to them than to Tova."

"The Zayta lands."

She was surprised I knew about them.

"A bit," I said, though by now it was a bit more than that.

* * *

Zayta was an Arab village near Hadera, which was Zichron's district capital, although back in the days when Avshalom Feinberg rode his horse between them, it was the smaller of the two places. To the east of it, between a swamp and the sluggish Hadera Creek, lay a large parcel of land belonging to residents of Zayta. The scandal caused by its sale brought about the end of Alexander Aaronsohn's brief political career.

It all began with Mary Fels, the rich American Jewish lady in whose honor Moshe Shatzman went to borrow a horse.

Mary was the widow of Joseph Fels, the founder and owner of the large Philadelphia and London soap manufacturing company of Fels-Naptha. Born in North Carolina to German-Jewish parents, Fels was an ardent supporter of the American reformer Henry George's "Single Tax" program. (It was George's theory that, land being the key to all wealth, a tax on it to force unexploited acreage into use would reduce its price for farmers, increase agricultural yields and the production of raw materials, push up wages by stimulating the demand for labor, lower housing and real estate costs, and raise sufficient revenue to abolish all other taxes.) Pooh-poohed by economists, the "Single Tax" was a popular cause in some circles, and the liberal-minded Fels, more reluctant to share his profits with governments than with the political progressives, suffragettes, and Russian revolutionaries he supported, found it appealing. Backed by his wife and lifelong partner, he was, from Henry George's death in 1897 until his own death in 1914, a leader of the Single Tax movement.

Land was thus something the Felses had thought about long before Mary decided to become a purchaser of it for Jewish farmers in Palestine. They had acquired it for benevolent purposes in the past, starting with a Philadelphia project for growing vegetables in vacant slum lots and on to grander schemes like Mayland, an estate outside London on which they settled poor city dwellers on five to ten acre holdings furnished with farmhouses, fruit trees, and agricultural instructors. If Mayland resembled a Rothschild colony, this may have been because the Felses knew of Rothschild's activities and interest in Jewish colonization – about which, however, they had their differences. Joseph, skeptical of the economic potential of Palestine, favored the return of Jews to the soil elsewhere; as an associate of Israel Zangwill, the Anglo-Jewish author and head of the Jewish Territorialist Organization, he traveled to South America to investigate possibilities there. Mary was a Zionist. She was friendly with American Zionist leaders like Stephen Wise and Julian Mack and joined them in sending a statement of Zionist aims to the Paris Peace Conference in 1919.

This statement was drawn up in consultation with Aaron Aaronsohn, who had close ties with Wise and Mack and had met Mary

Fels in New York. Mary was also introduced there, during the war, to Alexander Aaronsohn's Jerusalem-born friend Itamar Ben-Avi, the son of the Hebrew language warrior Eliezer Ben-Yehuda and the first child since antiquity to speak Hebrew as his mother tongue. Asked by Ben-Avi if she intended to visit Palestine after the war, she replied – so he wrote years later in his autobiography – that she would do so gladly if he would agree to be her guide and secretary.

In 1922 she kept her promise, accepting an invitation from a newly founded group called "The Sons of Benjamin." In the history books this was an organization remembered, if at all, as a private farmers' lobby that fought to obtain land and other benefits from a Palestinian Zionist leadership that favored collective agriculture. Yet though ending up as that, it started out more ambitiously. As recalled by Ben-Avi, then editor of the right-wing Palestine Daily Mail, established together with Alexander Aaronsohn and several other young partners in 1920, the Sons of Benjamin's beginnings lay in a strike staged by left-wing immigrant workers to protest the introduction of a new, labor-saving printing press. Ben-Avi wrote:

"This strike so embittered me that I decided it was time to realize the old dream of establishing a political movement for us Palestinians natives.... In several articles, I spoke of the need for a fascist party. These articles were not aimed at the workers or their trade union as such, but at the 'Reds and Bolshies' who were fomenting strikes and riots and endangering, I thought, the country's future.

"At that time, Alexander Aaronsohn had the similar idea of uniting Palestine's native sons. One day we met...and laid the groundwork for a party to be called 'The Sons of Benjamin' in honor of Theodor Herzl and Edmond de Rothschild."

"Benjamin" was both Herzl's and Rothschild's Hebrew first name. Subsequently, Ben-Avi related, a founding meeting was held and "representatives of the younger generation of the farming villages...unanimously nominated Alexander Aaronsohn to be president, while I agreed to be vice-president. Alex's influence on the youth was enormous and it truly seemed that we had found ourselves a leader."

"Fascist," of course, did not mean in those days what it came to mean later. In 1920, Mussolini had not yet come to power in Italy, although his Fascio di Combattimento was a force to be reckoned with and had taken to violence and street fighting in its campaign against the Communists and Socialists. In hoping to model a movement on it, Ben-Avi and Alexander were not thinking along totalitarian lines. Neither, however, did they have in mind a loyal Opposition. "Fascism" meant the excitement of rough-and-tumble extra-parliamentary action – just what was needed, they believed, to combat a Zionist Left that dominated Jewish life in the country.

There was indeed, on the Right, a vacuum waiting to be filled. The Left was well-organized and headed by experienced politicians, Second Aliyah leaders versed in tactical struggles. Although its two major parties received only a third of the votes in all-Jewish elections held in 1920, they formed a united bloc that easily controlled a National Assembly and National Executive Council that were split into numerous ethnic, religious, and ideological factions. The Right lacked a dominant figure. Avshalom Feinberg was dead. Aaron Aaronsohn, soon to be killed in an airplane crash, was busy pressing Zionist claims in the international arena. Vladimir Jabotinsky, the founder of the Jewish Legion that had fought with British troops at the First World War's end, did not launch his Revisionist Party until 1925. Nor did Jabotinsky, a Russian Jew who never set foot in Palestine until the Legion entered it, have a following among its "native sons."

Alexander did. Dashing and commanding, he was known and admired in all the Rothschild colonies. He had the Aaronsohn aura. Hostility to the Left was in his blood. There wasn't a better potential Duce.

He cut a splendid figure on the day Mary Fels arrived in Palestine. On hand to greet her with the Sons of Benjamin when she stepped off the train that brought her from Egypt, he was, Ben-Avi wrote, "dressed as a Muslim sheikh, a sword on his hip…. This handsome young man, a brown cloak on his lean body and a gold circlet on his proudly worn Arab headdress, looked like a true Oriental prince. We all felt sure that his exotic gallantry would sweep Mrs. Fels off her feet and bring about the fulfillment of our hopes."

There followed the *fantaziyya* that Moshe Shatzman had told me about. "A squadron of horsemen from the Sons of Benjamin performed on their noble steeds," Ben-Avi wrote, "while our 'sheikh' viewed their perfectly executed maneuvers with our guest of honor."

Moshe Shatzman remembered it differently.

"An opera! Alexander lined us up in columns, and the train stopped, and out climbed a dumpy little woman in a funny hat, and he stepped up to her and kissed her hand as if she were the queen of England. Then he gave a signal and we all shouted 'Long live Alexander!' 'Long live Mary Fels!' and fired our rifles and galloped around."

From the train station they proceeded to Petach-Tikva, where The Sons of Benjamin held its first gala convention. On the second day, following a lecture on the Single Tax, Mary Fels announced her intention of purchasing ten thousands dunams of land near Hadera for a new settlement of private farmers. It would be called Josephia in memory of her husband. "The excitement was boundless," Ben-Avi wrote. "The hundreds assembled let out deafening cheers. The convention broke up with a *hora* that was danced until dawn. Mary Fels gaily joined the circle while Alexander whirled in the middle of it, flashing his Bedouin sword."

* * *

The Zayta lands were bought with Mary Fels' money. Then no more was heard of them.

"Alexander double-crossed us," Ben-Hayyim said. "He secretly registered the land in Tova Gelberg's name. They divvied it up, Tova, Rutman, Alex, and Rivka. The farmers never got any of it."

It was Rutman who dealt with the Zayta landowners. He and Alexander were "thick as thieves." The transaction was complicated. There were legal difficulties. Sentiments, too. "It was Tova's dowry," Ben-Hayyim said darkly.

Moshe Shatzman was more forgiving. Alexander, he said, had had "a moment of weakness." You could blame his enemies for that. "They hounded him from public life. They made him feel it was himself against the world."

Yet Shatzman's memory had turned things around. The "moment of weakness" came first; Alexander's abandonment of public life later. Between the two, Yanko Epstein went to jail.

* * *

"What?" Epstein asked me one day. "I never told you how I beat the crap out of Sam Aaronsohn?"

Sam was the black sheep of the Aaronsohn family. He had kept aloof from the Nili ring, didn't get along with his brothers and sisters, and was known in town as a ne'er-do-well.

"I was talking one day with Yosef Davidesco and Itzik Leibowitz when someone came up to me and said, 'Yanko, Sam Aaronsohn is in front of the synagogue, badmouthing you to a crowd of people. He says it was you who broke into the Sons of Benjamin.'"

The organization had an office in Zichron, in a shack behind the pharmacy. One night it was broken into and all its records were stolen. The village was in an uproar. The break-in was assumed to have to do with the Zayta lands. For months there had been rumors of underhandedness. The thousands of dunams promised by Mary Fels hadn't materialized. Alexander denied having received any money for them. Zichron was split between his supporters and his opponents.

"They walked with me to the synagogue. Sam was talking to a circle of people. I pushed my way into it and kicked him." He flicked a leg to show me how he had aimed for Sam Aaronsohn's groin. "Then I knocked him down and stomped on him. As soon as I stopped to catch my breath, he got up and ran away. 'Yanko,' Davidesco said, 'you let him off too easy.' 'Any harder and I'd have hanged for murder,' I said."

The three men were arrested and jailed in Haifa. A few days later they were brought before Governor Anders. "He handed us a piece of paper and said he'd release us on our recognizance if we pleaded guilty. 'We're not signing,' Davidesco says to me in Hebrew – and in English he says, 'Governor Anders, sir, I need to talk this over with my parents.' His mother was dead and he didn't speak to his father, but the governor let us go and ordered us to come back the next morning. We went home and told the village council that unless the charges were dropped, we'd light out across the Jordan and become outlaws." *

"Who broke into the office?"

He grinned. "That's a military secret."

I found, in August 1924, the minutes of the council's meetings dealing with the three men's arrest. It had nothing to do with Sam Aaronsohn. It had to do with the stolen records containing a document that

Alexander wanted to get back. In a council session held on August 24, the night of the arrestees' release from jail, Sons of Benjamin member Ya'akov Ben-Tsvi, appearing on the organization's behalf, expressed a wish to "restore quiet to the village" but stated that, "Nothing could be done before Mr. Davidesco returned to Alexander Aaronsohn the letter of Mr. Aaronsohn's that had come into Mr. Davidesco's possession and that he was threatening to show to outsiders – an act that could prove 'highly damaging.'" A heated argument followed:

Councilman Karniel: "Why didn't the Sons of Benjamin seek to restore quiet from the start instead of filing a complaint in Haifa against Davidesco, Epstein, and Leibowitz?"

Mr. Ben-Tsvi: "Why didn't the village council take immediate action when the organization's records were stolen from its office?"

Mr. Karniel: "It's easy to criticize others. Why are the Sons of Benjamin even now not restraining members from continuing to stir up feelings in the village?"

Mr. Ben-Tsvi: "I repeat my demand that Mr. Davidesco hand over the letter."

Councilman Schechter: "And I repeat my conviction that it was the Sons of Benjamin who instigated the false charges against Davidesco, Epstein, and Leibowitz."

Councilman Sternberg: "I accuse the council of standing idly by while Mr. Davidesco launched wild attacks on the Sons of Benjamin and its leader...."

Councilman Goldstein: "During the war, too, the council was accused of standing idly by and letting a spy ring operate in the village...."

Councilman Neiderman (to Messrs. Ben-Tsvi and Sternberg): "Before my last trip to India, I tried privately to make peace between the young people, and perhaps I would have succeeded if my departure had not cut short my efforts. Back then Epstein was your good friend, and when the council took him to task for not properly fulfilling his duties as a field guard, you all stood behind him. Yosef Davidesco was your good friend, too. Now he is suddenly your enemy...."

Councilman Lerner: "The council is being accused of not obtaining a letter from Davidesco. But even now the council has no idea what this letter is!"

Councilman Sternberg: "I wish to call the council's attention to the fact that there are eavesdroppers outside the door."

Councilman Goldstein: "Jewish law says you do not comfort a mourner while his dead are before him. The young men have just been released from jail and have not yet stood trial. It's too early to talk about reconciliation. Let's continue this another time."

"Councilman Sternberg," the minutes ended, "moved to terminate the discussion and it was agreed to proceed to other matters."

The council never took up the matter again because the three accused men returned to Haifa the next day with Councilman Neiderman, who posted bail for them. Subsequently, the charges were dropped.

The incriminating letter found its way to Yosef Sapir, head of the Sons of Benjamin's southern district. The timing was perfect. At the organization's second convention, held the last week of August, Sapir accused Alexander in an angry speech of stealing the Zayta land. Alexander left the hall in a huff and resigned as president of the organization – whose members, he declared, were unworthy of the land because they had shirked their political mission and cared only for themselves. For several weeks he sulked in Zichron, surrounding the Aaronsohn property with a wall of straw mats to express his displeasure. Then he sailed for New York and Mary Fels.

* * *

Mary stood by Alexander. She was in love with him and they had grandiose plans, next to which Palestine and its politics paled. In New York they were visited by Itamar Ben-Avi, who wrote this remarkable account:

"Upon arriving in New York, I began to notice strange things happening to my friend Alexander Aaronsohn. He brought me to the home of Mary Fels, who had fallen completely under his spell. Mrs. Fels, whose guide, secretary, and companion I had been in Palestine, took me around her apartment and showed me the photographs of her dream man in every room and on every wall and table: now in his army uniform, now as a Bedouin sheikh, an English athlete, a theater director. Above all, she wanted me to see his bathroom – which, done in red marble, was the sanctuary of 'my adorable Zichronite,' as she liked to refer to him.

"'He is my Jesus,' she said to me one day from the couch on which she was sitting in an exquisite dress by the side of her Irish-German maid.

"I tried making light of the remark, but she went on:

"'Would you like to be his Paul?'

"'No, my dear lady,' I replied. 'I'm not prepared to be anyone's evangelist, not even my friend Alexander's.'

"'You're making a mistake,' she said. 'You have no idea what you'll be losing, both materially and spiritually. I've decided from now on to spend not only my entire life in his delightful company, but my entire fortune on the world movement he soon will found…. Alexander will be the Jewish Krishnamurti and I will be his official patron. Have you considered' – she laid her hand on mine – 'that my name is Mary, the same as the mother of Christ's, and that my late husband's name was Joseph? Isn't that curious? We had no children. My only, my omnipotent son is Alexander – a Galilean by birth, too.'"

"As she spoke, I stared at her glazed eyes as though at someone temporarily deranged. But when I mentioned this that same day to Alexander, sure he would be astounded, he burst into laughter and replied:

"'Why pretend? Far be it from me to think of myself as "God-summoned," at least for the moment. But the time has come for a great inner revolution. I hear a voice calling to me from the depths and the heights at once – those of an ailing humanity and a vigorous Divinity. Why should we bother, Ben-Avi, with a wretched, nitpicking thing like a newspaper? Here you are in New York, with Mrs. Fels' bankbook at your as well as my disposal. She has millions, tens of millions! Let's use them for the creation of a new movement that will conquer the world…. I'll follow in the footsteps of Bar-Kochba and raise high the banner of Judean freedom in all its pristine religiosity, a blend of the best in Judaism, Islam, and Christianity – and you, why not make yourself a modern Jewish master, a second Rabbi Akiva? We'll have the world at our feet!'

"Thus spake Alexander, not from the hilltops of Nazareth or the shores of the blue Sea of Galilee, but from the fourteenth floor of the Ansonia Hotel, while the lights of the great metropolis winked bewitchingly outside the window with their millions of eyes. I stood and gaped at him, bewildered and at a loss. Could this be my old friend, the idol of so many young men and women from the foothills of Lebanon to the

Negev, the brother of the great and tragically short-lived Jewish scientist Aaron Aaronsohn – or were his words those of a man driven mad by a windfall of imagined wealth?

"I felt the ground give way beneath me. My head began to spin – and I passed out.

"When I came to, Alex was bending over me and murmuring in my ear:

"'Wake up, Ben-Avi! We have only to will it – and, with the help of our friend Mary, the world is ours.'

"I was still trying to recover from my shock when a clock on a distant tower struck twelve.

"'Rubbish!' Alex exclaimed suddenly. 'It's all rubbish! Look at those streets down below, at all the traffic, the men and women, the lust for life pulsing in them all! The only life is the life of pleasure. Come, let's throw ourselves into it! There are so many lovely girls.... We're both young and our lives are still ahead of us....'

"I had no idea what I was in for. Alexander's leap, within a space of seconds, from the ecstatic pinnacles of a modern religious renaissance to the abyss of debauchery had left me aghast. In agreeing to accompany him to the street, my only desire was to get away and to do it as quickly as possible....

"And yet our old ties, as well as my curiosity and journalist's passion to observe, cajoled me into witnessing what this mercurial man, in whom I had had so much faith, was capable of. I wanted to see it with my own eyes.

"What I saw that night surpassed all imagination.

"I went with him from one girl's house to another. Some were high-society debutantes, thoroughly enslaved to their master and his lashes. It was one of the strangest spectacles that human life – the life of the human animal – could have to offer. When I finally parted from him and returned to my hotel in the wee hours of the morning, I couldn't sleep...."

Ben-Avi rose from his bed and wrote Alexander a letter, dated December 11, 1924, in which he severed all links with him. "You and I must part forever," he wrote. They never spoke to each other again.

For a while, the Sons of Benjamin continued to contest the Zayta lands. The organization's general secretary, Oded Ben-Ami, appealed to Mary Fels in writing. She answered curtly:

"We must go our separate ways.... You have blindly sold out your members by seeking to destroy Alexander Aaronsohn instead of combating the National Executive Council and the Zionist Organization as he wished you to."

There were legal suits and court cases, but the Zayta lands were lost. Alexander's career as a latter-day Savior was never launched. He and Mary Fels lived together in New York and then moved to France, where their relationship continued. What kept him with a "dumpy little woman" twenty-five years older than himself did not seem a mystery in Zichron. "He wanted her money," Ben-Hayyim said. "She wanted his dick."

Perhaps it was that simple. Yet reading Mary's biography of her husband, *Joseph Fels: His Life and Work*, written after Joseph's death and before meeting Alex, I was struck by a passage in it – one of the few in which she spoke of herself:

"One day in the year 1873, Joseph Fels, then age twenty, while pursuing his work as a traveling salesman, found himself in the little town of Keokuk, Iowa. During casual conversation with one of his customers, mention was made of the fact that there was in the same town another family of the name of Fels. As Joseph had thought that he had no relatives in America beyond his immediate family, the circumstance struck him as so unusual that he felt interested to seek them out and make their acquaintance. This acquaintance was renewed on each succeeding visit to the town.

"Upon his approach to the house at his very first call, his attention was attracted by a little girl of nine standing in the doorway, who confidently ushered this stranger into the home of her parents.

"Mr. Fels loved in after years to tell how, at that moment, he felt this child was destined for him and that no sacrifice would be too great to win her and make her his wife. This resolve grew into a devotion which continued unabated for the next nine years.

"In his attitude as elder brother and his solicitude to assist in her development, there lay a dormant romanticism which ripened into a love and companionship of rare tenderness and mutual inspiration. They were married in the year 1881.

"In July of 1884 a son was born to Mr. and Mrs. Fels, but in December of the same year the baby fell ill and died. It was naturally a serious blow, as Mr. Fels had a passion for children, but this misfortune was a significant turning point in the lives of both. To fill the gap caused by the loss of the child, Mrs. Fels occupied herself with social activities and intellectual pursuits. In this way the home, which had hitherto been consecrated to domestic ideals and business interests, became a center of intelligence and progressive ideas."

Was it only money for sex, then? And the symbolic incest of same-name marriage? The little girl wed to the man with a "passion for children" who loved her like an elder brother and the elder brother who loved little girls? The son lost to his mother in America in 1884 and reborn in Palestine in 1888? The dowager queen and the gigolo prince?

There were hidden channels, wormholes, that ran between lives. They followed strange inversions, parallel lines that met, fates that reproduced themselves on each other like strands of DNA and RNA. Immortal myths of forbidden longing and impossible fulfillment – Isis and Osiris, Ishtar and Tammuz, the Holy Family – turned rancid in ordinary flesh and blood.

Without Alexander, the nativist "fascist" party failed to get off the ground. Jabotinsky and his Revisionists formed the right-wing opposition. Yet Jabotinsky spent little time in Palestine, from which he was permanently barred in 1930 by a British edict. His main base was Eastern Europe, in the teeming ghettoes of Warsaw, Lublin, and Lodz, whose Jews clamored for the visas to Palestine that "perfidious Albion," as he called England, denied them while reneging on its Balfour Declaration commitments. In places like Zichron, the Right remained without a leader. Alexander died in France in 1946.

* * *

"Oh, those Zayta lands!" Rivka Aaronsohn hadn't touched her tea or cake. "All those trials that went on and on! Alex only wanted to help. But they had to bring in their politics, all that wheeling and dealing. He hated that...."

Her brother loved nature, solitude. So did she. She couldn't understand how anyone lived in cities, away from the soil, from birds and trees. "Do you know your birds?" she asked as if for a password to assure her that we belonged to the same secret society.

We walked back across the gravel courtyard in the fading light and stood by the gate. "I've disappointed you," she said.

"Not at all. Why – "

"No, no, I have!" She knew it. It was always like that. She hadn't told me the things I wanted to hear. She had talked too much and never to the point. I shouldn't have let her go on. She needed to be stopped, to be asked precise questions....

"It isn't easy to interview a historic figure. Or to be one," I said. You didn't put your arm around one and give it a comforting hug.

She agreed with a small suck of her breath, an inhaled French *oui* from her visits to Paris.

From a treetop came the last, wistful notes of a bulbul. They sounded again and fell silent, like taps.

"I've always loved the night," she said. "That's when I'm most awake."

There were stories in Zichron of her dancing in the gravel courtyard, ghostlike, in the moonlight. A sadness hung in the air, a decree of unfulfilled expectations.

Chapter fourteen

Nisan Rutman's *brother* married Perl Appelbaum's *daughter?*"

"Yes," Ora Rosenzweig said. She wetted the clay she was modeling with a finger dipped in a bowl of cloudy water. The Appelbaums had four children, two sons who were no longer alive and two daughters. The elder daughter, now in a geriatric home and senile, was married to a man from Binyamina. "Her sister married Haim Rutman. They live in Hadera."

Epstein, in telling me Nisan Rutman left behind a brother, had failed to mention this.

An improbable couple: the brother of the man whose hiding place was betrayed and the daughter of his betrayer!

I had been thinking about that man. Alexander Aaronsohn would not have carried out Sarah's plea for vengeance with his own hands. He wasn't the type to dirty them.

Alexander would have looked for a henchman. Nisan Rutman fit the bill. He had his own score to settle with Perl Appelbaum – and his Tova Gelberg's parents lived next door.

This last point was crucial. Not long after my tea with Rivka Aaronsohn, I came across a headline in the back pages of the newspaper that said, "Man, Died Half-Year Ago, Suspected Poison Victim." The story related:

"The police have reason to believe that Ya'akov Solomon, 36, of Kiryat Shalom, who died half a year ago, was poisoned by his wife with the help of a neighbor.

"The neighbor, Natan Baranes, was arraigned yesterday in Tel Aviv District Court. Half a year ago, a police official testified, Solomon died of complications reported by his wife to have been caused by encephalitis. The police did not investigate the case because there were no grounds for suspicion. Several months ago, however, information came to their attention incriminating the accused in Solomon's death. A check of the deceased's medical file revealed symptoms more characteristic of poisoning than of encephalitis."

I asked our family doctor if he knew of poisons capable of causing an encephalitis-like death. "Lots," he said. "Any number of alkaloids could do it. Nicotine, morphine, cocaine, quinine – all have similar properties. There's a plant growing wild around here called Golden Drunkedness because of its extreme muscle-relaxing and narcoleptic effects. The trick would be to mix small doses into something hiding the taste, like sugar or honey, so as to produce worsening symptoms over time."

Golden Drunkedness, or *Hyoscyamus aureus*, was listed in the copy of Aaron Aaronsohn's *Florula Cisiordanica* that I had found in Alexander's pavilion. Aaron had collected it for his herbarium from several Palestinian locations, including a specimen picked near Crocodile Creek in January 1906. Someone with easy access only had to sneak several times into Perl Appelbaum's kitchen with the alkaloid of Alexander's choice.

Ora shook her head at the tassels of the fez she was working on. "I can't get them to fall right," she fretted. The man wearing the fez was holding a clay basket. "It's for his whirligigs," she explained. "I'll make them when I finish him."

The whirligig man appeared from time to time with his bright toys. The child with two Palestinian mils in his pocket could buy one. Held by its handle, the sturdy stem of a weed, it spun in the wind. If his stock ran out, the whirligig man sat down on the ground, took colored paper, scissors, wire, and glue from his basket, and made more.

Alongside its jams and preserves, Ora's pantry was filling up with clay figures of types remembered from her childhood. Zeydl the green-grocer. Azar the shoemaker. The itinerant gypsy and his dancing bear. She was working on them constantly now. As if word had gotten out that here was a woman who turned away no one, they came flocking to her door, clamoring to be released from the indignity of oblivion, bringing with them their implements, animals, work tools, and accessories, the benches, stools, bowls, jars, pitchers, baskets, and basins that their maker, they were sure, would find room for too. "What a good soul Zeydl was!" Ora exclaimed as if that were her reason for taking him in. "He was our post office. He took the mail to Haifa when he rode his donkey there for fresh produce and came back with the mail that arrived."

Zeydl had a contented smile. So did all of Ora's sculptures. Refugees from the persecutions of Time, they gathered on her shelves, each week welcoming a new arrival, such as Mr. Shababo the schoolteacher, Yafia Cohen's father, standing by his desk with a ruler in his hands, or Sukkar Amba, the Arab peppermint candy vendor with his striped, sticky sweets. Each day more and more of them knocked on her door and the lines outside it grew longer.

*   *   *

At the top of the stairs to the agricultural store, the last building before the winery at the bottom of Benefactor Street, I spotted Ben-Hayyim and Epstein. Arms folded on their chests, they flanked the entrance like the stone lions of a museum. As I started up the stairs, the lion on the left started down, tipping his hat to Epstein and me.

"Ben-Hayyim and I had important business," Epstein said without volunteering its nature. He liked to sound mysterious.

I bought the grafting tape I had come for and walked him up the street into town. On the corner of Wine Street, across from the Rosenz-weigs', he stopped by the cellar of an old house, its entrance blocked by a heap of rubbish. I had once tried exploring it, only to be turned back by a solid wall of old cartons, planks and boards, empty paint buckets, broken furniture, rusted bedsprings, and the wheels of bicycles and baby carriages.

"That's where Fidi and her husband Fu'ad lived," he said.

Fidi was the bridesmaid he had snatched the flag from at the wedding of Mustafa, the brother of Alya.

"I'll tell you," he continued as we started up the street again, "how Fu'ad went to jail for stealing Fidi's dress to give to Fidi."

The first posters for the approaching national elections were plastered on the billboards along the street, covering older ads and notices. Each with the identifying letters of its party as they would appear on the ballot – EMeT for Labor, GaHaL for the Likud, DaSH for a new reform ticket – they resembled giant flash cards in a reading drill.

"Fu'ad was the foreman of Fauzi Bek's farm and slept there much of the time. That was fine with Fidi, because she and I had the cellar to ourselves while her husband was away. She didn't know he was carrying on with a married woman himself, a Bedouin. And no one knew about her and me, because I came after finishing my rounds, when the rest of the town was asleep. She'd leave me a signal outside her door to let me know when Fu'ad wasn't home.

"Fidi owned two dresses, a plain, everyday one and an embroidered one, kept in a chest, that Fu'ad had given her. One day the embroidered dress was stolen. Although Fidi didn't suspect Fu'ad of being the thief, he was. His Bedouin woman had complained that he would give her a dress, too, if he loved her, and since he didn't have the money for a second one, he took Fidi's and pretended to have bought it for her.

"Well, time goes by and Fidi is out walking in Zichron and sees the woman in her dress. She's doesn't make a scene, because she knows she can't prove it's hers. She waits for me to come that night and tells me about it.

"'You're sure the dress is yours?' I asked. 'Of course,' she says. 'I know the pattern of the embroidery.' 'Then all you have to do,' I say, 'is go to that woman's tent when she's away and take it back. It's your property.'

"I told her where the tent was and Fidi went and stole her dress back. Now it was Fu'ad and his woman who didn't know what had happened to it. They had no idea it was back in Fidi's chest until one day she stepped out in it. And who should be passing by just then but Fu'ad's woman!

"'Thief! That's my dress!' says the woman. 'You're the thief! It's mine!' Fidi says. Pretty soon they've torn off each other's kerchiefs and are pulling out each other's hair. Someone goes to get the police and a British sergeant hauls them off to the stationhouse.

"Fu'ad doesn't know what to do. His wife and his woman are both locked up. Neither knows the real thief was him, but they'll find out when they tell the police their story – and he's in trouble when they do. He comes to ask my advice – and I'm in trouble, too. If Fidi says I told her to take the dress, Fu'ad will blame me for it.

"I have to think fast. 'Look, Fu'ad,' I say, 'one way or another, the police will find out you stole the dress. But if you say you stole it from Fidi to give to your woman, Fidi will know you cheated on her.'

"'Then who did I steal it from?' he asks.

"'From your woman,' I say. 'To give to Fidi.'

"'But it is Fidi's,' he says.

"'*Ya* Fu'ad,' I say, 'use your head. You'll tell the police you saw a fine dress on that woman and stole it as a present for your wife. That way you protect a married woman's honor, Fidi thinks you're a good husband, and I'll see to it you get a light sentence.'

"That's just what happened. I talked to my policeman friend Kalman Radin, and Fu'ad pleaded guilty to stealing Fidi's dress and got thirty days."

"But then the dress would have been awarded to the woman," I objected. We had reached the post office and Epstein had taken out his mailbox key.

"It was. And who do you think was waiting for her when she walked out of the police station with it under her arm? I told her the truth and I said, 'And now give Fidi her dress back if you don't want your husband to know the truth, too.' She handed it over on the spot. That's why Fidi lowered the flag for me."

He had to stand on tiptoe to reach his mailbox. There was a single letter in it. He opened and read it silently in my presence, a grin spreading over his face. "Here," he said, giving it to me to read too. "What do you make of this?"

Written with a fountain pen on blue stationery, it said:

Dear Mr. Epstein,

I'm sure you remember me, although we have not met for

quite some time. I am the daughter of Perl and Avigdor Appelbaum, the youngest one, Rivka. My older sister is Leah.

I'm writing to you because your name was mentioned to me in a telephone conversation by a man who said he was doing historical research on Zichron and would like to speak to me about my family. He said he was your friend.

I'm writing to ask if this is true. I don't mind talking to this person if you recommend him. Please let me know if you do.

Sincerely,

Rivka Rutman.

Damn! It had never occurred to me that she might get in touch with him.

"Well?" he asked.

I stood holding the letter.

"Perl wasn't with the other three."

"I know," I said. "You've told me that."

"Then what is it you want from Rivka Rutman?"

"In Sarah's farewell letter, Perl is accused of informing on the Nili ring. I thought her daughter might know something about it."

"There were no informers in Zichron. The only one to blab was Na'aman Belkind."

"You've told me that, too."

"Sarah heard the Turks talk about Perl helping to find Rutman. That's all she was referring to."

"That doesn't square with what she wrote."

He cut short the argument:

"What shall I tell *madame*?"

"Tell her I'm your friend."

He took back the letter, slipped it into the breast pocket of his jacket, and patted it to let me know that the matter was under consideration.

*   *   *

Yellow mustard. Gold chrysanthemums. The purple gloves of the hollyhocks, climbing hand over hand. White parasols of Queen Anne's lace so high you looked up at them from below. Sky-blue chicory. Slim candlewick. The whiskered filaments of the caper blossoms that bloomed and wilted in a day, their lives a sunrise and a sunset. Like constellations of the zodiac they swept the earth, bringing summer, tolling its passage.

Talya and I watched the harvester ants at work. Each day they reaped in wider circles around their nests, bringing the harvest to its underground silos, to which they descended on ladders of dry stems. If one stumbled behind its load, another came to its aid, pulling while the other pushed so that their cargo jerked along like a boxcar between two locomotives. Skins of chaff lay scattered on their threshing floors.

So summers had once passed in the "Burj," the big yard with its fortress-like enclosure near Binyamina where the farmers had worked together. Farming was not all orchards and vineyards then, the way it was now, the fruit packed into crates and brought to market or the winery. It was grain, pulses, a household's daily bread. Wheat, barley, and sorghum for flour; chickpeas and sesame for *hummus* and *tehina* paste; beans and lentils; hay, vetch, and lupine for fodder. In the days before the mechanized reaper, it took months to get in the field crops. The work began after Passover with the cutting of the barley and ended with the sesame that was flailed in late September, its yellowed branches knocked together until the tiny seeds dropped from their pods. Under the sun and stars the farmers worked, rested, ate, and slept; cut and baled the grain; pitched it onto wagons and drove it to the threshing floor; pitched it off again; threshed, winnowed, and piled it in three stacks, one of kernels, one of fine straw, one of rough; re-divided the first stack into eight.

When the harvest was done, the Turkish tax collector chose one of the eight. Every evening he stamped the rising mounds of winnowed grain with a wooden seal, printing on them the words *barakat Allah,* "the blessing of the Lord." At night a guard slept on the threshing floor, the seal beneath his pillow. In the morning, he checked to see that Allah's blessing was still there.

It was a work space, the Burj; a clubhouse; a place for the young men to flirt with the Arab girls who came to glean after the reapers; an amusement park for the children who pushed each other off the piles of grain, laughing as they tumbled into the beds of straw, their hair full of prickly wheat. Sometimes they were allowed to climb aboard the threshing sled, take hold of the reins, and ride in bumpy circles. The sled was pulled by an ox, horse, or mule and inlaid with sharp stones that popped the kernels from their husks and crushed the stalks. It circled the growing crown of them as though following the brim of a sombrero.

Moshe Shatzman had liked it all: plowing the long, double furrows; sowing both at once, his arm swinging like a pendulum; leaning into the ripened stalks with a sickle, one hand seizing them below their spiky ears while the other hand flicked the blade low. He had especially liked the hard parts – straining every muscle to heave the bales onto the high-wheeled wagons, or sowing the sesame in spring. The seeds were planted close to the surface to allow them to sprout through the heavy soil, with which they were covered at once before its last moisture dried out. You had to prod the oxen quickly along to prevent the plow from cutting too deep while exerting an even pressure on the handle to keep it from jumping, maintaining a steady flow of seed through a funnel-like container, and brushing the upturned earth back into place with a rake that moved behind you like a tiller. It took strength and coordination.

The one thing he didn't like were the first minutes of winnowing each day, when the morning sea breeze began to blow. The gnats that had settled in the threshed grain overnight rose in great swarms when you tossed a forkful in the air. Not even the *keffiyeh* you wrapped around your head could keep them out of your hair.

"Say!" said Moshe Shatzman.

He grabbed me so hard that I jumped back in alarm. "Does this old man have a memory! How many years is it? Sixty. No, seventy! I was walking with an Arab field hand in this exact spot when he jumped in the air about ten times higher than you just did. 'What's the matter?' I asked. 'I nearly stepped on a snake,' he said. It's funny how you remember such things."

We were crossing a field of young trees on our way to the Burj. Shatzman hadn't been back to it in years. "Avocados!" he said of the trees. "In my day no one had heard of them."

Three boys were in the field. Two were emptying sacks of fertilizer at the base of the trees and spreading their contents with hoes. The third sat watching them. He looked about eleven or twelve. Shatzman asked:

"These are Eli Goldstein's trees, aren't they?"

"Yes," the boy said. "I'm his son."

"Well, tell him Moshe Shatzman sends regards. And don't work your Arab field hands too hard."

Not much remained of the Burj. The two-story wings of the yard were crumbling. Shatzman was disappointed to find little left of his old barn. Its flat roof, on which he had slept on the hot summer nights, had collapsed and wild blackberry canes covered most of it. "I thought there'd be more to show you," he said. He went over to inspect something. "Well!" he said, brightening. "Look at that."

He ran a finger along a gray line of grouting.

"This is my work. I put these stones back in place after Fauzi Bek's men stole our ox."

Fauzi Bek's farm had been nearby. One night some of his workers broke through the wall and made off with the Shatzmans' best ox. The family complained and Fauzi returned it.

"He had a big farm. After he died, his wife needed help. Ben-Hayyim and I went partners with her."

"The two of you and Epstein," I said.

He swiveled a wrist.

I recounted Epstein's story of Faida Bek.

Shatzman knew of their affair. "He tried hiding it, but it wasn't any secret. He was afraid we'd want to go halves in that, too."

He gave a merry yip, then stiffened like a pointer and said:

"Say! Up there – " he pointed to the Nose of the Carmel above us, half-eaten by a quarry – "was a Bedouin tribe that sent its cows down to graze in our fields. One night we decided to teach them a lesson. There were four of us: myself, Lulik Berkovitz, Davidesco, and Dov Leitner. We took our rifles and opened fire and killed some cows.

"In the morning we rode to Caesaria to see the governor. The Bedouin were already there. We told our story and put a pot of honey on the table. Ahmed Bek went to the next room and shouted at the Bedouin, 'You're liars, every one of you! Get out of here with your tall tales!' How's that for Turkish justice?"

The nose of the Carmel looked eaten by leprosy.

"Listen!" He was reminded of something else. "This happened the same year. I even remember the day of the week. It was a Saturday night. My brother and I relieved each other then; we each spent a week here and a week at home. The grain was nearly ripe and we slept in the fields to guard it. It was white sorghum. That was all the Turks and the locusts had left us. You couldn't get wheat seed at all.

"I rode straight to the field to tell my brother I had come. It was over there, where you see those orange trees. I planted them in the thirties.

"My brother wasn't in the field. But I noticed that some stalks had been cut and that there was blood on the stubble.

"I ran back to the Burj to look for him. In the end I found him without a scratch. Thieves had come the night before to harvest the grain, and he had shot at them and wounded one of them.

"Later, we found out who it was. He was a big black fellow. I even hired him as a field guard. There's an Arab saying that if you want a good watchman – "

" – take the thief from the hangman's rope," I said.

The black field guard made him think of Sa'id el-Bukei'i, the murderer of Benjamin Kruppik who fled across the Jordan and was sentenced to fifteen years in prison after being caught by Yosef Davidesco. From there he jumped to Rashid el-Ahzawi, the Bedouin sheikh in whose tent Davidesco had stayed; then to Hamid Abu-Warda, Sa'id el-Bukei'i's sidekick who broke a leg trying to escape from jail on a knotted sheet; and back again to el-Bukei'i, with whom Davidesco had another encounter after his release from prison, at a *sulha* in Pardes-Hanna.

"The *sulha* for Badrak."

"For who?"

"The young man from Poland who killed a Bedouin."

"Was that his name? Imagine! I was there and you remember it. Davidesco brought a group of us. I had never been to a *sulha*. We formed a circle around that fellow and they charged. Sa'id el-Bukei'i was a cousin of the dead man's. He came at us with a sword. Davidesco was half his size, but he grabbed him and held him tight. I'll never forget it: the murderer wrestling with the man who jailed him!"

Shatzman remembered another black Bedouin, who killed his own sister. Everyone thought it was an accident until he and Ben-Hayyim were sitting one day in the family tent. "The brother and his mother began to quarrel. She got so mad that she forgot all about us and shouted, 'You'll see! God will pay you back for what you did to your sister.'"

"What falls from heaven lands on earth," I said. "It was Mustafa, the son of Ahmed Ali."

He did a double take. "Who told you that? Ben-Hayyim?"

"No."

"Epstein?"

"Yes."

"But he couldn't have! No one knew but Ben-Hayyim and me. We agreed to keep it a secret. There was an investigation. There would have been a trial if we talked."

"Well," I said, "Epstein knew all about it. He was at the autopsy Dr. Cohen performed on Alya."

"Alya?"

"Mustafa's sister."

Two crinkles formed in the corners of his lips.

"That was how the family found out she was a virgin. She wasn't pregnant as Mustafa had thought."

The crinkles ran to join each other. Moshe Shatzman threw back his head and laughed. He laughed until he cackled like a chicken. He put a thumb on each shoulder and wagged his fingers like wings. "Lord Cock-and-Bull!" he crowed. "It wasn't Alya who was killed. Alya is still alive. It was Dibi! Mustafa hit her and killed her."

"It was Dibi!" The fingers, peacock's feathers on a rooster, wagged so hard that he seemed about to fly. "Her husband, Abdel-Halim, was my field hand. I was in their tent all the time. He died young and Dibi was left a widow."

Alya was Dibi's younger sister. She never married and was still alive, as far as Shatzman knew, in a refugee camp near Tulkarm. He had seen her there a few years ago.

"I suppose Epstein confused their names," I said. I felt like a lawyer who, though having lost all faith in his client, still feels obliged to defend him.

"Confused? You bet he is! Lord Cock-and-Bull! Dibi was a young widow with children. Alya is alive to this day."

He grabbed my shirt. "Say! Let's go visit her."
He would have set out on the spot had I agreed.

*   *   *

So it wasn't just the odd stretch. Yanko Epstein was a liar.

Not an ordinary one. He didn't fabricate his stories. He stole them.

A plagiarist, then.

Or perhaps, as Ze'ev Neiderman had called him, an artist. He improved on things.

What he stole had no intrinsic worth. The added value was his. He took what he heard and reworked it, adding detail, color, weaving different accounts into one. He had a gift that he felt compelled to use. He could not listen to a dry description of the shooting of Bedouin cows, or the killing of a woman by her brother, without itching to get his hands on it. The things that could be done with it – the opportunities for development, embellishment, reversal, surprise! *No one cared about a massacre of cows?* Then make it one cow instead of many; and give her a calf for bovine interest; and let her die in a comic accident; and add suspense with a race to the governor. *It was the widow Dibi who was killed by her brother?* But there was nothing romantic about a widow. It should have been her sister Alya – and she should have been as young and proud and provocatively beautiful and unexpectedly chaste as he imagined her. If life hadn't gotten it right, it was the storyteller's job to do better.

He put himself at the center of everything. Like counterfeit checks, all his stories were made out in his name. But what novelist didn't do the same, if not by means of the three characters called "I," "he," and "she," those alter egos dispatched with forged papers into the pages of books, then by the very act of narrative – at the back of which, no matter whom it was about, stood an author stealing the show like the joker making donkey ears in a photograph?

His imagination was more combinatory than inventive. He stripped other tales for their parts. Most probably he knew or had heard of a fire lit under a cow, a horseman fatally caught in the stirrups. He might have walked around with such pieces for years before finding the place for them.

I would never know where most of these came from or their proportions of falsehood to truth. It was only by chance that I sometimes found out. His story of deserting the Turkish army, for example. From talking to Rivka Leitner, Micha Rosenzweig's aunt and the widow of Epstein's old friend Dov Leitner, I learned that it really had happened – to Leitner. Dov belonged to the group of volunteers for the Turkish army organized by Alexander Aaronsohn. Aunt Rivka remembered their going-away party. The young folk sang and danced all night and walked the volunteers at dawn to the winery, where the Turkish transports were waiting. They were taken to boot camp and treated like galley slaves, even put into harness and made to pull wagons like mules. After a few days Dov deserted and walked back to Zichron. His father bribed the right people and he got through the war unmolested. Aunt Rivka had never heard of Amhamed Sa'id or the telegraph poles.

Back in Zichron, Dov Leitner ran errands for the Nili, carrying messages, opening and closing the shutters of the pavilion in the olive grove to signal the British freighter, driving spies in his wagon. Just before the ring was cracked, Sarah asked him to do her a big favor. "Dov," she said, taking his face in her hands, "it's all over." (Was it he, then, who took the abortive drive south that ended with bringing Lishansky to Atlit?) But it was not Sarah that Dov was in love with. "It was Alexander," Aunt Rivka said. "He would have done anything for him. I said, 'Dov, he sold you into the Turkish army and ran away to America,' but he didn't wake up until that business with Mrs. Fels."

She and Dov were out walking one night when they saw the woman in the park with the Turkish officer. The woman was a poor soul, in need of love. Her husband had left her and was living in Egypt, and she came from a home in which she was never given anything. Her father, _____, was mean-natured; though one of the better-off farmers, he refused to spend a cent on his children. Aunt Rivka remembered his wife coming to Mizrachi's general store with little cans of olive oil hidden beneath her dress that she sold to earn pocket money for them. "Oh, dear!" she blurted. "Now I've told you who that woman was!" She was so upset that she made me tear the page I was writing on from my notebook and hand it to her. She crumpled it and put it in her purse.

Aunt Rivka had worked in the general store, doing everything from operating the cash register to rolling cigarettes in a hand-turned machine. Among her customers at the time of the spies' arrests was one of Sarah's torturers – "a nice soldier," she recalled. It was his job to hold Sarah's legs while the soles of her feet were beaten with a rubber hose. "The beautiful lady," he called her.

Aunt Rivka saw everything from the store. She saw Sarah being led down the street, pulled by a chain. She did not hear the suicide shot, but she saw a horse-and-carriage take off at a gallop and return a moment later with Dr. Yoffe. She had never seen a carriage fly like that.

She saw the incident of the four women, too. That is, she saw two of them, Tsippora Lerner and Gita Blumenfeld, taunting Nisan Rutman. She did not have kind words for any of them. Adele Goldstein was "a nut case." Gita Blumenfeld was "like a top sergeant." Tsippora Lerner "wasn't fit to wipe her husband's shoes."

"And Perl Appelbaum?"

"There was nothing special about Perl."

"How did she die?"

"Something happened to her."

Perl sat on her front porch, drooling. Flies buzzed around her. That was all Aunt Rivka remembered.

* * *

I was chatting with Nissim Carditi in the library when Epstein walked in, mellow-mooded. He had something for the archives. He placed a thin, homebound notebook on the librarian's desk, across which was written: "Account Book and Minutes of the Hatikvah Athletic Association, 22/12/14."

"Read this," he said to me, turning pages to a paragraph that stated:

"On the 17th of Nisan the steering committee met to discuss the party on Saturday night. It was decided to charge each member of the association ½ metlik for refreshments. We were informed that Mrs. Wilder might give us a room for the party. Two members of the committee were asked to look into it...."

"And who," he said, "do you think the two members were? Itzik Leibowitz and yours truly."

It was the party, he declared, pleased to find it in the historical record, at which Arn Klarineter had failed to show up.

Nissim Carditi did not react with the same enthusiasm. He was frustrated. Aryeh Samsonov's widow had moved to Tel Aviv and was stymieing his efforts to locate the missing documents. Although she had met with him in her empty house in Zichron and let him go through her husband's desk, he had found only notes and scribblings in Samsonov's own hand. "She didn't offer to go down to the basement," he reported. "I told her the material could facilitate a revised edition of the book, but she didn't take the bait."

"Try putting money on it," Epstein said.

"I don't even have a budget for acquisitions."

"Well," he said, "Samsonov had some diaries of mine. I'd like them back."

Nissim limped off to help a reader.

"When were those diaries written?" I asked.

"I started them after the war."

"There's always the Sons of Benjamin method."

He gave me a probing glance. I had meant only to tease him, but he took me seriously. "Let's go have a look," he said.

"At what?"

"The Samsonov house. It has to be in that basement."

I walked with him out of the library and down the seaside slope of the hill.

The house in which Aryeh Samsonov had lived with his third wife was surrounded by a stone wall. Its gate was shut. "Wait here," I told Epstein. The stone had easy toeholds. I clambered over the top and down the other side.

I circled the house. It had two floors, the top one reached by an external staircase, with a basement on the uphill side. Its door was locked. Beside it was an unbarred window.

The windows on the ground floor, where Nissim had sat with Mrs. Samsonov, were shuttered with Venetian blinds. The top floor looked newly rented out. Laundry hung on a balcony.

Returning to my starting point, I found Epstein inside the stone wall. "You should have given the gate a push," he said dryly.

We walked back to the basement. He bent to examine the lock on the door. "It's a plain Yale," he said, "but you'd need steadier hands than mine to pick it. We'll have to go through the window."

"We can smash it," I agreed. I didn't ask where he had learned to pick locks.

"Smash it?" I amused him. "I'd use a putty knife. If you do it right, you can lift the pane right out."

But the family on the top floor was an unexpected complication. Even with a putty knife, there was no guarantee we wouldn't be heard. "I'm too old to go to jail again," he said.

We decided to think about it. The basement wouldn't run away.

*   *   *

We had a new daughter, Michal. Talya was cranky, resentful. I had to work to convince her that, at the age of three, the best years of her life weren't over.

One day we walked to the Bedouin shack in the hollow. Three little figures came running from the goat pen to greet us. Each had two legs and a coat of thick mud. Snatching Talya from my hand, they ran back to the pen with her. There they slipped and slid in the dark ooze, playing with the baby goats.

Their names, their mother told me, inviting me into the shack, were Walid, Ibtisam, and Iman. They were the only Arab family in Zichron.

The room was furnished with some chairs, a table, a television set powered by a generator, and a few mattresses stacked against a wall. I had never sat in an Arab home with an unaccompanied woman. It wasn't socially accepted. Nor was the easy familiarity with which she touched me lightly and begged me not to go. It was as if the window her eyes kept returning to, which framed a light-haired child gamboling with three dark ones, revealed possibilities, never glimpsed before, that she wished to partake of with me. She was long-lashed and good-looking in a lazy way, if you didn't mind her cheap perfume or the gold in her mouth. The skirt and blouse she wore formed a strange land around her, the heft of her spreading in the wrong places.

In the end, I took Talya home and washed her off with the garden hose. Then, the smell of muck and mutton still not purged from her, we drove to the beach.

An offshore breeze slapped at the water. The small bay of Tantura stirred beneath it. Out where the limestone reefs ran into the sea, three Arabs were fishing from a *hasaka,* a raft-like boat propelled by a long, double-bladed oar. Standing athwart it, a man dipped the oar in easy loops. He swung the craft in a slow circle while a second man knelt on the stern, feeding a net to the sea, and a third drummed on the prow to scare the mullets and breams from the rocks into open water. The drumming drifted over the sluggish waves like an ancient rite.

We walked by the wet sand at the water's edge, keeping clear of the tar line where the bilge of the big tankers had left a sticky black gum. The little fishing fleet of Faradis rested in the shallows, its outboard motors flipped out of the water, the iron octopuses of its anchors gripping sand. By the single stone house that was all that was left of the village of Tantura, a fisherman was unrolling his net.

We stopped to watch. You never knew what the nets would reveal. There might be checked folds of nothing, and then a fish, and more empty folds, and a plastic bag and some seaweed, or a little flurry of striped *saragus* or bearded *sultan ibrahim.* The catches were poor nowadays. They once had been better, the fisherman said.

"I guess we Jews spoiled even the fishing," I said. He had grizzled hair and heavy brows. The eyes were gray, the forehead broad.

"Don't take it personally," he answered. "The Nile used to bring the fish nourishment. Now it sinks to the bottom of an Arab dam." He chucked a mullet into a crate. "Jews, Arabs, what's the difference? We're all brothers, no?"

"Of course," I agreed. "The children of Abraham."

"Where are you from?" he asked.

"Zichron."

"Zichron. Do you know _____?"

I did.

"Take a good look at me."

I did.

"Don't I remind you of him?"

He did.

"When I say brothers, I mean brothers," said the fisherman. "None of that children of Abraham stuff."

Chapter fifteen

To my surprise, Rivka Rutman phoned to invite me to Hadera.

A plump woman, she did not at first glance resemble the mother whose picture hung on the wall in the ensemble of founders in Epstein's museum. The walls of her own apartment were hung with her paintings, those of an amateur of modest endowments. There was a scene of Hasidim praying in Jerusalem; of an alleyway in old Safed; of snow melting on a rooftop; of boatmen fighting an angry sea. All were done in the same bright colors, like the drawings of a child who uses her favorite crayons for everything. Noticing me regard the red and blue waves of the sea, she remarked:

"That's my latest. Friends said, 'It's a Van Gogh!'"

A Van Gogh it wasn't. We sat at a table by a window looking out on Herbert Samuel Street, a main thoroughfare of the city. It was a hot, dry day and Rivka Rutman complained about the weather. From behind a closed door came the hum of water in bathroom pipes. Presently, a freshly showered Haim Rutman emerged from his afternoon nap and sat beside us. His wife went to the kitchen to put on the kettle and left the weather to the two of us. By the time she returned with coffee and a package of cookies, it had been disposed of and Haim Rutman was asking what I did for a living.

I was in a delicate position. Rivka Rutman had impressed me over the phone as a good-natured, straightforward woman with no particular interest in the past, and I had planned my approach accordingly. I needed a reason for talking about her mother that would engage her curiosity and trust. For this I was prepared for a deception.

I had decided on a simple one. Even if she had little knowledge of the Nili years, at the time of which she was a small girl, she surely knew of Sarah's accusation. I would pretend, therefore, that I believed it to be false and was looking for evidence to refute it. Even if she had none to give me, this would encourage her to be open.

A sensible tactic, it failed to take into account two things. The first was Haim Rutman. I hadn't anticipated that – a compact man with small, watchful eyes – he would sit through our conversation like a chaperone, never budging from his wife's side even when, barely listening, his mind appeared to be elsewhere. The second was Rivka Rutman herself. Told I wished to discuss an old charge against her mother, she clapped a hand to her mouth and turned toward her husband, whose glance had strayed to the window. Their eyes met like those of two bridge partners dealt a worrisome hand.

"How did you know about that?" she asked.

"It's a matter of record," I said. "But I don't believe your mother was guilty."

She relaxed, the worry leaving her shoulders. "You see?" she said to her husband. "How many times did I tell you? And each time you argued!"

She had never expected to be vindicated. "My family always insisted my mother would never have done such a thing to Haim's brother," she said. "I just wouldn't have thought there were people in Zichron…that it was still possible to prove…."

Too late, I realized that she had never read or even heard of Sarah's letter. The only accusation she knew of, of which she now believed her mother to be exonerated, had to do with Nisan Rutman. Hence the quickly masked smirk on Haim Rutman's face as it turned back to the window. Its contempt was for me. I had to be an awful fool to look into the Nili affair and decide that Perl Appelbaum had nothing to do with his brother's arrest.

"The first Haim and I heard about it was when his mother flung it at me after our wedding," said Rivka Rutman. It had started with a quarrel. "She said I came from a family of traitors. Haim almost divorced me when he found out."

She reached out to squeeze his hand, bemused that an old marital spat, long rendered innocuous by time, had been belatedly decided in her favor.

But if he took me for a fool, what was she? He had to have known about Perl and his brother, had to have lied to her in feigning ignorance. The truth she was shielded from in her own home would not have been a secret in his. Her parents, she said, had never talked to her about the Nili years. She had few memories of them. One was of the searches at the time of the arrests. The Turkish soldiers emptied her family's closets and drawers and threw everything on the floor. She couldn't understand how her father could be treated that way. Ahmed Bek even came to apologize.

It was an unusual gesture for the Turkish governor to make while rounding up a spy ring. And it wasn't as if she didn't sense something. She had the feeling that her family was talked about in Zichron, that things were said behind its back. She just didn't know what they were. They eluded her even when dangled in front of her. Once she was standing with her mother in the doorway of their house when old Fishl Aaronsohn walked by. "We had a dog, a little black poodle, that began to bark at him. Fishl stopped and said, 'Your dog has a mouth like its owners.' My mother didn't answer. When he was gone I asked, 'Mama, what did he mean?' She didn't answer that either."

Perhaps Haim Rutman had that protective attitude toward his wife that allows men to regard what would they would consider obtuseness in others as charming innocence in the women they are married to. He had met Rivka Appelbaum by chance, several years after her mother's death. She was visiting a girlfriend in Hadera, and when the friend said she knew someone who owned a horse and was fun, they decided to drop in on him. "I'll show you what I looked like then," she said, going to fetch an album from another room. Haim Rutman went on staring out the window. I said to break the silence, "I heard your brother died not long ago. I'm sorry I never met him."

"You shouldn't be." The gaze shifted to me while remaining as blank as if I were a traffic light on Herbert Samuel Street. "He wouldn't have told you anything. He didn't like to talk about those times. He spent a year and a half in prison in Damascus and was beaten there twice a day. It made him a hard man."

His wife's footsteps were returning. "If he hadn't been squealed on," he added in the nick of time, "the Turks would never have found him."

It was easy to see why, the day Rivka Appelbaum dropped by with her friend, Haim Rutman was smitten. The photograph she showed me was of a young beauty. On the verge of plumpness then, too, she wore, its sleeves bunched at the elbows, a dress of dark velvet whose low collar was trimmed with white lace. Her cheeks had the downy curve of fruit; the lace rose with the swell of her breasts, lifted as though by a breath retained to steady herself for the shutter. "I call this my Renaissance portrait," she said. You wanted to reach out and touch those cheeks. Haim Rutman must have wanted to, too. Perl Appelbaum was dead. Her husband had remarried. Nisan Rutman was busy with the Zayta land. Haim kept silent and married the traitors' daughter.

"I had long hair like my mother," Rivka Rutman said. "This is her when I was a baby." Perl in the album looked more like her daughter. Younger and fuller than in the museum, her musing lips almost sensual, she was at that point in a woman's life where the first ripeness of motherhood edges her to a physical peak. "I used to love watching her comb her hair out. She did it by the light of her bedroom window."

Their house had four rooms: two bedrooms in the back, a living room, and a kitchen. The front door was in the kitchen and faced north, toward the Gelbergs. But although it was never locked, her mother wasn't friendly with the neighbors. She was a lonely woman in the years before she died. "She once said to me, 'If money could buy friends, I'd spend all I had.'"

"What did she die of?" I asked.

Haim Rutman's eyes snapped back from Herbert Samuel Street. This time his wife's did not seek them.

"It was some kind of palsy. She was sick for nearly half a year."

"Encephalitis?"

She wrinkled her brow.

"That's an inflammation of the brain."

"What kind of inflammation! It was palsy. There was nothing the doctor could do."

Haim Rutman's eyes drifted back to the window. After a while, they shut.

Rivka Rutman told me what she knew about her mother's origins. Perl Cohen was born in a small town near the Russian-Polish border. A sister and brother had emigrated to America, but Perl wanted to live in Palestine and traveled there alone at the age of sixteen, staying first with relatives in Hadera and then moving to Zichron. It was Tuvia Kruppik, the father of Gedalia Kruppik the real estate agent, who introduced her to Avigdor Appelbaum. The Appelbaums were an educated family. There were even rabbis in it.

Her parents stressed the value of learning. They weren't like the other farmers, who thought only of their vineyards and fields. They encouraged their children to get ahead. When Rivka's elder brother wanted to study veterinary medicine in America, they paid for his passage. Shortly before the war, her mother visited him there. She liked it well enough to want to stay. "My father almost agreed," Rivka said. "Years afterwards he told me that his mind was changed by the grape harvest. In those days the pickers sang Hebrew songs when they worked and he thought, 'I'll never have this in America.' He wrote my mother she'd have to live there by herself."

They were strict but loving parents. Perl was the disciplinarian. "She was old-fashioned. She didn't like the way young people in this country never bothered to say 'thank you' or 'please.' She taught us to respect our elders. But she had a sense of humor. My younger brother was always getting into mischief. Once she threatened to spank him and he said, 'Go ahead, being bad is worth it,' and she laughed so hard that she hit me by mistake. My sister Leah – she's not in her right mind any more – always said, 'What a home we had!'" Haim Rutman didn't open his eyes until I rose to go.

"But you haven't told me how you know my mother was innocent!" Rivka Rutman protested.

I promised to do that when I finished my research. We parted by the elevator and Haim Rutman took me down in it. It was like being escorted out by a prison guard.

* * *

Moshe Shatzman was already at Ben-Hayyim's when I arrived at eight o'clock that morning. Although the refugee camp where Alya lived was only an hour's drive away, the two of them had wanted to get an early start because Ben-Hayyim had promised his wife to be back for lunch. She was already at work on it, peeling potatoes at the kitchen table, her lips pursed stubbornly. She didn't look up when Ben-Hayyim told me he was feeling poorly and Shatzman said:

"Don't believe him. He's feeling fine." He winked at me. "Ben-Hayyim, there's nothing wrong with you. Come on, don't back out."

But backing out was precisely what Ben-Hayyim's wife's lips were telling him to do. "Honestly, Moshe," he said. "I think I'll stay home. I feel a cold coming on."

Even though it was a quiet time in the occupied territories, she didn't want him going to a refugee camp in the West Bank.

"Did he look sick to you?" Shatzman asked when we were out of the house. "Did he? He's no sicker than I am! I could see she wasn't going to let him go the minute I walked in."

Although he and Ben-Hayyim were old friends, they weren't at all alike. Shatzman had an adventurous soul. Ben-Hayyim was prudent. A cattle trader for much of his life, he had made it his business to stay out of trouble and thought little of those who got into it.

You could see the difference in their attitudes toward Yosef Davidesco, about whom Shatzman and I talked as we drove. A legend in Zichron, Davidesco was not thought of highly by everyone. Some justified his murder in 1946 by the "Stern Gang," the underground organization known in Hebrew as Lohamei Herut Yisra'el or Lehi, "The Freedom Fighters of Israel." He was accused of turning in one of its men to the British and there were those who believed it was true.

Ben-Hayyim was one of them. "He was guilty as hell," was his opinion. The motive was greed. Davidesco had worked at the Arab desk of the CID and was paid extra for intelligence on Jews. "He had a sweet tooth for money. It's the root of all evil, my friend."

But Shatzman, who knew Davidesco better, thought better of him, too. Not only did he not inform on the underground, he passed British secrets to it. "It was all a mistake," Shatzman said in the car. "He happened to be in a Tel Aviv café when a Stern Gang member was there. The British were tipped off and he was blamed, even though he had nothing to do with it."

Davidesco was shot through the window of his living room, now in the paint section of Benedik's hardware store. Ora Rosenzweig, hearing the shots, jumped up from her front porch and ran into the street just as four figures, three men and a woman, dashed by her in the direction of the winery. One brushed her shoulder as he ran. "It was awful," she said of the scene at the murdered man's house. "He was still flopping around in his pajamas."

They seemed to her, those pajamas, the very symbol of his degradation. "Like an Arab!" she said. Who else received guests in their pajamas? He had stayed at home in them in the weeks before his death, going out only when others were with him in the hope no assassin would risk harming them. It was a sorry end for a man known for his courage.

Yanko Epstein scoffed at this. "Ora!" he said, as if it took a woman to think Davidesco could be afraid. But it was true he had a weakness for money. While working for the CID he had moonlighted by selling information from his Arab sources to its rival, British Army Intelligence – and when this was discovered, the CID set him up. "The man arrested in that café was named Sitner," Epstein said. "His wife went to the CID to protest his innocence and it told her, 'Why come to us? Go to Davidesco.' She passed that on to the underground."

He knew this from David Tidhar, a private detective with underground connections. "Yanko," Tidhar had confided, "tell your friend there's an x by his name. He doesn't have much time."

Davidesco prepared to leave the country. Army Intelligence was looking for an agent in Iraq and agreed to transfer him there. The plan was to establish him in Baghdad as an Arab businessman. He began to settle his affairs and to look for a buyer for his farm. "I told him to hurry,"

Epstein said. "He said, 'Don't worry, I'll be gone in a few weeks.' I said to him, 'You don't have a few weeks.'"

Epstein was in the bathroom when it happened. Stepping out, he was told by his daughter she'd heard shots. By the time he dressed and ran outside, the whole town knew. The man he was closest to, his only role model, had been killed while he showered.

* * *

The Nur Shams refugee camp straddled a hill overlooking the Tulkarm-Nablus road. Much of its population came from the villages and Bedouin tribes around Zichron that had fled to Jordan in 1948. (It was here, in '67, that Epstein had met the exiles from Sindiani, their fate unknown to him since the night he came for their weapons and found them gone.) Yet "camp" was a misnomer for the shantytown built by them, the impermanence it suggested having been replaced long ago by a more solid squalor. Although Nur Shams had no streets and streamlets of sewage ran in their place, it was encrusted irrevocably on the rural landscape, a third-world slum among olive and fig trees, its concrete houses, most only a room or two, the only homes ever likely to be known by the children who surrounded our car when an outcrop of rock blocked its progress along the dirt track we had taken, following instructions given us upon turning off the main road.

Shatzman and I walked the rest of the way, leaving the children to guard the car for a promised recompense. They fought for the job and the losers ran ahead to announce us. The woman who stepped from the house they ran to, however, was not Alya. She was Alya's sister-in-law, the widow of her younger brother Muhammed. Alya was visiting next door.

More children ran to fetch Alya and we sat down to wait on a concrete porch, joined by some neighbors and a teenage girl with a metal rod and a basket of eggplants. While Shatzman chatted with the widow and the neighbors, the girl prepared the eggplants for stuffing by hollowing them with the rod and rinsing them in a bucket of water.

Alya appeared bit by bit. At first, like a mast and sail coming into view on the horizon, she was no more than a walking stick and the square, white front of a kerchief. This was because, as she slowly climbed the stairs to the porch in a dress as faded as herself, all that showed of her bent frame was a forehead that was level with the top of the stick. A small girl held her hand and more children circled around her, helping to push her across the porch and into a chair like a fleet of tugboats towing a crippled vessel to its berth.

All this time, Moshe Shatzman barely stirred. He accompanied Alya with his eyes, which seemed less to follow than to lead her, as if he were offering them to her to lean on. Only when she was seated beside him did he reach out and seize her hand. Three times he pressed it to his lips and exclaimed:

"Alya! Alya! Alya!"

He was more excited than she was. But perhaps the children had garbled his message, leaving her unsure who he was. Her sunken eyes, the dull maroon of dying embers, rolled inward like a blind woman's as though searching in a storeroom of memories for one to match his voice. Her nose, broad at its base, was short and straight, the lines splaying from it like cobwebs. The cheekbones were high and slanted; the pointed jaw, though sagging, well-formed. And even finer than her features, which had the tilted planes of an African mask, was their color. Mottled and stained like an old table, its golden brown, compared by Yanko Epstein to fresh bread, had the burnish of ancient mahogany.

"*Weyn, ya Alya, el-ayam?*" Shatzman asked.

Where, O Alya, are the days?

The eyes glowed and dimmed like fanned coals. "*Rahu,*" she said. Gone.

The word seemed dredged from the very abyss into which the past had fallen.

"*Wa-kif inti?*"

"*M'nihi. Nushkor Allah.*"

She was all right, God be thanked.

"*Wa-ahuki Saleh?*"

"*Rah. Allah yirhamo.*"

Her brother Saleh was gone, too. God rest his soul.

"*Wa-marrato?*"

"*Rahat kaman.*"

Saleh's wife – gone as well.

Rahu, rah,. rahat: the conjugations of the dead. Of her brothers and sisters, she alone was alive.

Shatzman asked about her nephews and nieces. Praise God, they were well. The men worked for the Jews and made money. Not enough, because everything was so dear. A son of Mustafa's lived next door and would perhaps stop by to say hello. Moshe Shatzman would recognize him. He resembled his father.

Shatzman slapped a leg. "*Isme'i!*" he said. Listen! Didn't Mustafa once have a child with a light-skinned woman who came out black as coal?

Alya smiled for the first time, revealing a single tooth that had grown for lack of rivals to almost fanglike proportions "*Kan ifrit kebir,*" she said. He was a great rascal, Mustafa. A thief and a womanizer. Not like Muhammed, who prayed every day and was the bravest of her brothers.

"*Isme'i!*" Did she remember the time Muhammed caught a thief stealing a sheep from the Burj? The thief shot at him with a gun and Muhammed charged him with his dagger, slashed him, and disarmed him.

"Was that in the time of the English?" someone asked.

"No," Shatzman said. "It was in the time of the Turks."

There was laughter. The time of the Turks seemed so distant that he might as well have said, "The time of the Prophet."

"Ask her now," I urged.

We had agreed that he would find the right moment. "*Ya Alya,*" he said. "*Bit'zakeri kif matat Dibi?*"

She adjusted the shawl on her dress and faced him expectantly. Of course she remembered Dibi's death.

"*Kanat tit'han kawa,*" he reminded her.

She was grinding coffee.

"*Wa-aja Mustafa wa-takatallu.*"

And Mustafa came and they fought.

"*Wa-ahad el-medakka wa-darabha wa-katalha.*"

And he took the pestle and struck her and killed her.

"*La!*"

Her "No!" was quick as instinct, stubborn as certitude.

"*Ma kansh Mustafa. Kanat tihlib el-bakara wa-rafas'ha 'l-heyl.*"

It wasn't Mustafa. She was milking the cow and the horse kicked her.

Moshe Shatzman reached out and touched her thigh gently. "Alya, Alya," he said. "*N'siti inno ba'aref?*"

Had she forgotten he knew?

The sunken eyes turned inward again, as if searching for what he might know. Perhaps she no longer knew herself. Yet finding it there, she said solemnly:

"*Na'am. Mustafa katalha.*"

Truly, Mustafa killed her.

An exhalation ran through the refugees on the porch, the sound of a secret released from long confinement.

"*Isme'i.*" Shatzman related Epstein's version in a few spare sentences, wrinkling his face as if chewing on spoiled food. There were some titters, though not as loud as the guffaws at Turkish times, and Alya said firmly, "*walow,*" "no way," as if the suggestion that it was she who was killed by her brother called for a vigorous denial. She had heard of Epstein – "Abu-Yussuf from Zamarin" – but had no idea where he had gotten such a story. Her father had never pressed her to marry anyone. On the contrary. She was the youngest child and her parents had wanted her to stay at home to do the cooking, cleaning, and milking.

The eggplants were stuffed with pine nuts and rice and swimming in a tomato sauce. "Ben-Hayyim doesn't know what he's missing," Shatzman said, eating heartily. "This cooking sure beats his wife's." He kept up his reminiscences, crowing each time they were confirmed. "Am I right? Am I right? This old man remembers! Not like Lord Cock-and-Bull. They say no one lies like a young man abroad or an old one who's outlived his age. Well, he hasn't outlived it yet!"

His victory was complete. He was just sorry he had forgotten to bring a gift. "I should have brought some fruit with me," he said. When we left he took a hundred pounds from his wallet and pressed them on Alya, who made them disappear like a magician in the folds of her dress. "No," he answered on the drive back to Zichron when I asked whether this wasn't an insult. "I could see they were hard up. Alya was like a sister to me. There's no shame in taking money from a brother."

He said with a chuckle:

"She was a looker. I would have started up with her if I hadn't cared for her family's honor. It would have been easy. She wasn't even a virgin."

"She wasn't?"

"No. She had an affair with an older man when she was young. The whole tribe knew about it. That was the real reason she didn't marry."

You had to hand it to Epstein.

*   *   *

I had obtained from Rivka Rutman the phone number of her brother-in-law Yehuda Ahiezer, the husband of her senile sister Leah. He lived in Binyamina and I called and asked if I could see him. Though cordial, he said he said he was going away for a few days and suggested I call again when he got back.

Meanwhile, I solved the mystery of the death of Nita Lange.

Or rather, it was solved for me on the beach at Tantura.

I had gone for a swim in the bay and was still dripping wet when I ran into Shosh Yisra'eli in her bathing suit. Shosh was the daughter of Thelma Yelin, née Bentwich, one of Nita's younger sisters. She and her husband lived in Jerusalem and had a weekend place on the Lange property.

We stood chatting on the beach. The Lange house had fallen into ever greater disrepair since the day I made off with its fireplace frame. The initialed washstand had been torn from its wall and the uprooted stairs to the top floor were unclimbable. Shosh remarked:

"Poor Nita! She'd need another shot of morphine if she saw it."

Seeing my blank look, she explained:

"That's what killed her."

She knew it from her mother. Nita had come down that winter day with bad stomach pains and Michael Lange sent for Dr. Cohen. Suspecting appendicitis, the doctor told them to prepare to go to the hospital and gave Nita a shot of morphine. Too much of it. She died from an overdose.

Suddenly it all added up. The doctor blamed it on a ruptured appendix. Michael Lange realized the truth and asked his wife's family to keep it a secret; it wouldn't bring her back to life and nothing short of an autopsy could prove it. Yet fearing he might ask for one, Dr. Cohen covered himself on the death certificate with a vague diagnosis of cardiac arrest. None of which was known to the townspeople – who, having seen Nita alive and well a few hours previously, thought her husband and the doctor had conspired to hide her suicide.

Written by a bungler like Cohen, "encephalitis" on Perl Appelbaum's death certificate indeed meant nothing.

*   *   *

Epstein and I hadn't returned to the subject of the Samsonov house. I didn't tell him I had bought a putty knife and was practicing on an old window acquired in a junkyard. Puttying the pane back into place was harder than taking it out. It was part of my plan, though. I would enter the basement by myself, take the diaries if they were there, and erase all signs of a break-in.

Neither did I did mention my trip to Nur Shams to him. Yet as though divining it, he proposed visiting his old friend Kalman Radin. Radin was the policeman he had accompanied to Alya's autopsy. He lived in Nesher, a grimy working-class suburb of Haifa, and Epstein hadn't seen him in years.

If he had hopes of having his story of Alya vouched for, however, they were dashed. "It sounds familiar," was all Kalman Radin would say, staring concentratedly at the table we were sitting at while his memory was unsuccessfully jogged.

A thickset, bull-necked man, he was delighted to see Epstein. "Ay, ay, ay, Ya'akov!" he exclaimed at our appearance. "What a surprise!" He couldn't get over it, not even when chided by his wife for keeping us standing in the middle of their apartment without offering us a seat or cold drink. "Nu, nu, nu!" he scolded, wagging a finger as though at a naughty child. He didn't say if the naughtiness was being out of touch for so long or turning up so unexpectedly without warning. "What a surprise! What a surprise!"

He had some catching up to do. The two men hadn't met since the death of Epstein's wife. Hearing that Epstein's eldest daughter was married to an executive in Solel Boneh, the big Histadrut-owned construction firm, he joked:

"What? A child of yours and a Bolshevik?"

Radin's wife laughed. "You have to admit, Ya'akov, that you didn't think much of us lefties. We felt the same about you. You were as kosher as pork to us. But who's looking after you now?"

Epstein said he was living with his son and daughter-in-law, a "fine lady."

"For how long?" Radin asked suspiciously. He clearly didn't think that a lady you did not share your bed with was an arrangement for a grown man.

"It's been a while."

"And you're all right?"

"I'm all right."

"Well, that's all right, then."

Still doubtful, however, he swiveled a wrist. "So how are you, Ya'akov?"

Epstein grinned. "You know me, Radin. I'm light. I've always been light. Whatever happens, I float."

"He was light," Radin said to me. "He was light as a feather – when it suited him. When it didn't, he was heavy as a freight train. Do you remember the time you clobbered those Arabs in Haifa?"

The grin widened. "I was at the movies with two girls. Three Arabs in the row behind us tried goosing one of them. I slipped on the brass knuckles I always kept in my pocket, turned around, and went *klunk! klunk! klunk!*" He mimed bringing down his studded fist on three heads. "They got up and walked out without a word."

"You were wild," said Radin's wife.

"I was wild. I didn't know Governor Anders was in the audience. After the movie he came up to me. I had just stomped on Sam Aaronsohn and was sure that this time he'd have me up on charges. But he only said 'Jolly good show, Epstein' and walked away."

Radin put his arm around Epstein's shoulder. "I spent days and nights with this man," he told me. "I rode down every trail with him, into every hole-in-the-wall."

"I liked being seen with a policeman," Epstein said. "It was good for my reputation."

It was then that he told the story of Alya. Afterwards, on the way back to Zichron, he said disappointedly:

"He didn't remember. He pretended to, but he didn't."

He thought for a while and said, "I'll tell you what made me so wild. It was a girl named Pnina Goldstein."

A cable car glided overhead, on its way with a load of limestone to the big cement factory in Nesher.

Pnina was the daughter of Itzik Goldstein, the uncle of Ezra Goldstein the tree murderer. She was gorgeous. You would never guess it from looking at her today, but she had a waist you could put your hand around.

He cupped a hand and held it to the windshield for me to see.

They had begun going out when they were teenagers and remained a couple for seven years. He was wild about her. He even took along her photograph to look at while making his rounds of the fields.

He was sure he would marry her some day. So was she. Her father was, too. "Keep Pnina for me," he had said to him. He was an excellent match, because Itzik Goldstein's farm did poorly and he earned a good living; besides being a field guard, he ran a small business trading in grain and other crops that took him as far as Egypt and Damascus. He just wasn't in a hurry. He and Pnina were young and his older brother Tsvi was still single. In those days, families married off their sons in order. Each had to be provided with farmland and a house, and it was a big expense.

But Itzik Goldstein was impatient. One day he appeared in the lean to in a vineyard that was Yanko Epstein's place of business. "Hello, Mr. Goldstein!" "Hello, Yanko! Will we be seeing you this Saturday night?" "Why not?" he replied. He came to pick Pnina up at the Goldsteins' every Saturday night. "We're counting on you," said Itzik Goldstein.

He arrived that Saturday night to find the house full of guests. His own parents were there, too. Tables were set for a banquet. "What's all this for?" he asked. "Congratulations, Yanko!" Itzik Goldstein said. "It's a surprise engagement party for you and Pnina. You're the first to know. The guests will find out when I make the announcement."

He turned pale. He wasn't ready to get married. He couldn't do such a thing to his brother. "Tsvi comes before me," he told Pnina's father.

They argued. He stuck to his guns. Itzik Goldstein was furious at having his party ruined and his daughter's future left hanging.

A last-minute excuse had to be found for the occasion, which left the guests wondering why so much food and fuss had been lavished on it.

The weeks went by. The quarrel wasn't patched up. Although he and Pnina continued going out, he no longer came to her house. They met at the "Club," a room in town set aside for the young folk. It had a canteen that sold food and drinks and the members supplied their own dance music.

One night he arranged to meet Pnina at the Club with his friend Mordecai Shapiro. He and Mordecai both played the harmonica. Sometimes one played while the other danced with his partner.

"That night," he said on the twisting road from Nesher, "Pnina was late. I played a few dance tunes for Mordecai and his girl. Suddenly Yitzhak Bronstein walks in. 'Yanko,' he says with this know-it-all smile, 'how come you're here? The whole town is at Pnina's house. Weren't you invited?'

"'To what?' I said. "Pnina is meeting me here.'

"'Well,' he says, 'she'll have a hard time getting away. She's celebrating her engagement tonight.'

"I was sure he was joking. But Mordecai Shapiro didn't like that smile and decided to have a look.

"He went to the Goldsteins' and came back and said, 'Yanko,' he said, 'I looked through the window. People were standing at a table and the rabbi was sitting and writing. Pnina saw me and came out. "Mordecai," she asked, "is Yanko with you?" "No," I said. "Then please tell him," she said, "that I can't meet him at the Club tonight because I'm getting engaged."'

He made Mordecai Shapiro repeat that three times. Then he took his harmonica and threw it at the wall so hard that it broke in two.

He was stunned. He could understand her father's wanting to marry Pnina off. But that she had gone on seeing him and saying nothing while betraying him...and with whom? "A pisspot from Jerusalem with a face like a baby's ass. He was a male nurse in a hospital and some patient wanted him to meet a cousin from Zichron. The cousin was a friend of Pnina's. Pnina went with her to Jerusalem and the pisspot liked Pnina better. Itzik Goldstein invited him to Zichron, and before you knew it they were engaged...."

It was a great blow. If he hadn't been in the middle of rehearsals for Moliére's "Miser," which was put on that year by the Drama Society, he would have left town and disappeared. By a twist of fate, he was cast as Valére, the servant of the stingy Harpagon and the secret lover of his daughter Elise. There he was in a play, his true love pledged to him against her father's wishes, while in real life she was marrying a pisspot. Itzik Goldstein had convinced her that he would never marry her himself and that it was foolish to wait any longer.

He made no attempt to see or speak to her. The Drama Society held its dress rehearsal and it was opening night. The play was produced in the cellar of the winery, the only place big enough for the whole village and its guests. Before curtain time he peeked out at the audience. Two couples were in the first row. "One was Moshe Kuperman and his fiancée. The other was Pnina and hers. I turned to the stage manager and said, 'Don't ask any questions, just bring me a glass of brandy in a hurry.'"

He downed the brandy in one gulp and managed to get through the performance. The play had four acts. His part ended with the third. When it was over, he went to the dressing room to remove his costume and make-up. Then, it still being intermission, he joined the audience. "I went over to Moshe Kuperman and his fiancée and congratulated them on their engagement. Then I turned to Pnina and said, 'I hear you deserve congratulations, too.'

"She was white as chalk. She took my hand and pulled me into the empty seat beside her and whispered, 'Yanko, we have to go somewhere to talk.'

"I said, 'Pnina, we can't. The intermission is almost over and the whole audience will see us walk out. Everyone knows us.'"

"'I don't care,' she said, getting up and pulling me after her. 'We have to talk.'

"I stood up and walked out with her. As we headed down the aisle I said, 'Don't look now, but every eye in the village is on you.'

"We found a quiet corner. She didn't beat around the bush. 'Yanko,' she said, 'it's not too late. My father's mule is saddled in our yard. We can ride to Haifa and find a rabbi to marry us.'

"Those were her words. I said 'Pnina, it is too late' and went back to watch the fourth act."

"Why?"

He didn't answer at once. We were heading down the other side of the Carmel, the blue sea in front of us.

"Why didn't you?"

"It was my pride," he said in his gruff voice as if finally finding the word that had eluded him. "It wouldn't let me."

Pnina had her wedding and went to live with her husband in Jerusalem. A year later he heard that she had given birth to a daughter. More time went by with no news of her. And then, as he was in the railroad station at Lydda to board a train to Kantara on the Suez Canal, from where he was to sail to Europe to visit his brother, he saw her. She was coming from Haifa and had gotten off to change trains for Jerusalem. "Hello, Yanko!" "Hello, Pnina!" "Where are you off to?" "To my brother in Switzerland." "But you're coming back? Promise me you'll come back!" "Of course I'll come back," he said. "But what difference does it make to you?" "We have to talk, Ya'akov," she said. "Pnina," he said, "we already did that after Act Three of The Miser." His train sounded its whistle and he jumped aboard.

He spent several weeks with his brother in Zurich and Paris and returned. He was having his liaison with Fidi at the time, and when her husband Fu'ad found work with Ya'akov Temshis and they moved from their cellar opposite the Rosenzweigs to a shack in the Temshises' yard, the liaison continued there. The Temshises didn't mind. They even befriended him.

One evening when Fidi had signaled that the coast was clear he came to spend the night with her. First, he knocked on the Temshises' door to say hello. "Good evening, Yanko," Frieda Temshis said. "Come in! I have a surprise for you." "What kind of surprise?" he asked. Since Itzik Goldstein's party he was suspicious of surprises.

"Go to the living room and you'll see," said Frieda Temshis. He went to the living room and saw Pnina. "Hello, Yanko!" "Hello, Pnina." "How are you?" "I'm all right. And you?" There was an awkward silence, broken only when Frieda Temshis entered the room and said, thinking Pnina had told him:

"Yanko, it's not so terrible. These things happen. The important thing is to look ahead."

He had no idea what it was about.

Pnina said:

"Yanko, I've left my husband. Let's start all over, you and I."

We had reached the Haifa-Tel Aviv road. Epstein said:

"I said, 'Pnina, I may have been to Europe, but I'm still a son of the East. I kept you pure for seven years because that's how I wanted you, and I wouldn't elope with an engaged woman even then. And now that you're second hand goods, you think I'll have you?'

"She started to cry. I hugged her and said, 'Know one thing. I'm still the same Yanko. I'll always have warm feelings for you. But it wasn't me who broke the glass at your wedding – and a broken glass can't be repaired....'"

Pnina Goldstein went back to her husband and he swore to remain a bachelor all his life. "That's what made me wild," he said. "For years I kept away from Jewish girls." After Fidi came his affair with Faida Bek, which lasted until he met his wife. "Faida wanted to go on seeing me. She said, 'What do you care? You'll have a wife and I'll have you.' I said, 'Faida, that, no. We Jews aren't Moslems. We have only one woman at a time.'"

* * *

Yafia Cohen had played Marianne, the country girl the miser's son is in love with, not knowing that his widowed father plans to marry her himself. She had wanted to be the beautiful Elise, but that part had gone to Leah Schechter. The miser's son was Ezra Goldstein, whom she didn't like. He had fat lips and was a "Don Juan." She would have preferred to be romantically paired with Yanko Epstein. Epstein was a "Don Juan," too, but there was a difference. Ezra Goldstein was always pawing her. Once he tried to kiss her on a staircase. Epstein was *galant*. She wasn't allowed to have anything to do with him, though: her father had made that clear to her. He was charming but a ruffian.

"He told me that came from being jilted by Pnina Goldstein."

"Oh, no," Yafia said from her folding chair. "He was always like that."

She didn't believe he had ever had a business. "What trading in grain? He sold what he stole from the fields. He was in cahoots with the thieves he was supposed to be guarding them from."

As far as she knew, Pnina's marriage was a good one. Still, Itzik Goldstein shouldn't have interfered. She and Epstein were in love. "Parents should keep out of such things. They think they're helping when they're only doing harm."

* * *

"I'll bet she didn't tell you the real reason," Epstein said of Yafia's father's dislike of him. "It was his fault I never finished school. He was a dirty old man. He felt up the girls during penmanship lessons while pretending to teach them how to write."

We were sitting in his museum.

"Once we were playing leapfrog during recess. There was a girl in the game and I pinched her behind jumping over it. She shouldn't have been playing with the boys if she thought her behind was so precious, but she went and told Shababo on me.

"After recess he walked into class, went straight to my seat, and started rapping my knuckles with his ruler. I broke away and said, 'You dirty old man! What I did was nothing compared to you.' I ran for the door but he got there first, so I ran to the window and jumped out. Then I went home and told my father I wasn't going back. The next morning I went to work with my brothers in the Burj. I learned more there than I ever did in school."

His first teacher was Sa'idi's new wife.

"My uncle had hired a new field hand, a big middle-aged Arab named Sa'idi. He wore his hair in braids and had a mustache like this." He twirled thick skeins of imaginary hair. "I was baling hay one day when two women sat down next to me. One was pretty and a few years older than myself; I could tell from the henna on her hands that she'd just been married. As soon as she went off somewhere, I asked her friend about her. 'That's Sa'idi's new wife,' she said.

"After a while Sa'idi's wife came back and we started to flirt. I could see that she liked me, because she gave as good as she got. That gave me the courage to propose meeting that night in the hay.

"I thought I was being grown-up. I had nothing on her. 'Why the hay?' she says. 'I have a bed. I'll wait for you there.'

"I said, 'But what about your husband?'

"'Oh, don't worry about him,' she says. 'He's like a dumb rooster. He falls asleep when the sun sets and doesn't wake until it rises. It's all I can do to roust him in the morning.'

"I was thirteen years old and took her word for it. When night came I waited for my brothers to fall asleep, went to her room, and tried her door. It didn't open.

"I wasn't a quitter. I took a ladder and some rope, climbed to the roof, moved a few tiles, and stuck my head in. Sa'idi was snoring below. There was a smell of kerosene from the oil lamp they'd put out before going to sleep. I tied the rope to the roof beam and slid down it. *Eeeeee!* That beam creaked like an old axle.

"It was so dark I almost stepped on Sa'idi. I could feel my foot touch his braids. His wife pulled me down beside her, covered me with the blanket, and snuggled up.

"Just then there's a grunt and Sa'idi turns over. Then he sits up and reaches for the lamp. Uh-oh, I thought, say your prayers! But he can't find a match and he goes to the door in the dark, bumping into a chair. He takes down the wooden plank that's propped against the door and steps outside.

"'The old fart!' his wife whispers. 'He put that plank back while I was sleeping.'

"'I thought he never woke,' I said.

"'Only to pee,' she says. Now she tells me! 'Stay,' she says. 'He's as blind as a bat in the dark.'

"He was, too. He came back in, put the plank against the door, lay down, and started to snore again. But by then I was so scared that I had to pee myself. I tiptoed out the door, climbed the ladder, untied the rope, put back the tiles, and went to sleep with my brothers."

The next night he lost his virginity – in the hay.

There was a new photograph on the wall of the museum. It was of a woman with a large, squarish head. Wrapped in a black shawl, she looked like a block of quarried granite. I went over to read the caption beneath her. It said:

"'If we have to eat stones we will eat them, but we will not budge from this place.'

Malka Aaronsohn."

Epstein watched me. "What could I do?" he said. "Go argue with history."

"But it isn't history," I protested. "I learned that from you."

"It is now. I'm tired of being contradicted by all those teachers who have been to Aaronsohn House." He looked away sheepishly. "Who'll know the difference? Let them believe what they want."

*   *   *

I revisited the barn at the north end of Founders Street in which, during our first year in Zichron, I had found thousands of old newspapers. It stood in back of an empty house with gothic windows that had once belonged to a family named Ribniker. The Ribnikers had sold it to the Aaronsohns and it still was owned by several Aaronsohn heirs.

Between the Ribniker house and the barn stood another house with a tin roof, built in British times. Whoever lived there kept a vegetable garden that was tended in neat rows.

The barn door was shut by means of a stick, thrust through two hasps, that was easily removed. I stepped inside and switched on my flashlight. The newspapers were stacked in crates. They were old issues of The Palestine Daily Mail – the paper, edited by his one-time friend Itamar Ben-Avi, for which Alexander Aaronsohn had written his column "From An Observer's Notebook."

The barn was dark and cool. Old farm tools hung on the walls. The crates were arranged in no special order and it took a while to find the one I was looking for. In it were all the issues of the paper from 1921. Perl Appelbaum was ill for several months before dying at the end of August of that year. The secret with Neiderman dated to the "Events" of either then or the year before.

In 1921 the Palestine Daily Mail, having just begun publication, was a four-page broadsheet with a front page composed entirely of advertisements on the model of London papers like the Times. Page two ran an editorial and local news; page three had the foreign news; and page four carried letters to the editor and more ads. There were no columns yet and no features, nor could there have been many newsstand sales, since the only price listed was for subscriptions – two Palestinian pounds per year, one pound twenty for half a year.

The year started out quietly, domestically and abroad. Page two dealt with such matters as the increase in Jewish immigration, up to a thousand newcomers a month; life in the Jewish colonies; the growth of Tel Aviv, now challenging Jaffa and Jerusalem as an urban center; and the performance of Herbert Samuel, the first British High Commissioner, criticized for being pro-Arab by the Jews and pro-Jewish by the Arabs. Major stories on page three were the new administration of Warren Harding and the war in Anatolia, where the Turks were battling to stem the Greek advance. The paper was brittle and I had to turn the pages carefully, piling them on the ground beside me when I finished them.

At the beginning of May, the country erupted. "DETAILS OF THE EVENTS IN JAFFA," said a large page-two headline on May 3. Riots had broken out during an Arab May Day parade. A Jewish immigrant hostel and Jewish shops and passers-by were attacked, and 16 Jews were killed and 98 wounded. Arab casualties at the hands of the British police were 3 dead and 12 wounded.

In the next two days the disturbances spread to other areas. Reporting the murder of Yosef Haim Brenner, the leading Hebrew novelist of his day, the Daily Mail lamented in black borders: "Y.H. BRENNER IS NO MORE!" "You have killed 50 of us and wounded 200," a defiant May 4 editorial addressed the rioters. "But do you not know – have you not heard – that the prophet Moses, who is revered by you too, called us a stiff-necked people? ... In vain! In vain! In vain are all your doings! We will never retreat!"

On May 5 the paper reported that the violence in Jaffa had stopped the previous afternoon. Yet the disorders continued to spread. May 7 brought attacks on Jewish property near Hadera. On May 8 there was news of outbreaks in Petach-Tikvah, with three Jewish dead and 11 wounded. A May 9 dispatch told of renewed pillaging in Hadera, where Jewish homes were burned and ransacked, and trouble in Rehovot in the south; Indian troops were called from their garrisons to restore order. By May 10 the disturbances had reached Hebron. The May 11 paper said, "We have been informed from Zichron Ya'akov that all the Jewish villages in the vicinity have been evacuated and their inhabitants brought for safety's sake to Zichron."

Gradually, however, the British army gained the upper hand. The tension subsided. The last incident, dispersed without casualties, took place on May 15. "Our special correspondent in the north," the Daily Mail informed its readers that same day, "writes that there is quiet in Zichron Ya'akov and throughout the Galilee." By the end of May, life was back to normal and Herbert Samuel had appointed a commission of inquiry.

The summer of 1921 was uneventful. There were Jewish protests when the High Commissioner temporarily halted further immigration. The Twelfth Zionist Congress was to be convened in Karlsbad in September. The Greeks were continuing their push and had taken Eshkishehir, opening the way for an attack on Ankara.

Wednesday, August 31, the day of Perl Appelbaum's death, was an ordinary one. On page one of the Daily Mail, Philip Kiefendorff, general agent of Hoffmann pianos for Palestine, Syria, and Egypt (*"Hoffmann, Hoffmann, ueber alles, ueber alles in der Welt"*), advertised "a new shipment of the best pianos," while the marching band of the Second Battalion of the Prince of Wales regiment invited the public to a concert in Jerusalem. An editorial on page two warned the Karlsbad conference to hide nothing from the Jewish people, "who demand the Zionism not of literary fiction and the cinema but of reality and truth." Page three reported a train crash near Rome, an anti-British uprising in southern India, the signing – to the distress of the French – of a separate U.S.-German peace treaty, the inauguration of airmail service between Cairo and Baghdad, and fierce battles along the Sakarya River, where the Turks were mounting desperate resistance. The British pound was trading for 37.60 French francs, 318 German marks, and $3.69. The grape harvest in the Jewish colonies was over. In Rishon le-Tsiyon a young man started a fire with an "electrical machine," nearly burned to death when his father tried dowsing it with a can of gasoline, and saved himself by rolling in the sand while the neighbors threw blankets and sacks on him.

The first half of May, then: if there was anything in Epstein's diaries, I would find it there. It didn't have to be *Saw someone suspicious stealing out of Perl Appelbaum's kitchen last night and told Neiderman in the morning.* This was not what you might confide, even to your diary, about a secret you had sworn to keep. You might simply write *N.R. outside P.A.'s,* or something like that, to remind you of it years later.

The sunlight was blinding when I stepped out of the barn. I slipped the stick through its hasps and stood blinking. Then I froze.

A man was hoeing onions in the garden. He was in shorts and an undershirt and had his back to me, but I knew who he was from the color of his hair. It was Bad Ginger. No one had told me he lived in the tin-roofed house.

I took a cautious step.

Bad Ginger went on hoeing his onions.

Another step. My sandal crunched a clod of earth.

He swung around.

What do you say to a policeman who sees you coming out of his barn with a flashlight?

"Hello," I said.

Bad Ginger stood gripping his hoe. You could kill a garden mole with a hoe if you swung it fast enough.

"I was just looking at the newspapers," I said.

"I could arrest you for breaking and entering," said Bad Ginger.

"I didn't break anything," I said.

What do you say to a moron with a flashlight if you are a policeman with a hoe?

"Get out of here," said Bad Ginger.

I got out.

Chapter sixteen

The directions given by a neighbor for getting to Yehuda Ahiezer's house were simple:

"Bear left up ahead and take the first right. You're there when you get to the cactuses."

You couldn't go wrong. Cactuses surrounded the little white house like a family of aliens that had taken over the property. It was a very extended family. There were cacti-parents and cacti-children, bald and hairy cacti-uncles, fat aunts, thin, desiccated grandparents, cacti-cousins with limbless trunks or arms and legs like centipedes, cacti-giants, midgets, and clubfeet. There were cactuses in pots; in cans; in painted jars; in old tires; in and around a large number of *objets trouvés*, on which some were impaled like skulls – rotted tree trunks, old boilers, rusted milk cans, telephone cable spools, electric light fixtures, plastic fruit boxes, garden tools, bits of machinery, the skeleton of an umbrella, the horns of a clothes tree. Between them, the sprayed ground was barren and bare. It was a demented scene, a vegetational ideé fixe.

"People say it's strange," Ahiezer said. He was sweeping the sidewalk in front of his house. "But I like cactuses. They're the camels of the plant kingdom. We waste too much water in this country. We throw too much out. A Jewish family creates more garbage in a day than an Arab one does in a month."

He smelled faintly of alcohol. Yet an old man with an Alzheimer's wife was entitled to a drink now and then and he seemed all there apart from his junk and cactuses. He was an individualist; this was why, although he had dreamed as a boy of being a farmer in Palestine, he had spent his first years there in Tel Aviv. In the agricultural commune in the Valley of Jezreel that he joined on arriving in 1919, everyone had left-wing views. He quarreled with them all the time. A main bone of contention was the Nili, still a fresh subject in those days. The communards spoke of espionage as if it were a deadly sin. He was a Zionist and he said, "What's wrong with it? War is war. Why is it all right to kill the enemy but not to spy on him?"

He moved to Tel Aviv and worked in a bank until he married Leah Appelbaum, whom he had met on a visit to Zichron the year before her mother died. Perl Appelbaum, as he remembered her, was a clever, energetic woman who ran an efficient household and took good care of her husband. Until she was sick, she brought hot meals to him on a donkey when he was out in the fields with his workers. Not many women in Zichron did that.

"Sick with what?"

"The sleeping sickness. She kept falling asleep. She was clear-minded when she awoke, but then she'd nod off again."

He didn't think Perl was as lonely as her daughter Rivka had said. The Appelbaums had good friends, like the Goldsteins and the Lerners. And the Neidermans. Avigdor Appelbaum and Yisra'el Neiderman were often together. They were even poisoned together.

"Would you mind repeating that?"

"Appelbaum and Neiderman were poisoned together."

"By whom?"

"The Nili."

It had happened during the hunt for Lishansky. The two men were traveling with some Turkish officers and were joined by an unfamiliar Jew. The Jew shared a meal with them and vanished. Immediately afterwards they fell violently ill. The Turkish officers were unaffected. "I heard it from my wife," Ahiezer said.

I took the plunge and said, "Perhaps I shouldn't be telling you this, but your mother-in-law may have been poisoned more successfully."

I told him everything, starting with the photograph of Tova Gelberg and *Sarah, Flame of the Nili*. "I grant you, it's all circumstantial," I said. "But you've added another link to the chain. The one thing I've kept asking myself was: how does anyone see a poisoning? But if Neiderman was poisoned too – and Perl had this strange illness – he only had to put two and two together."

Ahiezer was doubtful. "Why would Perl have informed on the Nili? It wasn't for money. I would have known if they had a secret stash. They were Jewish patriots. They could have gone to America and didn't."

"Perhaps they were acting as patriots."

He didn't follow.

"They could have thought the Nili would end badly for the Jews and decided to do something about it."

He wasn't buying that. "Look," he said. The arak on his breath had the delicate scent of perfume. "I don't believe Perl ratted on the Nili. But if she did, she deserved it. She got what was coming to her."

A man of impartial judgments.

* * *

Kalman Radin was skeptical, too. He had known the Appelbaums. "They were a solid, respectable family. Perl was a decent woman. Why would she have done it?" He had been a policeman; he knew about such things. "There's always an element of desperation in them. If you told me that a widow, or a woman who was alone, had informed on the Nili, I might believe it. Even an unhappily married one." But he would have known if Perl's marriage was unhappy. "You develop a sense for these things, in the children if not in the parents. And even if she had decided to inform, she wouldn't have gone to the Turks herself. She had a husband. She would have sent him."

"Maybe she did."

I recounted what I'd heard from Ahiezer. All along I had assumed that Perl and the Appelbaum of Sarah's letter were the same person. "But the informer could have been Avigdor. Alexander might have tried to poison them both."

"Alexander," Radin said, "wasn't capable of poisoning a mouse. He wasn't capable of anything."

That was that as far as he was concerned.

It wasn't just Perl Appelbaum I had gone back to him to talk about. It was also Yanko Epstein. He had known Epstein well – and he wasn't from Zichron, which gave him a different perspective.

He had first come to the village in the same year Ahiezer did, an immigrant from Russia looking for work. He had liked the place the moment he set eyes on it. There was something special about it, unspoiled. He had worked in other First Aliyah villages – Rehovot, Pet-ach-Tikva – and had felt the farmers there were just biding their time until they could exchange their lives for a middle-class existence. The farmers in Zichron weren't like that. They were happy being what they were.

He found work with the Zimnavoda family in Meir-Shfeya, across the valley. He enjoyed every minute of it. Each morning, before turning to their chores, they sat down together to breakfast – a glass of wine, a bowl of olive oil, and all the freshly baked bread you could eat. "To this day," he said, "nothing tastes better to me than fresh bread dipped in olive oil." He would sit there and think: where else in the world are there Jews who live by the sweat of their brows, eating bread from their own wheat and dipping it in oil from their own trees and washing it down with wine from their own grapes? He would have stayed had it not been for the Zimnavodas' married daughter Sarah, whose husband had gone to America and disappeared. She was lively and pretty and they fell in love, but she couldn't divorce her husband without his agreement – and he couldn't be found. It was the romantic disappointment of Radin's life. To get over it, he moved to Jerusalem.

It was by chance that he became a policeman. One day he ran into three young Jews from America, ex-soldiers in Jabotinsky's Jewish Legion, who had heard there were jobs with the British police. He went with them and was the only one to pass the interview. "Let's see what you look like in a uniform," he was told. "Get one from the storeroom and come back in an hour." He was given a uniform, bought a can of shoe polish and a bottle of Brasso, and went to work. When the hour was up, he reported back. An officer looked at him and said, "Bless my soul, Mr. Radin! I've never seen such a shiny policeman in my life." He got the job and was stationed in Zichron at his request.

He and Epstein became friends. "There were two things I liked about him," Radin said. "The first was that he could keep a secret. You could tell him anything and it would stop there." In those days, Zichron was full of tall tales about the Nili. But although they spent hours together on horseback, Epstein never talked about the spies, even though he knew a lot about them. "Not that he was a model of virtue. He was a trouble-maker. Once he got into trouble with my chief, Captain Redding. Redding lived on the town square and didn't like the young people keeping him awake at night – so one night Epstein and Pnina Goldstein stood outside his house and sang duets at the top of their lungs until he came out in his pajamas and threatened to run them in. Epstein was what we called in Russian a *shkolnik*, a bit of a wise-ass. All in all, though, he was more serious than other people his age, more honest."

The second thing he liked was Epstein's loyalty. "He'd do anything for a friend. If he gave you his word, you could count on it. That was something Arabs valued more than Jews – and he was more Arab than an Arab in some ways."

I said I would like his opinion about something and described Epstein's reaction when I asked about the death of Perl Appelbaum. "He went like this," I said, tensing my jaw until the blood backed up in my throat and making a sound to release it.

"That's him!" he exclaimed. "When he didn't want to talk, he had a mouth like a steel trap."

"So?"

He took his time answering. "She didn't die of natural causes. But it wasn't the way you think."

He wouldn't say any more.

* * *

Radin was anti-Davidesco. He had never liked the man. "Epstein should have worshiped him less," he said. "It worked against him in Zichron. Davidesco wasn't popular there."

Davidesco had his charms. "He was small, but strong, and a good storyteller – he could keep a room laughing for hours. And he didn't have to make a thing up, because it all was true. But I kept away from him. He bought and sold people like potatoes."

He had once tried to buy Radin. "She's the witness, she was there," he said, pointing to his wife. They were already living in Nesher and he was active in the Haganah. One night they were in their apartment when Davidesco appeared. "Hello, Yosef." "Hello, Radin! I have a proposition for you."

Radin told me:

"I could see he wanted to be alone with me, but I just said, 'I'm listening.' He talked – and what he said was that the British would pay me well for information on the Haganah. 'This isn't a temporary job,' he said. 'It's a steady income.' He was lucky my wife was there, because I might have put a bullet through his brain if she wasn't. 'Yosef,' I said, 'I've listened. Now get out and don't come back.' He had the skin of an elephant, though. A while later I ran into him in the street and he made the same offer."

By now I knew that, although Davidesco's official job was heading the Arab desk of the C.I.D. in Haifa, he had a wider clientele. To the Jaffa and Jerusalem branches of the C.I.D. he reported on the left-wing Haganah, the semi-clandestine defense force of the organized Jewish community, and on its two rivals, the right-wing Irgun and the extremist Stern Gang. To all three of these organizations he passed on information about the Arabs, the British, and one another. Army Intelligence learned from him about the C.I.D.; the C.I.D. about Army Intelligence. He was not so much a double as a quadruple and quintuple agent.

It was debatable where his true allegiance lay. Admirers like Epstein and Shatzman were sure it was with the Jews; if he had worked for the British, this was because it was a Jewish interest, and if he had revealed Jewish secrets, it was in return for more valuable ones passed the other way. His detractors were certain he had betrayed everyone until, in the case of Tsvi Sitner, he did it once too often.

Yet I now had in my possession a set of documents that threw new light on the Sitner case. It had been given to me by Davidesco's daughter Rakhel, a childhood friend of Ora Rosenzweig's who lived in Haifa. Ora must have recommended me warmly, for at our first meeting she handed me photocopies of some letters that she had never, she said, shown anyone. She had received them from Aryeh Samsonov, to whom they were written by a man named Moshe Rothstein in order to clarify the circumstances of Davidesco's death.

Before the establishment of Israel, Rothstein, now dead, had been an intelligence officer in the Irgun, the underground military arm of Jabotinsky's Revisionist Party. Formed in 1937 in reaction to the Haganah's alleged passivity in the face of Arab terror, the Irgun had launched a counter-terror campaign of its own, to which it added attacks on British soldiers and officials when the Mandate government shut the gates of Palestine to Jewish immigrants in 1939. But when Great Britain went to war against Germany soon afterwards, Jabotinsky ordered the organization to suspend its anti-British activities until the fight against the Nazis was won.

Although Jabotinsky died in 1940, the Irgun stuck to its ceasefire until the end of World War II. The year of his death, however, a breakaway faction led by a young Hebrew poet named Avraham Stern founded a splinter group that continued to target the British as the enemy. Its most spectacular strike was the assassination in Cairo of the British minister for Middle Eastern affairs, Lord Moyne, in 1944. By then Stern was dead too, having been gunned down by the British police, and the group's leadership had split into a right wing that dreamed of an expansionist "kingdom of Israel" and a left wing that identified with the anti-imperialism of the Soviet Union and regarded itself as its spearhead.

Davidesco, Rothstein wrote to Samsonov, was the c.i.d.'s main liaison with the Irgun. He had begun coordinating contacts with the Revisionists in 1931, and by the decade's end he and Rothstein were engaged in a covert operation to infiltrate Axis intelligence networks by pretending to pursue an anti-British alliance between the Irgun and Fascist Italy. When the British went to war, Irgun dossiers helped them to round up numerous German and Italian agents.

Politically, Davidesco sympathized with the Zionist Right. After the assassination of Lord Moyne, the Haganah, anxious to clear the "organized Jewish community," gave the British the names of 250 Irgun and Stern Gang members considered to be possibly involved. The c.i.d. passed the list to Davidesco to be vetted. That night, Rothstein wrote,

"I was awoken by a knock on the door. It was Yosef Davidesco, who had brought me a copy of the list so that I could alert everyone on it." The next day Davidesco attended a British intelligence conference and persuaded it that the list was worthless, "even though it would have been child's play for him to pick out the names of those behind the assassination."

While conceding that Davidesco had his "dark side," Rothstein stressed that he was a key figure, a man "in total control" of the C.I.D.'s Arab sources. Moreover, his importance grew as the war ended and fear of the Germans yielded to fear of the Russians. "From all over," Rothstein wrote Samsonov, "disturbing reports were flowing in of Communist preparations for widespread uprisings against Western imperialism." Arab nationalist leaders like the Jerusalem Mufti Hajj Amin el-Husseini and Rashid Kilani, the head of the powerful National Brotherhoood Party in Iraq, "abandoned the Nazi for the Communist horse. These reports roused the British lion from its lair. It was decided that Yosef Davidesco should leave Palestine, travel to England, be given an assumed identity, and start life anew as a wealthy Arab in Baghdad." Kilani had almost succeeded in engineering a pro-Nazi coup in Baghdad in 1941, and the British feared a pro-Soviet repeat. Davidesco was slated to be their chief agent there, the man in charge of foiling Communist efforts.

This contradicted what I had been led to believe – that is, that the transfer to Baghdad had been initiated by Davidesco because of the Stern Gang's threats on his life. The truth, Rothstein wrote, was the opposite: Tsvi Sitner, who was on the British wanted list, was betrayed because of the new role Davidesco was being groomed for... and by his own organization. More precisely, by its pro-Soviet wing, which arranged for the two men to meet in a café, informed the British about it, and leaked a false account that caused the rival wing to execute Davidesco as a traitor.

Rothstein didn't claim that Davidesco's framers had gotten wind of the C.I.D.'s plans for him. His point was merely that, as British Middle East intelligence shifted its scrutiny to Soviet activities, the Russians wanted him out of the way. He gave them the time they needed. Although he was, Rothstein wrote, "nearing the climax of his career, his farmer's blood did not permit him to leave the country before the end of the grape harvest. He saw it approach with a heavy heart, knowing that many years would pass before the next one. He never realized it would be the last harvest of all in his short but action-packed life."

* * *

I was in no position to evaluate Rothstein's letters. Their private nature, the only apparent motive of which was telling the truth, was a point in their favor. But while their author ranked high in Irgun intelligence circles, he had a reputation there for imaginativeness. "Anyone wishing to spend sleepless nights," the Israeli historian Shabtai Tevet once wrote of him, "might devote them to separating the chaff from the wheat in his résumés."

Yet even if not totally reliable, these letters put the Davidesco affair in a broader context. For the second time in the space of two world wars, a small town in Palestine was the venue of a drama pitting the Zionist Left against the Zionist Right against a background of international intrigue. One wondered what in the specific gravity of the place attracted such forces from afar.

A week before the elections, I saw Moshe Shatzman leaning against a billboard in town. Each of the parties running for the Knesset had plastered itself over the others so many times that the billboard's surface was crumpled like papier maché. I asked Shatzman if he had been hired to hold it up.

"No," he answered. "I'm hiding the truth."

He stepped aside to reveal the Labor Party's letters "EMeT," which also spelled the word "truth." "That's the closest to the truth they'll ever get!" he said.

Shatzman was a Likudnik, like all the farmers. He planned to vote for Menachem Begin, the ex-commander of the Irgun who had led the Right for three decades, losing election after election yet never the esteem of his followers. Even greater than their esteem for Begin, however, was the farmers' hatred of Labor. This went back to the days of the Second Aliyah and had grown worse under a government that burdened them with high taxes, discriminatory crop quotas, obligatory marketing cartels, and a host of bureaucratic restrictions. "Do you know why Ben-Gurion went into politics?" Shatzman asked of Jabotinsky and Begin's great opponent on the Left.

"Why?" I had heard it a dozen times.

"His first day in this country he was handed a hoe by a farmer and told to dig irrigation holes. An hour later the farmer came back and found three holes and Ben-Gurion in one of them, giving a speech. The son-of-a-bitch was too lazy to work. *That's* the truth!" He stabbed at it with a finger. "Where are you off to?"

"The bank."

"I'm waiting for Ben-Hayyim. Come have coffee with us."

Ben-Hayyim appeared and we went to Pomerantz's café. Waiting for us there was the sardonic man whose wife had been one of Alexander Aaronsohn's little girlfriends. This was hard to imagine, because she was now a huge, ailing woman who occupied most of the double bed she spent her days in. Shatzman urged her husband to bring her to the voting booth.

"How can I bring her?" he asked. "She can't walk."

"On a stretcher," Shatzman said. "Ben-Hayyim and I will pay for it."

"She won't fit through the door."

"Every vote counts," Shatzman said.

Although the latest polls showed Begin still trailing Shimon Peres, the gap was closing.

Yanko Epstein walked by in the street, wearing his blue beret.

"Do you know why he wears that French hat?" the sardonic man asked. "It's because he thinks he's Napoleon."

"The man of truth," Shatzman said.

Everyone knew Epstein would vote Labor.

"Little Napoleon!" The sardonic man had switched on the radio the other day and there was Epstein, talking about the Nili ring as if he had commanded it.

"I don't know how he gets away with it," Shatzman said.

"Don't you worry," said Ben-Hayyim. "No one gets away with anything in this world. There's a law and a judge." He laid a trembling hand on my arm. "You don't believe me? Listen, my friend.

"I had a goatherd, an Arab from Sindiani. One day he invited his friends to a meal and served a goat of mine for the main course. How did I know? From a neighbor of his. 'There's a smell of roast meat coming from your goatherd's kitchen,' he said to me, 'that I thought you should know about.' I counted my flock, saw a goat was missing, and fired the man the next day.

"A few days later a new olive grove I had planted was uprooted. I knew who had done it. Who else could it be? There was nothing I could do about it, though.

"But leave it to God. What happens next? My goatherd's son starts up with a girl from his village, one of the Mukbil clan. The girl's brother gets wind of it and takes a sword and goes looking for the boy. He finds him in the middle of the village and the boy takes to his heels. The brother chases him all the way to my goatherd's house. The boy opens the door and runs inside and his father reaches out to shut it – and the brother swings the sword and cuts off the father's hand.

"His hand! What's the Moslem punishment for theft? You tell me!"

He bore down on my arm. "Wait! There's more. I replanted the trees. One day I went to have a look at them. There's my old goatherd, standing and hoeing them. '*Ya hawajja,*' he says, 'I was just passing by and saw your trees needed weeding.' Just passing by! A one-armed man with a hoe! It was his conscience. And you say there's no law and no judge?"

"Well," Shatzman said slyly, "I once saw a judge try someone for theft. Some cows had been stolen and the tracks of a horseman who was with them led to the yard of Yosef Davidesco. I went as his witness and told the court, 'Your Honor, Mr. Davidesco could not have ridden that horse because he was at my house the night the cows were stolen.' The judge acquitted him and said, 'Mr. Davidesco, I'm letting you go for lack of evidence, but the next time you invite guests, try to be home.'"

"But how did he die?" Ben-Hayyim asked. "How did he die, Moshe?"

They argued while I tried to remember where I had heard that anecdote before.

It was in Epstein's story of Abu D'nein and the cattle thieves. *Your Honor, the night was not just mine.* Was it the death of Davidesco that had transformed him from an eschewer of tall tales to a confabulator of them?

Davidesco had been his idol. His was the life he would have liked to have lived instead of his own, a village field guard's. And then, while the field guard was in the shower, that life was ended, cracked like the binding of a book whose stories fell out of it without a title page. What was to keep him from picking them up?

Perhaps he had started with a few of them. In time he might have come to believe himself. This was common. You told a fib. You told it again. By the third time, it sounded to you as if it had happened. By the sixth, you couldn't swear it hadn't. By the tenth, you were certain it had.

And yet all along all he remained as tight-lipped about some things as he lost all caution about others. The secret with Neiderman. *He took it to the grave and so will I.* Why?

He was loyal, Radin had said. To what? A promise made to a long-dead man?

I wished I hadn't parted with Tova Gelberg. Those clairvoyant eyes hadn't yet told me all they knew.

There were still Epstein's diaries. I would wait until after the elections.

*   *   *

The bank was crowded. It was one of three in town, which should have been enough. But people in Zichron congregated in banks. They liked to look in on their money, which suffered from inflation and devaluations. At ten in the morning, Bank Le'umi was filled with housewives, pensioners, shopkeepers, farmers, plumbers, carpenters. They stood in front of the tellers' windows and flocked around the savings plan desk, the securities desk, the foreign currency desk, filling the available seats and talking in quiet tones like visitors in a hospital.

I spotted Ze'ev Neiderman at the end of a line and joined him. Shifting his straw hat from hand to hand as he fanned himself, he complained that he was feeling weak. He should be going for medical tests instead of standing in line for a lot of worthless money. "9.53 to the dollar!" he said. "Would you believe it? You walk out with a thousand pounds and have nothing. In my first teaching job I earned eight pounds sterling a month and lived like a lord."

He had taught at a Jewish school in Baghdad after graduating from the American College in Beirut. He had never wanted to be a farmer, not since the night in his teens when a hyena howled as he was threshing sorghum with a team of mules. The mules took off in two different directions and he landed in the sorghum. "This isn't for you, Ze'ev!" he told himself.

He didn't regret the decision. But he was sorry he had become a schoolteacher. "I wasted my life being a nursemaid," said the former principal of the Nili School. "I always wanted to leave this town. What a dump it was! I was bribed to stay. Seventeen and a half pounds a month! Do you have any idea what that was in those days?"

At the teller's window I checked my bank balance while I listened to Mr. Sepen, the manager, talking to a customer. The balances were written on slips of paper with stick-figure faces, smiley black and sulky red. Though my balance came back a sulky red, the teller's face remained a smiley black. "I tell you," Mr. Sepen was saying, "we're on the brink of disaster. The country is sinking into debt." "We've always been in debt," said the customer. "Once Rothschild took care of it, now it's America. Why worry?" Mr. Sepen, who was as pink and fat as a well-fed baby, did not look worried at all.

*   *   *

A few days after Menachem Begin's surprise victory, our friends Uri and Ya'ara came up for the weekend from Jerusalem with their two children, Daniella and Itamar.

They were upset about the elections. All our friends in Jerusalem were. Some felt panic at the Right's coming to power. There was talk of war, "creeping fascism."

I found that silly. Four years in Zichron had changed me.

Uri brought with him an antique bottle catalog sent by his brother in America, a collector. The Barnett & Foster Niagara Bottle was in it. It was of a type, known as a "Codd bottle" after its inventor, the Englishman Hiram Codd, that was in use from 1872 to circa 1920. Its market value was about thirteen dollars.

"Of course," he pointed out, "that's without the names and local trademarks on your bottles. That makes them worth more."

Fifteen dollars? Thirty? There were thousands of them buried below old Betsalel Ashkenazi's house. I only had to dig them up.

We spent long hours on the beach at Tantura. Daniella and Talya built sand castles and swam with their water wings in a lagoon with a little island you could wade to. We made up a story about a mermaid who lived there. Her name was Eleanora and we searched for her. "Eleanora! Eleanora!" the two girls called. The still sea listened without comment.

It was good to see Talya with a playmate. Although she was now in nursery school, she still had few friends. Sometimes the three Bedouin children came to visit from their shack. They arrived shyly, the two girls clinging to their brother as if not sure it was permitted. Apart from splashing in the mud with their father's goats, they had no concept of play. At first they stared at Talya's Fisher-Price dollhouse and dolls as at implements whose purpose was unknown. Ibtisam and Iman learned quickly and were soon bossing the little dolls around. Walid preferred working in the garden. He knew the uses of my tools. It was as if he understood that they were his future and that it was pointless to postpone it.

Uri and Ya'ara went back to Jerusalem. One afternoon, after the three children had been to our house, Talya said:

"I can't find my Fisher-Prices."

We searched for them under the bed, in the closets – they were gone.

"All right," Marcia said. "Those children were your idea. Go get those dolls back."

I set out for the Bedouin shack. Turning into Wine Street, I saw the children's mother coming up it with a plastic bag. We met by the bakery. I said:

"Look, don't be …."

But she was. There were hot tears of shame in her eyes.

"They're only children," I told her.

"I thrashed all three of them."

"You shouldn't have."

"Walid the hardest."

The little dolls lay, pale and breathless, at the bottom of the bag.

"I hope …."

She didn't know how to say what she hoped.

That you will accept my children's atonement? That you will not turn them away if they come again?

"Of course," I said. I knew they never would.

Marcia was furious.

"Calm down," I said. "I have the dolls."

"What am I supposed to be calm about? My daughter's friends stealing her toys?"

"Come on. They're nice kids. The temptation was too much for them. Their mother spanked them and they learned their lesson."

"Their mother is a whore."

"How can you say that? She – "

The cheap perfume. The easy manner. No ordinary Arab woman would have sat alone with me like that. No ordinary Arab husband would have allowed it.

"…is a whore. She sleeps with the farmers' sons."

"Are you sure?"

"Of course I'm sure. Everyone knows except you. You'd know, too, if it had happened fifty years ago."

That night we slept on opposite sides of the bed. We might have gone the next day without talking had she not woken me in the morning and said:

"You'd better get up. There's a police car in the driveway."

I jumped out of bed. There was a police car in the driveway. Two policeman had gotten out of it. One was Bad Ginger.

I threw on some pants and ran outside. Bad Ginger was at the bottom of the stairs, holding a burlap sack and examining a sickle.

"Could be," he said.

"Ticket it," said the second policeman.

Bad Ginger took what looked like a batch of baggage tags from his pocket. He detached one of them, wrote on it with a pen, tied it to the sickle, and dropped it in the sack.

"Can I help you?" I asked, descending the stairs. My heart was pounding.

"We'd like a look around your yard," the second policeman said. He was a sergeant.

"That sickle is mine," I told him. "It's from Benedik's hardware store."

"You can explain that at the police station."

Bad Ginger peered into the sack with a little smile as if I were inside it with the sickle.

I ran up the stairs to tell Marcia and came back down. The policemen were already circling the house. They weren't interested in large objects. Or in new ones. Bad Ginger chose the little old ones. A bent-handled spade. A rusted pruning saw. A horseshoe I had found. "Ticket it," the sergeant said. Bad Ginger dropped the spade into his sack.

He took a pair of old garden shears. A wooden ox yoke. A metal canteen purchased for a bicycle trip when I was in college. "I bought that in an army surplus store in New York," I said.

"Ticket it," the sergeant said.

When they were done, I was taken to the police station. The sergeant let them know we were coming. "Pariente speaking," he said into a two-way radio. "We're bringing in the accused."

The accused! I didn't have a name any more. It was in Bad Ginger's sack, too.

I was questioned by a detective. "At what hour did you break into Mr. Rom's barn?" he asked.

Mr. Rom was Bad Ginger. "I don't remember the hour," I said. "It was a month ago. I only did it to read old newspapers. I – "

"I'm asking about last night."

So that was the reason for my arrest. Someone had broken into the barn the night before and taken some things. "It wasn't me," I said.

"Mr. Rom says the items found in your garden are from his barn."

He wasn't called Bad Ginger for nothing. "They're mine," I said.

"We'll see about that," the detective promised.

I signed a protocol of my testimony and was released. Marcia drove to the station to pick me up. "I can't believe this has happened," she said.

"Never mind what's happened," I told her. "They may get a warrant and search the house. We have to work fast."

The fireplace frame. The pirate's chest. The wagon wheel. The threshing sled. The Codd bottles. The old books. They had all been taken from somewhere.

We covered the chest with a bedspread and took everything else down to the car, tying the fireplace frame to the roof as I had done years before. It was a jest of fate that, after combing every abandoned building in Zichron, I was in trouble for something I hadn't touched. And I could forget about recovering Epstein's diaries. It would be crazy now even to think of it.

I drove the cargo to a safe house. Then I drove back, bracing myself for the storm.

It never came.

Marcia had made up her mind. She didn't want to live where she didn't belong – where her children didn't belong – where her husband spooked the houses of the dead. She wanted to be near people like ourselves, with children like our own. She needed places to go to, things to do. There wasn't even a movie theater in town. You couldn't eat out unless you chose between falafel at the falafel stand and kebab and soggy fries at the bus station. She had had enough.

"You'd leave all this?" I asked. "The house we built?"

I went to the picture window in the living room and looked out. There was a haze in the air. Once, on a brilliant winter day, the kind that came when the rain scrubbed the sky like a carwash, I was astonished to see, beyond the farthest hills, a level line that could only be the Golan Heights, rising from the shore of the Sea of Galilee sixty kilometers away. I had never seen so far before; I never saw so far again. Even in the clearest weather, the level line did not reappear. Was it a mirage or an irreproducible moment?

It was all like that, the whole view, out over the valleys and fields. We had seen it once in the moonlight and thought we would see it again, over and over, the same way. We never did.

I turned from the window. Fine, I said. We would move back to Jerusalem.

Chapter seventeen

We found a place to rent outside Jerusalem. It was on the same pleasant street on which Marcia and I had once inspected a dwelling that looked like a converted chicken coop. We would move in mid-August.

Our home wasn't searched. I didn't hear again from the police.

The town quieted down from the elections. So did our friends in Jerusalem. Menachem Begin formed a government and the apocalypse lingered.

The grape harvest began. The tractors on Wine Street lined up in long queues, waiting to disgorge their grapes. The farmers stood beside them in their jungle hats, grumbling about the delays. The weather was hot and sultry; the sugar content in the vineyards was climbing like a fever. Outside the winery, a conveyer spat out skins and seeds. It shook, clattered, and spat a purple stack that rose each day like the grain on the old threshing floor.

From the winery's rear, a purple effluvium ran downhill. I followed it one day to where it overflowed its ditch in a redolent marsh. A flock of egrets waddled there like geese. Big birds that roosted in dead trees, patiently arranging themselves in perfect pyramids, they now staggered aimlessly. Now and then they gave their wings a puzzled flap and went to take another sip from the marsh. They were quite drunk.

I was at the checkout counter in Aminadav's grocery one morning, standing in line behind an old woman I had never seen before, when Yigal Shvartzman parked his tractor in the street and strode inside. Shvartzman was the farmer who owned the apricot trees on our hillside, a burly man with the manners of a grizzly bear. He lumbered to the back of the store, grabbed a loaf of bread and a fish, and marched to the head of the line.

"Aminadav!" he growled. "Is this fish fresh?"

Aminadav looked up from his cash register. "Fresh? It was caught this morning."

Shvartzman gave him a suspicious look. He waved the fish as if to see if water dripped from it. "That's impossible," he said. "It's smoked."

"If it's smoked," said Aminadav, "how can it be fresh?"

Shvartzman was a farmer, not a wit. "Charge it! I'm in a hurry!" he growled, lumbering back to his tractor.

Aminadav entered the sum in his account book. He rang up the woman's purchases. "You'll have to excuse some of my customers," he apologized, looking for her name. "Here we are. Sarah Zimnavoda."

The woman saw me staring at her. Small and frail-looking, she wore a kerchief like the founding mothers in Epstein's museum. "Do I know you from somewhere?" she asked.

"Perhaps you've seen me around town," I said.

"I don't think so. I haven't been here long. I spent most of my life in America."

Her Hebrew phonemes were native, their intonation foreign and flat.

"In that case," I said, "regards from Kalman Radin."

"From whom?" She put a hand to her ear.

"Kalman Radin."

"Rabin?"

"Radin."

"Where does he know me from?"

I told her.

"You say he stayed with my family?"

"In 1919 or '20."

"I don't remember him."

"He remembers you, though," I said. "He says you were lively and pretty."

"Lively and what?"

"Pretty."

She weighed the likelihood of that. "He couldn't have meant me. He must have been thinking of one of my sisters."

"He mentioned you by name. He said your husband had gone off to America."

"Yes, that was me. In the end I joined him there. I came back because he died. Well, say hello for me to... what did you say his name was?"

"Kalman Radin."

"To Mr. Radin. Tell him thank you."

I stopped at Benedik's hardware store to buy a new sickle. "Save the receipt," Meir Benedik counseled. The police had questioned him about me. "Do you know what the Zichron farmer said when he was asked if he enjoyed sex with his wife?"

I had no idea.

"He supposed he did, because otherwise he'd have his field hands do it for him.'"

Meir's blond hair was turning grey beneath its army fatigue cap. He was standing in the spot where Yosef Davidesco had fallen in a pool of blood.

In the copse of pine trees at the start of our dirt road I spied Ora Rosenzweig peering through a binoculars. Supposedly a vest-pocket park, the copse was frayed and needed mending. The lower branches of the trees hung contorted where they had died in their loopy struggles for light, and soda cans and sandwich wrappers littered the faded benches. Yet weekend painters still set up their easels here, ignoring the remains of lunches for the view that Ora was staring at from beneath a summer bonnet.

She hailed me when she saw me. "I'm on sentinel duty," she called. She was keeping watch on the valley, where a sewage pipe was being run down the hill from Shfeya. She and Micha had obtained a court order to stop it because it encroached on a wheat field of theirs. Now, though, they had heard that work was being resumed.

"It's to the left of that tree." She handed me the binoculars.

The wheat field, its upper corner pricked by a silver needle, was a yellow patch in the green quilt of the valley.

"Do you see anyone down there?"

"No one," I said and walked her back up the street. In front of her house Sonya Bloch was scolding her cocker spaniel. She and Ora ignored each other. Back in the days when she worked in the town library, Sonya had accused Ora's daughter of failing to return a borrowed book. By the time it was found, the two were enemies.

Ora had a new sculpture to show me. Three little figures, seen from the back, sat on a bench, arms and heads pressed against a rectangular block. Facing them was a man with one hand on the block and the other gripping a handle. It looked like a stocks, some primitive punishment machine.

Ora laughed at the idea. "We couldn't wait to be punished. Before Alter Graf's cinema, this was our movie theater. An Arab brought it to the village. This block of wood was hollow and had peepholes. Inside was a metal drum turned by a crank and fitted with rolls of illustrated paper. The Arab turned it while telling us stories about the pictures. One was about the beautiful daughter of a sultan who was kidnapped from the palace. The sultan's soldiers galloped after her and freed her in a grand fight."

The movie theater was painted bright colors and decorated with round little mirrors, chains of clam shells, and tinkling bells. "We came running at the sound of them. I can't decide whether to add them." She turned the base of the sculpture to view it from all sides. "I don't want to spoil it with too much detail. But I do want to show how things were. They're only a memory now."

"If Elfie Samsonov has her way, they won't be even that," I said, telling her of my aborted plan.

She regarded me in surprise. "You don't know?"

"Know what?"

"What happened to all that material."

"Do you?"

"Moshe Shatzman burned it."

"*What?*"

"Shatzman burned it. Elfie gave it to him because his youngest daughter is married to Samsonov's son from his first marriage. A while back he came to me and said, 'Ora, I think I did something stupid.' I said, 'Moshe, how could you?' and he said, 'Well, it was taking up room in my shed and I didn't think anyone cared.' Stupid isn't the word!"

It was too painful to think about: the entire history of Zichron – documents, memoirs, correspondences, notebooks, records, diaries – Epstein's diaries – gone up in smoke. No wonder it had been impossible to get a straight story from Elfie.

"Shatzman!" I said. "I wouldn't have guessed it in a million years."

"A man without guile." There was as much affection as irony in her voice. "Here, this is to remember us by in Jerusalem."

She handed me an orange scroll wrapped in wax paper.

Only the old-timers still bothered to make it. First you boiled the fruit for hours until you had a sticky liquid. Then you set it out in trays to harden slowly in the sun, covering it by day with mosquito netting against the flies and taking it in by night to protect it from the dew. Finally, you hung it out to finish drying and rolled it like a poster for safekeeping. Every June, the laundry line in Ora's yard was draped with what looked like orange underwear.

"What's that?" Talya asked when I brought it home with the groceries.

"Apricot leather." I took it from its wrapper and unrolled it. "It's like a Torah scroll without writing."

"Then it can tell any story I want."

"What story would you like it to tell?"

"Once upon a time there was a family that lived on Apricot Hill at Rainbow Valley. And it was very, very."

"Very, very what?"

"Just very, very," Talya said.

* * *

Looted, burned, smashed. The past stood no chance.

On the land above us, a bulldozer appeared without warning. The couple from Haifa had started to build.

It was over within hours. The plot was leveled and cleared. The big power scoop tore up trees, roots, bushes, hedges, shrubs, rocks. The Barnett & Foster bottles lay shattered on the surface, broken slivers bright in the sunlight like the bellies of dynamited fish. They had crossed the seas from London and quenched the thirst of the Levant, only to be trampled by a snorting ox of a machine with the strength of four hundred horses. A fortune! Lost forever!

*   *   *

Wooden packing crates stood all around. The books and dishes were disappearing from the shelves. The furniture not being taken to Jerusalem had been moved to the basement for storage.

The house had gotten smaller. It was an odd thing about houses. You would think they would become roomier as they emptied out. But it was just the opposite. It was as if each object in them had stretched the space around it, which contracted when it was removed.

With the rugs and much of the furniture gone, our brick floor lay exposed in all its folly. It was unique, the only one of its kind in the country. The idea for it came from a week in the south of France on our way to Israel in 1970. Brick floors were common there. But the only suitable bricks we could find were made by a factory that was going out of business, and we were horrified when they arrived. They were humped, crooked, mottled, chipped, no two the same shape or color. Before shutting its doors, the factory's owners had scraped together every last reject and shipped them to us.

There was no one to return them to and we decided to use them. They so unnerved the Arab floorer that he ran away twice and had to be coaxed back with blandishments and threats. The results had more in common with the woven texture of basketry than the flat surface of paving. Some people loved it. Most suggested we tear it up or cover it with concrete. Like Edmond de Rothschild, we had tried transplanting Provence to the Middle East and made a botch of it.

It wouldn't help sell the house. But we weren't up to that. As far as our neighbors in Zichron were concerned, we were simply taking a year's vacation. This was why, handing me a parting drink on his terrace, Izzy Traub said:

"Don't look so doo-er, lad! You'll be back before you know it."

"And you may have a phone by then," Rhoda said.

"Of course," I replied. "We've nearly made it to Category 6."

There was a page in the telephone book listing eight degrees of priority. Number 1 included prime ministers and cabinet members; number 6, all applicants waiting five years or more.

"And a book," Izzy said. "By God, I can't wait to read it."

That was part of our story. We were going to Jerusalem to help me write my book. I would rent a workroom and be out of the house all day, away from Marcia and the children, away from Zichron. I would have the perspective I needed.

"Have you decided what it will be about?" Rhoda asked.

"It's a murder mystery," I said.

"Don't tell me you still think that what's-her-name was poisoned!"

"I'll never know. I've lost my last chance to find out."

I related the fate of Epstein's diaries.

"You'll think of something," Izzy said. "What would Hercule Poirot do?"

From the great carob tree came the snores of a barn owl. A soft breeze from the east blew the ferment of wine. Toward morning it would have the tang of yeast in it.

"Well, good luck with the writing," Izzy said. "Just leave us out of it. We don't want any pesky journalists knocking on our door."

"It's too late for that," I told him. "I've written the first chapter and you're in it."

"Oh, no!"

He sounded more pleased than alarmed.

"It's an introduction. It tells how we came to Zichron – how we met you by chance as we were walking down the road, and how you invited us for supper, and how the land next to you was for sale and we bought it the next day."

How long ago and crazy it all seemed!

"But that's not what happened," Marcia said.

"How do you mean?"

"We didn't meet Izzy and Rhoda by chance. We hàd their telephone number and called them from town. And we didn't buy the land the next day. Gedalia Kruppik took us to see some other properties and we went back to Jerusalem and thought for two weeks before making up our minds."

"What two weeks?" I said. "Kruppik met me with Ashkenazi the next morning. We bargained and shook hands."

"You're imagining it. You're becoming like Epstein."

"Izzy! Rhoda!" I appealed. "Didn't we buy the land the next day?"

Neither of them remembered. "Children, children!" Izzy said. "No arguments, please. Let's speak only of happy things. I hear you've gotten your driving license, dear. That's marvelous. Now you can scoot up to see us while…'Tsati, shame!"

Matsati had a dead lizard in his mouth. Rhoda Traub bent over him, gently pried his jaws open, and released it. The lizard stopped playing dead and scuttled off. Matsati whined petulantly. "Izzy," said Rhoda, "go fetch 'Tsati his bone."

"A bonus for the dogus," Izzy said. "Just listen to old Tito. He's sleeping on his back again. Here, I'll fetch you a refill while I'm at it."

*　*　*

The real estate agents were the first to glimpse it dimly. By the time we left for Jerusalem, one or two had set up shop in competition with Kruppik. They opened small offices for the prospectors who had heard that land and houses were cheap in a quaintly shabby town with fine vistas on the Carmel.

But even the agents had no inkling of what was to come when the pioneer prospectors were followed by a gold rush: the new streets of swanky villas facing the sea, the row cottages running down from Founders Street, the developments sprouting on the hills – suburban estates named Eden Bluffs, The Baron's Manor, and Zichron Preserve, instant neighborhoods of three-bedroom homes, take-home lawns, golden retrievers, and children on bicycles, of squash – court-sized gardens bright with bougainvillea and loop-around streets called Almond and Anemone whose engineers set out each morning for a high-tech park outside Haifa and whose lawyers took the 7:36 from Binyamina to Tel Aviv. Zichron would become a commuter town.

Who knew it then, though? Who knew there would be a renovated town center, a pedestrian mall with imitation cobblestones and faux-antique streetlamps, a *route touristique* grandly called "The Wine Way" running from the south end of Founders Street to the winery? Not Marcia; not I, taking a last walk past the cemetery, past the museum, past the bus station, though we had tried telling whoever would listen, like a beachhead calling for reinforcements that never came, that the place had a future and now was the time to buy. But while I dreamed often in those years (even dreamed that our valley had become a great lake in which the yachts bobbed at anchor like the boats at St. Tropez while behind us, up the hill, a great market took place and slim-waisted women walked among its stands, dappled points of bright color like the figures in Seurat's *La Grande Jatte*), I never dreamed that here, where the town once began and Ezra Goldstein, a ten-year-old boy (gone now!), welcomed Edmond de Rothschild with flowers ("*j'ai l'honneur*," he had said, declaiming it for me from a bench in the park, for we had made up since the day he cut down the plum trees, "*de vous présenter ce bouquet de fleures en témoignage de votre reconnaissance à notre pays, à nos parents, et à nous*"), a visionary architect would erect, as though the Wine Way threaded the gate of a medieval city, a formal white archway, floodlit claret purple at night, its astral glow touching the houses past which Yanko Epstein rode on his way home from his rounds, past the Schwartzes, past the Appelbaums, past the Gelbergs.

Past Ben-Hayyim's (gone now, Ben-Hayyim!), past Epstein's (gone!), Founders Street lined with cafés and restaurants, the decrepit farmyards restored, their collapsing barns and sheds turned into pubs, bakeries, gift shops, boutiques, jewelry and health-food stores, antique shops, art galleries, arcades ("my God," a Californian friend said, "you've been Carmelized!"), little signs hung on poles for handicrafts, leather goods, garden sculpture, decorative fountains, stained glass windows, therapeutic massage, feng shui, rice paper, harp recitals, jazz concerts, wine festivals (Shatzman gone! Neiderman gone!), the Graf Hotel knocked down for a supermarket, second stories on all the old houses, historical plaques on their walls, the farmers gone too (Tishbi! Ephraim Ashkenazi! Micha Rosenzweig!), their lands sold or leased, their grandchildren professors, playwrights, mathematicians, software designers, tour guides, their Arab field hands replaced by stocky Thais who caught the stray cats that crept through the town and roasted them over their campfires, the streets full of wine cellars, ice cream parlors, espresso bars, pizza places (Ora Rosenzweig gone! Rhoda Traub gone! Izzy Traub gone!), and everywhere, everywhere the realtors, the prices doubled, tripled, ten times, fifty times higher, you wouldn't believe what a dunam was worth.

Past Aaronsohn House. Past the old water tower. Past Esther-Leah Berkovitz rocking on her porch. Past Aminadav's grocery. Past the falafel stand and the kiosk on the corner ("Vance, Begin Meet Today") and down the Street of the Benefactor. Gift Bear. Wine Bear. Asheri taking in his vegetables, early risers in need of their beauty sleep. Miriam's wool store. On her folding chair on the sidewalk Yafia Cohen was taking the declining sun. The success of her operation had left her troubled, for a better lawyer might have advised her against signing a new lease on life. "I don't know what God gave me so many years for," she had grumbled the last time I saw her. "What did He think I was going to do with them?"

Now, though, squinting upward, her mood was better. "Hello, sweetheart," she said. "Don't bump your head against the sky. My, you're a pretty girl! Talya's your name, isn't it?"

"No," I answered, since the daughter on my shoulders didn't talk yet. "This is Michal."

*   *   *

The movers were due in two days. I stood in the driveway burning trash in a metal barrel like a diplomat destroying the files of an evacuating embassy. Then I showered and went to pick up Epstein.

I had invited him for a farewell lunch and he chose to go to Goldenberg's, by the railroad tracks in Binyamina. It had better food than the bus station's. "Besides," he said, "it's Friday. There'll be soup and fish." Mrs. Goldenberg's Sabbath specialties, chicken soup and gefilte fish, were to be had once a week.

Two men were paying their bill as we arrived, leaving us the only customers. Mrs. Goldenberg, an autocrat by nature, was in a bad temper. "You may as well put down those menus," she said, "because I don't have anything that's on them. You can start with the soup or the fish."

"Well," Epstein said, "I wouldn't want to miss your fish. Your fish is what I've come for. But I like your soup, too. I'll start with that and then have the fish."

She had never heard of such a thing. "Soup and then fish?" she asked. "Soup *and* fish? That's new to me."

"There's always a first time," he said. But when I made it a second time by asking for the same, she walked off angrily. "You can start with fish and you can start with soup," she complained to the kitchen doors as they opened ahead of her, "but who starts with both?"

We were facing the railroad tracks. "The land Ahmed Bek and my father quarreled over was across those tracks," Epstein said. "Or it would have been if they had been there. They were laid by the British."

The raised arms of a traffic barrier escorted the road across the tracks. It wasn't that men like him or Shatzman lived in the past. It was that the past lived in them. It made for a kind of double vision – not like that of bifocals, which required you to see near or far, but like that of a transparency, one thing imposed on the other so that you saw them both together.

Two bowls of golden soup arrived, thick with noodles.

"It smells delicious," I said.

Mrs. Goldenberg spurned the compliment.

"Did you have a chance to look at that correspondence?" I asked Epstein.

I had made copies for him of Rothstein's letters to Samsonov.

He nodded, his mouth full of noodles.

"And?"

The letters confirmed what he had thought: Davidesco was set up. He repeated his reasons for believing it, adding a new one. "They were planning to kill him long before Sitner's arrest. If I could find a certain young lady, I'd prove it to you."

The young lady would no longer be young by now. She had come to work as Davidesco's housekeeper several months before his death and had disappeared right before his murder. He was sure she had been involved in it.

Mrs. Goldenberg cleared away the soup bowls and brought the fish. With it came a plate of horseradish and two bottles of beer I had ordered.

I filled our glasses and raised mine. "Well, here's to Zichron," I proposed. "May it never lose its charms."

We clinked and drank.

"I want to thank you for all your stories," I said. "I hope I haven't been too much of a nuisance."

His hand flicked away the possibility. We both knew our friendship had its motives. We had stalked each other from the start. He had wanted to be the hero of a book as much as I had wanted to write one.

"There's still one story you owe me," I said.

He waggled a wrist.

"That woman in the park and the Turkish officer – "

"Adel Bey."

"The army doctor. You promised to tell me how you made him pay for it."

"I captured his tent in the battle of Zichron."

"What battle was that?" I lunged for his bait one last time.

"It was this time of year, the end of summer. The British were already in Hadera. They were planning to move on Damascus through the Valley of Jezreel, up Wadi Milikh. For that, they had to take Zichron." His hoarse voice flowed smoothly down the streambed of the memory. "I had gone to the Burj to bring home a load of sorghum. On my way back, I heard guns. A shell landed on the hillside. A British warship was firing from the sea. I thought it might be aiming for the road, so I left the wagon in the Aaronsohns' olive grove and rode the mule into town through the fields.

"The warship wasn't aiming for anything. It was only trying to scare the Turks. And it did, because they gave the order to pull out. That's when I remembered the doctor's dispensary. It was in a big tent behind the administration building. I rounded up some friends and we took it apart. We were dragging it away when the last Turkish troops left town and the first British ones entered. It was made of good, strong canvas: for years we winnowed sesame on my share of it. That was the battle of Zichron."

He sliced a piece of fish to mark the end of it.

"But the war still wasn't over. I had one thing left to do."

He finished the story with a deft twist:

"I took that mule and lanced its boil. If it could have talked like my horse it would have asked, 'What's taken you so long?'"

It was time to set my plan in motion. "I've been back to see your friend Radin," I said.

His fork paused on its way to the horseradish.

"He thinks the world of you."

It resumed its journey.

"Especially of how you keep a secret. He says you have a mouth like a steel trap."

The trap opened. The fork slid in and out.

"I didn't need him to tell me that. You've kept three secrets from me, even though each was so old that it couldn't possibly matter any more."

He took a sip of beer.

"The first was that woman in the park. I had to find out who she was on my own."

I mentioned her name. He was impassive.

"She had lost her honor. But you had yours. If anyone was going to know about it, it wasn't going to be because of you."

The second secret had to do with the Sons of Benjamin. "You wouldn't tell me who stole their records. You did."

He looked at me sharply. "Why would I have done it?"

"To find out what had happened to the Zayta land."

"There was no need for that! Everyone knew what had happened to it. Alexander bought it with Mrs. Fels' money and registered it in Tova Gelberg's name. It all came out in Petach-Tivka. Sapir accused Alexander publicly."

"The break-in came first. Who told Sapir what he knew?"

He was saved from having to answer by Mrs. Goldenberg, who came to clear away our plates. "For your main course," she said, "you can have the flanken or the goose. Just don't tell me you want both."

"I don't want either," Epstein said.

"You-don't-want – *either*?"

"I'd like something sweet. What do you have for dessert?"

"I knew it!" said Mrs. Goldenberg. "I knew it! What could any-one expect?"

Certainly not a healthy appetite. Soup *and* fish!

"Some compote, perhaps."

"Compote! If you wanted compote, you should have asked for it. Did you think I had nothing better to do than wait to bring you compote?"

"You know," he said when she was gone, "that's one woman I wouldn't marry even for her cooking."

"You'll have to marry someone else then."

He blushed, the red staining his cheeks as it did on the day he talked to the woman named Bella. Did he love her? Could you love a woman if you loved a place more? It struck me that I knew nothing about him. He had never discussed his feelings with me any more than I had discussed mine with him. What kind of hero would he make? The problem was that he was real. If he were a fiction I could delve into any recess of him – could fashion it like a glass blower spinning space from a drop, expand it, shape it, twist and twirl it as I wished. People thought it was easier to write about "the facts" because then nothing needed to be "made up," but it was just the other way around. The imagination took you anywhere you wanted. Reality dug in its heels. It was an eighty-year-old man with a half-drunk glass of beer who knew more about the past than anyone and couldn't be trusted to tell the truth about any of it. And the truth was dense, shapeless, impenetrable. You could only grope your way around it.

Mrs. Goldenberg came back from the kitchen with two bowls of stewed pears. "Here," she said. "Just don't dawdle. If you want to talk all day, go to a hotel lobby."

We didn't need all day. "There's one secret left," I told Epstein.

He regarded me gravely.

"It's the big one. What did you see that night – what did you tell Neiderman about in the morning – that made you both swear to take it to the grave?"

He said nothing.

"It was during the first Events – let's say on a warm summer night. You were riding home from your rounds, starting at the south end of Founders Street. The town was asleep. You lived halfway up the street to the synagogue. You had to pass a dozen houses on your way."

He didn't dispute that.

"You saw a person come out of a house. It had to be that. You wouldn't have run to Neiderman because of someone in the street, even in the middle of the night."

There was a look in his eyes, of alertness or apprehension, that hadn't been there before.

"It was someone you knew. We can agree on that, can't we?"

He shook his head. I was drawing him in.

"Of course we can. A stranger would have been challenged by you. You had your Enfield. You would have pulled it out and called, 'Who are you in the night?' Even if he had gotten away, you would have thought he was only a burglar. You wouldn't have been in a predicament."

He waited for me to go on, one finger tracing a crooked line through the moisture on his glass.

"Whoever it was had no business being there. If he wasn't a thief, who was he? A clandestine lover, like the woman in the park's? You told me it was more serious than that. What's more serious than theft or adultery?"

The finger rested on the table.

"It was something that threatened the whole village. It had to stay a secret forever."

The farmers were hungry for land. Alexander had promised to obtain it. Mary Fels was planning a visit. Nothing could be allowed to spoil it.

"In a minute," I said, "I'll tell you what it was. But first you'll tell me something."

His hand gripped the glass. Now! Either I caught him off-balance and pinned him with a throw or he had slipped away from me forever. Hercule Poirot couldn't have done it any better. I shifted my weight in my chair and asked:

"How did you know Perl Appelbaum was murdered?"

The muscles around his chin hardened. He lifted his glass to his lips. And then, as I watched the blood run through the rivers of his veins to his ears and the wattles of his neck, he took the slowest sip I had ever seen a man take of anything. It was so slow he had to ratchet back his head until he was staring at the ceiling – so slow it made you wonder, as if he were a diver under water, how long he could go without air – so slow that, watching the sluice of his Adam's apple open and shut, I thought of the lizards who hunted moths on my window by the light of the reading lamp, their startled prey aflutter inside their translucent throats. He drank until his glass was empty – until only the froth was left – until each bubble even of that had passed through his patient lips. Only then did he put the glass down and answer in a voice from which all that beer hadn't washed the gravel:

"I don't know what you're talking about."

Zichron Ya'akov – Jerusalem – Zichron Ya'akov, 1974–2004

About the Author

Hillel Halkin

Hillel Halkin is an author, critic, and well-known translator whose journalism and essays from Israel have regularly appeared in *Commentary*, *The New Republic*, and *The New York Sun*, for over thirty years. His first book, *Letters to an American Jewish Friend*, the recipient of a National Jewish Book Award, caused spirited controversy. His much-acclaimed *Across the Sabbath River: In Search of a Lost Tribe of Israel*, received the 2002 Lucy Dawidowicz Prize for the writing of history.

The fonts used in this book are from the Arno family

Other works by Hillel Halkin
available from *The* Toby Press

Adjusting Sights by Haim Sabato (trans.)

Breakdown and Bereavement by Yosef Haim Brenner (trans.)

To This Day by S.Y. Agnon (trans.)

Whither & Other Stories by M.Z. Feierberg (trans.)

The Toby Press publishes fine writing,
available at leading bookstores everywhere. For more
information, please visit www.tobypress.com